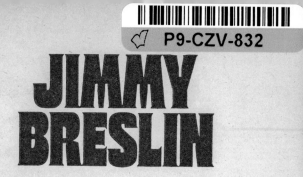

JIMMY BRESLIN

"WHO BETTER KNOWS THE CITY'S UNDERBELLY THAN BRESLIN, GRITTY COLUMNIST, TIRELESS CHAMPION OF THE DOWN AND OUT? . . . *FORSAKING ALL OTHERS* CAN SCARCELY BE SURPASSED."
Los Angeles Times

"A DEADLY SERIOUS BUT VERY FUNNY BOOK . . . HOORAY FOR THE NEW UPTOWN RUNYON!"
Houston Chronicle

"A SAVAGE UPDATE OF *ROMEO AND JULIET* . . . HOLDS YOU ENTHRALLED TO THE BITTERLY IRONIC END."
Cosmopolitan

FORSAKING ALL OTHERS

JIMMY BRESLIN

"NO ONE KNOWS THE UGLINESS, DRECK AND HORROR OF NEW YORK LIKE BRESLIN, AND NO ONE WRITING TODAY LOVES IT MORE."
People

"Excellent . . . In FORSAKING ALL OTHERS Breslin has forsaken no one . . . a major accomplishment."
Philadelphia Inquirer

"BRESLIN IS A . . . CONTEMPORARY DICKENS, a keen observer of the grim and the outrageous . . . Reading this book is like walking through New York City with him . . . what you will see will be stark, clear, and unforgettable."
Chicago Sun-Times

FORSAKING ALL OTHERS

JIMMY BRESLIN

"BRESLIN IS BRILLIANT . . . ADVENTURE, EXCITEMENT . . . A COMMUTER VERSION OF *WEST SIDE STORY*."
Time

"A romantic novel with very sharp teeth . . . in the tradition of vintage Manhattan tale-tellers from O. Henry to Damon Runyon."
The Washington Post Book World

"BRESLIN'S BEST WORK TO DATE . . . The drug wars that pound the streets of the Bronx are drawn in black and white and blood . . . it's a shoot-'em-up in more ways than one . . . An authentic, groin-tightening thriller."
Playboy

FORSAKING ALL OTHERS

FORSAKING ALL OTHERS

JIMMY BRESLIN

With the Cooperation of Team C Homicide

FAWCETT CREST • NEW YORK

A Fawcett Crest Book

Published by Ballantine Books

Copyright © 1982 by Rodene Enterprises, Inc. and Team C Associates

The author gratefully acknowledges permission to use the following:

MANANA by Dave Barbour and Peggy Lee, © 1948 Criterion Music Corp. © renewed 1976 Criterion Music Corp. USED BY PERMISSION.

Fermata International Melodies, Inc.: Excerpt from "Toro Mata." Spanish lyrics and music by Carlos Soto De La Colina. Copyright © 1975 by Consorcio De Editoras Musicales Peruanas S.A., Lima, Peru. All rights for U.S.A. and Canada assigned to Fermata International Melodies, Inc., 6290 Sunset Boulevard, Hollywood, California 90028.

Library of Congress Catalog Card Number: 82-3274

ISBN 0-449-20250-x

This edition published by arrangement with Simon & Schuster

Manufactured in the United States of America

First Ballantine Books Edition: May 1983

FOR ROSEMARY

The author and publisher gratefully acknowledge the assistance of:
    Thomas Davis
    Kevin Hallinan
    Alfred Howard
    Ronald Marsenison
    John McCann
    Michael McTigue
    John Meda
    Richard Paul
    Charles Summers
Team C, Bronx Homicide

---- • • • •

Tito Solivan took a pint bottle of whiskey out of the hip pocket of his baggy brown pants, swigged it and then spoke while his lips still glistened with drink.

"In Texas, most men become rich," he said.

He took another drink from the bottle, which was *pitorro*, a moonshine. Solivan was a man of local olive drab skin, but with the blue eyes, snub nose and perpetual thirst of his grandfather, Michael Sullivan, a United States army soldier stationed in Ponce in 1916. Sullivan married a local black Indian and his name was refined over the years to conform to community standards: at death, he was listed as Colon Solivan.

"In Mississippi, you get jobs and money," Sullivan's grandson, Tito Solivan, now said.

"Maybe I'll go to America," Teenager said to him.

"In Seattle, Washington, it should be a sin for people to live," Solivan said. "The life is so easy it makes God mad."

Solivan stood in front of his shack, which was built high off the ground in an attempt to make dampness keep its distance. Chickens kept appearing at the top of the high wooden stoop and then turning to go back inside the shack. A couple of hundred yards away, the orderly spacing of streetlights and phone lines came to an end, with sneakers and tin cans hanging from the wires. Solivan was the town lecturer on the riches of America, and peo-

1

ple came to him for advice even though Solivan had been
born in this shack and had spent his entire life standing
under the ceaseless sun on these mudflats running to the
Caribbean. That his grandfather had been American,
New York Irish, was qualification enough for Solivan to
inform everyone of the life awaiting them on the other
side of the land and sea from this town of shacks, La
Playa de Ponce in Puerto Rico.

"Where is the best place?" Teenager asked Solivan,
who was his cousin on his father's side. He had asked
Solivan this many times, but Teenager had a need to hear
it again, for then he could walk away knowing that his
future was assured.

"In New York, the priests are ashamed when they find
out how poor the Pope lives," Solivan said.

Teenager, however, was not yet ready. He stood holding the hand of a beautiful, vacant fourteen-year-old
named Lydia, but there were so many others in the town
whose hands he held and did not want to relinquish.
Teenager's life was in the town square, a place of cement
walks and low tropical oaks called robles trees. The tree
trunks were painted white and the walkways were lined
with globe lights on tall posts. A bandstand was in the
center and each evening the girls walked counterclock-
wise about the square and the boys went clockwise. In
their strollings, boys and girls always would be face to
face and the boys would be able to make remarks to the
girls. Not remarks about the beauty or great charms of
the girls, but rather boasts of how strong they were, of
how easily they would destroy anybody who came near
the girls, of how much they would like to have sex with
the girls.

Teenager at seventeen walked the square, shoulders
swinging, voice declaring to the night sky that all this
belonged to him, that all the girls there were to be his
pleasure. Rising out of a blank life, he found his identity
depended upon his level of violence. Therefore he told
his women in the square not of flowers, but of whom he
beat up. His search was for domination, his basic urge
was to destroy; sexual conquest for the sake of humiliating a woman was the first duty of a man to himself.

"You see that bus over there?" Teenager one night said to three men who had come over from the larger town of Ponce to capture women in the square. The three looked at the old bus and nodded.

"You have five minutes to get out of this square and onto this bus," Teenager told them.

"What are you saying to us?" one of the three from Ponce said.

"I am telling you that you have five minutes to get out of this square and go onto the bus. If you are here in five minutes I will kill you."

Teenager walked over to the El Cacique Bar, at the corner of the square nearest the water. It was a shed, with a thin bartender dozing on a high stool. The people drank Corona beer and Zorro rum and shot pool. Outside the open rear of the bar was a muddy path that ran through the weeds to the start of the sea, ten yards away. Teenager stood in the bar, stared at a pool game and guessed time in his head. He looked at the clock over the bar and saw that four minutes and forty-five seconds had passed. He looked out of the door of the El Cacique and saw the three from Ponce standing under a light in the square. Nonchalantly, staring at the ground, he walked out of the bar. The grass plots of the square had wire strung around them knee-high, held up by metal pipes driven deep in the ground. The wire went through holes at the top of the pipes. Passing one plot of grass, Teenager suddenly reached for a pipe. The wire did not go through this particular pipe; it was simply looped around, and when Teenager tugged, his special pipe slid quickly out of the ground and up through the wire loop.

When the three from Ponce saw the pipe in Teenager's hand they began to run. Teenager caught the tallest between the shoulder blades. The tall one stumbled and started to go down. Teenager brought the pipe onto the back of his head and the tall guy lay there, stunned, the blood matting his black hair. Teenager said to him, "Now you get up and get onto the bus or I am saying to you that I am going to kill you." The tall guy pulled himself up and wobbled across to the bus stop. Teenager took the pipe back to its spot, stuck it back into the ground, looped the wire over it and, taking a deep breath, looked around the square to see which girl he wanted to own.

One night, Teenager decreed that Lydia would take her clothes off only for him, and that if she ever did it for another he would kill both her and the male. Early one Saturday, Teenager's mother and stepfather left for the shopping boat to Saint Thomas, and an hour later Lydia was in Teenager's bed in his house. In midmorning, tropical rain crashing on the tin roof gave to the couple the feeling of being protected by castle walls, causing them to burrow deeper into drowsy privacy. They heard only the sound of rain, not the dripping hair of Teenager's mother, who had returned from a swamping at sea. On Monday morning, she took Teenager and Lydia to the judge in the city of Ponce and had them married. As they were not in a state of grace, they could not be married in the Catholic Church. Nor would the mother allow time for confession and other regulations necessary to the sacrament of matrimony, because she wanted the young people married immediately so that if one of the beauties of their Saturday was pregnancy, the child would be legal from first cell onward.

Teenager had a job in a car repair shop owned by El Negro Bobo—Black Bobo—in the Belgica section of Ponce, the part of town for those with skin color running from bitter chocolate to blue coal. In this setting, Teenager appeared as pale as paper. People with his color, faded khaki, lived primarily on the West Side of Ponce. On the hills rising sharply at the edge of the town there lived the Castilians, or people who pretended to be, and they would not allow their skin to be touched by the light from a heavy candle.

With no car, Teenager went to his job by bus. While he loved cars, and thirsted for the day he would own one, he despised working on them. His huge arms and great back muscles could lift up a car engine, but if he awoke with a stuffed nose, he said to himself that he had pneumonia and remained at home in bed. On days Teenager did show up, he was late, and he often went out to lunch and did not return. He was paid fifty-five dollars for a six-day week. Black Bobo thought it was cheap, as long as

Teenager showed up for Saturdays, when at day's end Black Bobo always went to a whorehouse in Belgica run by Mirta La Negron—Black Mirta. Black Bobo would get drunk at the bar and have Teenager, who sipped only a beer or two all evening, stand guard.

One night, a month or so after Teenager was married, he was at the whorehouse bar when his boss got into an argument with a man named Ralphie, who worked at the ironworks. Black Bobo slapped Ralphie in the face. As Ralphie picked up a beer bottle, Teenager reached out and got a hand on Ralphie.

"That's all right," Teenager said.

"You go away and I'll fix this bastard," Ralphie said.

"That's all right," Teenager said.

"I come back here with a gun and I shoot him," Ralphie said.

Black Bobo laughed and returned to his drink. Thirty minutes later, Ralphie walked through the door with a pistol in his right hand. Ralphie walked down the bar toward Black Bobo. Teenager dived for Ralphie's gun hand. Teenager's left hand clamped onto Ralphie's right wrist and Teenager's arm muscles rippled as he pushed Ralphie's gun hand out, as if opening a door. Teenager took a step to his own right, moving his body away from the wavering gun. Suddenly, Ralphie found himself with his right arm held far out to the side and with the entire front of his body open to Teenager, who was off to the left. Ten thousand years of male instinct caused Ralphie's knees to clap shut in front of his groin.

Teenager's right elbow rose and his right side moved in one piece. The elbow hit Ralphie like an iron bar on the bridge of his nose. Ralphie did not go down. He simply doubled up, hands over his face, the blood running out from beneath the palms.

Black Bobo threw his arms around Teenager. "The champion of this whole whorehouse!" he yelled. He banged his glass on the bar for another drink.

Black Mirta, watching Ralphie shuffle out, said, "I don't like this. It is not the end."

"Bullshit," Black Bobo said.

"You're the one who is bullshit," Black Mirta said.

Teenager was bored. He had to stand at the bar with a
beer that was warm and listen to Black Bobo boast and
babble. When is this man going to have sex with some
girl and let me go home to sleep, Teenager kept saying to
himself. After 1:00 A.M., with Black Bobo still at the bar,
Teenager was in the bathroom just starting to piss when
he heard a shout that drowned out the juke box. He came
out of the bathroom on the run. He saw Black Bobo
scurrying out the whorehouse door. Behind him, a gun in
his hand, was Steve Alvarez, Ralphie's brother. Steve
had on a yellow shirt. Teenager ran for the yellow shirt.
He could not get through the people in time. The yellow
shirt was out the door and running over the rutted dirt of
the whorehouse parking lot. Up ahead, racing for his car
in the corner of the lot, was Black Bobo.

"I get my gun in my car and I kill you," Black Bobo
yelled at the yellow shirt. The yellow shirt did not stop
chasing him. Black Bobo ran up to his car and pulled the
door open and put his head into the front and shrieked,
"Now I have my gun, you mother-fucker." Steve Alvarez stood in his yellow shirt directly over Black Bobo.
He fired the pistol. It sounded like a tray falling on the
floor. Teenager's hands went out for Steve Alvarez' yellow shirt. The tray kept falling. By the time Teenager
pounded on the yellow shirt, Steve Alvarez had emptied
his gun into Black Bobo. Steve Alvarez walked backward. Teenager did not touch him again. Teenager looked
into the car and saw the blood in the darkness and Black
Bobo down on his left ear on the floor of the car.

"What happened?" somebody shouted from the door
of the whorehouse bar.

"I just lost my job," Teenager said.

At four the next morning, Teenager and Lydia left in a
pickup truck that Teenager had taken from Black Bobo's
auto repair shop. They drove across the mountains to San
Pedro. Teenager was not yet eighteen and Lydia was not
yet fifteen. Teenager had with him the address of a
brother of his late father. The brother lived in Manhattan
and would do anything to help, Teenager's mother told
him.

Two hours later, as Teenager was about to turn into

the airport, he swerved out of the line of traffic and rode alongside the airport until the road turned to dirt and ran under coconut palms. He remained on the dirt road, which became even more rutted. Vegetation brushed against the sides of the truck. People and cows walked in the road in front of the car and it was futile to blow the horn because there was no room for anyone to stand on the side of the road.

All the people on the road were quite black, descendants, the mixture undisturbed, of the slaves brought by the Spanish to Puerto Rico to work in the sugar fields. Upon being freed, this group of slaves left the fields and moved to the coast, where they were shunned by the Taino Indians, who felt no need of any deeper shade of skin. Nor would the white Spanish do more than glare at them. Perhaps out in the mountains nobody cared. And in America's South the white farmers, born of Irish and English sheep violators, had no inhibitions about rolling among cornstalks with a field nigger. But in this particular spot along the Atlantic Ocean, the Castilians were truly afraid that it would rub off. An Indian or so was all right; high cheekbones were not catching. But black was untouchable. So now, two centuries or so later, those living in this jungle area were as dark as the day their ancestors had the chains taken from their necks.

Teenager drove to the village of Loiza Aldea, consisting of a street, then an old gray fort of a Roman Catholic church, St. Patricio's, a town square, a shed with a Corona beer advertisement and, two blocks from the church, a green wooden house with an old sign on the front porch: "Templo Espiritual de Sanidad Divina." The person inside practiced positive witchcraft; if Teenager had wanted anyone hurt he would not have come here, to Loiza Aldea, but instead would have driven along the other coast, from Ponce directly to Guyamo, which is where the evil voodoo people live.

A plump woman on the porch motioned Teenager and Lydia into a dim living room, where Teenager sat on a straight chair which was under a large cloth banner of Jesus, whose garments were held apart to display the Sacred Heart. Another banner was dedicated to the

Blessed Virgin, a third showed Christ being attended to by St. Michael the Archangel.

An inordinately short woman, a measure away from being a pygmy, looked out of a bedroom that had a curtain as a door. The woman smiled, displaying top front teeth missing.

"I soon be out," she said.

A few moments later she appeared, full set of white teeth gleaming. She carried a glass of water. The spirits drink the water, although you cannot see the level of water go down even if you leave the glass out for an entire day. After settling their thirst, the saints talk to her through the water. She placed the glass of water on a saucer on the small table and sat on the opposite side from Teenager, who pulled his chair up to the table. Lydia remained against the wall.

"You require a session?" the woman said. She yawned. "You are the earliest today."

She rubbed her eyes and stared at the glass of water. There was no conflict in her mind between her glass of water and the banners of Jesus and the Virgin Mary hanging on the walls. The Spanish priests, trained and sharpened at Salamanca until the edges of their faith sparkled and could cut through the thickest jungle, still found the beliefs of slaves in Puerto Rico to be unsplittable. Therefore, over the centuries, mergers were allowed, and people prayed to Christ and listened to water, as the woman was now doing.

There were two ways for the spirits to speak to Teenager: they could whisper to the woman and she would relate it to Teenager, or the particular spirit could overtake the woman and begin speaking out of the woman's mouth, and thus directly to Teenager. The spirit the woman was talking to was Changó, the saint of war, power, prisoners and sex. After several minutes, the small woman shivered. Teenager sat forward. He knew the woman's body was tingling with the presence of the spirit who spoke to her.

The little woman, watching the water, said, "Soon you will make very much money. There is a person you admire most in the world who made very much money and

soon you will make this money too. That is what you
want. Do you remember the day you first admired this
man? You were at a place where children play and you
admired this man. You cannot make the money here.
You must make it in the city in America. The man you
admire most is there.''

Teenager knew that the woman was speaking to the
proper spirit. His hero was Rockefeller. Once, in the yard
behind the school, Teenager sat on a bench with a book
from the library about Rockefeller. The other students
were playing softball; Teenager read over and over one
passage about John D. Rockefeller, Sr. It said that early
in Rockefeller's life he imported more opium than the law
allowed. Rockefeller, the book said, was using the opium
for a patent medicine. Teenager decided it was for pure
drug selling. Rockefeller, Teenager believed, made his
fortune with opium and then caused all the laws to be
passed against it in order to prevent anybody from becoming rich that way. Teenager remembered sitting in the
schoolyard for a long time and thinking about how smart
Rockefeller was.

Now the small woman said, "You must use your
strength to get these riches in America."

Teenager nodded. "I am going there now."

"Do you have someone to advise you in America?"

"This woman called Mama. She is going to be a saint.
They give me her address."

"Listen to her. She will tell you what to do."

Teenager paid the woman five dollars. Lydia and he
got into the pickup truck and started for the airport.
Teenager's arm hung out the window and the sun warmed
it. It was October of 1966 and another life fashioned by
the sun and the water was coming to the place made of
cement and steel.

.... **Chapter**
1
.....

State of New York, Department of Correctional Ser-
vices.
4/6/76
Parole Hearing, Albion Correctional Facility.
Case of Ramon Solivan, 73C748
Commissioner: Lewis Constable

Q. How old are you, Teenager?

A. Twenty-seven.

Q. For a guy of twenty-seven you were in and out
of trouble for a long time, right?

A. Yes sir.

Q. I can tell you straight out, Ramon, that this board
looks at your record very seriously. And you were
found guilty by a jury verdict.

A. Yes sir.

Q. Well, we take the jury system very seriously
around here. If a jury says you're guilty, then we give
that quite a bit of weight.

A. Yes sir.

Q. Do you admit your guilt at this time?

A. Yes sir.

Q. How do you feel about this crime you committed?

A. I am sorry.

Q. For selling dope.

A. Yes sir. I am sorry for selling dope.

Q. You are now credited with six hundred and eighty-one days jail time. And you were found guilty of possession of drugs and conspiracy to sell drugs and assault second on a police officer. And you received a five-year maximum sentence on each count, but they are to run concurrent.

A. Yes sir.

Q. Are you a junkie?

A. No sir.

Q. Why on your misbehavior report does it show that you entered another inmate's cell and beat him?

A. That was a bad guy started a fight with me.

Q. Let's get back to your crime. How many fellows were involved with you in your crime?

A. Three.

Q. Benny Velez, Nector Lopez and Ramin Negron.

A. Yes sir.

Q. So far as you know did any of them go to trial?

A. Nector Lopez and me.

Q. And Ramin?

A. He copped out.

Q. Took a plea?

A. Yes sir.

Q. It doesn't say here that he took a plea. It says here that he was found cut into parts and left in an empty lot.

A. Yes sir.

Q. Why do you say he took a plea?

A. Because that is what he did, he told them he was guilty.

Q. And then he got killed?

A. This I don't know.

Q. It says here that he got killed before he got to court.

A. This I do not know.

Q. Let's go to the start. Here you are nineteen and you assault and rob a cab driver. Was this in the Bronx?

A. Yes sir.

Q. Was narcotics involved here?

A. Yes sir.

Q. You were involved in quite a few assaults prior to this?

A. Yes sir.

Q. How many would you say?

A. Not many. I just come here then from Puerto Rico.

Q. So when you started your criminal career, you were about nineteen?

A. More or less, yes sir.

Q. And those other fellows with you belonged to a gang called the Teenager gang?

A. Yes sir.

Q. And you are known as Teenager?

A. Yes sir.

Q. Considering the fact that you were continually in trouble in Bronx County with crimes of narcotics and assault, how can you expect to get parole today?

A. I don't have any plans of associating with these people I was with before.

Q. Well, you saw enough of Ronald Schiavone while you were here. He has an organized crime folder. Seemed you were his bodyguard around here. Do you plan to see him on the outside?

A. Never.

Q. Now your gang was named after you?

A. Yes sir.

Q. And you are going to stay away from them.

A. Yes sir.

Q. The New York Police won't be happy to see you coming back to the Bronx. Certainly the reports from this institution or even the reports from the reception center weren't too good.

A. Yes sir.

Q. And you were given one month credit for jail time before your trial. So you are locked up almost two years now.

A. Yes sir.

Q. And on a five-year bit you'll have until October of 1977 to go on parole.

A. Yes sir.

Q. That's over a year and a half from now.

A. Yes sir.

Q. I wonder, I really wonder, and so does the board wonder, whether you can make it on parole over that period of time. What do you think?

A. I want to try.

Q. Why?

A. Because when the parole is over I plan to go back to Puerto Rico and live again with my mother.

Q. You weren't working.

A. I was working.

Q. I see no jobs listed here.

A. Well, I worked.

Q. How much were you making at this job of yours?

A. This guy gives me one hundred fifty.

Q. Apparently you weren't making enough to satisfy yourself if you became involved in the crimes that are explained here.

A. It wasn't the need for the money. It was just the guys I was hanging out with.

Q. How do you plan to support yourself and your wife and children while you're on parole?

A. I have this job painting rooms in apartments.

Q. I see that. Now, do you think you have done fairly well in here despite your background and your ability?

A. Yes sir.

Q. In what way?

A. I was thinking about when I get out on the street to finish school out there. Go to a community college.

Q. Do you have a drinking problem?

A. I didn't ever do that.

Q. Do you have a drug problem?

A. No sir.

Q. But when we look back at the crimes you committed, robbery first, grand larceny first, assault first, assault second, possession with intent to sell, and these were just a few of the things you did out there. Three homicide arrests. Now you know and I know that you don't get arrested for homicide for nothing. Even if you're let go immediately, the arrest still indicates you're around serious trouble.

A. No sir.

Q. No?

A. The police break my chops.

Q. With homicide arrests.

A. Yes sir.

Q. They arrest you for murder just to be pests.

A. Yes sir.

Q. This is the longest period of time that you ever were in prison.

A. Yes sir.

Q. And you feel you learned something out of this.

A. Yes sir.

Q. All right, Ramon, we'll take everything into consideration when we make our decision.

A. Yes sir.

Q. Think there's any chance at all that you'll stay out of trouble?

A. Yes sir.

Q. Or would you get yourself right back in?

A. This is the last time I will ever be in these places.

Q. You can't afford it, whether you are here or in Puerto Rico, with this record.

A. My record will be good enough to let me out.

Q. You're pretty sure of yourself.

A. Yes sir.

Q. I have to tell you that I've seen a lot better records.

A. Soon I will be out.

Q. You're pretty sure of this, aren't you?

A. Yes sir.

Q. Well, we'll let you know.

A. That's all right.

——————....Chapter 2

——————————————————————— ....

The collect call from prison came at six o'clock at Ana's Bar on East 138th Street, in the South Bronx. Benny Velez, who worked for Teenager as a drug peddler, shrieked when he heard the voice. He slapped his hand on the bar when Teenager told him that he had a chance for parole.

Two others, Boogaloo and Albertito, got on the phone, and Benny Velez, deciding to make the world a total delight, put a small plastic box, large enough to hold a ring or some medicine, on the bar. Using a dollar bill, he took cocaine out of the box. Without bothering to go to the men's room, or even to turn his back to the window on the street, Benny made lines of cocaine on the bar, put the bill to his nose, bent down and took a great sniff of barroom air that became enchanted as it went inside him.

"Teenager!" Benny Velez shouted.

Maximo Escobar, the tallest person in the place, sauntered to the phone, grinning. Everybody in Ana's Bar watched as the neighborhood celebrity, Maximo, shouted in Spanish to the neighborhood legend, Teenager. Teenager wanted his wife taken to see Mama, so that Mama could pray to the saints and get Teenager released. Of course he could do that, Maximo said, for he had intentions of seeing Mama himself. To say hello, not for voo-

doo. But he would see to it himself that Teenager's wife,
Lydia, saw Mama for a ceremony.

"Mama told him on the phone he would be out of jail
by July," Benny Velez said. "His saint is always right."

"The prisons are so crowded that they let everybody
out when they do minimum time," Maximo said.

"His saint, that's the one who must do it," Benny said.

Maximo didn't want to argue. "What does he do when
he comes home?" he asked.

Benny shrugged. "He comes here to be home."

Maximo picked up his beer. He would not embarrass
Benny by saying anything bad about Teenager. Maximo
despised drug peddlers; at the same time, he loved Teenager. Maximo was twenty-three, four years younger than
Teenager, and he came from a shack in Ponce that was
two doors down from the one in which Teenager had
been born. One of Maximo's first memories in life was
being five years old and watching Teenager climb to the
roof of a car and sit there, cross-legged, as the car
bumped down the street without the driver realizing anything. When the car paused at the corner, Teenager
jumped off. Over the years, no matter what Teenager
perpetrated, Maximo never could feel total disgust; that
they had sprung from the same landscape was more important. And if asked to choose between Teenager, even
if found selling heroin to babies, and some fat Irish detective or little Jew judge, Maximo found it no contest. And
as he thought of Teenager now, Maximo smiled. He
began to realize how much he had missed Teenager, with
those fifty-two-inch shoulders and the eyes that turned
into cat slits when you told him something funny.

Maximo could see Teenager, his chin rising, his great
head sitting on those huge shoulders, on the morning the
clerk in the subway change booth started trouble.

Maximo, his right arm wrapped around a pyramid of
schoolbooks, had gone into the subway at 8:00 A.M. and
held out his high school pass.

"That's no good until tomorrow," the man in the booth
said.

"They just gave it to me yesterday," Maximo said.

"I don't care when you got it, it's no good until tomorrow."

"What should I do?" Maximo asked.

"Pay thirty-five cents."

"I don't have any money," Maximo said. He didn't. Nor was there any money in his house. His mother had been laid off for two weeks, and each day she went out into the hall and borrowed two dollars and used it for dinner.

"Thirty-five cents," the change-booth man said.

"Have a nice day," Maximo said. He walked to the turnstile, lifted himself onto it, swung his legs over and began walking down the platform. He looked into the darkness at the head of the tracks to see if the train light showed.

There was shouting behind him, from the change booth, and Maximo heard footsteps. He turned to see a stocky policeman coming after him.

"I have my train pass from school," Maximo said, holding the pass out.

"What did you jump the turnstile for?" the cop said, walking toward him.

"I have my pass," Maximo said.

The cop's hand came out and grabbed Maximo's hair. The cop yanked the hair and Maximo's books spilled from his arm. The cop dragged Maximo off the platform and into an alcove by the change booth used for storing cleaning equipment.

The cop pulled Maximo's head up. "You're going to get the beating of your life," the cop said. He slapped Maximo across the mouth. The slap made a noise so loud that a woman near the change booth, seeing what was going on, gasped. Hearing her, the cop let some of the anger drain from his eyes. He pulled Maximo to the stairs, kicked him in the shin and sent him up.

"I dropped my schoolbooks," Maximo said.

"Why don't you come down and get them?" the cop said.

Maximo, his eyes wet with frustration, went back to his building. He was about to go into the doorway when he heard Teenager calling him from the corner.

"Hey, what's the matter with you?" Teenager said.

Maximo told him. Teenager punched Maximo on the arm. "That's all right. Come on with me."

Teenager went down the stairs to the subway two at a time. Maximo followed him. Teenager went by the change booth, loped up to the turnstile, slapped his palms on it and vaulted the turnstile, his legs folding under him, more easily than Maximo had ever seen anyone do. The cop, standing by the change booth, watched closely.

"Come on," Teenager said to Maximo.

Maximo went up to the turnstile and lifted himself over it.

"Go get your books," Teenager said.

The cop called to them.

"That's all right," Teenager yelled.

As Maximo picked up his books, the cop came up to the turnstile.

"That's all right," Teenager said again.

"You didn't pay and that kid didn't pay," the cop said.

"That's all right," Teenager said.

"I said you didn't pay," the cop said, his voice rising.

"That's all right."

The cop took a closer look at Teenager and remained on the other side of the turnstile. His voice went high enough to quaver. Teenager swung his shoulders and he and Maximo walked away from the cop, who did not come after them.

Maximo preferred to think of Teenager in this way, the protector on the subway and the kid sitting atop the car in La Playa de Ponce, rather than as a drug seller to be hated.

Besides, on this day in the bar Maximo Escobar had more important uses for his anger. Earlier in the day, before he had taken his five-hour bus ride home from school to start the Easter recess, Maximo had been interviewed by a man from Mobil Oil. It took place in a room on the second floor of the Law School building. The man from Mobil Oil was in his midforties and his name was Bo Watson. When Maximo entered the room, Bo Watson stood up. Bo Watson's handshake was firm and his gray-blue eyes locked on Maximo's. Watson then looked Maximo up and down. Bo had no trouble with Maximo's color, which was a shade off white. His eyes paused on Maximo's shoes, which were black, pointed, high-heeled and spit-polished.

"Maximo," Bo Watson said, "I am very glad to meet you."

As Maximo sat down on the near side of a chrome and wood desk, he pulled an envelope out of his shoulder bag. He handed the envelope to Watson, who pulled out the resumé, and took a pair of bifocals out of the inside pocket of his suit jacket.

Maximo's resumé gave his address: 1523 East 138th Street, the Bronx, New York. It said that he had attended La Escuela Maria Puente, Calle Colon, Ponce, Puerto Rico. Then P.S. 263, the Bronx; Intermediate School 224, the Bronx, DeWitt Clinton High School, the Bronx; Lehman College, the Bronx; and now Harvard Law School, Cambridge. He was presently in the top tenth of his class. Under the section headed "Work Experience," Maximo had listed that he had worked for the last three summers at Cutti's Superette on East 138th Street.

"This is very impressive," Bo Watson said. "Is this the South Bronx?"

"Yes," Maximo said.

"Is it as bad as they say?" Bo Watson asked.

"It is very bad," Maximo said.

"Have you ever been arrested?" Bo Watson asked.

"No," Maximo said.

Bo Watson jotted down a series of notes on a Mobil Oil employee interview form. Maximo saw that next to the word "Appearance," Watson wrote, "student, Spanish, medium build."

Watson put down his pen, looked up from the form, held out his hand and walked Maximo to the door.

"You'll be hearing from us," Bo Watson said.

Sure would, Maximo knew. A Harvard Spic was the hire of the year. In the last two months, he had received one hundred letters from corporations. Two days before, the man from ITT hadn't even bothered to make notes; he simply asked Maximo to let them know when he

would like to begin his career with them. Maximo was
tempted to go back inside the room and tell Bo Watson
that he had lied, that in fact he had been arrested in the
South Bronx. He wanted to see Bo Watson nod and say,
"Well, I'm sure that's all done with and you'll have a fine
new life with us."

It had been that way all through school. Nobody at
Harvard openly patronized him; they were beyond that,
and they even had seen one or two live Puerto Ricans in
the years before Maximo. But they did want him to know
at all times that he was different from his people, that he
was better. This was done best at wine and cheese parties. For three years, every time he turned around, there
was a wine and cheese party thrown by some woman
named Pebble, whose husband taught Constitutional
Law. Maximo decided that wine and cheese was the standard Protestant way to teach a Puerto Rican how to dis-
pose of Spic-ishness.

Maximo met Teenager's wife, Lydia, two nights later
in front of the building where Mama lived on Southern
Boulevard.

"Have you got the picture?" Maximo asked.

Lydia stamped her right foot several times on the sidewalk. On the phone, Mama had told her to get a picture
of the judge who sentenced Teenager and to put it in her
shoe and walk on it. Lydia didn't know where to find
such a picture, but she went through a newspaper and
found a photo of Senator Russell Long at a natural gas
hearing and, figuring that judges and senators were the
same, tore out the picture, tucked it into her shoe and
went around stamping her foot on the face of Russell
Long, as extension of the judge. This act, Mama had
assured her, would cause the judge to become seriously
ill and the prison gates to open for Teenager.

Maximo took her into the building and down a lightless
basement corridor, at the end of which a red votive candle played across the heavy-boned ebony face of Mama.

"Entra en la casa para que los santos te ayuden,"
Mama said.

When she saw Maximo, her religious demeanor

dropped and she gave a toothy smile and a howl. She placed the candle on a small table inside the door and held out her arms, demanding that Maximo allow himself to be hugged.

"I asked your saint to see that you pass all your subjects in school," she said. "This I do for you."

"I didn't take the exams yet," Maximo said.

"Then when you take the exams, your saint will see that you pass them."

"We will pray to Changó and bring Teenager home to his house," Mama said, waving Lydia into the darkened basement apartment. Lydia wore a skirt and blouse and carried jeans and another blouse; she thought it would be simpler for the skirt, rather than the jeans, to be cut off her during the ceremony. In the darkness, somebody took the jeans and blouse and Lydia stood uneasily, arms folded. As she grew accustomed to the darkness, she noticed two women in white dresses and three young men in white suits. Mama was in an old print blouse and dark pants. She padded about in gray socks. There was a noise at the door and a tall young man in a white suit pulled a goat on a rope. Mama waved him away and followed him out into the hallway, giving orders. Then she came back and stood in the kitchen and watched Maximo peer into the refrigerator.

"Orange juice, grapefruit juice, something like that," Maximo said.

"When the boy comes back, I'll send him to the store," Mama said.

"Maybe I'll go out myself," Maximo said.

"You do not stay?" Mama said.

"No, I'll just go for a walk," Maximo said.

"Changó helps you in the school, too," Mama said.

Maximo smiled. Mama had such great sense in this big old body of hers, yet she persisted in identifying any thoughts of her own as being messages from her saints; in his first year at Harvard, with his insides crying for something familiar, Maximo had called Mama simply to talk to someone, and she listened to him for a few sentences and then told him to regard himself as a prisoner and move immediately into the Spic group. "When you go into the yard, you stand only with them," she said. By yard, she meant any area similar to the one at Attica; she had no idea that Harvard had a Yard. When Maximo told her there were no Puerto Ricans at the school, Mama then insisted that he move out of his dormitory and into a Hispanic neighborhood. Maximo took a room in Roxbury and regained his ability to breathe.

"Maybe you helped me by yourself," Maximo now suggested to her.

"But you did what I told you to do."

"I guess I did."

"And you are still doing the workout?"

"I am." Mama had told him that to defeat the effect of Harvard whites, he must use pushups, just as Puerto Ricans in Attica, their loins screaming, try to exercise the sex out of their systems. Maximo would come to Constitutional Law with aching biceps.

"If you did what I told to you on the phone, then you did what Changó said," Mama said.

"Whatever it was, it helped."

"The saints now will help Teenager."

"I don't know who'll help him," Maximo said.

"You still let them fool you," Mama said. "It is not an American religion, so you think something is bad. If some Puerto Rican people believe in this religion, why cannot it be good? You are as bad as the people who go to the market and they say, 'Don't give me that little tomato. That's a Spic tomato. Give me the big one over there, the American one.' That is what they have done to the minds of the Puerto Rican people. If it is Puerto Rican it is no good. Only American is good. You do not believe *Santeria* even it helps you. Prove to me that Mama cannot do more for you than the priest in the church."

"I guess I can't."

"You see? Tonight, I will have the saints help Teenager."

At this, Maximo decided to go for his walk. He wanted to do it casually, for he couldn't insult her. She had been part of his life since childhood. When he was ten, three blacks with baseball bats walked up to him in front of the projects on 137th Street and began swinging. One of Max-

imo's ankles broke and he pitched onto a patch of dirt
and crab grass in front of the projects and began screaming, his hands ripping at the crab grass. He heard Mama's
voice call out that she would help. His hands kept ripping
at the crab grass, and Mama went into the street and
stopped an ambulance. In later years, Maximo understood that the ambulance had happened onto the street at
that time, but on that day Mama had claimed that the
saints had sent it, and no one, particularly Maximo, dis-
puted her. Since then, whenever he felt like displaying
cynicism toward her belief, he remembered the time he
was ripping at the crab grass. For that day alone, he
never could hurt her.

"I have to go out for something anyway," Maximo told
Mama. "You take care of your ceremony."

As he walked out of the kitchen, he heard a fluttering;
in the doorway, the young guy now stood with a bird of
some kind. *"Gallina?"* Mama asked. The young guy assured her that it was a hen. Maximo went by them and
into the hallway.

"When do I see you?" Mama said.

"Soon," Maximo said.

"I will pray to the saint for you," Mama said.

Case of: Ramon Solivan 73C748
Date: 6/15/76

The subject is to be conditionally released on the
marginal date (9/1/76) from the Albion Correctional Facility. On the day following the marginal date, the subject is to make his Arrival Report to the New York
area office. He is assigned to report to the Bronx Parole
unit, Bronx County Courthouse, 161st Street and
Grand Concourse.

————————.... Chapter 3

——/ ....

Maximo had just walked out of his house and was looking at the headlines on the newsstand when the arm came under his chin and pulled him back. The moment Maximo felt the size of the arm, he knew who it was.

"I feel the presence of an evil personage," he called out.

"I am saving you again," Teenager said. "I am pulling you up from a deep hole."

Teenager released his arm and spun Maximo around. "Let me see you. You look smart. The school has made you look very smart."

"You look terrific," Maximo said.

"Of course. I have been away to school too."

"I think you were with nicer people," Maximo said.

"I was with lice. Never have I had to be with such people. All bums and lice who get caught. Never will I be there again. Mama said this time she will watch for me every day and save me."

"This time you ought to try watching yourself," Maximo said.

"Mama will do it for me. You helped me get out, Maximo. For taking my wife to Mama, I will buy you something. Here, we'll go down the block to Eddie Hernandez and I will buy you all new shirts. Yes, I will do that for you right now, I will buy you something."

"I don't want to go there," Maximo said. "Not today. I've got things to do."

"What have you got to do? You're finished with school?"

"I still have to take the test, the bar exam."

"After this, you will become an *abogado*."

"If I pass."

"You will pass everything. Then when you pass, I will hook you up and you will make millions. You will keep Teenager out of jail."

Teenager held out his hand. Maximo, laughing, slapped it.

"You are so brilliant that the judges will see you come into the courtroom and they will say, 'Oh, we cannot go any more with this case against Teenager. Here he is bringing Maximo with him and Maximo is too smart for all of us.' "

"I don't think your business will be my business," Maximo said.

"Anything you do I will make sure that you earn millions," Teenager said. He saw something out of the corner of his eye and he turned around and gazed at the other side of the street. "Is that Pat?"

"Where?"

"That one." Teenager pointed to a young woman, growing heavy in the waist, pushing a baby carriage.

"That's Pat," Maximo said.

Teenager roared. "Pat!" he called out.

Across the street, the young woman with the baby carriage stopped, focused, and then gave a whoop as she saw Teenager.

"You are very beautiful," Teenager called.

Pat waved her hand.

"Is that Maximo's baby?" he called out to Pat.

Pat put a hand to her mouth and shook her head no.

"That is too bad. Maximo is going to make millions. You and your child would be very rich."

Pat seemed uninterested in Maximo.

"Your next baby will be with Maximo," Teenager shouted. Pat turned the corner quickly.

Teenager said to Maximo, "I am going for a drive."

"I'm going to sit down someplace and read," Maximo said. He carried a thick law book.

"Come on, you can read in my car," Teenager said.

"Where are you going?" Maximo asked.

"To New Jersey," Teenager said.

"What for?"

"What difference does it make? Wherever I go, you just stay in the car and I promise you it'll be all right. It's nothing. Just a ride."

The Mercedes was parked around the corner. Maximo slid into the car, put his head back on the seat and closed his eyes as Teenager drove up toward the George Washington Bridge.

"Who are you going to see?" he said.

"Mariani," Teenager said.

"Some wop," Maximo said.

"You could call him that," Teenager said.

Maximo was uneasy now. Maybe you better make this the last, he told himself.

Teenager drove onto the George Washington Bridge, a structure meant for splendor, but now, loaded with Sunday afternoon traffic, just another crowded federal highway. Beneath the bridge, people furiously enjoyed themselves on small boats. The traffic moved into New Jersey, where somewhere children ran through grass. To find this place, one had to know the proper muffler shop or fried chicken stand to use as a turning point.

Louis Mariani lived in Swiftbrook, and Teenager had been given his phone number by a son-in-law of Mariani's named Ronald Schiavone, the inmate at Albion who lived in continual trouble with the blacks and Hispanics. Usually, Teenager was the only object between Schiavone and the hereafter. When Teenager called, Mariani first said he would meet him the next day at the bar next to the funeral parlor on Pleasant Avenue in East Harlem. When Teenager said he wanted to see Mariani right away, Mariani said he was home cooking Sunday dinner for his family, but he could spare a few moments from the gravy to welcome a returning veteran, particularly one who had done so much for him. If Teenager had not

assisted Schiavone, Mariani would have placed land
mines on his front walk before allowing a Hispanic into
his house.

Mariani was the boss-in-fact of the Mafia family running the Bronx. News and law-enforcement people call it
the Lucchese family: Lucchese had been dead for years,
but cops and reporters have decreed that the Mafia, like
prestigious Protestant law firms, goes under the names of
founders even though those heroes have been dead for
decades. The man with the actual title of boss in this
particular family was a man named Albert who was in
prison. The family, run by Mariani, had no name other
than its newspaper and police file name, and its members
operated in "crews" whose lives revolved around finding
the right black to sell dope to; the wrong black being an
undercover agent. Little else mattered, for importing and
selling dope always has been the only serious occupation
of the Mafia.

Teenager stopped at Burger King on Route 4 in New
Jersey and asked directions to Mariani's house, which
was difficult to locate because a golf course cut off many
of the streets. Teenager and Maximo had a hamburger
and onion rings, each tasting like cardboard, and then
turned off the highway at a transmission repair shop and
several minutes later wound up at Mariani's, a large yellow brick home on a corner lot in a neighborhood of
houses set far back from the street. Teenager put his
Mercedes 300 directly in front of Mariani's house, got out
of the car and stretched. If you came to a neighborhood
like this, there is no reason not to let everybody inspect
you, Teenager said to himself. The windows of the
houses of the street were covered, but Teenager could
feel people: suburban eyes can look through velvet and
still make out a Puerto Rican or black.

Teenager had on a red silk shirt from Eddie Hernandez' store. His great upper torso, which seemed to carry
half his hundred and ninety pounds, was outlined sharply
against the shirt. Light tan gabardine pants without a
wrinkle sat on his thirty-one-inch hips smoothly.

His hair was a thick black mane, shaggy and striking,
that, through mustache, sideburns and full beard, allowed

the hairless part of his tan-yellow face to be covered by
the palm of a hand. Hooded eyes seemed sleepy. He
grinned as he looked at Mariani's house, the high cheekbones rising even more.

Teenager knew that his hair was part of the reason why
Mariani changed his mind and invited him to the house.
Teenager had *pelo lacio*, which is straight hair. If he had
pelo malo, Mariani undoubtedly would have made it plain
that he did not want Teenager in his house. *Pelo malo*
means bad hair: wiry hair, kinky hair, African hair. There
is a crazed regard for *pelo lacio*, while *pelo malo* causes
people to withdraw.

Teenager did not have to ring the doorbell. Louis Mariani appeared with his arms spread. He threw them about
Teenager's shoulders. His capped teeth gleamed.

"I love you like a son," Mariani said, "for what you
done for that kid."

"It is good to see you," Teenager said.

"Where'd you leave the car, in front of this house?"

"Yes. It's all right. Parole officers don't work on the
weekend," Teenager said.

"I didn't mean that. I meant that you can't put the car
in front of anybody else's house. Some of these neighbors, they're citizens. They beef when they got cars from
this house in front of their house. You one of my babies."
He pinched Teenager's left cheek and blew kisses with
his mean mouth.

The pinching annoyed Teenager. Who is this little man
to touch me when I could snap his arm off?

Mariani suddenly withdrew and waved his hand.
"Look at her, will you?"

Walking across the lawn from the driveway was a
young woman with a long cheerful body.

"My daughter Nicki," Mariani said. "She's my baby
doll."

In the car at the curb Maximo raised his head and
looked out the window at Nicki. Immediately, Nicki noticed that Maximo was looking at her. With a glance, she
saw that Maximo's hair was combed straight back; it def-
initely was not nigger hair. His close-cropped beard was
almost exciting. Whoever he was, he was taller than most

Puerto Ricans, and he sat erect in the car, not slouched down like some common Spic. He might even like my nose, she thought. Hers was prominent, although not as prominent as she had once thought, and its ridge was delightful, and important, to gray-green eyes that rested above strong cheekbones. At thirteen, she had been embarrassed by her nose, and when an uncle had his nose flattened by a baling hook at the Fulton Market, she dreamed of going down to the market and having hers, too, flattened by a hook. As she grew up, she realized that the nose was far less obtrusive than she imagined, and most people even liked it. As a carryover from youth, however, she still thought of it each time a man looked at her, as this one now was.

"Nicki," her father said.

"Yes."

"Say hello to Teenager."

Nicki had a catalogued greeting for this sort of person: she smiled, nodded, said pleasure to meet you and walked away from them. "A pleasure," she said to Teenager and then, walking away, she concentrated on her step and how she held her head in the presence of the steady gaze that she felt coming from the car window.

"Nicki," her father said.

"Yes, Daddy."

"What's the matter with you? This is Teenager."

"Oh, you're the one," she said.

"*Que paso,* Nicki?" Teenager said.

Oh, I hate this dirty Spic and I have to be nice to him. For a moment, she saw her husband, so much smaller, standing in a cellblock with Teenager in front of him. She was suddenly furious with her husband for being caught and having to place everybody in the debt of this Puerto Rican. Look at this, now I have to reach out and touch his hand.

"Have some coffee with us?" Nicki said.

"Why not?" Teenager said.

Nicki walked into the house ahead of him, sorry that she was no longer in the eyes of the one in the car. She wanted to get a good look at him.

Mariani swaggered down the hall and into a kitchen

paneled with wood and aluminum oven doors. A kitchen towel tucked into his belt flapped on his pot belly as he moved. The sleeves of an initialed white-on-white shirt were rolled up. His bald head glistened in the kitchen lights.

The wife cut onions and the daughter moved swiftly from cabinet to coffee pot, her long hair swinging across her shoulder blades.

Nicki pulled out two fresh dishtowels and draped them over the trays of food she was taking up to her husband at prison the next morning, thus removing, she hoped, the husband from as much of the kitchen conversation as possible. Her long cheerful body, the legs beginning at the hips, moved inside Bloomingdale's jeans and a ninety-dollar gold silk shirt from Saks Fifth Avenue. As she waited for the coffee, her wide mouth was set in a young matron's smile that was an attempt at protective coloration, a very good attempt, too, except there was bleakness at the core of her eyes. Her husband had to live with people like this Puerto Rican in the kitchen with her, and then tomorrow, when she visited him in prison, where he ate and slept among these Spics and niggers, he would touch her.

"Want fruit?" Mariani's wife said.

"Just coffee."

"You can't have just coffee," the daughter said.

"You got to have gravy. We got to build you up," Mariani said. "Genoese gravy. You ever had it?"

"I don't know this gravy," Teenager said.

"You don't know what living is until you had Genoese gravy my way," Mariani said.

As this might have been taken as an invitation to dinner, the daughter stiffened.

"I thank you very much, Louis, but I cannot stay today," Teenager said.

The daughter relaxed.

Mariani's son, who was about seventeen, came into the kitchen.

"You know Teenager."

The son's face was embarrassingly pretty, with pink cheeks and large soft eyes. "I think so," he said.

"You think? You don't know Teenager?"

"You got very big, Ralphie," Teenager said.

"I play baseball," Ralph said.

"What team is it?" Teenager said.

"School team."

"He goes to DePaul Academy," Mariani said. "I go to the game and see him hit the ball. I say, geez, my own son can hit a ball like this?"

"I get a tryout with a scout next year my pop says."

"He got to finish school first," Mariani said. "But he don't mind that. This kid got school spirit. It ain't like when I went to school. All I cared about was gettin' into the girls' room. This kid, you ought to see this kid, he got school spirit. He goes to school, he wears the school jacket with the name of the school right on it. That's one of the biggest things a kid could have. School spirit. Ralphie, get us a drink. Me and Teenager need a boost up."

Mariani went to the stove. "Teenager, you got to excuse me for a second. I'm just in the middle of making the gravy. See these? Neck bones. That's what I use. I put neck bones in here. Three pound of neck bones to every pound of linguini. Neck bones, three pound of onion. Someday you eat this with me. Eat my way. You'll die. I make baked sausages with peppers to go with this."

"That sounds delicious."

"What are you, kidding? I'm speaking to this guy the other day, Barker. He got some car insurance business. He says to me that his wife has him eat macaroni with American cheese on it out of a can. I says to him—*Madonna!*—you ought to put your wife's head in the oven."

His son Ralph brought in brandy. Mariani, wiping his hands on the towel, held out his glass.

"*A salud.*"

Teenager nodded and sipped the brandy. "You know what respect I have for you," he told Mariani.

"You listen to me, you'll become rich. You're smart. You not like these other Spanish guys."

"I try to use my head to see what is coming," Teenager said.

"That's what I mean. You think. You're not like the rest of your people."

"I got to make money."

"You listen to me, you'll make millions."

Mariani's wife said, "You should see the people makin' money today. People got no class at all are getting rich."

Mariani wiped his hands on the apron. "Here, let's get out of here so we talk."

He led Teenager down the hall and into a study whose shelves were lined with porcelain figures. Two chess tables with hand-carved ivory figures flanked a large television set. Mariani sat in a large chair. Teenager leaned against the wall. Nicki walked past the door, on her way to the back of the house.

"They don't know nothing about what I do," Mariani said. "Keep the women and children out of it. They're nice. Let them live nice. Right?"

Teenager nodded. "Right," he said.

"We're men," Mariani said. "We have to do what we can do. But that don't mean you bring in the wife and the children. Only scum do that."

"That's right," Teenager said.

"So what do you want?" Mariani said.

"I want to do some business with you."

"*Babania,*" Mariani said.

"You have?"

"I got."

There was a small noise in the hall. Mariani held up his hand. "Ralphie." There was no answer from the hall. Mariani's hand came down.

"I got the best white in a long, long time."

"Uh huh."

"You could step on it seven times."

"Seven."

"That's right. Seven times."

He held up his hand again. "Ralphie!" This time there was a squeak in the hall.

"I smack out his brains," Mariani said. He smiled at Teenager. "You could hit my stuff seven times."

The one particular of arithmetic that Teenager had

been carrying in his mind, in prison cell and mess hall and exercise yard, stirred in his mind. A kilogram is one thousand grams. A gram is a thousand milligrams. This makes a kilogram a million milligrams. Thirty milligrams is a dose on the street. Take one kilogram and step on it, how many times is that you step on this one, seven? Step on this one seven times and you have, what is it, 230,000 doses to sell? This is over two million dollars. *Business*.

"Seven times is very good," Teenager said.

"Very good?" Mariani asked. "This will make you rich."

"Thank you. I won't forget."

"You better not. Because I'm helping you."

"Yes."

"So what are we talking about?" Mariani said.

"A unit."

"That much? You always go an eighth maybe. From an eighth down."

"This time the whole."

"That costs fifty."

"That's a lot of money."

"Fifty."

"I thought like forty for pure."

"This is pure. Ninety-seven five."

"Ninety-seven five? To this city it doesn't come," Teenager said.

"It does this time."

"Ninety-seven five for forty you say?" Teenager asked.

"I said fifty."

"That's too much money for me. I just come out of jail."

"What can I tell you?" Mariani asked, shrugging politely.

"Couldn't you give me a little less of a price?"

"It's out of my hands."

"Whose hands could it be in? The clouds in the sky? You are the highest man on earth."

"I speak the truth. It's out of my hands."

"Such a figure to pay when I just came out of jail."

"So you'll wait until you have it. This stuff don't come

by subway. It takes time to get here. I got guys everywhere waiting for it. Guys down your way. Pedro Torres' been *begging* me.''

Teenager made certain his face showed nothing when Torres' name was mentioned. Pedro Torres was on 149th Street, and while Teenager was in jail, Torres had told people that he, Torres, would take over the entire South Bronx. Teenager had said that he would slap Torres in the face for such talk. But this made it different. This was beyond talk: Torres was dealing directly with Mariani.

Mariani said, "You know him. He's a nice boy. I help him out if I can. I help out a lot of people. *No poca di petrosino fabone duti di puti minestra.*'' Mariani laughed. "You know what that means?''

"No.''

"Sicilian. It means, I'm like parsley. A little parsley makes all kinds of salads good.''

Teenager smiled and held out his hand. "Fifty.''

"You'll make a million,'' Mariani said, shaking the hand.

"I can get it today?'' Teenager said.

"Give me the money. Then leave your car at the Sunoco station on Castle Hill Avenue. You know the place. Where Paulie stays. Leave the car there, somebody picks it up. They call you, tell you where the car is. The unit'll be in the car.''

"I pay you soon,''·Teenager said.

"Fine. Then you'll get the car back soon.''

"I wanted the car back tonight.''

"Then pay the money before tonight.''

"I give it to you soon.''

Mariani held out his hands.

"I'm reliable in business,'' Teenager said.

Mariani smiled.

"Wasn't I reliable in how I helped out Ronnie in jail for you?''

"My son-in-law's not here in this room with us,'' Mariani said. "Ronnie's got nothin' to do with this.''

Teenager shrugged. "I don't know what to tell you.''

"You're a smart boy,'' Mariani said. "You can see that I just can't *do* it.''

"How am I going to get my business started unless you help me?" Teenager said.

"I will," Mariani said. "An eighth. Tonight, you could have an eighth. You want the whole thing, I can't do it."

"For an eighth I could have time?"

"All the time you want. In fact, I tell you what. Don't even leave the car for an eighth. Tell me where you want it and I'll have a guy bring it to you."

"At the bar," Teenager said.

"When?" Mariani said.

"Tomorrow. Just give it to Benny in the bar if I'm not there. He is as good as me."

"Beautiful," Mariani said.

"How much do you give Torres?" Teenager said.

Mariani held out his brandy glass and tapped Teenager's. "Let's be nice."

"Could I use your bathroom?" Teenager asked.

"Sure, go right outside down the hall. The second door on the left. Guest bathroom."

Teenager went to the bathroom and Mariani walked the opposite way, to the kitchen. When Teenager came out, he walked soundlessly down the hall.

"What does he think you got, Louis, a delicatessen?" the voice of Mariani's wife said.

"Will you shut up?" Mariani's voice said. "He got it in him to bargain. He don't know any different. The Spics is like Arabs. They got to bargain."

"You said it was the best you had in a long time, didn't you, Dad?" the son's voice said. "You told us you could step on it six times, right?"

"Seven," Mariani said.

Teenager made noise now and the talking stopped. They all smiled at him as he stepped into the kitchen.

"Could I trouble you for the phone?" Teenager said. "I just want to call my wife to tell her I am coming home."

There was no answer at home. Lydia probably had the kids out for a walk, he thought. "I go now," he said.

Now, Nicki walked into the kitchen, hand out, the protective smile wide on her mouth. "I feel terrible that you couldn't even stay and eat with us," she said.

Teenager held out his hand in farewell and walked out of the kitchen. He glanced over his shoulder and saw Nicki pick up a washcloth and begin to rub hard on the receiver that he had just used.

Nicki crumpled up an empty pack of cigarettes on the kitchen table, paced about looking for a full pack and began muttering when she could not find one. She was bothered, as she always was, by this empty Sunday of cigar smoke and garlic, a day made all the more uneasy by the meaningless Saturday that had gone before it and by the Monday that was ahead, with its lonely drive to prison. Waiting through a weekend for the humiliation of standing in a jailer's gaze.

She picked up sunglasses from the kitchen table, pushed them atop her head and went to the front door. Her father and Teenager were still standing there talking. Teenager had his hand on the door, but Nicki knew this was meaningless; gangsters rarely have anyplace to go after meeting each other, and their notion of terminal ability is to spend a half hour exchanging afterthoughts.

"Where are you going?" her father said to her.

"To get cigarettes."

"Got money with you?"

"Yes."

"Then get out of here."

Mariani and Teenager laughed, and Nicki went out the door and her long cheerful body tripped down the stoop. She was going to cut across the lawn to her father's car in the driveway, but instead she strode all the way to the front sidewalk.

As she walked closer to Maximo she saw a good leather jacket, a knit shirt and a gold chain. She was conscious of the look Maximo gave her as he looked up from his book. It was not the domineering, possessive look that always came from her husband; this one was pure sex. She was about to turn on the sidewalk and walk over to the driveway when Maximo smiled at her.

He looks like a fucking movie star, Nicki thought to herself.

Her eyes met Maximo's and stayed on them.

"Hello, I'm Maximo."

The accent, as slight as it was, caused her to flinch. It reminded her of dirty little Spics with thin greasy mustaches huddled in doorways, or leering at her on the subways, and of all the things she had heard about what Puerto Ricans do to their women.

"Your friend should be right out," she said coldly.

"Thank you," he said. Said it with this glad face and sexy eyes.

"What are you reading?"

She was ready for him to bring up some gang-bang magazine. Instead he held up this thick textbook. *The Uniform Commercial Code for the State of New York.*

"My law book."

"I'm sure," she said.

"No, look. That's what it is."

Even the Ivy League hadn't fully erased a slight "thas," a sound that caused the chamber of Nicki's ear to flinch. If there was one thing she could not stand about Spics, aside from nigger hair, it was that they said "thas" and "New Jessey." When she glanced at the pages of the book Maximo was holding, she saw that it was some kind of law book all right.

"Trying your own case?" Nicki said.

"No, I'm studying for the bar exams."

"Sure you are."

"Unfortunately, it's the truth." He smiled at her.

Just don't say *New Jessey,* she thought. Oh, you're a fucking movie star.

"That's fine," she said. "It was a pleasure to have met you."

Maximo watched her walk up to the Cadillac parked in the driveway. What does she smell like, Maximo thought.

Nicki dipped elegantly, provocatively into the Cadillac. She slid out with a pack of cigarettes in her hand.

"Saved me a drive," she said. "Right on the dashboard." She walked back, opening the cardboard box of cigarettes and stuffing the cellophane into a jeans pocket.

"Want one?"

"No, thank you."

"Well, I'm going in now. It was nice to have met you."

"I love your shirt," Maximo said.

She wanted to retreat behind the lighting of a cigarette, but she had no matches. "Isn't it pretty?" she said. "I just got it Friday."

"You should go shopping every Friday."

There was such a strong sexual undercurrent being caused by his eyes that she felt it pushing against her ankles, causing her to dig with her toes to prevent herself from being lifted off the bottom and floating helplessly.

"Maybe I will. Right now I have to go in."

"You never told me your name."

"Nicki."

"I will see you again, Nicki."

Boldly, unblinking, he kept his brown eyes riveted on her. She felt herself basking. This was not a look coming from a pair of raw streetcorner eyes that reached out and ripped her clothes off. This was a softer look, one that could not be brushed away, a look that was gently, but firmly helping her to undress.

Inside the house, Nicki took the cigarette cellophane out of her pocket and dropped it in the garbage. She pulled the towels off the trays of food. On each tinfoil covering was a piece of paper with her husband's name and prison number. Ronald Schiavone 327C19. The prison demanded that the food be delivered in this form, so that it could be checked for guns or knives or more important contraband, such as packets of cocaine. The guards were very watchful for drugs, because so much of a prison-town economy is based on guards selling drugs to inmates for outrageous prices that any interference with this process causes greater anger than an escape. The three trays Nicki was taking to prison this time contained lasagna, sausages and peppers, and chicken *scarpariello*, which meant that Ronald the prisoner would be eating like Palermo royalty.

This time, there even would be wine, for Nicki's visit was going to be an overnight stay with her husband in the trailer parked outside the prison fence—"the fuck truck," the inmates called it—and for twenty dollars to a guard, the arriving wife always could bring in a few bottles of wine.

When she had told her girlfriend Angela about these periodic visits to the trailer, Nicki had said, "For two days all you do is drink wine and get raped." But it had not been exactly that way. It had been more, bring him his running suit, iron his clothes, serve him food and listen to him complain. On the last visit, he had put on the Kelly green Adidas jogging suit she had bought for one hundred thirty dollars in Bloomingdale's basement and sauntered around the trailer in it. When Nicki said that he looked terrific in it, that the color was nicer on him than that of the crimson jogging suit she had brought up to him on the last visit, Ronald said, "Yeah, and look where I got to wear it."

"Come on, Ronnie, it's a lovely day."

"I got to wear this like I'm a dog in a kennel. Guys are out on the street making fortunes of money, and I got to eat and sleep with niggers."

"Ronnie."

"Ronnie my ass. You could talk. You sitting home like a queen. Where am I? I'm stuck in with niggers. Do you call that fair?"

If, as Nicki had been brought up to believe, a friend in need is a pest, then a husband in need turns out to be a carrier, passing his troubles onto her as if they were the flu; insisting that she suffer with his ailment, coughing full in her face to bring it about. Ronald complained for nearly all of the remainder of her visit; and at one point, three hours before she was to leave, Nicki went into the small shower because she had to be alone and she let the water run off her long body while she stared at the wall. "I'm the one that's in jail," she said.

On the drive home, she played an FM station so loudly that even with a feline howl, she could not make her voice sound above the music. Nor did the music have any effect upon her feelings. She considered herself a woman on her way back to a girls' camp.

"You'll do it right," her father had said to her on the day her husband went to jail. This meant remaining home, or being seen only with female friends whose husbands, too, were in jail. Under the rules of their upbringing, these prison wives were to spend their time shopping

and going to the movies or, most often, sitting at home
with a kitchenful of women in the same circumstances.
She had been raised to marry only "one of the men," as
the women refer to hoodlums. An arrest is considered
part of the business overhead. The job of the woman is
to go to court, listen stoically as the man is sentenced and
then visit him in prison, bringing along large amounts of
carefully prepared food. On visits, it is important to take
Polaroid shots of the husband and to ask a guard to take
the standard picture of a young woman and young man
together. The photo is taken in a prison waiting room,
but it follows the traditional two-shot of school gradua-
tion day camera art: male and female with arms about
each other's backs, smiling, the male smiling much more
broadly, as if he had just learned, under an elm tree on
the great campus, that he was graduating cum laude. The
prison version Polaroids are shown all the next week to
girlfriends, who then dig into purses and produce new
Polaroids of their own husbands, who are in other jails.

After many stacks of Polaroids, the man returns and as
a reward the wife is given diamonds, which she can admire as she sits through the nights while the husband is
out resuming business. And somewhere, she knows, is a
snub-nosed Irish precinct kid driving an old car, or an
insurance-faced federal agent in an undented car, waiting
to grab the husband again. While the poor may commit
felonies and then evade jail, the Mafia does not embarrass
the criminal justice system. They are convicted frequently, and they always serve.

Now, standing alone in the kitchen, she thought
bleakly of her trip to prison the next morning and, more
depressing, of what the ride home would be like. Driving
home to a house where she was supposed to find great
satisfaction in helping her mother clean the entire house
each Saturday. She had a song in her body and they
wanted her to spend her life in a laundry room.

She stared at the trays of food with the paper slips on
them, then sat down and slowly took out a cigarette, lit it
and immediately thought of the movie star outside in the
car.

"Can you imagine me being with a Spic?" she said.

* * *

"Maximo!"

Teenager finally walked out of Mariani's house. "I kept you waiting a long time, Maximo."

"I was reading," Maximo said.

"I had to talk to him about his son-in-law," Teenager said. He began driving.

"That's all right. Because I'm coming up with you again the next time."

"What do you mean?"

"I said, I'll be with you next time."

Teenager's eyebrows bunched together. Then his eyes widened as he realized what Maximo was speaking about. "Your school turned you into a crazy man. You can never go near that female."

"There's nothing crazy about wanting her," Maximo said.

"He would have to kill you if he knew you were even talking of his daughter," Teenager said.

"Who says he has to know?"

"And she has a husband. To save his honor he would have to torture you."

"How could he torture me if I were already dead?"

"They would take you into a freezer in the meat market and hang you on the hook like a lamb and then they would cut you up a piece at a time. They would make sure to keep you alive for a long time. They would torture you all week. Then on Sunday they would cut off your nuts and stuff them in your mouth."

They were going across the George Washington Bridge and Teenager was effusive, often letting the car drive itself while he used both hands for sweeping gestures to illustrate how horrible was the death that Maximo faced, and Maximo sat wordlessly and stared out the window at the flat gray river, spring sunshine splashing the edges, and thought about the lovely warm color that ran through Nicki's face when he smiled at her.

Maximo was surprised that he had the power to bring this into a white woman's face. What does she smell like, he wondered. Certainly not like the women at Harvard. He remembered one named Cora, the skinny one with pale white skin and gray eyes, who had smelled like the shopping mall under Rockefeller Center where his father had once taken him to see people ice-skating.

"The Italians cannot control themselves when it comes to their women," Teenager said.

Maximo nodded. As the car came off the bridge and onto the first singed blocks of the city, he was thinking of Nicki's breasts and long legs. This one, he decided, had to smell good. She would not smell like a shopping mall. He smiled as he heard Teenager rambling. Perhaps for the first time in his life he would do something that Teenager would be afraid to do. He would stand in danger and guffaw at Teenager, who would remain outside.

When they got to Ana's Bar, Maximo walked right to the phone and called to Teenager, "Give me the phone number of that female's house."

"You're crazy," Teenager said.

"She is in love with me," Maximo said. "I have to call her or she will kill herself tonight."

"Sit down here, I buy you beer," Teenager said.

Maximo remained at the phone. "What are you afraid of?" he said.

Teenager called out the number and Maximo, with the calmness of a general starting a war, dropped coins into the phone.

She answered on the third ring. Her voice became a fire alarm when she heard Maximo ask for her.

"Who is this?"

"I am Maximo. Teenager's friend outside in the car."

"Are you insane calling me here?"

"Your look lingers," Maximo said.

"What?"

"All the way home across the bridge I could see your face on the surface of the water. That is how you have captured my thoughts. This has never happened to me before. Only a particular person, a very wonderful person, could do a thing like that to me."

"Thank you."

"I meant it," Maximo said.

"Maybe I have thoughts about you," she said.

"Tell me about them."

She laughed. "Not now. Do you want to get us killed?"

"Tell me about them tomorrow."

"I'm away tomorrow and Tuesday."

"Then Wednesday," Maximo said.

"Well . . ."

"Wednesday."

"You could meet me by where I work," she said.

"Where?"

"I work on Fifty-third Street," she said.

"And where?"

"Third Avenue."

"So I go to a bar review course in the Statler. Over on Thirty-third Street. It's right on the subway from you."

"I go to lunch at twelve-thirty," she said.

"After work," Maximo said.

"What time after work?"

"There's a bar review class I go to at seven," Maximo said.

"Then you could meet me at five."

"Wednesday night at five."

"There's a place in the basement of the Citicorp Building. The European coffee shop."

"Where do I get you in case something happens and I have to call you?"

"Continental Bank. I'll give you the number direct to my department. Plaza 1–2592. I'll see you at five."

"Thas lovely," Maximo said.

When she hung up, she told herself that if she had not taken charge of making the arrangements, this guy would have had her meeting him in a social club full of Puerto Ricans someplace. Some kind of law course he's supposed to be taking, she thought. He and his friend must have some sort of a case together and they're trying to read up on it behind the lawyer's back. Oh, what does all that matter? *A fucking movie star.*

Maximo was beaming when he hung up.

"What did she say?" Teenager said.

"That she loves me very much."

Teenager laughed. Maximo said, "It's nothing to fool

with. She is in love with me. I am playing with this poor girl's life.''

"You are playing with your own," Teenager said.

All Maximo could think about was Wednesday.

Upstairs, he stopped at the apartment at the other end of the hall, where his mother sat with neighbors and watched a Mexican movie with Marie Felix and Jorge Negrete on the Spanish-language channel. Maximo then went into his apartment, made a cup of tea and sat down at the kitchen table with his textbook. His eyes wandered for a moment, falling on his father's old radio–record player which sat atop a chest. The wooden case had a furniture polish luster, which was wrong, Maximo felt, for it now was over a quarter of a century old and should have been covered with dust. In memory of his father, however, his mother kept it clean and prominent. Glancing at it now, Maximo immediately remembered his father, short and stocky, his chest swollen with anger, standing next to the machine and listening to the record that to him was the symbol of all that was against him and whose sound, over the many years, rang against his arteries so often that leaks began springing inside his head. The father became an invalid and then a memory. Which now drew Maximo from the kitchen and caused his hand to search through the cabinet at one end of the chest and take out the old record, a disc as hard as rock candy. He put it on the record player and turned the switch. After allowing the machine to warm up, he played the record, which produced whirring and static and then the clear voice of Peggy Lee:

> . . . the faucet, she is dripping,
> the fence, she's falling down,
> My pocket needs some money,
> so I can't go into town.
> My brother isn't working,
> and my sister doesn't care,
> The car, she needs a motor
> so I can't go anywhere.
> Mañana, Mañana, Mañana is soon enough for me.

Somewhere about this point in the song, Maximo remembered, his father would appear to be fighting off a seizure. His tense voice would call out, "You see what they think of us? This was a great big popular song. They still play it. They make fun of us right on the radio." The voice's volume would rise as Peggy Lee, in an attempted Hispanic accent, came to this part of the song Maximo now listened to closely:

> *My mother, she is working,*
> *she is working very hard,*
> *but everytime she looks for me,*
> *I am sleeping in the yard . . .*

When Maximo was young, his father's hand would start whipping the air as he shouted about the insult that the song represented, how his son would be ready to fight these insults for the rest of his life, for the insults would surely come, from a cop, a messenger, a radio, from anyplace that could make a sound. But as Maximo listened to the record now, he wasn't as bothered by it as he once was, although the part about the mother working hard still caused his insides to sting. Give the father a job and the mother doesn't have to work so hard, he said to himself. In the six years since his father died, however, Maximo had tried to look at life from a place a few steps away from where his father had stood. The view remained the same: Puerto Ricans on a cold street with nothing to do, looking up at the train whistling through East Harlem and the Bronx on the way to the suburbs, a train with windows made white by newspapers held by white suburban people who through their working lives, twice a day, five times a week, sat on this train and made certain to keep their papers as high as a fighter's left hand to keep away the view of burned-out buildings and Puerto Ricans with nothing to do on the cold streets.

The South Bronx was separated from Manhattan by an oily river, on the Bronx banks of which there rose a wall of highways and sullen factory buildings. Behind them was a forest of tenements. Once, the South Bronx had a half million Irish and Jews with one only having to glance at the street names to see who was on top; it was the only place since the creation where Jews lived on St. Mary's Street. The area also had an institution that people felt made them important and different. The South Bronx had Joe DiMaggio, who was seven blocks to the West, on the other side of the Grand Concourse, running down a flyball in deep centerfield at Yankee Stadium. And each morning, for people in the South Bronx, the act of opening a newspaper and looking at the Yankee box score—DiMaggio, two for four again—was to allow them to pass over the unlived-out potential of their own lives.

DiMaggio was replaced in the South Bronx by buildings afire that were shown on the World Series telecasts at Yankee Stadium. The burning of the South Bronx was started by landlords looking for insurance, and at the end, the fire belonged to the children. In one year, while Maximo was in college, fire drove out twelve hundred people from the single block between 140th and 141st on St. Anselm's Avenue. The people forced to flee were Puerto Ricans, and the ones setting the fires were Puerto Ricans working for landlords, and for mischief. Once, migrations caused statues to be erected and poems to be written in honor of the journey by sea to the new land. There is no monument, however, to the new immigrants, the blacks who came to the South Bronx from Jacksonville, Florida, and Americus, Georgia, and the Puerto Ricans from San Pedro and Santurce and Salinas and Ponce. There is not even official recognition that these new immigrants accomplished something that nobody else could do: turn the United States into two actual nations, one country of about one hundred ninety-five million whites and the other, the second America, of about sixty-five million, their skins running from faintest tan to ebony. The history of the first America can be found in any schoolbook; that of the second America in unemployment figures, aid-to-dependent children payments, and penitentiary records.

Maximo was young, and while he wondered how much difficulty he would encounter with his own people, raised in poetry praising the white heart, and also how many traps were hidden in the murky established order of

Bronx politics, of which he knew nothing, he still was certain that someday he would place his standard atop the rubble and the breeze would cause the colors to dance and the people would be attracted. He was certain that someday New York would be the first part of America to approach a European city, with almost all citizens speaking more than one language. In New York, it would be English and Spanish; the people who now resented most the bilingual signs and education in the city would be the ones who someday would have to sit across from their children at night and watch them learning Spanish as a grammar school requirement. Ask any hospital maternity ward. Always, Maximo remembered the night at Lenox Hill Hospital, with Park Avenue traffic just under the windows, when Eddie Hernandez, eighteen then, ran to the bank of phone booths, dialed nervously and then shouted, *"Es macho! Seis libras, quatro onzas,"* and the other people in the hallway looked surprised at the Spanish, but Maximo now knew that this was the way it would be more and more, a new father calling the grandmother and speaking in Spanish, until someday the heads in the hallway would turn only when they heard the strangest of sounds, a guy screaming into the phone, "It's a boy! Six pounds, four ounces." As Maximo sat down at the kitchen table with his tea and textbook, he thought about Nicki. That long happy body. Marvelous of me, Maximo thought. I start my life among my people by filling my mind with a white woman.

.... **Chapter**

4

.... :

Maximo called Nicki Wednesday from the bar. He said he would be downtown in a half hour. Nicki told him it would be good to see him and Maximo said it would be wonderful to see her. Teenager, watching Maximo's face, could see that he was not speaking to a relative.

"Come with me and I'll buy you a shirt and some other things at Eddie's," Teenager said.

"I don't have time," Maximo said.

"I want Eddie to get you all dressed for the last big time of your life," Teenager said.

Maximo smiled.

"I told you they put you on a meathook," Teenager said.

"Courage before caution," Maximo said. He swaggered past Teenager and went out the back door.

Why should boundaries formed by color apply to him? He had just spent three years among the most favored—among? Striding far ahead of most of them—and he was therefore certain that he would continue in this position throughout his life. How, then, could some law of ignorance have anything to do with him? Particularly, when the woman involved, this Jersey Italian, had looked at him as if she were standing in a field of dust and saw suddenly the approach of heavy rain clouds?

On a matter of simple experience, Maximo also could not understand Teenager's warning about the danger of

49

Italians because, between the Bronx and Harvard, he had never seen more than two or three Italians at a time in his life.

Mostly, however, this cavorting exit in front of Teenager was caused by a need for vanity. The idea of going down to Eddie's store, disturbed memories that Maximo would prefer remain hidden.

Eddie Hernandez grew up two blocks from Maximo and was in the same class through grammar school and high school. After school one day, when both were in junior high school, Eddie was at Maximo's house, having soda, when Teenager banged on the door. Maximo's father, sitting alone and damaged in the dim living room, laughed as Maximo let Teenager in.

"Aha!" Teenager shouted quickly.

Eddie Hernandez quickly swallowed his soda and reached for his coat.

"Where are you going?" Maximo asked him.

"Home to my mother."

Maximo's father and Teenager didn't notice that Eddie walked out without even throwing his eyes toward them. In school the next morning, Eddie Hernandez seemed to have more nervous energy than usual, and when Maximo came up to talk to him in the back of their homeroom, Eddie pulled a gray sweater over his head and his arms became entangled while he was getting out of it and time for talk was lost. That afternoon, Maximo walked over to the basketball court in the projects and found Eddie taking shots with some other boys.

"Why did you go home so quick yesterday?" Maximo asked him.

"I wanted to," Eddie said.

"Is that all?" Maximo said.

"No. My mother told me that I can't be anyplace where Teenager is."

"Why?"

"Because that's what she says."

"My father likes him," Maximo said.

"My mother told me, that's all I can say," Eddie said.

In July of 1970, Maximo's mother went into the bedroom at about eight P.M. to see her husband and came running back with a hand to her mouth. She opened the door and wailed for neighbors. Maximo went into the bedroom, where his father was on his back with his mouth open and his eyes looking out like those of a mounted fish. The body was removed to the medical examiner's office and the night was spent with Maximo's mother weeping on a kitchen chair while women from the neighborhood made tea.

At one A.M., Maximo went downstairs to the bar, where Benny Velez was in an argument with three men.

"Where is Teenager?" Maximo called from the doorway.

"He isn't here," Benny called out, without turning his head.

"Where is he?" Maximo said.

"It is none of your business or my business," Benny said.

"When will he be back?"

"When he comes back from going away with a female."

Maximo walked to the projects, woke up Eddie Hernandez and sat talking to him for a half hour.

"I won't leave you alone in this thing," Eddie Hernandez told him.

The next morning, Maximo looked out his window and saw Eddie Hernandez and his sister sitting at a card table set up on the sidewalk in front of the newsstand. They were collecting money, dimes and quarters, to pay for the funeral of Maximo's father. For two days Eddie and his sister, and a couple of kids from school and the basketball court, sat at the card table and asked people for money to pay for Rafael Escobar's funeral.

They collected eighty-seven dollars, which meant that the bill for a Rivera Chapels funeral, one hundred and sixty dollars, could be paid. Maximo and Eddie Hernandez went to the Rivera funeral chapel, paid the bill, picked out a white plastic casket and had Rivera go to the morgue for the body. Back at Maximo's building, a familiar voice came out of the apartment's open doorway. Eddie Hernandez began to linger at the top of the staircase, but Maximo took him by the arm and forced him into the apartment. There, pacing back and forth in the living room, was Teenager, his hands moving, breath snorting.

"You should have called me," he said to Maximo.

"Nobody knew where," Maximo said.

"You should have called me."

Teenager stopped and put his hands on his hips. "Now what is this funeral?"

"Eddie and I just came from Rivera's. We paid him."

"How much did you pay him?"

"One hundred and sixty."

"That is a cup of coffee. That is no funeral for your father. I will see that your father has a funeral."

"We already paid," Eddie Hernandez said.

"You will get your money back now," Teenager said. He pulled a thick packet of folded bills from his pocket.

Shaking his head, Eddie Hernandez backed away from Teenager and became lost in the general confusion of the room. Maximo did not see Eddie again until the funeral. Maximo's father was laid out in a polished brown mahogany casket in Rivera's big chapel. Maximo, sitting in front, happened to glance back and see Eddie Hernandez sitting in a row of children who sat in the heat and kicked their legs. The people went to church in three limousines. Teenager sat in the hearse and held a microphone into the air and allowed the sound of funeral music to blare through the streets.

Maximo did not see Eddie Hernandez for several weeks after that. When he finally went to Eddie's house one night, Eddie stood in the doorway and did not ask him in.

"My sister and I collected money from the people, but you wanted your father buried with drug money," Eddie said.

"I do not know what Teenager does," Maximo said.

"My mother does," Eddie said.

Maximo only saw Eddie now and then after this. He was with Eddie in the hospital waiting room the night Eddie's first baby was born, but otherwise they were generally apart.

And now, on the sidewalk outside the bar, Maximo

could remember the look on Eddie Hernandez' face at the hospital that night. Maximo glanced at the newsstand and this suddenly caused him to remember something else: the afternoon two years ago when he was home from Harvard for the summer, standing here on this same patch of sidewalk, and Eddie Hernandez' wife, Fela, began to walk past him, but then her curiosity overruled. Her generous mouth in a smile, her eyes bright atop high brown cheeks, Fela walked up to Maximo.

"I haven't seen you in a long time," Fela said.

"That's because I haven't been here," Maximo said.

"Oh, this I know," Fela said. She put her hands to the back of her neck and lifted the long black shining hair. "It is only June and it is as hot as it is in PR," she said. Fela's chunkiness strained a white sleeveless blouse. The rest of her, covered in black jeans, was ample enough to please her husband, who, as do most Puerto Rican men, regarded a little extra weight in a woman as a sign of health and something a bit more pleasant to hold onto at night than bones. Fela had not, however, gone over the line with her weight; she had stopped just short of that point where the amount of flesh causes the husband to go out looking for a woman right away.

"What is it like in that school you go to?" Fela asked.

"Pretty good." As Maximo spoke cheerfully, his head nodded to others he knew who were passing by. The corner was daylight busy: Nemo, who started as dishwasher and saved his money and bought the Ramona Coffee Shop, the best in the Bronx; a soda-truck driver carrying cases into a *bodega;* Carney, overweight, her teeth stumps, the mother of the last white family on the street; Medina, twenty-eight now, his skin surfaces torn by a past of dope and street gangs and prisons, but able to walk with a looseness and a smile, the scars inside perhaps faded, as he headed for the playground he and his friends operated since the city abandoned it; women in twos and threes going into the subway for their jobs downtown and, standing for all the hopes and all that is right, Valentin Perez, walking proudly in the hot sun, his plaid shirt buttoned to the top, a blue tie pulled flush with the neckline, not a semi-inch of shirt fabric showing, let-

ting the world understand that he was going to the subway to ride downtown, where he held the most important
thing of all in the life of a person in the South Bronx, he
held a *yob*.

And there were the slow-walking, their eyes soaked
with resentment, who understood that the major event of
their day could be what they were doing right now, walking the street with nothing to do.

"How's Eddie?" Maximo asked Fela.

"He's good. You know Eddie. He's always dreaming.
Now he says someday maybe he will own a store."

"That would be great," Maximo said.

"Then he could use you as a lawyer," Fela said.

"I hope not," Maximo said.

"Oh, you'll be very good for Eddie," Fela said.

"No, I want him to own a store long before I become
a lawyer."

Fela laughed. Unconsciously, she took a step backward and bumped against one of the people walking to
nowhere. He was about twenty-five and he had on a black
undershirt and orange tattoos on his biceps. His hair was
long and tangled. He stopped walking, with Fela stacked
against him for an instant, and his mouth became a leer.
He put his left hand between Fela's legs. Then he brought
his hand up to his nose.

"That smells nice, man."

She jumped away, and he stood grinning at Fela and
Maximo. The grin showed pride in what he had done, and
also a desire that it would lead to something else, a
chance to hurt somebody. He was only slightly heavier
than Maximo, maybe only ten pounds heavier, and he
stood grinning and looking at Maximo and Maximo
looked at him and did not move. Inside Maximo, natural
fear was fed by memory and justified by time spent in
another atmosphere. Where Maximo was now, on a sidewalk of the hopeless, a stare held too long, a careless
elbow, a misheard phrase, could lead to anywhere. "I
only asked you for a dollar, man," the young guy named
Johnny Gomez had said to Ruiz at this same newsstand
five years ago. "Go fuck yourself for your dollar," Ruiz
had said. "I ought to get a gun and shoot you," Gomez

had said. "Go ahead. You a *maricón*. You wouldn't know what to do to me," Ruiz had said. Gomez, eyes blazing, spun and ran away. He was back in ten minutes, his manhood and a shotgun in his hands, and he blew most of Ruiz' head away while Ruiz was counting change. Gomez was twenty-two when he went to prison; he might be free as early as his thirty-seventh birthday. That Maximo was violence-shy had kept him from jumping at this guy who stood grinning at him. That he had learned, through thousands of hours in other places, that there was more to being a man than the instant, the right to revenge had been traded for the protection of law, that it was insane to stake your life on a matter so stupid that sensible people would not remember it an hour later, assured him that his initial fear, while not a sign of heroism, could pass for the beginnings of maturity. Throw a punch at this guy and you might cast him in the only drama of his life, and he would produce a gun.

The guy's grin became broader and his chin stuck out and Maximo, looking straight at him, still did not move. Then he took Fela by the arm and walked her quickly to the side door of the bar. Inside, there were only two old men and a woman serving them drinks. There was no Teenager; Teenager was in prison at the time. Fela looked around the bar and then her eyes returned to Maximo and prosecuted him in silence. Fela abruptly walked out the front door of the bar.

Fifteen minutes later, as Maximo stood in the shadows of the doorway, Eddie Hernandez came along. He walked with his head up and his face showing nothing and a baseball bat swinging easily in his right hand. He noticed Maximo, but acted as if he had not. Maximo watched Eddie walk down the street in the direction in which the guy with the tattoos had walked. Maximo still was in the doorway when Eddie Hernandez came back, from a search that had found nothing.

Maximo started to say something and Eddie Hernandez cut him off.

"That was my wife," Eddie said.

"I'm trying to say something," Maximo said.

"Say what? Say that you have to wait for your friend Teenager to come home so he can hit the guy for you?"

"I didn't mean that," Maximo said.

"Well, we know what you are," Eddie said. "Now I have to go back to my wife and tell her I couldn't find the guy. She'll make me as bad as you." He walked off in disdain and Maximo stepped back in the bar and knew he had to sit there until nobody was around and he could leave without somebody's glare stripping him to his bones.

Now, remembering this, Maximo became irritated by the size of the stone that had caused him to stumble. Small, stupid. Producing stupid pressure. Maximo knew that he would have no way to overcome this memory until he could look at Eddie Hernandez and speak to him and somehow dissolve the past. Which had to include Teenager. But he had no way to do that now. Now he had to ride downtown and see a white woman.

When Nicki hung up the phone at her desk, she was surprised, as she pulled out a cigarette, to find that her fingers were so calm that they barely disturbed the cigarette box. In all of her life she could not conceive that she ever would say yes to a Puerto Rican about anything, and yet she just had, and here she was, lighting this cigarette as if she was passing through just another part of the afternoon.

She looked at the administrator's terminal in front of her and tapped the display function. On the screen came the production sheet for Crowley, J. He had been working in the charge cards department for only two weeks, and he was placed at a terminal in the center of the great room, but Nicki despised him. She had smelled him once when he brushed past her out in the hallway in the morning and she had been unable to drink her coffee as a result. He must have chickens hidden under his jacket, she had decided. Anyone that sloppy about his personal cleanliness had to be careless about his work, she thought, or worse than careless. He was Irish; he must be a liar.

Her eyes went down the calls listed by Crowley and she stopped at account number 867132. The production sheet note after it said, "Called home, spoke to card member who promised immediate payment." Nicki took the name and phone numbers of the card member, a man in Louisville, Kentucky, named Landau.

As it was before five, she called Landau at his business number.

"Who's calling Mister Landau?" a voice said.

When Nicki identified herself and said she was from the bank's credit card division, she immediately caught the hesitancy in the voice on the other end. After eighteen months of running the delinquent accounts, sixty-five to ninety-four days, department for the bank, she was familiar with even the most trifling signs of weakness from people who owe money.

"Mr. Landau just stepped out," the voice said.

"I'm calling because we have a problem with our computers," Nicki said.

"Yes," the man said. The smallest hopeful sign puts timbre into the voice.

"Because of the computer problem, which of course is our fault, I merely want to check out something with Mr. Landau."

"You can check it with me," the voice said.

"Well, I'd like to know first if someone from our bank had the courtesy to call Mr. Landau today and inform him of our computer malfunction."

"I got no call from your bank today," the voice said.

"Well, I'm calling you now in reference to an unpaid balance of $975.63 cents. This balance now has been outstanding for eighty-three days, our records show, and we would like to know what Mister Landau intends to do about it. If we don't receive payment shortly, I'm afraid we will have to turn the matter over to our collection agency."

The voice on the other end of a man screwed rose many decibels.

"Listen, you dirty fucking bas—"

"Mister Landau, *I'm* not a dirty fucking bastard." She smiled as she heard a grenade go off in his mouth. She aimed her words carefully through his shouting. "Mister

Landau, I am today turning your account over to our collections people for proper action. Good afternoon."

Immensely satisfied, she hung up. It had taken her months to figure out that while she was not allowed to react to any personal abuse from delinquent credit card members, nowhere in the bank rules did it say that she could not deny a charge and do so in a way that would leave her, as always, the one holding all the tools of torture. Furthermore, on this call she also had nailed Crowley as the liar that he was. Nicki made a note on her pad. "Crowley lies re account 867132." In the morning, she would again bring up the Crowley production sheet on the display function, show it to Mr. Means, the officer in charge of personnel for her department, and start Crowley towards dismissal. Let him buy soap with his unemployment.

She glanced over the hundred and twenty-five people at video terminals. She was immensely proud of having risen this far in the bank, and at the same time had trained herself to think as little as possible about any job beyond this. She was being paid twenty-six thousand five hundred dollars a year and gave the men over her the same feeling of reliability that they got from their cars. However, the next step up for Nicki someday would be an assistant vice-president of the bank, and she had been told repeatedly that it was a job for which she was unqualified because of her educational background. "You don't have the pedigree," the chief of personnel once had told her.

His use of a courthouse word such as this caused her to flinch. Nicki had only two years of high school. When she began in school, her father was a gangster of little substance, he was in prison, in fact, and Nicki was living with her brother, mother and an aunt named Cia Concetta on 105th Street in East Harlem. Her aunt, Cia Concetta, enrolled Nicki in Cathedral High School, but on the first day Nicki went to the school, she was greeted by a huge black nun standing in the doorway. Nicki backed away, turned and fled up the street. When Nicki told her of this, Cia Concetta said, "The school mustn't be Catholic anymore." She took Nicki all the way downtown, to St.

Anthony Girls Commercial High School on Sullivan Street in Greenwich Village. It was a two-year school, with twenty-two girls in a classroom, and when Nicki graduated at age sixteen the nun in charge of placing girls in jobs sent her up to the bank, where she started as a file clerk, then moved to teller and now, at twenty-six, with eight years of diligence reflected in her file, she had gone as far as her drive, street sense and instant familiarity with figures could take her without the greatest of all assets, a pedigree.

At times she became incensed at the wimps who were placed in jobs over her merely because they had college backgrounds. This was in contradiction to her upbringing, which was one of being servile to men, but common sense overruled the past when she was confronted with a person like Dalton, who had come onto the floor as an assistant vice-president a year before. He scheduled so many productivity meetings that there was no production, for which his memos blamed her. At one such meeting, an interminable one in the morning, Nicki rose to go to the ladies' room out of boredom.

"Ah, Miss Mariani," Dalton said.

"Yes?"

"Could you please tell me where you're going?"

The six other faces in the room were all watching Nicki, and for a moment she felt the embarrassment rise to her face, but she quickly overcame it and let her instincts show.

"Out to buy you a new head," she said.

As an assistant vice-president, Dalton immediately took this matter to personnel and Nicki was called in and the chief of personnel said to her, "We understand that Mr. Dalton's work has not been conducive to achieving the results we have come to expect from your department. But there is a management principle here, and we simply cannot pass off charges of insubordination. At the same time we know how valuable you are. Perhaps could this be settled privately, ah, with a discreet apology?"

The next morning, Nicki went into Dalton's office, looked at his blue watery eyes and said in a dry tone, "I'd like to apologize personally for yesterday."

Dalton grimaced and began running his hands together. He was about to start a lecture on his own importance that he undoubtedly had spent the night preparing when Nicki walked out of the office and went back to work. You did what you had to do, she assured herself.

Even now that her father was home and turning over large amounts of money with his business, she needed the job more than ever. While she would live with him, and sometimes allow her mother to make large purchases for her, she would not take cash directly from her father. This was her settlement with the life about her. All of it was based on this one achievement of her life, her job.

Now, at her desk, Nicki picked up her pocketbook and went to the ladies' room out in the hallway. As she put the key in the door, she looked about her to be certain no one was trailing her. She then pushed the door in and entered hesitantly. Only when she saw female legs in one of the stalls did she relax. In the past two months, two women had been mugged by filthy Puerto Ricans in the building's hallways in the late afternoon. Probably someone in Maximo's family doing it, Nicki said to herself.

She looked in the mirror at her green-gray eyes and carefully put light blue eyeshadow on her eyelids, a little under the eyes, and in the creases she put dark blue for contrast.

"I'm going through a lot of trouble for some Spic. Even if he does look like a movie star," she said to herself as she inspected her eyes.

Below the eyebrows she put on more light blue, which she covered with white. She then melded the two colors with her index fingers, working her fingers outward, so that the eye-shadow gently faded near the top of her cheekbones. Always, she did this unthinkingly. This time, she could feel the pressure of her fingers on her eyebrows. As she put on mascara, she began to think what she would say to Maximo when she had coffee with him.

"Who says I want to talk to him?" she said to herself.

Back at her desk, she called her mother and said that she was meeting her girlfriend Angela for a drink at five-thirty and would be late for dinner. Then she called her girlfriend Angela, who worked in the garment center. Angela had grown up across the street from Nicki and had been divorced for five years. She found that at thirty a woman in New York was wrapped in a shawl of loneliness even in the most crowded places. Angela, with long dark hair and the near-Oriental eyes of the Sicilians, had exactly three dates in the first two years, the nicest of them turning out to be fighting a losing battle against gayness. When Nicki's husband went to prison, Angela moved into a garden apartment in Fort Lee so she could be near Nicki.

"I'm meeting you for a drink at five-thirty," Nicki said to Angela.

"Where?"

"I'm meeting you for a drink at five-thirty, but you're not coming."

"What do you mean I'm not coming?"

"Because I'm going out to have a little disgrace tonight. I'm using you."

"You're going out?" Angela said.

"Good-bye," Nicki sang.

"I can't believe it," Angela said. "You?"

"Good-bye," Nicki said again.

There was a crowd of shoppers in the arcade and when she pushed through them and came into the coffee shop, she saw Maximo at a front table, a vision, his head turned from her so that the slope of his neck taunted her. When he turned and saw her and smiled, her breath quickened. Maximo's nose was slender and his lips thin. Oh, of course they had to be. She knew that she could not have fooled herself the first time she saw him by overlooking big fat lips or wide nostrils. She knew that she could never have made such a mistake, thank God for it too, but at the same time the mere thought of such a thing, just a quickened shred of thought made while turning her head on the pillow the other night, was enough to keep her awake for hours. Oh, could you imagine if his lips were thick! But now as she looked at him, the face aristocratically slender, she was elated.

"Your eyes are lovely," he said.

"Thank you. Wouldn't it be better if we went to the back? There's too many people walking by here."

"Fine." He stood up and his face showed no suspicion. This pleased her, because she was moving the table in order to keep people passing by from seeing her with a Puerto Rican.

Nicki led him to a table in the rear corner of the shop, by the swinging wooden doors that led to the kitchen.

"Cappuccino," Nicki told the waitress.

"Espresso," Maximo said.

"You want any pastries? They got good pastries," the waitress said.

"Bad for the figure," Nicki said.

"Thanks, but I'd prefer not," Maximo said. He smiled at Nicki. "I don't like to eat before this course I'm taking," he told her.

"Say the truth," Nicki said.

"What?"

"You really go to school?"

"Yes."

"Come on."

"What can I tell you?"

"Say the truth."

"I'll tell you what. When we leave here, you come with me and see what I do. And if I'm not sitting in a bar review course for three hours—"

"All right, I believe you." The surprising thing to her was that she did believe him. A cold, factual quality to his voice convinced her. She was of course going to tell him anyway that she believed him, for honesty was the last objective of this meeting. But now she was in more wonder as she looked at him.

"Are you always this suspicious?" Maximo said.

"I don't want to say anything, but look who you were with when I met you," she said.

"And look who you were with," he said.

"I guess we're both busted valises," she said.

"No, we're not," Maximo said. She loved the confidence in his voice.

"This morning when my mother woke me up, I was

going to throw her, the alarm clock and everybody else right out the door,'' Nicki said.

"Why?"

"I don't know. I hated to get up. You ever get like that? You hate to even go out?"

"No."

"You don't? Why?"

"Because I can handle anything that happens that day."

"My father's that way. He doesn't let anything faze him. He could be going to meet the King of Italy and he'd be the same way. You know what my father did the day I was getting married? He was shaving. Holding up the whole wedding. We're late for the photographer to take pictures, for the car to go to the church, for the mass, everything. My father's shaving. My mother starts screaming at him. You know what my father says. 'Make coffee for the *Duce*.' My mother starts screaming and he says, so quiet, 'Make coffee for the *Duce*.' Just like that. She had to go into the kitchen in her long gown and make coffee for my father. At least she cheated and made instant.''

"When did you get married?" Maximo asked her.

"Forty-two months ago. He's been gone thirty-six of them.''

"What for?"

"What for?" She lit a cigarette. "What do you think for?''

"Drugs," Maximo said.

She inhaled slowly, her eyes looking out the window, and said nothing.

"When does he get out?" Maximo said.

"He got four to life. The Rockefeller law. He can get work release next year. Maybe."

"And you wait?"

"Of course I do."

"Then maybe I shouldn't be bothering you," Maximo said.

"Did I say you shouldn't?"

"No."

"Then you just wait until I tell you."

"Fine with me," Maximo said.

"How often do you go to this course?"

"Three nights a week."

"For how long?"

"Until November. That's when I take the test."

"Is it a hard test?"

"I'll pass it."

"One good thing. You'll make a lot of money. Big bucks."

"I don't imagine I will," Maximo said.

"Come on. My father always says that the lawyers get all the gravy and leave us macaroni with nothing to go on it."

"It depends on what kind of lawyer you are," Maximo said.

She studied Maximo's face and couldn't think of what more to say to this Puerto Rican who was going to be a lawyer.

"Were you born here?" she said, finally.

"La Playa de Ponce. Ever been to Puerto Rico?"

"No. I've been to Vegas."

Examining him, she decided that he was not a pure Puerto Rican. He was more like a Spaniard from Spain. That would be all right, to be in love with a Spaniard from Spain.

Maximo had been studying her as they spoke. He knew that each time he smiled, her face flushed.

"What do you do in the bank?"

"I'm in charge of people who collect money."

"I can't like that so much."

"There's lots about you I probably don't like. I'm not here to talk about my job, anyway."

When they had finished coffee, Maximo said, "Are you coming to check on my course?"

"I'm going home."

"That's a great waste."

"Isn't it?" Nicki said.

"I'll say."

"Next time you can take me to your course," she said.

"When will that be?"

"Soon."

"How soon?"

"Call me at work. At night you could call my girlfriend Angela at her house. Here, write the number down." She waited until he took a sheet of paper out of a notebook. "She lives in Jersey. Two oh one. Seven three three, five eight oh two. You call her up and leave a message where you are. She'll call me and I'll call you."

"Why can't I just call your house?"

"So you could get the both of us killed?"

Maximo took the check.

"Are you sure?" Nicki said. She had her wallet out. This irritated Maximo, who answered with a grunt. He must be a Spaniard from Spain, Nicki said to herself. He gets insulted just like an Italian.

Outside, he smiled at her and her face flushed and she reached out and took his hand.

"You'll call."

"Fine."

He smiled again and she walked down the hall. She was going the wrong way, but she wanted to walk someplace slowly. Maximo went to the subway entrance and on a whim, just because he felt like it, put one hand on the banister and then sent himself far out into the air, so that he landed half way down the first flight of stairs.

When she got home, Nicki put her pocketbook on the dresser and crossed the room to the closet. She opened the folding doors and took an empty shoebox from the shelf above her neatly hung clothes. The shelf had several dozen boxes, stacked perfectly, like the stockroom of a good shoe store. Nicki kept all her shoes in these boxes until the shoes were old, at which point she threw out the box and replaced it immediately. Nicki took off her shoes and put them in one box and took down another. She took out her white canvas Tretorn sneakers that had only been out of the house once, when her sister Phyllis had borrowed them. Nicki had caught her right away, even though Phyllis had washed off the bottoms, because Phyllis had not lined the box up properly when she put the sneakers back.

Nicki put the sneakers down, took off her pants and

put them on a hanger. She tugged at the bottoms so they
hung right. From a bottom drawer Nicki pulled out a pair
of Levi's and a white T-shirt with the initials USC on it.
She never thought what the initials meant; what was important was that this was her cleaning shirt. She took off
her silk shirt, put it on a hanger and hung it on the closet
doorknob. If she aired the shirt, it could be worn again;
after all, she didn't smell. Then she took a pair of white
sweat socks from a top drawer and put them on. From
the same drawer she took an elastic band, brushed her
hair and pulled it back into a tight ponytail.

In the next drawer, hidden under Nicki's underwear,
was her special soap, toning lotion and moisturizer. Her
sister Phyllis couldn't find it here. Nicki was sure that if
she left it in the bathroom, her sister would use the soap
in the shower and throw the moisturizer all over her
body. On the instructions it said that these items were
only for the face. With Phyllis using the soap in the
shower, the bar would become all mushy on the bottom.

In the bathroom Nicki followed the three steps as she
cleansed her face, just as the instructions read, wiped off
the box that held the soap so that no water was on it, and
put the three items back beneath her underwear in the
drawer. Before she left the room, she tugged at the bedspread. It was a little wrinkled, as if someone had sat on
her bed. Even her sister knew better than that. Then she
walked out into the kitchen and wondered what Maximo
was doing right now.

_____.... **Chapter 5**

_____ ....

"Look at this trombernick," Weinstein said. He was watching Teenager, who was across the street in front of Eddie Hernandez' clothing store. Teenager's car was triple-parked on the street. "Trouble," Weinstein said again, as he watched Teenager walk into the clothing store.

Weinstein was standing in the window of the linoleum store where he had spent his last twenty-five years. Once, when Puerto Ricans first began to outnumber whites in the neighborhood, Weinstein bought a delicatessen in Far Rockaway and ran it at the same time as the linoleum store; his idea was to build up the grocery and then leave the Bronx before the Puerto Ricans cut him up for stew. But in Far Rockaway, the housewives said to him, "Oh, Mr. Weinstein, this milk says it was delivered on Monday and now it's Wednesday; if I give this old milk to my child and she gets sick, I'll have to send you the doctor's bill."

Weinstein used to twist like a rope inside. I keep my own milk a week, nobody gets sick, he would say to himself. He would, however, have to smile at the women because they were, like his insulin pills, something without which he could not live. And at the same time in the South Bronx, an old Puerto Rican named Malabe worked until 3:00 P.M. each day for Weinstein, but then never left. He stayed in the store until Weinstein closed and

then escorted Weinstein to his car and did not leave until
Weinstein was safely gone. One day, Malabe had a doctor's appointment and left at 3:00 P.M. As Malabe left,
his wife and eighteen-year-old son arrived and stood in
Weinstein's window until 5:00 P.M., and then walked to
the car. When Weinstein tried to pay Malabe extra for
this, Malabe refused to accept the money. And then early
one morning, Weinstein went to install linoleum in an
apartment in the housing projects and the Puerto Rican
woman handed him the house keys and left for the day.
Never in my life have I seen people who trust you like
this, Weinstein said to himself. He closed the delicatessen in Far Rockaway and stayed in the Bronx.

And now, disturbed, he walked out of the linoleum
store and went across the street to Eddie Hernandez'
clothing store.

"Aha!" Teenager called out as Weinstein walked in.
Weinstein stood by the door and said nothing.

"This is Eddie's store now," Teenager said.

"I know," Weinstein said.

"He is going to have a very good store, believe me,"
Teenager said.

"It's a good store already," Eddie said.

"It will be better now that I am here," Teenager said.

Weinstein wanted to say something, but he knew the
first rule of the retail business was to agree with everyone. He stood in silence at the door and thought bad
thoughts about this lazy bum, this criminal, daring to say
he could help Eddie Hernandez. Weinstein got him a job
at this clothing store, which had then belonged to Aaron
Samuels. Eddie worked a seven-day week for a long
time, and then one morning Weinstein saw Eddie, face
drawn, eyes narrowed, opening the store for Samuels. It
was 7:30 A.M.

"What's the matter?" Weinstein said.

"I was up all night, some kind of a virus," Eddie said.

"Why don't you go home?" Weinstein said.

"Man, we got Father's Day coming up," Eddie said.

Weinstein went into his linoleum store on that day and
said to himself, all the people who ran away from here
are shit. They took all the money out of here and ran

away and left vacant stores. Weinstein will not run, Weinstein will leave a statue here with his name on it—I will leave this Spic kid with a store, he told himself.

Two months later, when Samuels, the clothing store owner, said he was leaving because he was afraid of holdups, Weinstein told Eddie Hernandez that he should buy the store. Eddie's eyes widened. He never had thought of himself as being like a Jew. Then Weinstein, lecturing in a voice that made his words sound like accusations, said, "If you buy clothes for your store and say that you will have the money by Friday noon, then you have the money by Friday noon. The full amount that you say you will have. Nobody wants money in little pieces. You never write a check if you do not have the money in the bank. If I ever find you writing a check without the money in the bank, I'll walk away from you and never see you again."

Weinstein put up seven thousand five hundred dollars of his own money and helped Eddie get a bank loan to start the business. He began repaying Weinstein on a schedule. "Eddie coughed up again," Weinstein said when he got home one night. He put the check from Eddie on the bureau.

"Wait till the check clears," his wife said.

"Eddie's checks are good. Eddie is a responsible businessman," Weinstein told her proudly.

Now, standing in the shop and listening to Teenager say how much he would help Eddie, Weinstein had to turn and look out the window. Jailhouse boasting, he told himself. And, oh, look at this. Now this bum has to show up. A guy with a shaved head and a pirate's earring carried two large boxes through the door.

"Want jeans, man?" the guy said to Eddie. "I got Levi-Strauss."

"No," Eddie said.

"Great jeans, man."

"I don't need them," Eddie said.

Teenager said, "How much are you going to charge my friend for his jeans?"

"Half."

"Half?" Teenager said. "Is this the way you treat a

customer? You are supposed to bring him these clothes for maybe twenty percent and then bring him more tomorrow."

"All right, twenty percent," the man with the shaved head said.

"That's better," Teenager said. "You see, Eddie? I am here only a minute and I help you already."

Weinstein was about to turn around and say something, but Eddie Hernandez said, "I don't want them for nothing."

"Eddie," Teenager said.

"So long," Eddie said to the man with the shaved head.

"No, you stay here a minute," Teenager said.

"No, you go," Eddie said to the guy.

With a smirk, the man with the shaved head walked out. Eddie Hernandez began arranging a pile of shirts. "If you let them in here once," Eddie said, looking at the shirts, "then they think it is you they own. They start hanging around. They are no good for business. People do not come in a store if they see bums hanging around. Who buys his son a confirmation suit if he sees a junkie in the store window? I work here seven days a week. Now this son of a bitch, who takes five minutes to steal something, wants me to give him money that I must make by working. I don't want him or his lousy jeans in my store."

Weinstein grunted. He saw that his monument stood on an even firmer base than he had realized.

Teenager smiled and walked around the store, looking at the clothes. A speech such as Eddie's was meant for others. Yet Teenager saw truth in what Eddie had said and he admired it. A man who runs things and works hard should not have to share so much of what he earns, Teenager told himself. This is how I will run my business. He bought three shirts for sixty dollars.

"Thank you," Eddie Hernandez said.

"I will be back in this store," Teenager said.

When Teenager left the store, Weinstein pointed at his back. "So him we have again."

"He's been in here a couple of times," Eddie said.

"You told me to sell clothes to the devil as long as the clothes are honest and the devil pays."

"That's right," Weinstein said.

"Well, I was just nice to the devil."

.....Chapter 6

Myles Crofton crouched down in the debris and picked up a brick. He thought of taking two of them, but he told himself, no, this one brick would be better; he would place it atop the television in his playroom and say to everybody that it was the last brick from the apartment house in the Bronx where he had been born and raised. As he looked around the empty lot where the apartment house once had stood, he could see that someday soon the brick in his hand actually would be the last. Already the piles of bricks and charred timber were nearly covered with auto tires, plastic Clorox bottles and broken glass blinking in a light from some distant place; the Bronx itself no longer has a sky. What once was an Irish proving ground, twenty-five apartments, a hundred and thirty-five tenants, nearly all practicing the religions of Catholicism and slander, now was becoming an Atlantis under garbage.

The place had carried the address of 508–510 Sycamore Avenue. When it was erected in 1930, the building's scale, taking up the entire block of Sycamore from 139th to 140th streets, caused the local Bronx postmaster to decide that two address numbers were required.

Now Myles was surprised at the true size of the neighborhood. The walkups, thrown against each other, were narrow, and the larger apartment houses that were still standing, which were of the same style as the one in

72

which he had lived, had apartments that were so small that he could imagine people raising their feet high as they walked about, in order not to step on the legs of somebody sitting. He had grown used to a parched lawn and split-level house in Barton, in Suffolk County, an outer suburb. He had driven down today with his wife and mother-in-law in a 1972 Chevrolet Impala to pick up Myles' six-year-old Le Sabre, which was being fixed at a transmission shop on Southern Boulevard.

With a finger, Myles measured the air to a spot a little to the left of where fire-blackened springs sat. Once, his apartment had taken up this area.

"Myles!"

His mother-in-law's voice caused him to look back over his shoulder. His wife and mother-in-law, sitting in the locked Impala, motioned toward the corner, where a group of Puerto Rican men suddenly had materialized. Myles' mother-in-law worked her index finger back and forth to indicate that Myles should get out his gun.

"It's nothing," Myles called to them.

"Well, I don't want any of them sneaking up on you," the mother-in-law said.

"Never happen," he told her.

Myles returned his attention to the debris. He listened for footsteps echoing in the stairwells in the late afternoons, as the kids he was growing up with carried grocery orders up to their apartments.

"Myles!"

His mother-in-law was waving her arm in distress. One of the Puerto Ricans up at the corner had just taken a step, or perhaps two, and now was almost two flagstones closer.

"Forget it," Myles said.

His wife got out of the Impala and tip-toed through broken glass covering the gutter and stood alongside Myles. "What do you want me to do?" she said.

"I don't know," Myles said. He had taught his ear to quarantine his wife's voice, but direct questions always cut their way in.

"We're here," she said. "I wish you'd tell me what you want us to do."

"I don't know what I'm doing," Myles said.

"That's just it," his wife said, "you keep us hanging."

He didn't answer. He ran his finger up to where the fourth floor had been. He traced the hallway to the right, to where the last door had been. That was his wife's apartment. When the father, great old guy, would sit at the dinner table, Myles remembered, he would wait until the mother was just sitting down, fanny just about to touch the chair, and then he'd say, "Before you sit down, Mae." He'd catch her just right with all her weight coming down and now having to be reversed, the backs of the knees suddenly having to push the whole works up again. And then the father would say, "Bottle of beer, eh Mae? Good girl yourself, Mae." Otherwise, the husband and wife almost never spoke until the night they carried the father downstairs on a wooden kitchen chair, doubled up with a heart attack, knees right up against his chest. The wife was right behind him on the staircase. Hand over her mouth. At the hospital, the father gasped for the mother, the mother wailed when he died. The mother went to live with the sister in Oradell, New Jersey, but she wound up spending half the time at Myles' house in Barton. At both places, the first thing the mother now did in the morning was to dust off the shrine to her husband that she maintained on the top of each dresser.

Myles thought that this perhaps might be the answer to his own married life. He had been married to Cathy for sixteen years, the last ten of which had been numbed by children, economics and an adherence to history. At thirty-seven Myles Crofton, graduate of St. Benedict's Roman Catholic grammar school and Cardinal Collins high, lived by the rules branded into him by these schools. They were ancient rules; the Catholic Church changes only in books or movies. Always, it is a religion of cold churches and windy cemeteries and the admonishment that you are not put on this earth to be happy. From age seven onward, he had been taught that there could be no adjustments therefore. He could be with his wife through limitless hours and not say as much as a sentence to her: for the length of a three hundred eighty-mile drive to a sister's house in Buffalo; through an obligatory night out, from car ride to dinner to drink at the bar and ride home, and he knew that it was futile for him ever to look hard at the darkness. Change was unlawful. Besides, he reasoned that the reaction of Cathy's mother to her husband's death meant that he, too, probably had some great emotion for Cathy somewhere inside him and the shame of it all was that it would take a tragedy to bring it out.

His wife's voice again intruded. "So what do you want us to do?"

"Why don't you go home? Let me stay here a while."

"Stay here? How could you stay here? It's bad enough you have to work here now, without staying on your own time."

"I'll be home on time for supper."

"Sure now?"

"What else am I going to do?"

She paused, and when he said nothing, she went to the car. As it pulled away, Myles saw his mother-in-law banging the door locks down. He was left with a brick in his hand and his beginnings in the air in front of him.

Myles went to his own newly repaired car, dropped the brick onto the seat and started off. Then for no reason he walked to the corner of 140th Street and halfway down the block, a street of burned-out buildings with junkies on the stoops, to the rear entrance of St. Benedict's. Its old gray stones belonged on a hill, with rain and mist, not on a block like this. Myles had not been inside the church in five years.

Inside, the church was empty in the Sunday afternoon. He walked to the last row, pulled out a kneeler and dropped onto it. A few steps away, the confessional booth he always had used was gone, replaced by a statue of a saint, St. Martin de Porres. I never heard of a nigger saint, Myles said to himself. They must have gone blind searching for a nigger they could put in church instead of jail.

Myles blessed himself and started to pray. He always said an Our Father and ten Hail Marys to pull his mind into the current where prayer ran, but halfway through the Our Father his thoughts drifted and he had to start

the prayer over. He decided to get up and light a candle
for his mother. When he walked over to the bank of candles by the Blessed Virgin's statue, he found tops on the
red glass jars and that, upon removing the top, the light
inside the jar was being made not by candles but by small
electric bulbs, cheap twisted Christmas tree bulbs, the
twists causing the light to appear to flicker. Bulbs from
Cheap John's store, any avenue. A sign in English and
Spanish said a person was to push the button on the top
of the glass jar to turn on the light, then drop the offering
into the slot at the base of the jar. Myles wondered why
the old candles had been replaced by light bulbs. Perhaps
the pastor had no one around to change the candles and
clean the wax that dripped over the sides of the jars and
onto the floor. No. The reason the pastor had to put bulbs
was that he had his bellyful of Puerto Ricans setting fires.

Whatever, Myles wouldn't push the button. Electricity
was too abstract to deal with the soul of his mother. He
knew he could feel no warmth from lighting a light bulb,
and part of the reason for lighting a candle is to warm the
heart of the one lighting the wick, just as much as it is to
create a light that asks God to ease the stay in Purgatory
of the soul of a most faithful departed. Here, however,
the connection between the living person and his God has
been broken by the introduction of electricity. Next, he
told himself, they'll take down the Cross and put up a
picture of an auto accident and claim Christ died in a hit-
run.

Myles had been back working in the Bronx for two
weeks now, as a member of the Twenty-ninth Homicide
squad, a position he got by using a hook strong enough
to tow the Queen Elizabeth II. At thirty-seven, Myles
still held a patrolman's badge and salary, but he had been
moved to the Twenty-ninth Homicide, with the promise
of a detective shield and pay soon, by a man he drove
three weeks each summer, Martin Scannell, a supervising
acting chief inspector. When Scannell's regular driver
went on vacation, Myles was pulled from his precinct,
the Ninth, out of a booth in front of the Panamanian
consulate and given the opportunity, as he drove, to put
his career furtherance as prominently as possible into

Scannell's mind. He wanted Scannell to put him into the detective division, which would mean an immediate pay raise of nearly three thousand dollars.

Myles lived a life of financial torment; he was about three hundred and twenty-five dollars short each month, and his nerves chafed each time the phone rang, for there was the chance of the caller being a finance company clerk who would take enormous pleasure in humiliating a cop. Scannell was easy to talk to, for he knew several of Myles' cousins from St. Raymond's parish in the Bronx. Ability to retain what he heard was limited, however, because at fifty-three he had fallen deeply in love with a woman who sold sweaters at Macy's. In his mind, Scannell was conducting an invisible romance, one that only he and the woman knew of, and Scannell denied her to himself so much that during the warmest part of sex he assured himself that it wasn't happening at all. Yet he had his car and chauffeur parked in front of Macy's so often that all the policemen in the area called him "Strauss," after the first owner of Macy's.

Discovery that Scannell's love was in sweaters was made on the day Croatians bombed the Yugoslavian embassy. Reached by beeper, Scannell used the phone extension at the sweater counter. In the midst of his hurried discussion with the office of chief of operations, Scannell had a saleswoman, not his true love, pick up an extension.

"You've got to get off, I got a bombing," Scannell said.

"No, *you*'ve got to get off. I've got a full-figured woman needs a thirty-eight cardigan up here right away," the salesgirl said.

"What are you so worried about being a detective for?" Scannell asked Myles one day.

"The money," Myles said.

"At least you tell the truth," Scannell said.

"I couldn't lie to a man like you," Myles said.

"I appreciate that," Scannell said.

"I couldn't lie to anybody you put me with, either," Myles said.

"You're supposed to get to the detective division by

narcotics or anticrime," Scannell said. "I don't know, what do you want? You have a nice spot now. They put you in a squad, you'll be someplace where you could get hurt."

"I'd rather get shot than stay the way I am," Myles said.

Scannell, remote, in love, shrugged. Myles talked about being a detective so much that he began to act like one. During Easter week, he was driving Scannell and wound up waiting at a table in Clark's, in Macy's basement. A woman brushed Myles as she bent over to reach for something on the floor next to his table.

"I'm going to make a phone call and I dropped my dime," she said.

Myles stood up. "Don't worry about it."

"I'm looking," the woman said.

"Forget about it," Myles said. He went to the phone booth, dropped in a quarter, dialed the operator and then grabbed the quarter as it dropped back. He motioned to the woman, a dark-haired woman of his age.

"Operator, this is a police call," Myles said loudly. "Shield number 1174. Detective Crofton of the Organized Crime Special Security Squad. I'm calling . . ."

"499–6272," the woman said.

"499–6272," Myles said into the phone. "Thank you." He stepped away from the wall pay phone and handed the woman the receiver. "There you are."

"Oh, thanks."

"Forget about it."

Myles let his jacket fall open so that the woman could see the gun. She was enthralled. When she was through, she sat with Myles and gave her name as Barbara Berger. She was thirty-eight and dreadfully alone. Myles was thirty-seven and with three kids. His will power was a cotton wall when Barbara Berger smiled at him. He fell in love with her on Holy Thursday and at home on Easter Sunday he had to invent a reason, expecting a call from the inspector, for not attending mass with his wife, mother-in-law and kids. If he had attended, he would have been unable to receive communion, for his soul was black from sin with Barbara Berger.

Who also tore the heart out of his financial system. The first night he took her out, on a Thursday, they went to an Italian restaurant on the West Side that looked cheap until Myles and Barbara began drinking wine and ran up a check of ninety-five dollars. One date a week later and Myles no longer had money for his car payment.

At home that week, the phone rang at eight o'clock in the morning.

"This is Mr. Peters from Beneficial Finance," the voice said. Myles owed a personal loan he originally had taken out five years before.

"I can't talk now," Myles said.

"We're interested in cash, not conversation," Peters said.

On Thursday, when Myles walked out of an eight-to-four tour at the Ninth Precinct, the air was so soft that the streets seemed like a public garden. Still, he was gloomy as he walked into the subway. He pulled out his patrolman's badge, which was on a chain as long as a lawn hose, and held it high so the toll booth man would know that it was a cop and not a turnstile jumper going through the gate. Police rules forbade off-duty men from riding the subways free, but Myles did not understand the purpose of any badge that did not gain at least small perks for the bearer. His badge was on this long chain so that when held high in a crowded subway, nobody bumping into Myles could cause him to drop the badge and lose it, a tragedy for which the police department penalty was five days' pay. Myles could not afford to lose an hour's pay. He had eleven dollars with him, and was fortunate to have that, and he was therefore in need of a plausible reason for not taking Barbara Berger, whom he was to meet in front of her office at five, for as much as a beer. He had settled on the word emergency by the time the train reached 34th Street. As he emerged onto Seventh Avenue, he saw Inspector Scannell's car parked in front of Macy's main entrance. The regular driver sat reading a newspaper. Myles walked behind the car, went into Macy's and took the escalator up to the fourth floor, where he found Scannell, leaning on the sales counter as if it were a bar, talking with Italian animation to a saleswoman with enough loose skin under the chin to indicate that once she had been fifty. Upon seeing Myles approach, Scannell jumped away from the counter and intercepted Myles.

"What are you doing here?" Scannell demanded.

"I had to come up and see you."

"How did you know I was here?"

"I just figured."

"Did you talk to my driver?"

"No, sir."

Scannell's eyes widened. "Are you sure you didn't talk to my driver?"

"You could ask him. He didn't see me. And you know I don't lie."

Scannell was silent. His voice lowered. "All right, what do you want?"

"I thought I have to tell you this. The other night I was working in a bar on First Avenue. I got this second job. I can't make it on my pay."

Scannell's face reddened. "You're here to give me this?"

"No, I was just saying. What happened was, I'm working in this place and one of your sons came up and said hello."

"Which one?"

"You got to forgive me, but I get mixed up with the names. The one we had with us one day. The twenty-year-old."

"That's Eddie. He goes into those places. So what's the problem?"

"Well, he knew me and I knew his face and he comes up and I have the bartender give him all the beer he wants. You know."

"So?" Scannell said. He was shifting back and forth on his feet.

"I have to tell you. He said to me, do I know anything about you having a girlfriend."

"He said that?"

"I'm afraid he did."

"When was this?"

"The other weekend. Of course you know what I said, Inspector."

"I know that."

"I told him, you're crazy, have another beer and stop listening to people who are jealous that your father is a successful man."

"So then what did he say?" Scannell said.

"No, that took care of it, Inspector. He was satisfied. In fact, I think I got it out of his mind forever."

Scannell nodded.

"I hate working that second job for money, but I guess in this case it was good I was there," Myles said.

Myles became silent, which to Scannell was more painful than a loudspeaker held to his ear.

"You know, you mentioned to me about wanting to be in the detective division," Scannell said.

"Yes, sir."

"Tell you the truth, I was just thinking about it the other morning. They got a way of putting a patrolman into a squad right away and then getting him a shield later. Make a good arrest or something. They do in special cases. Say there's an organized crime case and one of the relatives is in the department. Or if the patrolman speaks a language and a squad needs him. It can be done sometimes right away, with no review boards or anything. Then later, you just give the guy his shield and his money."

"I have special knowledge of the Bronx," Myles said.

"A lot of guys know the Bronx," Scannell said.

"I was on a softball team my last year in the neighborhood and I went out and got this kid Flores, he didn't look Spanish, just so when we played a Spanish team he could listen to them talk and tell us when they were going to bunt, things like that."

"That was good," Scannell said.

"Maybe I could do something like that again," Myles said.

"Maybe," Scannell said. He squeezed Myles' arm, winked and gently pushed Myles toward the escalator. As Myles went down, he saw Scannell walking to the sweater counter again. Myles was proud of the way he had made up the story instantaneously, standing right there on his feet, putting the key into the lock with his eyes closed. Scannell was so terrified of having his romance uncovered that he would shoot himself before asking his son, even most casually, if he had bumped into Myles lately.

On the following Monday, Myles was assigned as a patrolman to the Twenty-ninth Homicide detective squad in the Bronx. The lieutenant, Martin, assured Myles that only time would be required before the gold shield and extra pay were forthcoming.

"With your hook, you could hump a nun and make it," Martin said.

"I was told I had to make a good case before that happened," Myles said.

"Put it this way. You won't be hurting yourself," Martin said.

"Then I'll make it on my own," Myles said.

"You won't have any trouble," Martin said. "We got a world war going on up here."

Now, in church, Myles shifted around in his seat and the squeaking reminded him that he had been sitting here for some minutes daydreaming in God's face. He got up and walked out of the silent church.

Outside, when he tried to start the car, nothing happened. He got out, but even before lifting the hood he knew the battery was stolen. He walked toward a group of men who were standing up at the corner. Without noticing Myles, they began walking away. They went down to 138th Street, stood in front of Ana's Bar for a moment and then two of them went in and the others continued down the street. Myles decided to walk into the bar. If it were night, he never would do it alone, for the procedure that Martin had set down for him called for the back of the bar to be checked, particularly the men's and ladies' rooms, before settling down to any business. But the place was so familiar to Myles that he walked toward it, remembering the day when it was called the County Cavan and a kid named Big Richie O'Brien, who had a forehead like a cement ledge, looked out the saloon window at the first Puerto Ricans in the neighborhood.

"You think they should come here?" he said to Myles.

"No," Myles said.

"To where we live?" Big Richie said.

Myles remembered that one guy in the bar, Jackie Walsh, tried to catch Richie by the arm, but Richie was out in the street, walking across to the Puerto Ricans, there were three or four of them, Myles couldn't remember, and there was a lot of running when Richie went after them with his huge cement head nodding in anger and the baseball bat he had hidden behind his right leg suddenly swinging out. Big Richie swung the bat and one Puerto Rican, in a white shirt, tried to raise a hand to stop it and the bat slapped through the hand and went onto the side of the Puerto Rican's face. The Puerto Rican's whole head bulged to the right, as if he had a pound of gum stuffed in his mouth. The Puerto Rican fell on his back. Big Richie O'Brien began to swing the bat, golf style, but not exactly golf because Richie didn't use a real backswing. He just kept bringing the bat back a little and slamming it into the Puerto Rican's head. Myles could see the Puerto Rican's white shirt turn completely red. He didn't count how many times Big Richie hit the Puerto Rican, and it all happened so quickly nobody stopped it. It was the first time in his life that Myles had seen somebody kill a man, and he had seen it from the window of this bar he now entered.

He took only two steps inside the front door and stopped. An old barmaid, wearing a white kerchief under a straw hat, stood with her arms folded. The two men who had walked in from the street drank beer near the door; three others sat in the dimness at the far end. The youngest in the place was in the back playing pool.

"I'm from the Twenty-ninth Homicide," Myles said. Everybody looked and said nothing. "Somebody just took the battery out of my car."

At the end of the bar, a voice muttered, "A homicide man trying to find a battery. Does that mean some dude took the battery out and murdered it?"

"What's that?" Myles said. The guy who had done the muttering looked like a lion.

"*Yo no sé de que hablas,*" Teenager said.

"I asked about a battery," Myles said evenly. "If somebody helps me find my battery now, maybe someday I can help with one of their problems. You know?"

"*Batería?*" Teenager said.

"Battery," Myles said.

"*Yo no tengo un carro.*"

The barmaid slapped a hand to her mouth. Myles could see that the young guy playing pool was smiling broadly as he lined up a shot.

"What's that?" Myles said.

"He say that he doesn't even own a car," Benny Velez said. The barmaid's hand remained over her mouth.

"What about you?" Myles asked.

"*Cancharra,*" Benny said.

"What's that supposed to mean?"

"I have a very old, bad car."

"I asked for a battery, not what kind of car you have."

Teenager, sitting on the far side of Benny, now gave a great yawn to attract attention. His left arm came in front of Benny, removing Benny from the conversation. Then Teenager threw his head back and stretched more, showing Myles his body. Teenager held his left arm high in the air and stretched that side of his torso.

"*Estoy esperando cojer el número para comprar un carro,*" he said.

"He said he is waiting to hit the number and then he will buy a car," Benny said.

"*Quatro dieciséis,*" Teenager said.

"His number is four sixteen," Benny said.

Teenager tilted his body, dropping his left arm and bringing up the right arm. He yawned loudly again.

Whistling, Myles went to the phone, and keeping his eyes off Teenager to let him know that he wasn't worth looking at, he called the precinct.

"What am I running, a car repair shop?" Martin, the lieutenant, yelled. Then he said he was sending a detective named Hansen down. Myles felt good; he liked Hansen. For an instant, he forgot his pose and his eyes went to Teenager's. The two looked at each other with distaste and Myles was ready to forget about it, just another Spic in a saloon, when Teenager yawned loudly again and then slammed his right hand down on the bar and caused the glasses to jump.

"Cojí el número! Ahora voy a comprar un carro."

"He says he hit the number and now he is going out to buy a car," Benny said.

Head high, sneering, Teenager slid off the barstool and walked to the front door. He brushed past Myles and, singing loudly, went out to his Mercedes, waved to the bar window as he got in and, tires shrieking, pulled away.

"What was that supposed to be, smart?" Myles said to Benny Velez, who did not answer.

"What was his name?" Myles asked.

"Some guy comes in here."

"I know that. I want to know his name."

Benny spread his palms.

"I asked you for the name," Myles said.

Benny said nothing. In the rear, the young guy playing pool put down the cue and stuffed his hands into his pockets.

"Officer, do you have reasonable cause to believe that a crime has been committed?" Maximo asked.

"Yes. Somebody stole my battery."

"Officer, do you have reasonable cause to believe that somebody in here committed the crime?"

"Who are you?" Myles said.

"That's not the question. The question is, do you have reasonable cause to believe that one of us here committed a crime?"

Myles fixed his eyes on Maximo as he would a motorist caught passing a red light, but Maximo's eyes, rather than waver or lower, grew more direct and intense. Myles knew that it was his turn to speak, and he considered some smart Bronx remark and then grew wary that this Spic would talk back and make him feel foolish. He turned abruptly, walked outside and stood on the streetcorner until Hansen drove up with the battery.

"Fresh punk," Myles said as he got the battery from Hansen's trunk.

"The bar?" Hansen said.

"Some fresh punk in there smartasses me."

"They'll do that."

"They won't do it again."

"You'll probably get your chance," Hansen said. "That place is always trouble."

"You wouldn't mind it if he did it on his own. He had this big guy going for him, so he puts on a show."

Hansen looked in the bar window. "What big guy?"

"The guy left already."

"Oh. Because I'm looking in there and I don't see any big guy. At least not the guy I'm thinking of."

"Who's that?"

"Teenager."

"I don't know. I don't know their names."

"Teenager is a guy with a big beard and a lot of hair. Powerful-looking body."

"That sounds like him," Myles said.

"I don't even like to give him the respect of using his street name," Hansen said. "To me, he's just another bum they build jailhouses for. He just got out of one. He'll spend all his time looking for ways to get right back in."

"Him and his friend with the mouth better stay the fuck out of my way," Myles said, with disdain, but with the size of the one and the tough eyes of the other making him uncertain inside.

"You won't get many chances to miss Teenager," Hansen said. "Before he went away the last time, he was in so many places around here we thought he was a whole family. They got him for narcotics. That left us with a whole lot of files on guys got killed around here."

"Where are the files?" Myles asked.

"We got an office full of them," Hansen said.

"Am I allowed to look at them?" Myles said.

"Of course you are. The cases don't belong to anyone."

"Let me take a look, then," Myles said.

"You may not have to. He'll give you plenty of fresh ones," Hansen said.

"I'll give this guy some personal attention," Myles said.

Hansen became preoccupied with his pipe. He was a man who preferred to conduct his life without turbulence. When he was fourteen, his parents moved from La Grange, Georgia, to New York, but when Hansen arrived he found he was going to be set back a year in school; instead of being a first-year high school student he would be back with the children in elementary school. Rather than face this humiliation, he went back to La Grange and lived alone through four years of high school.

He grew used to the silence of living alone, and by the time he finished high school and came to New York, he seemed to be a man whose nervous system had been scraped out of him. In his first summer as a policeman, he chased an armed man who had just robbed a grocery store. The man ran with a bag of money in one hand and a gun in the other. Hansen, running on country-boy legs, drew close enough to the gunman to be able to fire at him and knock him down even if the shot were taken while in full stride. Hansen, however, told himself that he would shoot only if the gunman turned around; until then he would keep running after the man. The gunman's legs began to wobble at 127th Street and 7th Avenue and he turned into a playground and saw fencing on all sides of him and, gasping for air, trying to think of some magic that would lift him out of this dead-end cage, he heard Hansen's voice saying to him, not shouting at him, but saying to him, calmly, "There's no way out of here. Now just throw the gun down so's neither of us gets hurt." The gunman dropped his weapon and turned around with his hands up. Hansen liked it that way. Stay placid and stay alive.

In 1958, on a day tour in Harlem, Hansen responded to the call of a man stabbed in Blumstein's department store on 125th Street. He found bedlam on the sidewalk and inside, Martin Luther King on a couch with a brass letter opener sticking out of his chest. Immediately, he saw that King, using Georgia-boy calmness, was not allowing any part of his body to move and thus risk further damage from the letter opener. The woman who had stabbed him,

Izola Ware Curry, sat in a haze in handcuffs in the next room.

"You just stay still," Hansen said to King, who heard clearly but did not move his eyes, lips or a finger in response.

Hansen then pointed out to a captain that the crowd outside by now was so large that it was impossible to have King brought out on a stretcher and not have people rush forward to touch him and, in doing so, perhaps drive the letter opener into his heart. The crowd most certainly would attempt to tear apart the deranged woman, Izola Ware Curry.

"How do we stop them?" asked the captain, Irish, looking to the black cop for special knowledge.

"I'd have more ambulances and patrol cars called to the front entrance. Let them come out there on 125th Street with their sirens going to attract all the people. Then we'll have one ambulance and a couple of patrol cars come to the back entrance on 124th. With no sirens or anything. Take Dr. King out that way and then I'll take the woman the same way afterward."

King was carried out to an ambulance on an empty street and the Ware woman moved to a patrol car with only a few store employees watching. The captain received so many commendations for his native Irish canniness in time of strife that he had the strange experience of being bothered by his conscience. He recommended that Hansen be placed in the detective bureau.

It was chance that placed Myles with Hansen, but now Myles wanted to make it a partnership. He had no trouble with Hansen's color, because when on duty almost all cops regard themselves as state issue. Besides, Hansen, a black, was disliked by Puerto Ricans more than whites, a fact that Myles found comforting. More important, Myles felt, was that in the vortex of a crisis, Hansen would seek to minimize rather than raise the possibility of danger.

The only negative point about Hansen was the way he could embarrass Myles about his secret relationship with a woman, as he proceeded to do now as Myles, the battery in, was about to drive away.

"When are you on again?" Hansen said.

"Wednesday night," Myles said.

"I guess that ties you up. No, I got it wrong. Thursday's the day you get with your woman."

"What are you talking about?" Myles said.

"I got you clocked," Hansen said. "Thursday's your female day."

"Wrong," Myles said. "Thursday I'll be going through those files on this guy inside."

────── .... **Chapter**
7
───────────── ....

Teenager's career in America had started when he arrived in New York, nine years earlier, at 2:00 P.M. of a fall day whose breezes, coming off the sparkling bay beside the airport and the ocean beyond the bay, carried hidden in them the first hints of winter. Teenager had thirty-seven dollars with him. On the plane, Teenager had shown a man a note with his uncle's address and under it the man had printed instructions: "Walk to 93rd Street and ask again." Teenager and Lydia rode the airport bus to the West Side Terminal and 42nd Street. In the men's room, he met a Puerto Rican who was changing paper in the towel machine. The Puerto Rican told him which direction to walk to 93rd Street.

"When did you come here?" Teenager asked him.

"Nine years ago."

"How long have you had this job?"

"I been working here three years."

"Is this a good job?"

"Only once in a while some drunk comes in here, pisses on your shoes."

Teenager and Lydia walked up Broadway to 93rd Street in bright fall sunshine and found number 330 West, a brownstone with a broken basement window and a bag of garbage spilled open on the bottom step. Teenager could make out the word "superintendent" on the bell to the basement door. His ring brought a gray-haired man in a sweatshirt to the door. A cigarette, half of it wet, hung from the man's mouth.

"No Olmo here," the man said, reading Teenager's note.

"My uncle," Teenager said.

The man handed him back the slip of paper. "Not here, pal."

"We are to stay with him," Teenager said.

"Not here, pal, because he's not here. I never heard of the guy."

Teenager caught enough of the English words to know what the superintendent meant. But before he could say something else, the superintendent shut the door. Teenager then walked up to the stoop and tried the glass doors, but they were locked. He shaded his eyes and looked in at the mailboxes, but he could not read the names. He and Lydia sat on the stoop and waited for people to come, so they could be asked where Luis Olmo, his uncle, could be found. Over the hours, people came to the house and each looked at the slip of paper and shook his head and went into the building.

Late afternoon shadows chilled the street. Lydia first tried to tuck her bare feet under her skirt. She then tried wrapping the cardigan sweater about them, but this made the rest of her cold. So she put the sweater back on, opened the suitcase and thrust her feet into it. Teenager took out another shirt and put it on over the one he was wearing, but he still had to keep moving his arms. By 8:00 P.M. the suitcase was as cold as the wind and Lydia's feet could stand it no more. They walked to Broadway and went to 89th Street, where he was sure that he would see somebody from Ponce who could help him. The steamed glass of the hot dog stand on the corner drew them in. The moment Lydia put her feet into the warm air the pain went out of her face. The stand was empty except for a Puerto Rican with a pencil mustache who was behind the counter.

"I was supposed to stay with my uncle," Teenager told him in Spanish.

"Everybody has an uncle someplace," the counterman said.

"I can't find him," Teenager said.

"Do you see him here?" the counterman said.

"Where is there a place to stay?" Teenager asked.

"I do not rent rooms, I sell hot dogs," the counterman said. "Why are you bringing your troubles to me? Go walk down Broadway, there are hotels. You just look and you see them with your own eyes."

The counterman walked away from them and began to wipe the griddle. Lydia started to leave, but Teenager remained motionless. He smiled at the counterman. The smile became a laugh. He saw his wife outside, changed expression and walked out.

At 79th Street there was a sign for the Hotel Orleans, a block over on Amsterdam Avenue. They went there and rented a room for a week at twenty-one dollars. The room had a bed, a night table, closet, toilet, hot plate with a dirty pot atop it and virtually no breathable air. The window, covered with soot, looked out at the brick wall of the next building and could not be opened. Teenager left his wife in the room and went out to a *bodega* on Columbus Avenue and bought one egg for a nickel and a box of rice for fifteen cents. He brought it back to the room and Lydia boiled the egg and rice. There was no fork or spoon, so Teenager went back to Columbus Avenue, walked into a Chinese restaurant, nodded at the hostess, watched her turn to lead him to a table, whipped up the nearest napkin wrapped about silverware and was out the door.

At 8:00 A.M. the next morning, Teenager walked into a candy store and asked if the man needed any help. The man pointed to his wife. "She is my staff."

Teenager went to the French cleaners next door. The owner, who had just opened for the day, locked the lock as he saw Teenager walking up. He motioned Teenager away. Teenager walked to 89th and Broadway and found the hot dog stand crowded with people drinking morning coffee. Two Jews, the owners, not the counterman he intended to smash, were working.

"What'll it be?" one of the Jews said to him.

"Nothing," Teenager said.

"Have your nothing outside," the Jew said.

For the next hour, Teenager stood on the corner and asked every Puerto Rican if they knew Fernando Lebron or Aros Blanco, Junior Quiñones. They shook their heads and kept hurrying to the subway. Teenager started walking. He went into coffee shops and supermarkets asking for jobs and then began climbing stairs to a dress factory and a novelty manufacturer and an upholstery place. The day became a man shaking his head and returning to his work and leaving Teenager standing in the doorway. He returned to the hotel at 4:00 P.M., with another nickel egg. Lydia had remained in the room all day, as Teenager had ordered. After eating, Teenager fell on the bed and was asleep immediately. At eight o'clock, he awoke and said he wanted to go out to the hot dog stand. The cold night air on her feet caused her to whimper at first. On Broadway, seeing all the other people with shoes, she became ashamed of the thongs she was wearing. They went home. In the morning, Lydia spent nine dollars on a pair of shoes, leaving them six dollars and change.

Teenager looked for a job in a fifteen-block radius of the hotel, in order not to spend carfare. He found that people had the same reaction to itinerant Puerto Ricans as they did to palsy victims. Even more disappointing to Teenager was his inability to find anybody on the corner of 89th Street who knew him, and who would give the respect and adulation he needed. He had been in New York for four days, and he found the disdain more alien than the climate. He did see one person who thought she remembered him. Her name was Mendez, and she came up the block with her child, went into an apartment house where the superintendent's mother babysits days and then came hurrying out to get the subway to work. Teenager walked with her for a half block. She was going to work in a belt factory.

"Is hard here," she said. "But it's way better, man, than Ponce."

Lydia dozed or looked out the window all day. Teenager would not allow her as much as to open the door without his being there. By Thursday, Lydia was in a haze from solitary confinement. Teenager came home early and after their egg and rice took her to the Manhattan Theater on Broadway, which cost a dollar and a quarter before 5:00 P.M. The movie was *The Victors* and they sat in the last row and whatever dialogue Teenager caught he explained to Lydia. When they walked out, the manager, standing by the ticket booth, nodded to them.

The next day, on Friday, Teenager was on Broadway because a man in the Daitch Shopwell had told him that he had heard that there was an A&P in the sixties that needed a delivery boy. As he walked past the theater, Teenager saw the manager and they nodded to each other. He walked to the A&P, found no job and was trudging back when he saw the manager again.

"Eat?" the manager said.

"Not yet," Teenager said.

"You look like you can eat something," the manager said.

He spoke slowly, and gestured with his hands, and Teenager was able to follow him. The manager took Teenager to a coffee shop on the next corner. When his hamburger arrived, Teenager nearly bit his own fingers as he snapped it into his mouth.

The manager's name was John Cohalan and Teenager called him Pedroito.

"Last night that was your wife?" Pedroito said.

"*Sí.*"

"Where is she now?"

"Hotel."

"Get her here tonight and I will buy her food," Cohalan said.

At 7:00 P.M., Teenager was back with Lydia. The manager bought them roast beef sandwiches. He said Teenager was a strong kid and would get work someplace. In the meantime, he made Teenager understand that he was to come to the theater whenever he and his wife felt hungry.

"You pay me back when you get a job," Cohalan told them.

Cohalan's eyes grew misty. This is how this country was built, he told himself, giving food, drink and shelter to some dust-caked, emaciated man walking out of the desert. The desert man's stomach eased, his body clean, he goes out and starts as a porter and winds up an international banker. God bless America, Cohalan said to himself.

"If I could find a job this weekend," Teenager said.

Cohalan smiled. "You keep on looking. You'll find something." Cohalan slipped back into his lovely haze.

"I must get a job on this weekend. I have no money and the hotel money I must have on Monday. Twenty-one dollar."

Cohalan was shaken out of his dreams by a fact that missionaries before him had known for centuries: when the natives light a fire under the pot, the water scalds. Cohalan focused in terror on these people who had grown, over a sandwich, into tormentors.

"I don't know about that," Cohalan said.

"I would never ask you for such a thing as money," Teenager said.

This made Cohalan sick.

"Just if you hear of a job this weekend, you could tell me," Teenager said.

In the mail on Saturday morning, Teenager received a letter from his mother with thirty-four dollars enclosed. When he and Lydia saw Cohalan for lunch, Teenager did not mention that he had any money. Cohalan was tight about the mouth. One loan of twenty-one dollars to Teenager, he knew, would begin a trend that would end with him eating out of garbage cans.

I thought all my relatives were dead, Cohalan said to himself.

To Teenager he said, "I'm looking all over."

On Sunday morning, Teenager and Lydia were asleep when Cohalan, pounding on the door with both fists, woke them with the news that he had met the man in charge of maintenance at the Parkview Towers apartment house, and the man needed a handyman immediately. Cohalan gave Teenager a piece of paper with the address, on Central Park West, and instructions on how to walk there.

"Pedroito!" Teenager said. He threw a headlock on Cohalan.

Cohalan left with the lightened stride of a man who has just felt a gun removed from his back.

When Teenager got to the apartment house on Monday, the maintenance boss had him fill out forms. He also handed Teenager twenty-one dollars and had him sign a voucher for it.

The boss, a white Cuban, spoke in Spanish to Teenager. "Cohalan said that you needed the hotel rent this morning. Take an early lunch and go to the hotel and give them the money for your room. I am doing this for Cohalan. He lets my children into the movies free all the time."

At 11:30, Teenager pretended to be going to his hotel. He already had paid for the room. He went into Central Park, had a hot dog and thought of how wonderful a person Pedroito was. He felt like running up to the theater and kissing Pedroito, but he thought that would be too sloppy, that it would make him appear too weak. You can be grateful without licking someone's hands like a dog, Teenager decided.

The job paid Teenager a hundred and eighteen dollars and he cleared eighty-seven. Whenever he was alone in the hallway, chipping paint, he prayed aloud to Changó. "Please let my friend Cohalan have sex with any woman he sees who he wants when she comes into his movie house." His days became the same. He and Lydia had breakfast in their room, then he left for work and Lydia returned to bed. Teenager was home for lunch and directly after work, when he took a nap, woke up to eat and then took out Lydia, his caged animal, for a walk. Each night, they stopped at the Manhattan Theater and saw Cohalan. Teenager always said the same thing, "Pedroito, I pray that you should have great luck in your life every day. I hope you have sex with all the women."

He had been on the job for three weeks when Teenager found himself one day in an eight-room apartment being painted for new tenants. The apartment had picture windows and a large terrace overlooking Central Park. At quitting time, Teenager stayed alone in the apartment and watched Central Park dissolve into dusk. The rich, lighted apartment buildings on Fifth Avenue, over on the far side of the park, started visions in his head. He gazed at the lights and imagined the money that was somewhere in the rooms with the lights. As far as he could see, left to right, there were these lights. There was money in baskets right next to the lamps, he thought. He shook his head and shoulders rapidly, a dog coming out of the water, and caused all those beautiful lights to swirl. He walked slowly about the dark, empty apartment. He kicked canvas off the floor so his feet would be on the fine old Central Park chestnut floors. The squeak of the wood and the lights on the dark sky on the other side of the park made him feel so good that he supposed he was at this moment very close to God, to Changó.

"I am living here," he announced. "I am here with my wife and now I have three children. I have great rugs from Persia in the middle of the floor, but I have no rugs right here where I stand because I like the sound of this wood. I have everything I need. If I want a drink, I have a nigger working for me who runs into the kitchen and gets it for me. If my wife wants anything, there is a nigger maid who runs when she hears her name called. I am very gentle in my house, but the niggers know to run because they can see that Teenager gets mad. Where is my wife? She is in the bedroom putting on her fur coat. We are going out tonight. To a place where they play Bugaloo music. I will go to this place with my wife and we will show to the people our clothes and our jewelry and Wilfredo's band will play. But I won't stay there for so long. Because I like my house so much that I come back to here and I send my wife to bed and I stand here and look out the window and then the doorbell rings and I go in and let in the door my girlfriend. We go to my hideaway room, on the other side of the apartment, and we love till I am tired of her. Nobody bothers us. My wife knows that she is never to leave her bedroom at night. Then when I am finished with my girlfriend, I send her home. She can go home alone because she does not have far to go. She lives in the apartment on the next floor. I am so rich that I have two apartments in this very same building."

Walking home, he thought of finding money or stealing

some, so he would no longer have to dream of two apartments. Suddenly he let out a shout. Fernando Lebron, whom he knew from Puerto Rico, was standing on the street corner. His girlfriend Leonida was with him. She now was fifteen and she stood proudly on Broadway with her second baby pushing her stomach wall out.

"I deliver drugs," Fernando said.

"How much money do you make?" Teenager asked.

"Not so much money as you think. I do not own the drugs. I only deliver them."

"Whose drugs are they?"

"Guineas. Guineas own everything."

"Why don't Puerto Ricans own some drugs?"

"The Puerto Ricans own the jails," Lebron said.

"That's bullshit," Teenager said.

"If I could make a living, do you think to my mind would come something like doing what I do?" Lebron said.

Lebron had his girlfriend write out Mama's address, on Southern Boulevard in the South Bronx. Fernando never was able to read or write. In Playa, his mother took him once a week to San Pedro for psychiatric assistance. They found the part of his brain having to do with erections in sensational condition and the rest badly clogged. New York air had not changed this: his girl was pregnant and he was illiterate in two languages now.

"Where do you live?" Teenager asked Lebron.

"On 138th Street. We are three blocks from Mama. You should come. Many people from Playa are at 138th Street. You remember Maximo? He lives in my building."

"Little Maximo?"

"He goes to school."

Fernando Lebron and his girl went down the street and got into a Mercedes car that was double-parked. He had a car like this, Teenager reasoned, and he only delivered drugs, and he needed his pregnant girlfriend to ride around with him so she could read for him and help deliver drugs. What kind of car, then, could a man drive if he owned all the drugs instead of just delivering them?

The next night, Teenager and his wife walked through

Central Park to the East Side and took the train up to the South Bronx. It was the first time they had left the West Side and they missed the stop and did not arrive at Mama's until nearly 10 P.M. Mama was in her bathrobe and did not want to let them in. When Teenager told her where he was from, and that he had just found out that his wife had a fatal disease, Mama let them in.

"I will cure the disease," Mama said.

"First I need money," Teenager said. "When I have money, I can give the money to you and then for sure you'll cure the disease."

Mama took out statues of Ochibia, the saint of all saints, and Changó, listened to seashells, read from the Bible, then moaned and shook with tremors.

"Soon you will have money," she announced.

Within a week, Teenager and Lydia were in a three-room apartment in the building over Ana's Bar on 138th Street and Sycamore Avenue in the South Bronx. They had a bed and television set and Teenager was standing in the evening outside Ana's Bar with Fernando Lebron, who handed him twenty-five dollars and a dozen bags of heroin: white powder in glassine envelopes used to keep stamps in. Teenager took them to 119th Street and Third Avenue and handed them to a fat man in a leather cap. Teenager did this for Fernando a couple of more times, and then one night Fernando took him into Ana's and introduced him to Ricardo who was shivering inside a gray overcoat. "I hope for the summer to come," Ricardo said. He handed Teenager thirty dollars and a pocketful of envelopes to deliver to a guy in a red Plymouth on the corner of East Tremont and Sheridan Avenue. The trip took twenty minutes. Teenager earned another twenty-five dollars later in the evening for bringing envelopes over to Minerva Avenue in the Hunts Point section.

"Where do you get the envelopes from?" he asked Ricardo.

"This is my business. Your business is to carry them," Ricardo said.

Teenager averaged four trips a week for Ricardo. One

evening, Ricardo took Teenager through a door at the back of the room that led to a short staircase, at the top of which was a storeroom. He gave Teenager a paper bag. "Take this to a man and I will give you a hundred dollars," Ricardo said.

"How much is in this bag?" Teenager said.

"A quarter key."

"How much sentence do I get if they catch me?"

"Nothing," Ricardo said. "They don't bother little guys. They only want the big people."

Outside, Teenager asked Lebron about this bag he was carrying.

"If you get busted with this amount they will give you years like they are days," Lebron said.

"Ricardo says they don't bother small people," Teenager said.

"They built the jail for runners," Lebron said.

"I should get more than a hundred dollars for taking a chance like this," Teenager said.

Lebron said nothing. Teenager walked off to the subway.

The man he was delivering to was named Jackson and he lived on the third floor of 498 Washington Avenue in the Bedford Stuyvesant section of Brooklyn. Teenager carried the paper bag on the subway as if it were a loaf of bread. Jackson was in a rear apartment on the fourth floor. Jackson was an old black man, a frizzle of gray hair atop a mostly bald head. And suspicious. He peered from a door that was chained in two places.

"Just give it to me," Jackson said.

"How do I know who you are?" Teenager said.

Jackson took down the chains and let Teenager in. There was nobody else in the apartment. A window in the kitchen, the glass frosted, had a hole in it. Through the hole, Teenager saw an airshaft. Teenager put the paper bag down on the stove alongside the window. When Jackson came to inspect the bag, Teenager got his hands under Jackson's armpits, lifted him up and pushed him through the frosted glass window. The breaking glass made a quick, clear sound.

Teenager kept the paper bag under his mattress in the

Bronx for three weeks. When he heard nothing about this old man Jackson in Brooklyn, he went up to East Tremont Avenue and said to the man in the red Plymouth, "Can you use a quarter key?"

"If it is good," the man said.

"How much do you give me for it?" Teenager asked.

"Thousand dollars."

The next night, Teenager brought the paper bag. The guy in the Plymouth took Teenager to an apartment on Sheridan Avenue where two others examined the heroin. Then the guy in the Plymouth handed Teenager a thousand dollars in fives and tens. A month later, Teenager asked the man in the Plymouth what he had done with the quarter key.

"Cut it and sold it."

"For how much?"

"Four thousand dollars."

"You made four times as much as me?" Teenager said.

"Yes. That is this business."

"Then it is mine, too," Teenager said.

_____ .... **Chapter 8**

_____ ....

And now, nine years later, in 1976, his life bolted together with villainy, he began the last of summer in a bar in the Bronx and waited for life to erupt. That it would do so was inevitable, despite all the concordats between Teenager and Pedro Torres, the man who had grown from street urchin into entity while Teenager was in jail.

There were three conversations between them, mainly clashes of ego and greed. The notion of strict control of drug territory, one block is yours, the next mine, was ridiculous, for legitimate life in the South Bronx was anarchy and thus the notion of controlling anything illegitimate was ludicrous. It was simply a matter of applying enough force about the flagstone on which you stood at the moment in order to ensure that you remained standing. For the third meeting between Teenager and Torres, the site was the Arecibo Club, which was converted from an old garage and stood between junkyards on Southern Boulevard. It took three days for the meeting to occur, for each time it was scheduled, the people on both sides arrived with so many weapons and were so certain that the other side plotted treachery that postponements were required. Finally, Torres and Teenager took places at the end of an otherwise empty bar and began haggling. They were able to agree on only one basic point.

"If you take off one of my pushers, then I take you off," Teenager said.

"If you take off one of my pushers, I take you off too," Torres said.

With this settled, they left, and the future of a loose, miserable and dangerous business in an unstructured area was left to whatever havoc the wind could stir.

When it came, it started with other people and it was over a windowshade.

One day Yvette, barmaid at the Caribe Casino on Tremont Avenue, told the owner, Octavio Turin, that she would be delighted to live with him, particularly if she could stop working as a barmaid and stay home in bed and watch television. At fifty, fat and one of the few Puerto Ricans using a toupee, Turin felt that leaving Yvette home alone at night was similar to allowing bank tellers to work unsupervised. He asked the landlord to move the shade down about two inches on Turin's ground floor bedroom window. At odd moments during the night, Turin would leave his nightclub and rush by gypsy cab to his apartment house, where he then would stand atop a crate on the sidewalk and peer over the top of the shade into the bedroom. Always, Turin found Yvette enthralled by Spanish-language soap operas or 5:00 A.M. reruns of Daniel Boone.

Yvette had a cousin named Luisa Maria Flores. Luisa Maria called Yvette one day to say that she had "fresh sexy movies," the "fresh" being her word for "French." Yvette said she couldn't wait to see them. That night, at 1:00 A.M., Turin stood up on a crate and looked over the windowshade and found Yvette and an unidentified male Hispanic in bed. Giggling told Turin another couple was on the bedroom floor. He saw Luisa Maria's head bobbing. On a projection screen was a man with a missing incisor tooth and an alert sixteen-inch penis.

Turin leaped from the crate and ran around to the apartment door. The inside lock, the Fox lock, held him out of his own house.

"Who is in the house with you?" Turin called through the door.

"Not you," his wife, Yvette, said.

Turin took out a .38 Smith & Wesson and fired three shots through the door. He hit nobody inside, but there was considerable screaming. Turin announced he would come back and kill everybody, but the one he blamed for the night, Luisa Maria Flores, her he would torture.

The next morning, Luisa Maria slipped out of the apartment and went to a place called the San Pedro Casino, where Pedro Torres, the drug dealer, sat with four men in the daytime empty club.

Luisa Maria told him a story she knew: some months before, Octavio Turin had sent people to rob one of Torres' pushers, a man named Junior. Luisa Maria told Torres that Octavio Turin's people had taken thirteen hundred dollars from Junior.

Torres' eyes told Luisa Maria that the figure she quoted was absolutely right.

"Octavio Turin also got an eighth key off Junior," she said.

Torres stood up. This, too, was a precise figure.

"Wait a second," one of the men at the table said. His name was Paulie and he was a Sicilian from Knickerbocker Avenue in Brooklyn who carried drugs and collected money for Louis Mariani. Paulie was dressed Puerto Rican, with a bright red shirt and gold chain, but it was clear by the manner in which he leaned back in his chair that he was in these clothes only for purposes of sales. Clearly, he regarded his blood as superior. He smiled, showing his newly capped teeth, and put a hand on Torres' arm.

"All right," Paulie said. "It looks like you got to do what you got to do."

"Shoot every one of the bastards," Torres said.

He motioned to the two Puerto Ricans who had been sitting in silence at the table. Their names were Gigi and Victor. They went over to another table with Torres. He had Luisa Maria join them. Paulie, sneering, above this, remained alone.

Three nights later, Octavio Turin arrived at the Mojujuo Bar at 1:00 A.M., a full hour earlier than the appointment he had made with his wife, Yvette. She had asked for this meeting at the bar in order to explain the French

movies, and as she intimated that she would bring Luisa
Maria with her, Turin had his toupee pasted firmly and a
Browning .9 millimeter automatic pistol stuffed in his
belt. He intended to shoot Luisa Maria many times. Octavio Turin sat over grapefruit juice and vodka. Into the
barroom came Pete Boogaloo, who sold drugs for Teenager. Boogaloo took a seat next to Octavio.

"I'm buying Octavio a drink," Pete Boogaloo told the
barmaid.

"It's my drink," Octavio said.

"No, I'm celebrating," Pete Boogaloo said.

"Oh, that's right. Your man is back," Turin said.

"Teenager!" Pete Boogaloo said. As he laughed, he
revealed missing bridgework on the entire right side of
his mouth. The dentist wanted $1,500, but Pete Boogaloo
had to pay the monthly bill for his leased Mercedes Benz
480, the car being much more important to him than the
ability to chew.

As Octavio Turin and Pete Boogaloo were having a
drink, a festival appeared in the barroom doorway. Two
barmaids known as Oligita and Inez were escorting Clarissa Martinez, a woman of prominence; the night before
Clarissa had unanimously won the Bronx Bar Owner's
Go Go Girl contest. There were twenty-five people in the
Mojujuo at this hour, but Clarissa Martinez, seeing a visiting bar owner, Turin, chose a seat next to him.

"Buy us a drink," she said to Turin.

"I'm just having a drink with Pete," Turin said.

Clarissa Martinez looked at Pete Boogaloo, who sat on
the other side of Turin.

"Then you buy us a drink."

"We are just talking," Pete Boogaloo said.

"These two are no good dirty bastards!" Clarissa Martinez said.

No one noticed Luisa Maria walk into the place with
two men. She stood just inside the doorway and pointed
to Octavio Turin. "Him," she said. She then fled to the
ladies' room and the two who had arrived with her, Victor and Gigi, two of Torres' men, walked toward the bar.
Gigi took a nickel-plated Colt .45 Combat Commander
from his waist and walked up and shot Octavio Turin in

the head. The toupee flew. Victor took out a black
Charter Arms .44 Bulldog and, deciding that Pete Boogaloo was as bad as Turin, shot Boogaloo in the head.

There was noise and a desperate rush for the door. Gigi
and Victor had trouble getting out because so many customers were jammed in the doorway ahead of them. Neither thought of getting Luisa Maria, who had been told to
stay in the ladies' room until one of the gunmen came for
her.

At the bar, Clarissa Martinez and her girlfriends did
not move. Clarissa went into her purse for part of her
topless dancing contest winnings, pinches of coke, and
placed the crystals on the bar for the others to share. The
bar owner, who had made a 911 call, stood in the middle
of the room and stared at the two bodies on the floor next
to the girls. The owner became ill and went to the men's
room. Clarissa and her girlfriends all took deep, delicious
breaths with cocaine crystals. They were chattering high
and the pleasant sounds caused Luisa Maria to look out
of the ladies' room. Clarissa Martinez absently swung her
lovely young legs back and forth over the two bodies on
the floor.

A cop blustered in, the visor jammed down over his
flat face.

"Did anything happen?" he asked.

"Sure," Clarissa said.

Statement taken by 41st Precinct on Sept. 10, 1976 by
Assistant District Attorney Irwin Weiss.
Statement of: Clarissa Martinez
Present: Detective Robert McGuire, Shield #1417,
29th Homicide Squad
Reporter: Patricia Curtin
Time: 7:00 A.M.
Examination Conducted by Mr. Weiss

Q. Your name is Clarissa Martinez. Is that correct?
A. Yes.
Q. Were you born on March 1, 1957?
A. Yes.
Q. Your telephone number is 767–4611.

A. Yes.

Q. Do you know your Social Security number?

A. I don't have one.

Q. Do you understand what an ADA is?

A. No.

Q. I am a prosecutor.

A. Pros—what? You a pros?

Q. Do you understand English?

A. A little bit.

Q. Anytime you don't understand what I am saying, I will try to explain it better for you, okay?

A. Okay.

Q. I call your attention to earlier this morning. Where were you?

A. In the bar.

Q. What bar?

A. Mojujuo—I can't pronounce the name.

Q. And what happened there?

A. Some dudes shot Octavio and Pete.

Q. Who shot who?

A. The dudes.

Q. You don't know who the dudes were?

A. I don't know their names.

Q. You saw someone shoot Octavio and Pete Boogaloo?

A. Yes.

Q. How many shots were fired?

A. Whole lot of shots.

Q. How many people did you see with a gun?

A. It was two.

Q. You were in the bar when the two dudes who shot Octavio and Boogaloo came into the bar?

A. Yes, I was in there already.

Q. What time did you get there?

A. About 1:00 A.M.

Q. Until about 5:30, right?

A. Yes.

Q. About 5:30 this morning, what did you see happen?

A. They started shooting.

Q. When you say they started shooting—I am going

to show you some pictures. Were the men that started
shooting any of these men? Look carefully.

A. Number four I saw.

Q. Did you see anyone else?

A. Not that I know.

Q. Look at them individually one more time just to
make sure.

A. Only number four.

Q. This fellow number four, what is his name?

A. His name is Primo.

Q. Did you see him at all before this day?

A. Yes.

Q. About how many times?

A. I worked once in this bar and that was—it's been
about four months ago. I meet him about two years ago
with my father.

Q. All right. Did you see him walk in?

A. Walk in when?

Q. When he came into the bar and shot Octavio and
Pete Boogaloo.

A. This dude didn't do that.

Q. I thought you told me that you saw him?

A. I saw him another time last month. My girlfriend
Gypsy walk over to kid with him. That's how I know
his face. He sat down first at the bar and they had a
couple of drinks and then he got up and put some quarters into the pool table. But that was another time. I
just know him.

Q. Why did you just tell me that you recognized his
picture?

A. I do. For the time when my girlfriend Gypsy kid
him.

Q. Why bring that up now?

A. Why show me his picture now?

Q. Do you know what acting in concert means?

A. Celia Cruz.

Q. Who?

A. Celia Cruz concert.

Q. I do not mean music. I mean that if these two
people who did the shooting, and if you were involved
with that, that makes you just as guilty as the one who

pulled the trigger. That's what the law is. That is acting in concert.

A. So?

Q. If we have evidence that you were in fact involved with these other people who shot and killed two individuals . . .

A. You make up lie.

Q. I can't understand why you don't tell me exactly who you saw in the bar.

A. I tell you I see two dudes shoot.

Q. What were they wearing?

A. One an army jacket. The other I don't see.

Q. Why?

A. I see his gun.

Q. The gun you saw, what did the guy do with it?

A. He was standing like about here, the dude that was shooting nearest to me. When I looked at Octavio Turin when he fell, I saw the dude shoot and he walked somewheres. Then I saw this other guy pull his gun, he shoot Pete Boogaloo, and then he puts the gun back inside his pants.

Q. And you didn't recognize him?

A. No.

Q. You weren't acting with him?

A. No.

Q. Do you feel at this time that you would like a lawyer?

A. It doesn't matter, I don't have no money to pay for the lawyer.

Q. Do you understand that you can talk to a lawyer free of charge if you want to?

A. I don't understand. I was in the place having drinks, something happens. I have nothing to do with it.

Q. It might help you to talk to a lawyer. Do you understand that?

A. All right.

Q. Would you rather speak to a lawyer first or would you rather talk to me right now?

A. The same thing I am going to tell a lawyer is the same thing I am going to say here.

Q. What's that?
A. Fuck you, I tell the truth.

The day outside carried the last summer heat. Lieutenant Martin's office was airless, the windows down.

"Leave it alone," Martin said when Myles went to open a window. "Planes come right over the building and you can't hear the game."

Martin sat in his office in a short-sleeved shirt, the underarms dark with sweat. Arms folded, eyes darting with each pitch, he watched the Yankee game on the small television that was atop an old refrigerator.

"Third inning," Martin said.

Myles sat down.

Martin returned to the game. In the squad room outside, a couple of detectives sat at gray metal desks and took phone calls. One of them, his face beleaguered, came to the door of Martin's small hot office.

"Lieutenant."

"After," Martin said.

"How much after?"

"After," Martin said again.

He grunted to Myles. "They got four girls in there."

"That's on the double from last night?" Myles said.

When Martin saw Myles' tenseness, he held up a hand. "You'll get all the work you need on this. You just stay here with me for a little while. I want to tell you a couple of more things about this job before you go running around not knowing what you're doing."

A long fly caused Martin to shift in frustration. A ground ball caused him to grunt. Between innings there was a commercial that featured a black baseball player with a goatee who sat on lawn furniture and extolled its comfort.

"Now they even use them in commercials," Martin said.

"They sure do," Myles said.

"Well, they sure use them the right way," Martin said. "Lawn furniture's just about perfect for them. I never seen them do anything but sit on their ass."

Martin sucked on his cigarette. In the fifth inning, the

Yankees had three men on and Reggie Jackson up and Jackson hit a line drive down the right field foul line. Martin came forward in his chair.

"Fair!"

He called it a half beat before the Yankee announcer.

On television, Yankee runners scurried across home plate and Reggie Jackson stood in the dust at second base and acknowledged the plaudits from the stands.

"They make him the Pope," Martin said.

"How many of them are in the crowd?" Myles said.

"What does it matter?" Martin said. "I knew we were through the first time I saw Jackie Robinson. You ever seen him play? Well I did. First World Series he was in. Nineteen forty-seven against the Yankees. He gets on base and he starts jigging around. Jigging and jigging. Here's poor Yogi Berra catching. First time Berra ever caught in the big leagues. He starts trying to pick Robinson off first. Ping! Throw to first. Ping! Pitchout, throw to first. Sure enough here goes the next throw into right field. Robinson runs to third like a bastard. To *third*. I said to myself, next thing you know they'll be living with us. Wow, was I right."

Martin stood up and stretched. "So, what's doing with you?"

"Nothing."

It was morning before the police were through questioning the four girls concerning the killings in the Mojujuo Bar. Clarissa Martinez was angry because they all had been kept so long. Luisa Maria looked for a cab, saw none, noticed the *bodega* up the street and decided that her mouth was smoke-parched. She asked the others if they wanted gum. No, they said. Luisa Maria started for the *bodega*. A man was walking toward her from the *bodega*. The man turned around and went back.

The *bodega* man had gum and candy on the counter as you walk in. Luisa Maria was reaching for a pack of gum when she was yanked the length of the store by this wide-shouldered bearded man who held a finger to his lips. Luisa Maria knew enough to keep quiet.

He took her out the back door, through an alley and to a Mercedes 300 that was parked by a fire hydrant.

Luisa Maria was frightened and tried to pull away. It was impossible to get out of the man's grasp.

"That's all right," Teenager said as he put her into the Mercedes.

"I like your name, Teenager, that is a good name," Luisa Maria said in the motel.

They were long past any questions and answers. In the car, Luisa Maria had taken one long look at Teenager and then told him immediately why his friend Pete Boogaloo had been killed: "I just happen to be in the club looking for a job and I hear this Italian guy Paulie tell Torres that he has to shoot Octavio Turin and Boogaloo right away. Paulie said, go ahead, you better do it tonight. Gigi and Victor said, yes, they would do it tonight."

Over brandy in the motel bar, Luisa Maria told Teenager every daily habit of the four, Paulie, Victor, Gigi and Torres, that she could remember. And now in bed with Teenager, Luisa Maria ran a fingernail across his chest and said, "Next time I think they want to shoot you."

"Who said that?" Teenager asked.

"I just think so," Luisa Maria said. She kept running her fingernails on the chest. "Teenager, I like that name."

"I will give you my name someday because you are so beautiful," Teenager said. "I will make you my wife."

"I have a husband," Luisa Maria said.

"Maybe I will make your husband go away," Teenager said.

"Oh, I like that," Luisa Maria said.

Eighteen months before this, in the first job she had in this country, as a floor girl in a factory where old clothes were cut into rags, the foreman one day asked her if she wanted to have sex. She said she had a husband. The foreman said, "Then go home and ask your husband if you can do it with me."

That night, she mentioned this to her husband and he said, "If he gives you money, then it is all right for you to have sex with this man." In bed with Teenager, Luisa Maria said to herself, fuck this husband I have.

"He should go away forever," Luisa Maria said to Teenager.

She looked into Teenager's eyes as she said this. Then Luisa Maria slid her hand between Teenager's legs and caused his great body to shiver.

In the morning, Teenager took Luisa Maria to Ana's Bar and told the old barmaid who wore her hat over a kerchief that he did not want her any longer.

"Do you know how to tend bar?" Teenager said to Luisa Maria.

She stepped onto the duckboards and picked up a rum bottle from the bottom shelf. She blew the dust off it.

"You keep this place dirty," she said.

"Here," Teenager said. He held up a dollar.

She bounced down the duckboard floor. "¿Sí?"

"You play the juke box for me."

She came out from behind the bar, punched the tunes and came back. As the first record came on, Teenager said, "Make the music loud." Behind the bar, Luisa Maria turned a key and the tune, "¡Toro Mata!" with Celia Cruz singing, blared into the small barroom. Luisa Maria began to sing with the juke box.

> Toro mata ahí
> Toro mata ahí
> Rumbanchero toro mata
> Toro viejo se murió
> Mañana comemos
> carne
> Toro mata
> Toro torito toro mata

Teenager wriggled his shoulders to the tune. *Toro mata*. The bull kills. The song said the bull kills, the old bull died and tomorrow we eat meat. Halfway through the lyrics the second time, with trumpets loud and high, Teenager let out a growl that came from the bottom of his belly.

..... **Chapter 9**

In the middle of the hot afternoon, the shoemaker stood in front of the small electric fan and let it blow on his wet face. Outside his window, the Brooklyn sidewalk was crowded with Italians and Puerto Ricans who walked slowly and street-shopped at the outdoor displays of fruit and summerwear and fish that the shopkeepers had set up. A Puerto Rican with large, menacing shoulders covered by a powder-blue knit polo shirt stood with his back to the shoemaker's window. The Puerto Rican turned and came into the shop. The shoemaker placed a hand to his mouth and spit the shoenails into his hand. He was proud of the shoenails; he was sure that he was the only shoemaker left in Brooklyn who still hammered nails to put new soles onto his shoes.

"Can I help you?" he said to the Puerto Rican.

Teenager did not answer. He opened a paper shopping bag and took out a white boat-captain's hat, which he jammed down over his eyes.

Teenager walked up two doors and then stopped at the outdoor counter of the Cafe Del Golfo. Around him, the narrow strips of sidewalk going past the outdoor stands were clogged with shoppers. In the windows of the five-story walkups, old women rested their arms on pillows and stared down at the street. A kid in a bathing suit sat atop an open hydrant and directed the water at passing cars by clamping his bare legs against the opening, seal-

ing it, then suddenly opening his legs and directing a
stream of water at the windows of the cars and delivery
trucks. The air was filled with the sounds of a changing
neighborhood, Puerto Ricans calling in Spanish and Italian merchants shouting out in rough English. A cockeyed
kid in a white apron came to the open window of the
cafe.

"Lemon ice," Teenager said. He glanced at his watch.
One fifty-nine. He had a full minute.

The cockeyed kid went to the refrigerator and Teenager stared into the Cafe Del Golfo. The cockeyed kid
was the only one behind the long counter. A squat orange
espresso machine sat like a tabernacle on the middle of
the counter. The far end of the counter was open. There
were phone booths, and then a space in a partition leading into the back room where the Italians sat and played
cards. Teenager watched the amount of smoke hanging
in the air over the partition.

When the cockeyed kid brought him the lemon ice,
Teenager fumbled in his pocket for change. He took a
step back and grimaced.

"I have a whole pocket of change someplace here," he
said.

The cockeyed kid stared out the open window and said
nothing.

Inside the cafe, one of the phones rang.

"Now I have the change," Teenager said. He stepped
up to the counter. Inside the cafe, the phone kept ringing.
Finally, a bald man in a short-sleeved shirt came out of
the card room and answered it. The bald man dropped
the phone and walked back into the card room.

"Paulie," he called out.

Teenager grabbed the cockeyed kid by the T-shirt and
yanked him so that the kid's chest and head were through
the window. The first Italian in my life I ever touch and
it is an idiot, Teenager said to himself. His right hand
went under the powder-blue polo shirt and brought the
black Browning .9 millimeter into the kid's face.

"Sit down on the floor or you are dead," Teenager
said.

He let go of the kid. Terrified, the cockeyed kid

dropped to the floor behind the counter. Now Teenager
gripped the Browning with both hands and aimed down
the counter, past the espresso machine, at the phone
booths. Paulie came out of the card room to answer the
phone, walking with his lips wide apart so everybody
could admire his newly capped teeth. Teenager didn't
know if Paulie saw him or not. Teenager had his eyes
riveted on Paulie's chest, a yellow shirt under a brown
lounge suit. It took a fraction over a second for the
Browning to fire nine shots at the chest. It sounded at
first, on the crowded street, as if a truck had backfired.
Then in people's minds came the realization that the
truck had a trigger. Women began to shriek. Teenager
was in the shoe repair shop by now. He stuffed the pistol
into his trousers and threw the captain's hat behind the
counter. The shoemaker, afraid it was a bomb, jumped
into his show window, which was filled with shoes and
posters for a soccer match.

Teenager ripped off the blue polo shirt, dropped it and
walked outside in a white undershirt. The screaming of
many voices came from the cafe. People on the street
were running toward the cafe to see what had happened.
Teenager walked away from the shoe repair shop, went
past a fruit stand and then mixed in with a group of Puerto
Ricans who stood at the corner.

One of them, bare-topped, held a quart bottle of Miller's beer. "The Guineas shoot each other," he said.

Teenager took the bottle from his hand. "I'll buy you
a dozen bottles," he said. He took a long swig of the
beer, the sun blazing against the clear glass. As he drank,
he had his eyes on the entrance to the Cafe Del Golfo.
Guineas kept running out, stopping, looking up and down
the sidewalk, seeing the flock of Puerto Rican faces, and
then running on to their cars. Flying out of the doorway
came the cockeyed kid. A hand from the doorway held
the cockeyed kid's black hair. A foot came out and
kicked the cockeyed kid out onto the sidewalk where he
rolled in pain.

"Come with me," Teenager said to the bare top. They
walked several yards up the sidestreet and into a *bodega*.

"Three quarts of beer for my friend," Teenager said.

He put a five-dollar bill on the counter and then walked out into the hot street and ambled up to a 1965 red Falcon. Benny Velez pretended to doze at the wheel, but his hands shook slightly. Teenager opened the door and stood in the sun and stretched. He watched a police car come the wrong way on the one-way street, siren sounding, roof light spinning, the bare-armed cops inside it motioning furiously for the crowd of Puerto Ricans in the street to get out of the way.

Teenager got in the car, slammed the door shut and put a hand on Benny's thigh to keep Benny from trying to reach ninety by the middle of the block.

"Just drive slow," Teenager said.

They went up the narrow, littered street, past stoops crowded with women who held babies and craned to see what was happening at the corner.

"Right," Teenager said at the end of the block.

Benny turned right and the car now was on the street with several old cars driven by Puerto Ricans. They drove for blocks until they no longer could hear the police sirens.

"Let's go home," Teenager said.

When Teenager walked into Ana's Bar, Luisa Maria slid off the barstool and looked at him. Teenager licked his lips and smiled. Luisa Maria put her hand on the juke box key. Suddenly, the music roared into the room.

Toro mata ahí
Toro mata . . .

"Aha!" Teenager shouted. His shoulders wiggled to the music.

"Call somebody on the phone," he said to Luisa Maria. "You are good at making phone calls."

Luisa Maria shrieked and clapped her hands.

Two days later, Gigi and Victor were having one of the best times in months. At 6:00 A.M., they were at the Myruggia Bar in Hunts Point, a desert by day and swamp by night, separated from the South Bronx mainland by an expressway and a slimy canal with an old drawbridge going over it. Hunts Point has a huge market area, fenced and closed at night; a high white building holding Spofford House, the detention house for kids arrested under sixteen, a few low apartment houses and empty lots around weary factories. Fire reduced Hunts Point to about a third of what it once was; the Myruggia Bar sat in the center of this like a truck stop in the middle of Nebraska. There were no sidewalks, and the bar had no other buildings near it. A lone streetlamp bathed the front of the building in a weak light. The Myruggia was a long one-story building with a steam table in front for factory workers' lunches during the day, along with several pool tables, and the rest of the place taken up by a rectangular bar that could fit two hundred. On a platform behind the bar nearly naked young women, women not as young as the trade called for, danced to Latin music. The women were listless and sad-fleshed, but this was no matter to Gigi; he sat with his friend Victor and they carefully braided five-dollar bills into paper airplanes. The way Gigi did it, he made the point as sharp as possible, and then he kept twisting the point until it seemed as firm as metal. When Gigi and Victor had many of these five-dollar planes, Gigi picked up one, squinted and aimed it at the dancer's bare right breast.

A smile came on the dancer's face and her body began to swing more. Big lesbian hips swung out, causing her chest to shake, a chest with contours suggesting more of fat than of beauty. She looked at the ceiling, smiling, knowing what was coming, but pretending she did not, so that she could give a greater kick to Gigi.

Gigi threw his airplane dart. The kneaded nose seemed to be going right for the nipple, but it landed lower.

The dancer gave a jerk, as if in pain.

Gigi exploded. "Yaaaaahhh!" he roared. The dancer smiled at him, and gave him a reproving look. Hips still moving, she bent down, picked up the five and tucked it into the little patch of cloth covering her pubic hair. Her gaze went to the ceiling again, so that she could be taken by surprise by another of Gigi's darts.

Gigi aimed carefully. She glanced down and caught him in the midst of this and Gigi giggled and covered his face

and hid the dart behind his glass of vodka. Then the big
hip-swinging lesbian looked up at the ceiling again and
Gigi threw. She swung her body to the right and the dart,
fading, landed just at the right hip. She gave a little start
that made Gigi smile slightly. Then as he took aim again,
she scooped up the five-dollar dart and tucked it safely
against her brown sugary hair. She straightened up to
dance and now, at once, Gigi and Victor Buenes aimed
and threw, Victor for the left tit, Gigi for the right. Victor's fell harmlessly to the floor, but Gigi's hit well, about
two inches from the nipple. The big lesbo dancer bucked
forward as if badly stung. She began to swing her body
as if in great pain. Gigi loved it. As the lesbo danced, she
indicated with a finger the bills that had just been thrown.
The barmaid picked them off the floor and stuffed them
down the dancer's front.

"That's all right," Teenager said. He was standing behind Gigi and Victor, pushing up against Gigi so that Gigi
would feel the pistol in the small of his back.

"You're coming with me," Teenager said to Gigi.

"I am here," Gigi said.

"That's all right," Teenager said.

"I don't see you when you are home from jail and now
you come to me like this?" Gigi said.

"That's all right," Teenager said.

Chita Gonzalez, in red blouse opened to the waist, was
at the opposite side of the bar. She looked up from her
drink and saw Teenager and immediately began to push
her way through people to get to him.

"I make money with him," she said.

As she came around the bar, Teenager was pushing
Gigi and Victor toward the door.

"You don't remember me?" Chita Gonzalez called to
him.

Teenager glanced at her, then marched Gigi and Victor
out of the bar. They stood outside the rear door in the
early morning.

"You have been in jail too long," Gigi said. He saw
that point reached Teenager. "Come on," Gigi said,
"would I be out in a bar such as this if I had done anything to you? I would be on the other side of the world."

Teenager slapped Gigi on the shoulder. "I don't know who tells me anything. I am so mixed up from prison. You are right."

"Where do you have to go?" Gigi asked.

"To the Cross Bronx Expressway service road," Teenager said.

Gigi knew where this was. It is a short, deserted street with no sidewalk that serves as a launch site for cars going out onto the expressway and, more prominently, a meeting place for Puerto Rican drug peddlers and Mariani's Italian suppliers who came off the expressway from the North Bronx, did business through car windows with these greasy Spics, then took the money and rushed off to their homes.

Teenager slid into the back seat and Gigi and Victor sat in front of Gigi's tan Mark IV Lincoln. The drive took less than ten minutes. Gigi pulled his car alongside a fence of a public schoolyard, whose asphalt sounded with the footsteps of the first basketball game of the day.

"You are just nervous from jail," Gigi said. "When I first come home from jail I cannot listen to a bus going by, I am so nervous."

Teenager shot Gigi in the back of the head with the gun in his left hand and Victor in the back of the head with the gun in his right hand. He fired once more into each head. He stuffed the guns into his belt and dove out of the Lincoln on the street side, so schoolyard kids would not see him. Benny drove up in his Mercedes. As the car pulled away, Teenager could see Gigi and Victor with their heads against the seatbacks. Teenager began to think of a place to get rid of the guns. Then, like a bored cat, he began to lick the blood from his hands.

At 7:45 A.M., the sector car lurched up to Gigi's Lincoln and saw what was inside. The patrolman called for a supervisor. When the sergeant arrived, detectives were called. Detective Lieutenant Robert Martin, his face red, but not from sunshine, drove up in a weary brown Plymouth Fury. Behind him was a blue Plymouth with two detectives and in the third Plymouth, black, were Hansen and Myles.

"Keep your hands off the car," Martin shouted at the patrolmen who were around the car. He went up to the window and looked in. "The *Cuchifritos* Brigade," Martin said. Noise irritated Martin. He turned around and saw that the schoolyard fence was now made up of rows of young white faces pressed against the chain link.

"They shouldn't be looking at a thing like this," Martin said to Myles.

Myles, walking to the fence, called out, "Get out of there."

"They got their brains blown all over the front of the car?" a kid said.

"Get out of there," Myles said.

"That's right. You wouldn't know what brains are," the kid said.

Myles slapped the fence and the kids jumped off and ran away. Martin's voice called him back. "Go round to a butcher shop and get a lot of wrapping paper," Martin said. Myles and Hansen drove to a supermarket in the Parkchester housing and came back with a roll of brown paper from the meat counter.

Martin nervously ripped off a large sheet of paper and pulled open the door on the driver's side. A patrolman winced as he saw Martin's hand covering the door handle, eliminating any chance of handprints being taken by the forensics unit. The patrolman walked away rapidly; he knew that if any of the lab men complained, Martin would blame the nearest uniformed patrolman. Martin leaned in and covered the face of Gigi and Victor. A tow truck raised the front of the car, then took it off the block, with Martin driving directly behind it and Myles and Hansen in the next car. Six blocks down, in front of St. Clement's Church, the nine o'clock mass was just getting out as the tow truck went into a pothole, swayed, causing the car being towed to shudder. Inside the car, a crystal of air snapped open and the hand of the devil reached out and caused the butcher's paper to fall from the faces of Gigi and Victor. A woman on the church steps, a woman with blue hair and both hands gripping her purse, swayed as if about to faint. Martin's siren went off, causing the tow truck to stop. Martin's hand waved for Myles, who ran up from his car as Martin ripped off a large sheet of paper and held it out the window. Myles went to the towed car, reached in with his eyes shut and placed so much paper over the dead faces that he appeared to be packing them in a barrel for moving.

As Myles walked back to his car, he found his hands covered with blood. Doing the work of the Lord, he told himself, but without conviction.

..... **Chapter 10**

When she awoke for work at 7:00 A.M., she was surprised to smell cigars, which signified that her father was up. As the hour was so alien to his habits, she felt that something extraordinary was taking place. She sat up quickly. At first, her guilt forced her to wonder if all this was over her seeing the Spic after work. Nobody saw me, she assured herself. Then she decided that it really didn't matter anyway, for she would say if questioned that all she had done was to have coffee with this guy who worked for her and was receiving a civilized last chance before being fired. At ease now, she got out of bed, her body motions dissolving the last of the night's sleep. He actually is a citizen, she said to herself, her mind going immediately and involuntarily to Maximo.

Putting on a white terry-cloth robe, she went into the bathroom to brush her teeth. She then followed the cigar smoke along the hallway from the bedrooms, past the den and into the living room, where the sound of her father's voice, arguing in the kitchen, caused her to stop.

"So you got two guys sitting in the same joint with Paulie, am I right or am I a fucking cabbage?" her father growled.

"Right," another voice said quietly.

"Yeah, the two was there," a third voice said.

"So Paulie gets clipped and then the next thing, the two guys go, too," Nicki's father said.

"Two fucking Spics," a voice said.

"I know they was Spics," the father shouted, "but Paulie ain't no Spic. He's one of us. What I'm thinking is that one guy does the whole job on the three of them."

A voice said something inaudible, then her father's hand sounded on the kitchen table. "What is it you're telling me?" he yelled. "You bring in some cockeyed kid which doesn't know the day of the week. We know he probably can't see a thing with that cockeyed eye. So you rely on him? Forget about him. I'm going with the fact that Paulie was in the room with two guys. Paulie walks out. Boop. Paulie's gone. Now out walks the two guys. Boop, boop. Now the both of them are gone too. That's three guys gone from the same room. I say they all got it for the same reason."

"I can't come up with an answer," one of the voices said.

"Yeah, we *axt* everybody," another voice said.

"Did any of you *ast* the Spics?" Nicki's father demanded.

There were murmurs. "I'll tell you what I think," the father said, "I think some fucking Spic done it. I know just the guy I'm thinking of. I'd like to bite my whole face off, I let him come into my own house."

"Teenager," one of the other voices said.

"Who else could it be in the Bronx?" the father said.

"What do you think?" one of the voices said.

"I think he ought to get buried," Nicki's father said.

Nicki silently went back into the bathroom, showered and dressed for work. When she came back out, she walked loudly, as warning to those in the kitchen.

"There she is," Mariani said, as Nicki came to the kitchen door. He was sitting over coffee with an old man named Sal, whom Nicki knew lived in Florida, and a big guy with thick black hair, the first gray showing at the fringes, whom she knew as Corky.

Smiling, Sal and Corky stood up and Nicki turned her fixed, vacant smile on them.

"Where are you going this early?" Mariani said.

"To work."

"At least have some coffee first."

"Thanks, but I have to be in early and I'm running late already."

"Take the car," Mariani said.

"No, thanks, I have my bus."

"Why don't you want the car?"

"Because I take the bus."

"Well, then, here. Wait a minute." Mariani stood up, his hand bringing out a sizable fold of money.

"I don't need anything," Nicki said.

"Take something. Take a cab into work."

"Thanks, but I don't need a thing. See you."

"How do you like this kid? Doesn't take a thing and runs off to work. She's a real citizen."

The other two laughed. Nicki did not. "That's what I am," she said. "A real citizen." The smile fixed, she went out the front door to walk to the bus. She would borrow the car for shopping, or for a trip to prison; she would not take the car to work for the day. That would be the same as owning the car. And most certainly, she would not buy one by herself. When they arrested her husband, they grabbed the car, and when she asked for the car back after the case was over, she was told that under the law there had been a trial to determine if the car had been used in a crime, and the car had been found guilty. A yellow Lincoln Mark IV and a husband went out of her life in one case. She earned enough money to buy a car of her own, but she was sure the agents or police would find some way to take this one, too. Once, a vice-president at work suggested to her that she attend night college in order to improve her chances of advancement. When she told him that her parents did not like the notion of her continually taking the bus home at night, the vice-president of the bank said that she should simply use a car. "I'll never pay for another car," she said. "Around here, even the police steal cars." The vice-president didn't understand it, but Nicki, who was minus a Lincoln Mark IV, knew exactly what she was saying.

Walking the three blocks to the bus station, she thought of Maximo again. No movie star should ever get killed, she reminded herself flippantly. On the bus, however, the realization that another's life somehow rested in her hands was bewildering. She thought of the first time she saw Maximo, sitting in Teenager's car. They mostly get killed in cars, she told herself. She shuddered. Across her years, she had overheard dark talk in her house, but it always was conversation through which she could walk without the words registering, a commercial playing for a product whose name never is retained. This was different. Supposing Maximo was sitting in a car with Teenager? Would I have to live with that on my mind? Imagine being haunted by somebody I hardly know.

As she knew no way to call Maximo, she sat at her desk, looked at the faces of the hundred and twenty-five people who were in her charge, and hoped that Maximo would call. He still had not called her by midafternoon, and she began to ask herself why she was so certain that he would call. It was ridiculous, she told herself, for he had only called her once, and now she sat here as if he were supposed to be calling on a schedule. Then she assured herself that he would be calling continuously, and for a long time, because she was a white woman. Call now, she said to herself.

When Maximo didn't call by five-thirty, she put her cigarettes into her purse and called her mother to say that she was going to shop for a few hours.

"Why don't you wait until tomorrow night and we'll go together?" her mother said.

"I just want to walk through Macy's for a while," Nicki said.

"What is this walk through Macy's? You come out of there at night, you could get killed on the street by some dirty nigger."

"Ma, it'll be light when I leave there."

"So they do it day or night."

"I'll be home by a quarter to nine," Nicki said.

"All right," the mother said reluctantly. There was a pause, caused by thousands of years of living by suspicion. "Are you sure you're going shopping?"

"Ma."

"All right," the mother said.

Nicki walked slowly to Macy's, arriving at six-fifteen to find the jeans department crowded. She bought one pair of Calvin Kleins that she did not need, but bought in order to show her mother that the evening was spent legitimately. She walked the one block to the Statler Hilton Hotel and entered the lobby at seven o'clock.

He calls it the bar course, she said to herself. If I ask for the bar course and they send me into a bar and I find him carrying ice around like some other Puerto Rican busboy, then my father's people won't have to kill him; I'll strangle him right here, she said to herself. She paused inside the lobby and thought about what she was doing. Are you crazy, she asked herself, talking to a guy you don't even know and telling him something like this? Supposing he runs right to this bum he hangs out with, this Teenager, and tells him? Oh, for sure he'll tell him. No, you can't be serious doing a thing like this. Daddy will *kill* me.

A cardboard sign tacked to the top of the bulletin board said, "Martense Bar Review Course, Manhattan Ballroom."

Without thinking, she stepped into the ballroom elevator, getting off in an entranceway that had been made for people coming to see Glenn Miller and now was a place where people stamped out cigarettes. She stood at one side of the doorway and looked into the ballroom and saw only a couple of people seated on folding chairs at long tables. She lit a cigarette and watched the elevator doors as they opened to allow bright young faces to walk off, the American faces that Nicki disliked so much. Their heads look like they all had just been rolling around in a clothes dryer, she thought. Neat, lifeless hair, long faces with almost no distinguishing marks and eyes that were, most serious offense of all, completely unmysterious.

She waited for fifteen minutes before Maximo arrived. She felt the sensation of somebody foreign, a beard, dark deep eyes that kept things hidden, prominent cheekbones. Nicki would have liked it even better if Maximo wore an earring.

Maximo pushed through the crowd. "The doors opened and I look past this guy and I got the best surprise I've had in a long time," he said.

"Thank you," Nicki said.

"Are you going to sit through this whole thing? It's long."

"No, I have to go home. I just have to say something to you." She stepped out of the doorway and went a few yards down an empty hallway. Don't leave him with any doubt, Nicki told herself. Say exactly what he has to know. And make sure that you don't tell him one thing he doesn't need to know.

"I'll make it fast because you have to go to school," Nicki said.

"I don't care," Maximo said.

"No, listen to what I say. I want to see you again."

"Terrific."

"But I can't ever see you again if you hang around your friend."

"Teenager."

"That's right. If you even sit down to have coffee with him, then you won't see me anymore."

"Why do you say that?"

"Never mind why I say it. Just listen to what I say. If you think that you want to see me again, then don't be on the same block with your friend. You're going to have to take my word for what I'm saying to you."

"I barely know you and here you're telling me who to be friendly with," Maximo said.

"It isn't that at all. Listen to what I say. I say the truth. So if you want to see me again, then you can't be near that Teenager. Even once."

"Tell me why," Maximo said.

"Because it's you and me against the world, dear." Her cheerfulness as she said it caused Maximo to forget about his concern for a moment and laugh.

"That's the way it is," she said. "So it's up to you. If I hear from you again, then I know you're listening to what I say." She looked into his eyes, cocked her head, smiled and walked to the elevator banks.

She moved to one side as a crowd came off the elevator. She stepped into the empty elevator and just before the doors closed she smiled out at him and said, "Remember what I say."

I see her twice and she cannot remain away from me, Maximo told himself proudly.

Inside the ballroom door, he met another student who had been at Harvard. His name was Woolcott and he was a bony frame fed by watercress. He had light hair as short as fingernails and wore a three-piece suit so severe and dull that it appeared to have been taken off the back of a retired Protestant as he dozed through the afternoon at some Ivy League club.

"What have you been doing?" Woolcott said.

"Thinking," Maximo said.

"No job?"

"I'm about to start looking."

"Where?"

"In the Bronx."

"What would you go to the Bronx for?" Woolcott said.

"That's where I'm from," Maximo said.

"But you're not going to stay there?" Woolcott said.

"I'll try."

"What will you do up there? You'll wind up with the Legal Aid trying to help one person at a time in some crummy robbery and you'll get nowhere."

"I was thinking of something broader than that," Maximo said.

"Well, you can't do anything broader than start with a large firm," Woolcott said. "I'd guess where I am does more public service work than the whole Bronx put together."

"Where are you?" Maximo said.

"My father's firm. You know that. Simpson, Thatcher and Bartlett. One of the partners was the Secretary of State. I consider that public service."

"I guess so," Maximo said. "What do they pay you there?"

"Thirty-two five to start. Come on, Maximo, you know what they pay people like us. What's the most you could get in the Bronx?"

"The place I'm thinking about, the Legal Services office, pays maybe fourteen."

"I'd say that thirty-five is a lot more than fourteen."

"What do they have you doing for that kind of money?" Maximo asked.

"You do legal research until you're admitted to the bar. Right now, I'm doing things on investment capital."

"I'm sure that's very good," Maximo said. "I believe I'd prefer something like the Bronx Legal Services. Maybe work on class actions. Get involved in community work. Politics maybe."

"Well, if you want politics, we have a partner who was a federal judge. And my father is on the bar association committee that picks judges. You can't get into heavier politics than that," Woolcott said.

"I'll see," Maximo said. He walked to a table and sat down.

Through the evening in class, the thought grew on Maximo that Nicki could have been telling him the truth, that there was serious trouble centering on Teenager. After the lecture, he went to the Bronx and started looking for Teenager. He found him in the ChibCha on Tremont Avenue, a nightclub that lived up to the definition: the cocktail hour at the ChibCha began at 10:00 P.M. and by 11:30, when Maximo found his way into the place, Teenager and a party of ten were just sitting for dinner.

"I want to talk to you," Maximo said.

Teenager held out his hands. He had Luisa Maria on one side of him and Benny seated on the other.

"First you have something to eat with us, then we will talk. We have all night to talk," Teenager said.

"I have to tell you," Maximo said.

"So you will tell me after we eat." He had Maximo sit down next to Benny, and immediately resumed holding court.

"I am the president of the business," Teenager said to Benny.

"Yes."

"And you are the vice-president. If something happens to me, you become president."

"What do you say this for?" Benny said. "Nothing ever can happen to you."

"An accident," Teenager said. "It happens to Kennedy. Someone is out there who does not like me. Maybe someday I will not see him in time."

"Never," Benny said.

"Or somebody could make up a lie and get me in trouble."

"We will take this guy off the count," Benny said.

Teenager said to Luisa Maria, "What would you do if someone made up a lie about me?"

"Everything between his legs I would chop off."

Teenager's eyes crinkled and he suddenly stood up and called out, "I am going to sing."

The bandstand in the ChibCha was a small circle in a corner of the dining room, and the three guitar players were nearly shoulder to shoulder and had to maneuver their instruments much as moving men do to fit a couch through a doorway. When Teenager got up and came to the bandstand, one stepped down to make room, which he knew he had to do, just as an Italian waiter would have to assign a large table on a crowded night to a lone Mafioso and his woman.

Teenager took a microphone and said, "I am going to sing this love song I like."

Benny clapped loudly and the bartender at the small bar in the rear of the place also clapped.

"Aha," Teenager called out.

"Sing!" Benny yelled.

Teenager looked at the lead guitar player. He hummed the song he wanted to sing. The man nodded, told his two partners, and they started to play. The guitar player on the floor stood on tiptoes and held his guitar as high as possible in order to get its sound into the microphone. Teenager sang low, almost too low to hear, with each note perfectly off-key. The guitar players smiled and nodded their heads, as if supporting the great Chucho Avallanet. Sometimes the smiles turned to winces as Teenager hit a particularly bad note.

> *Yo la quise, muchachos,*
> *Y la quiero,*
> *Y jamás yo la podré*
> *Olvidar*

The song was about a man getting drunk because he loved his woman and could not forget her, while at the same time the woman was experiencing no difficulty at all in doing so.

When Teenager was finished singing, the three guitar players all applauded and the people in the dining room picked it up and Teenager proudly bowed and went back to his table.

"Did you like my song?" he said to Luisa Maria.

"Yes, but it is not my favorite song."

"This favorite song of yours is what?"

She began to hum "*¡Toro Mata!*" Teenager laughed. "Ah hah. That is not for here. Here is for love." As Teenager laughed, everybody at the table laughed with him and all around the room of the ChibCha restaurant people smiled in approval, for Teenager was a person of status. He was an outlaw.

Maximo saw that it would be a mistake to say anything to Teenager that would disturb his egomania at this moment; a threat, such as the one Maximo carried, would cause Teenager to assault the messenger and then go thrashing into the night with guns waving to prove his invincibility. Even if Teenager shot Mariani and all with him and became absolute ruler of his world, Maximo knew that he would be remembered forever as the one who brought bad news. Maximo also told himself that if Teenager went after Mariani, that would end the chance of ever seeing the girl again. Maximo now wondered if he was giving these reasons to himself as an excuse for remaining silent, an emotional defense against being drawn into a matter that could only provide danger. Looking at Teenager, Maximo saw that in the gold chains and brandy and music and laughter—laughter immediately picked up by the others at the table—there could be no disturbing news, no matter how gently given. Mama, Maximo said to himself. He knew that she could give a center to his confusion.

"Maximo is having no fun," Teenager said.

"I'm falling asleep," Maximo said.

"Wake up, then."

"I will. Just long enough to get me home."

As he left, they laughed at him as if he were still in grammar school. Pausing in the doorway, Maximo searched the street, then became irritated with himself for being dramatic. His mind had allowed a warning to grow into a shadow stalking him. He smiled at this, walked across the sidewalk and hailed a gypsy cab. When he realized that he was directly under a streetlight, he suddenly felt exposed, as if the light were coating him with typhoid, and he hopped into the shadows. She had warned him not to be around Teenager even once, he reminded himself.

When he got to Mama's house in the morning, she answered the door in a new blue pants suit and seemed impatient that he would be at her door at such an hour.

"Where have you been?" Mama said. "You come now. Now I have to go out and see a new apartment."

"I just felt like seeing you for a couple of minutes."

"Why didn't you call me?"

"I didn't know you had a phone again," Maximo said.

She frowned like a duchess being asked if she owned polo ponies. "I have had this phone for many weeks now. You can come in anyway. I'll give you coffee." Maximo followed her into the kitchen, where she cleared dirty dishes into the sink and set two mugs of coffee on the small kitchen table.

"How is everything?" she said.

"It's all right. I'm studying hard for this test. Then when I leave here this morning, I'm going over to see about a job."

"Oh, I know you do all that," Mama said. "The rest is what is very hard for you. I told you that. You are from this world and you are in the other world too."

"Mama, that's all I saw in school."

"You did not see everything I tell you about."

"Mama, the day I was in Harvard learning about wills of ten million dollars, my Aunt Ramona died and left eighty-five dollars in an envelope. So I know what two worlds is."

"A book cannot tell you these things I tell you about,"

Mama said. "Don't tell me about wills in a book. Tell me about how you live with the other people."

"I tell you, that's why I'm here," Maximo said. "One of these other people said something to me."

Mama had been looking at her coffee, about to sip it, and now her eyes, schooled in the primitive, watched Maximo for a sign, a trace of complex things that she somehow was able to see.

"What did this person say?"

"I have to tell you like a lawyer and client," Maximo said. "Only between us."

"A lawyer? I am better than a lawyer."

"All right. Like a priest in the confessional."

"That is what I am like all the time. If I were to tell something that someone tells me, then people would pray to the seven powers and I would turn into a pile of worms in my bed."

"All right," Maximo said. "One of these people from the other world told me to stay away from Teenager."

"Ah, that is because they don't want you to be yourself."

"No, I thought that. But I was wrong. This person told me that Teenager has a man very mad at him."

"Who is this man?"

"An Italian. His name is Mariani. Teenager knows him." Immediately Maximo saw that Mama knew the name, too.

"Who told you about this?"

"Somebody who knows."

"Female," Mama said.

"That's right," Maximo said.

"And she knows?"

"Absolutely."

"She told you so you could tell him?"

"No. Not even close."

"She told you to protect you?"

"No question."

"You must be very close to this person."

"I'm not. Not now, anyway. I don't know what it is right now. I know that she doesn't want me to get hurt. That's obvious."

"And you did not tell this to Teenager?"

"Mama. How could I do that?"

"No, you couldn't do such a thing," she said. "Teenager would, oh boy, he would be so mad."

"So you tell him," Maximo said.

"Yes, I'll tell him."

Maximo put his empty cup down. "So now I've told you. Now you can go out and get your apartment."

Mama smiled. "This female, does anyone see you with her?"

"I don't know. I had coffee with her in a restaurant."

"Here in the Bronx?"

"No, not in the Bronx."

"Oh. Your trouble begins when Puerto Rican people see you with this woman."

"I'll worry about that when it happens."

"You better worry before that," Mama said. "You played in a vacant lot. Now those who played with you in that lot will become very angry if they see you with an American girl. They will not let you help anybody. Do you tell anybody about the girl?"

"Only you. Teenager thinks that I saw her, but he never saw us together. What am I talking about, anyway? I only saw her twice, no three times in my life."

"You'll see her more," Mama said. "If she wants you to be safe, then she wants you for her. Then you will have trouble with yourself because you cannot live both ways."

Mama got up and walked into the living room. "I'll be just a minute," she said. Maximo stood in the doorway and watched as she went into one of her jugs and began taking out seashells. She held one up for him.

"The people die and the souls turn to rainwater and drop into the river and the ocean and become stones and seashells," she said. "They can speak to me."

She spread a straw mat, an *estera,* on the floor and held up her shells and, praying, began to drop them on the mat. Maximo went back into the kitchen and sat down. In a few minutes, he heard the shells being collected and then Mama came back.

"Are you ready to go?"

Maximo followed her out of the apartment.

"The shells told me the proverb for Teenager," Mama said. "The shells told me, 'You are defeated through your own fault.' That is the proverb of Changó, Oya, Yewa. I will tell this to Teenager and he will be safe from this Mariani."

Outside, Maximo said, "Now tell me something else, where is this new apartment you're going to get?"

"Mosholu Parkway."

"Hey, that's pretty good." He had a dark notion of where her fresh money was from.

Mama's chin came out proudly. "Soon I will not have to walk to a subway."

When Maximo left Mama at the El steps, he had a feeling of accomplishment. He had done his duty to Teenager and from now on would please Nicki and try not to see him anymore.

Two days later, Maximo was at the Bronx Legal Services, which were one flight over the Santurce *cuchifritos* stand on Cortlandt Street. The director of the Bronx Legal Services sat in a large cubicle decorated with a poster for the Puerto Rican Day parade. The director's gray pinstriped suit was an attempt at being that of a successful lawyer's, but was so wrinkled from belt-line to knee that the quality of material had to be more suspect than his fat legs. His name was Arthur Lefkind, and in a droning voice he explained that the office was federally funded and that it was allowed to deal only in civil matters for clients who either were on government assistance or whose earnings were under one hundred dollars a week.

"I don't see any reason why we couldn't use you," Lefkind said, studying Maximo's resumé, "as long as there's nothing that isn't kosher here."

"If my name goes on anything, it has to be absolutely proper," Maximo said.

"It's like I get Harvard people walking in here every day," Lefkind said.

"I am here because I am going to spend my life here," Maximo said.

"Don't say a thing like that," Lefkind said. "Nobody

ever did anything so bad that they had to spend their
whole life in the Bronx.'' He scrawled something on a
memo pad, ripped the page off and handed it to Maximo.
"Go over and see Luis Jimenez. You know him? You
don't? Well, you better. He's at the Bronx All Services
Center. On Westchester Avenue. I put the address
down.''

"What do I tell him?'' Maximo asked.

"It isn't what you say to him, it's what he says to me,''
Lefkind said.

As Maximo walked down the street, he imagined that
Nicki was walking in front of him. There was no purpose
for her being on such alien flagstones, yet she walked as
if the surroundings were hers; she slowed as she approached a candy store, a hand going into her pocket to
find if she had enough cigarettes. Yes, she did. Her grace-
ful step resumed. Maximo kept looking at her hair, which
was untied, unclasped, and moved just enough to cause
the light to skip across it. Once he allowed himself to
draw even with her. At first he felt her attitude of domi-
nance over anybody who would dare step into the flight
area about her body. As she saw it was Maximo, an intensity came into her eyes and the air about her softened.
He could not believe that she would allow him to be this
close, to let his hand reach out and touch her hair. She
sighed inside.

A moment later, when he was alone again, he felt foolish with the memo paper in his hand, the note a child
carries to the grocer, or, more disturbing, the slips that
cheap employment agencies hand to someone being sent
out for a restaurant porter's job. He crumpled the note
and threw it in a garbage can. The note, Maximo thought,
would have caused his father to expire on the spot.

Now, with his father dead nearly six years, Maximo
walked under the El, looking for the Bronx All Services
Center, musing over what he felt were the differences in
life between the times of his father and now. It was no
longer a matter of how far down you bent in order to
receive something. Today it was wine and cheese parties,
as long as you kept your personal life away from the
party; no one wanted to subject himself to some plump,

Puerto Rican woman shrieking and kissing people, as if
equal with them. Of course nothing else but personal sur-
vival for the few invited to the parties could be accomplished. Maximo believed that if he did it the other way,
if he took the jobs no one wanted, worked to advance the
people everybody shunned, carried the causes that others
found too heavy, he could accomplish things for all that
would last forever. Teenager tried his way and Puerto
Rican pain only increased. Maximo would accomplish so
much more with the mere rustle of paper; he loved Sei-
gelman, the high school teacher who had forced him to
say "present" instead of "*yo.*"

He found the office entrances to the Bronx All Services
Center, double glass doors opening onto a flight of stairs
that were covered with linoleum and led up to what once
was a ballroom or bowling alley. A uniformed security
guard and a black Hispanic woman sat at desks in a reception area, with the woman busy at a monitor board
that kept buzzing and lighting each time she attempted to
talk.

Finally, she said to Maximo, "You must lead a very
good life. He has a few minutes to see you now."

The security man opened a door and directed Maximo
down a hall to a secretary, who indicated an office behind
her. Sitting at a large desk, the wall behind covered with
plaques, was Luis Jimenez, his skin of perfect color, light
enough not to unsettle a white and yet dark enough to
satisfy even Hispanics most black. He was about forty-
five, with black curly hair and a smile that had preten-
sions to warmth. The face was round, and reminded Maximo of pork.

"Oh, you're a smart boy," Jimenez said, reading Maximo's resumé. "Oh, a very smart boy."

"Maybe someday," Maximo said. "Right now I'm still
learning."

"Oh, you are much smarter than anyone already. This
I can see."

"Do you run the Legal Services office?" Maximo
asked.

"Oh, no. I have nothing to do with them. I am not a
lawyer. I am the one who helps all the people in the

Bronx who are poor. I help welfare people, I help drug addicts, I help sick people. I help all the poor. All the government money comes to me."

"What am I supposed to talk to you about?" Maximo said.

"About the job," Jimenez said. "In the Bronx, if somebody is Hispanic and he is to get some sort of job, they usually ask me to see that the person is an honest person, and a smart person, so that he will not embarrass the Puerto Rican people in this job."

"I see."

"But this does not concern you, for you are so smart that we know you are honest, too. So you will get this job."

"Thank you."

"There is one thing you must do," Jimenez said. "When there is an election, you must come and help us get the man elected. A smart boy like you could do such tremendous things for us in an election."

"Oh, I intend to work in politics," Maximo said.

"That's good. Then in an election, you will work with us."

"Of course," Maximo said, "I would have to know the man running and the issues. I just wouldn't back anybody I did not think was good."

Jimenez threw back his head and laughed. "Ah, you are so smart. That's wonderful to be like this. I can see that you are not a sheep who would follow everybody else."

"Never," Maximo said. "I've heard about our people being sold out too many times for me to just go along."

"You're so smart!" Jimenez said. He came out from behind the desk and put an arm around Maximo's shoulders and walked him to the door. "Yes, the Legal Services. That would be a good job for you." Smiling, he walked back toward his desk. "Call me tomorrow," he said.

In the morning, Ana's Bar was not yet open at 9:30, so Maximo leaned on a car by the phone booths on the other side of the street, took a breath and went to the phone and dialed Luis Jimenez. The secretary that answered

said he would not be there until ten. At 10:05, Maximo
called again. Jimenez would be in at eleven, the secretary
said. Maximo went for coffee, read a paper and talked to
Ralph at the newsstand; when there is no phone in the
house, there is a cost to each missed phone connection.
At 11:15, Luis Jimenez' voice came on the phone.

"Oh, I'm so sorry. But we just gave this job to this
other guy. You were very smart, but everybody wanted
this other guy so we just gave him the job."

"You told me yesterday that I had the job," Maximo
said.

"No, I never said such a thing to you," Jimenez said.

"Yes, you did."

"No, I remember exactly what I said," Jimenez said.
"You didn't listen to me. I said that the Bronx Legal
Services would be a good job for you. I didn't say you
had it. I just said it would be a good job for you. Maybe
you don't listen to everything. Maybe you are not so
smart."

Maximo hung up with the anger rising in him.

Over the next four days, Maximo applied for work at
the Bronx Legal Aid Society, the New York State Substance Abuse Center, the New York City Department of
Buildings and the district offices of State Senator Antonio
Flores, where a woman named Sarita Velazquez looked
up from her desk and said, "You have not seen Mr. Luis
Jimenez before coming here?"

"Not for this job?"

"Do you go into a church without blessing yourself?"

"Well, I don't know."

"Let me put it this way. Never mind you. But do most
people walk into a church without putting their fingers
into the water and blessing themselves?"

"No, they bless themselves."

"Then how can you come into a political office unless
you first have seen Luis Jimenez?"

He decided to call Jimenez back, but this time with an
awareness of the consequences of his language. If asked
to work in a campaign, he would give a Jimenez answer:
of course, I will work in this political campaign, for it is
my duty as a citizen to do such a thing. Which candidate

will I work for? Of course I will not work for any candidate until I have seen you. Maximo was angry with himself that he had not delivered this answer when he was
asked the first time. Promise to see the guy. To see means
many things, particularly, Maximo thought, I'll see you,
you sonofabitch.

When he called Luis Jimenez' office, he was able to
get only the secretary this time.

"He is very busy for you to bother him," she said.

"Would you tell him that I've thought over what he
told me the other day and I now agree with him?" Maximo said.

"Just a moment," the secretary said.

Luis Jimenez came on the line. "You are the smartest
young man in the whole Bronx!"

"If I learn from you long enough I might be," Maximo
said.

"Oh, no, you're so much smarter. Someday you will
be governor of this state. Bankers will hold you up as a
hero."

"I'd like to start at that job first," Maximo said.

"Well, that cannot be done so quickly now. First, we
must see what is what."

"How do we do that?"

"We have this meeting on Friday night. All the citizens
can come. The meeting is here. Why don't you come and
we will speak after it?"

Maximo, who had no lecture on Friday night, came
home from the library, took a shower and changed
clothes. He found he had three dollars in his pocket. He
walked out of his bedroom and saw his mother's purse
on the dining room table. His mother had gone down the
hall to visit another woman. Maximo stared hard at the
purse and then went downstairs with the three dollars in
his pocket and stepped into the bar.

"Aha!" Teenager called out. He was sitting in a booth
with three men Maximo never had seen before. Skinny
men with faces that reflected the dirthills that filled the
insides of their heads.

"Can I see you?" Maximo said.

Teenager slid out of the booth.

"I need ten dollars. I can give it back to you the day I get paid from my job."

"You will take a hundred," Teenager said. "What is this job?"

"I said I wanted ten," Maximo said.

Teenager smirked and tried to put the hundred into his hand. "Ten," Maximo said.

Teenager withdrew the hundred and handed Maximo the ten. "Now what is this job?"

"I have to go see Luis Jimenez tonight. All the jobs I want are up to him."

"Who is Jimenez?"

"You don't know him? You were away too long. He runs the Bronx. At least as far as Hispanics are concerned."

"Who runs the Bronx?" Teenager said.

"Jimenez."

"I never heard of him. He has never met me. Who is he to say he runs the Bronx?"

"He doesn't have to say it," Maximo said.

"And you are going to see him now?"

"Yes."

"Show me where he is."

"He's going to be at a meeting on Westchester Avenue."

"To hell with these meetings."

"That's where he'll be."

"I'll drive you there. I just want to see the face of this man, he says he runs the Bronx."

Teenager walked out as if the three ugly men in the booth were not there. In the car on the way over, he listened to Maximo tell of how Luis Jimenez knocked him out of his job, at least temporarily, and the moment he finished speaking, Maximo knew he had made a mistake.

"He screws you, he screws me," Teenager said.

"Forget it. I can straighten it out, I think," Maximo said.

"He makes you beg," Teenager said.

"Well."

"Nobody begs," Teenager said.

He double-parked in front of the Bronx All Services

Center and Maximo tried to get away from him, but
Teenager insisted on going upstairs with him.

"Then I'm not going," Maximo said, standing on the
sidewalk.

"Why is this?"

"Because you'll blow everything on me."

"I am the strongest man in the world," Teenager said.
"Do not be afraid."

"This isn't a fight."

Teenager's voice softened. "I just want to look at this
fellow who is a boss. I will do nothing else."

Maximo went upstairs with Teenager behind him and
followed the cardboard sign to the weekly citizens meeting of the Bronx All Services Center. It was being held in
a large room where men sat on folding chairs and smoked
cigarettes. Luis Jimenez sat down at a table in the front
of the room. A large black man in a blue shirt took a seat
a few feet away. He folded his arms and his eyes, heavy
with sleep, appeared to close. On the wall behind Jimenez, starting from one corner of the room and running to
the other, was a set of framed sequence photos, a dozen
in all, showing Luis Jimenez advancing across the floor
at a political meeting and, arms out, embracing John F.
Kennedy and his wife, who held one hand to her hair and
the other against Luis Jimenez' fat chest. Maximo, hands
stuffed into the pockets of a blue zipper jacket, slipped in
quietly. He felt Jimenez looking at him. Teenager stood
for long moments, then scraped a chair across the floor.
He remained standing, for all to see his upper torso
wrapped in a skintight yellow shirt open to the chest. Only
a couple of people seemed to know him, but those who
did not seemed to sense immediately that Teenager did
not have as his primary interest the field of public safety.

Luis Jimenez, befitting a man who had decided many
years before this that his constituents were primarily
scum, and thus unworthy of any reaction stronger than
slight indignation, smiled tolerantly as Teenager finally
took his seat. The man in the blue shirt, sitting near Jimenez in the front of the room, opened his eyes and
pulled his chair closer to Jimenez. His eyes stared steadily at Teenager.

"We must discuss the festival that we are having at Randalls Island," Jimenez said.

Before Maximo could put a hand out, Teenager was on his feet. "I want to speak of something else."

"Tonight, we discuss the festival," Jimenez said evenly.

"I want to discuss with you why people go to great colleges and learn many things and they come to you and you do not help them."

"Are you a man who went to a great college?" Jimenez asked.

"I went to the greatest college where the greatest teachers are," Teenager said. "I do not want your *porquería*. But this man here, he went to Harvard. He is to be a lawyer to help all the Puerto Rican people. You do nothing for him."

Maximo forced himself to stand up. "He is talking for me and he means well, but he does not understand," he said.

Teenager became furious. "I understand that this man will not give you a job."

Jimenez, his smile ready, held out his hands. "We have a legal committee that helps boost all Puerto Rican lawyers." He nodded his head, causing a thin man with neat black hair and skin that was quite pale to arise. "This is Luis Ortiz, who is in charge of seeing that all Hispanics have the proper chance in law.

"I take care of all problems," Jimenez said.

"Why don't you give Maximo a good job?" Teenager said.

Jimenez nodded to another part of the room and a short, fat man popped up. "I move that these people are talking too much during this meeting."

Three people, in different parts of the room, stood and called out to second the motion.

Luis Jimenez, his smile ready, said, "I am sorry. The business tonight must be the festival at Randalls Island."

Teenager's finger counted the heads in the room.

"Fifty," he said in a low voice. Then he called out to Jimenez, "I want a vote."

Jimenez smiled. "You see for yourself that this is a

waste of time. Please do not bother us so much now. You have heard what the others have to say."

"No, I want a vote on whether I should shut up or not," Teenager said. "Here is how we will have this vote. I will hit you on the chin and break your fucking jaw. Then I will hit him on the chin and break his fucking jaw. Then I will hit this man over here and break his fucking jaw." He swung around. "I will hit you and break your fucking jaw. I will break fifty fucking jaws in this room. Then we will have the mother-fucking vote and I will win by 1–0."

The large man in the blue shirt next to Jimenez stirred. Teenager pointed at him. "I will break your fucking jaw, too. And I can see that you have a gun. You think you are the only one with a gun. Now I am going to show you something that you are not the only one."

Teenager bent down, pulled a Walther PPK/S automatic out of his sock, held it over his head and fired into the ceiling. Maximo froze, but nearly everybody else in the room dove to the floor.

Teenager again bent over, pushed the safety down and put the gun back into his sock, and now stood up and surveyed the room. The people on the floor, the fear finally draining out of them, reassembled their bodies on chairs. The next to last man to show his head was Luis Jimenez' bodyguard. The last man to appear, rising like a victim of a mine cave-in, was Luis Jimenez.

Teenager kicked the chair out of his way and stomped down the hall to the staircase. Maximo was in the hallway, slumped against the wall, listening to the carhorn blaring out on the street. He knew it was Teenager waiting for him. Maximo was in pain until the horn stopped blaring, signifying Teenager's impatience had won and he had driven off into the night.

When Luis Jimenez stepped out of the meeting, Maximo said softly, "I couldn't stop him from coming in here."

"Oh, I know it is not your fault," Jimenez said.

"Really. The guy just walked in. I told him not to."

"Oh, I know this," Luis Jimenez said. "You are a smart boy. You would never do such a thing. Come in with me. I want to talk to you about your career."

Maximo was badly shaken by his having been on a bough in a forest fire. The naked power that had taken him through subway turnstiles as a schoolboy and had been exhilarating to watch, now caused him to be terrified. He had prepared himself for a complex life and here he could lose it at the very outset to common thuggery. Yet, as he followed Jimenez down the hall, he could feel that Jimenez, who lived closer to the ground, was reacting differently: these things happen, and were best served by compromise, his body motions indicated. Maximo thought of his father. His father would be pleased. This was Carlos Tapia's way. Now Maximo smiled for a moment. He had just been on a ride he never again would take, but it was clear that it had left him where he wanted to go.

"Mister, are you the man I am to see?" The first client of his career, a thin Puerto Rican woman, clutching an old purse, stood in the doorway of Maximo's cubicle at the Bronx Legal Services two weeks later.

"I guess I am," Maximo said.

"You are an attorney?"

"I hope to be soon. But I am allowed to handle your matter now, however. Sit down. What can I do for you?"

"My husband leaves me."

"Oh, I see."

"I have nothing. No food at home. No rent. I walk here. I do not have even the bus fare."

"Well, something has to be done about that," Maximo said.

The woman's hands dug into a purse.

"Look."

She held out a large color picture of a woman with long dark hair covering bare shoulders. A great bosom pressed against a red strapless evening gown whose front was sprayed with sequins. The woman in the picture had her head back and was laughing with joy.

"This is the woman your husband ran away with?" Maximo said.

"No, this is my husband."

For the next week, Maximo looked for a furnished apartment, but the number of burned-out buildings made it difficult to find anything inhabitable. Dirt could be scrubbed. Rats could be contended with; he had grown up to the sound of their scratching inside the bedroom wall at night. But a half-empty building, with the threat of fire in the night starting in an empty apartment, was not for him. Then a man named Roy in the *bodega* said that he had a cousin named Chino on Pinto Avenue who had a furnished apartment and was giving it up.

"It's a wonderful place for me," Chino said the next day. He ruffled the coat of a large German shepherd. A couch and two chairs in the living room were covered with plastic. In the bedroom, the bed had a light-colored headboard and the tables alongside it were from a different set.

"I hate to do this thing, but I must give this place up for fifteen, sixteen months," Chino said.

"Where are you going?" Maximo said.

"Wherever the judge sends me."

The apartment was on the second floor of a three-story brick building that stood on a street that had been nearly razed by fire. Directly across the street was a sandwich shop that was opened in the daytime, but at night was covered with corrugated metal. Over it, in frontier loneliness, lived two families. The rent for Chino's apartment

147

was $212.50 a month and Chino said he wanted forty a month to cover the furniture.

"Fine," Maximo said.

"Give it to my cousin in his *bodega* and he will keep it for me," Chino said.

"Every month," Maximo said.

"What about the dog, man?" Chino said. "You got to pay me ten dollars a month for my dog."

"I don't know whether I want the dog," Maximo said.

"When you see him bite some guy's ass tries to get in here, man, you'll want the dog."

"What's his name?"

"Duque."

The dog panted as he heard his name.

"He only speaks Spanish," Chino said.

"*Bájate!*" Maximo said. The dog sat. "That's good," Maximo said.

"You just feed him and he's yours," Chino said. "Anybody else, he bites, man."

Maximo moved into the apartment about a week later. On his first night there, he went downstairs to an outdoor phone booth and called the number that Nicki had given him for her girlfriend Angela. He gave Angela the number of the phone booth and hung up. A few long moments later, the phone rang.

"Where have you been?" Nicki said.

"I'll tell you tomorrow."

"I thought you didn't call me because you weren't going to take my advice. You did what I told you, didn't you?"

"I haven't seen him or said anything to him."

"Ahead of all the schools you went to, that shows you're smart. So now let's forget that. We don't need to talk about that anymore."

"Right. Am I going to see you tomorrow?" Maximo said.

"I'll be in the same place at five o'clock," Nicki said.

Nicki was there fifteen minutes early this time. She took the same table in the back, by the doors leading to the kitchen. It was all right for her to maneuver Maximo to this table the first time, she told herself, but if she had allowed him to arrive first this time, and then again had to make him move to this back table, he would almost certainly realize what she was doing to him. He probably would start hollering "New *Jessey*" all over the place, she thought.

She wore a maroon velour shirt from Macy's and blue Calvin Klein pants from Bloomingdale's. Around her neck were two thin gold chains given to her by her father. She ordered a cappuccino, lit a cigarette and stared over the heads of people at the door. When Maximo appeared in a gold knit shirt, smiling across the room at her, Nicki felt her face become warm. As she watched Maximo slide between tables, hips swaying to avoid people's elbows, she thought of him as a jungle animal, a long black panther. Do they have panthers in Puerto Rico? It doesn't matter, she thought, whatever it is, as long as it is something direct from the jungle.

"I got a job," Maximo said.

"That's nice," Nicki said.

"And I got an apartment."

"That's nice," Nicki said.

"I'm going to be working in a poverty law office in the Bronx. It will give me a great chance to work at some of the things I want to do. Housing. I can't wait to try some class actions in housing."

Nicki saw him on a wide screen, his eyes and beard commanding.

"Where the poor get screwed is on Section 235 housing funds. The city uses them for the white middle class. They're supposed to be used for the poor. Did you ever hear of Section 235 housing rehabilitation?"

Nicki said nothing.

"Did you ever hear of it?"

"No," Nicki said finally.

"I'll explain it to you. When I was in law sch—"

"—Where did you go?"

"Law school? Harvard?"

"That's in Boston, isn't it?"

"Cambridge."

"Cambridge, Boston, it's all the same to me. You went to a sleepaway school?"

"Yes."

"My father never would let me go to sleepaway school. We're conservative at home. Sleepaway school is all right for liberals like you."

"What's a liberal got to do with it?"

"You're Puerto Rican."

"Of course I am."

"Then you got to be a liberal. We're not. We're conservative and we don't go to sleepaway colleges."

They lapsed into silence for several moments. At first their eyes were moving from coffee cup to cigarette to ceiling lights and then, simultaneously, they locked on each other and remained there. Maximo saw a forbidden white orchid, and she saw a panther striding across a wide screen.

"A professor I had in law school told me," Maximo began. He then told her of a law school view of housing in poor neighborhoods and he was pleased that her eyes showed so much interest in the subject. His hand rose and he gestured as he spoke and now, awash in knowledge, deeply proud of his ability to relate it to this woman and to hold her interest, he went into what he felt were the organizational weaknesses of the Department of Housing and Urban Development.

Oh, you can see he has to be an animal, Nicki reassured herself as Maximo spoke.

She must find it a relief, Maximo thought, to be away from all those morons in her house and be able to listen to some intelligent conversation. He then had a great thought about Section 235 housing and he was in the midst of it when she said to him, "Where were you born?"

"Huh?"

"Where were you born?"

"La Playa de Ponce."

"Is that near jungles?"

"It's right on the Caribbean."

"They have wild animals near you?"

"There's no such thing in Puerto Rico."

"There isn't?"

"No."

"Do they have sharks in the water?"

"That they have. I don't remember seeing any, I was too young. But it's warm water. They have to be there."

Maximo was sure he saw deep interest in what he was saying. It was, he told himself, the first time he ever had used this power he had, this special background, on someone like Nicki. He was in awe of his ability to enchant her mind, to bring such total attention out of an Italian girl on a subject as distant from her life as slum housing. Maximo was pleased with himself. Good Ivy League smugness seeped through him. The air in the coffee shop was sweet.

"Sharks make big bites," Nicki said.

"Where were you born?" Maximo said.

"Hun' fifth, first and second."

"Harlem," Maximo said.

"I loved it. I was there till I was fifteen."

"Did your parents like New Jessey better?" This time she didn't notice the Jessey.

"My mother hated it."

"Then why did you move?"

"You know, the neighborhood changed."

Maximo laughed.

"I say the truth."

Maximo thought she was as open as the sea. He wanted to touch her.

"You know what I used to do growing up?" she said. "We lived on the fifth floor and my mother would throw my lunch money down to the street and she'd say, 'Get milk and a sandwich.' I'd say, 'Yes, ma,' then I'd run to the candy store, hun' ninth and fifth, and eat potato chips and Coke. I never ate anything else for lunch when I was growing up."

"It didn't stop you from growing," Maximo said.

"I bet you did the same thing in the Bronx," she said.

"We lived on the fourth floor, but my mother never threw any money down to me on the street."

"They'd steal it on you?"

"She didn't have any to throw down."

That he liked, a small ambush to display his command. And at the same time to recognize the past that had shaped him, a harshness, and to point to what he had placed atop it, something which she could surely see and be greatly impressed with as she sat across from him, this palace of high knowledge he had.

She looked at her watch. "Will you look at this? It's six-thirty already."

"So?"

"I'm late for dinner. I have to call."

"My course starts at seven," Maximo said.

"You're not going," she said.

"No?"

"Not tonight."

"Where are we going?"

"You said you just got an apartment."

"Yes."

"That's where we're going. Just stay here until I call my mother."

She went to the phone and told her mother that she and Angela had decided to stay in town and see a movie. Then she called Angela and said that she would need her first for an alibi, and then later for transportation.

They took the subway uptown, the number six line that has the narrowest of cars of the subway system. The interiors were so coated with graffiti, the windows blacked out by it, that Nicki felt she was inside a crowded truck. To her eyes, the graffiti meant a Puerto Rican with a knife. Maximo stared at it. He thought much of it was pleasing; certainly some of the red, blue and silver swirls from a spray-paint can were easier on the eye than the dingy municipal green with which all cars are painted. Maximo, however, knew that graffiti was the loser. Whites had been taught that it was evil and saw no imaginative lines. Maximo felt this was serious, for while people argued over graffiti, the undercarriage of the trains went unattended, the tracks uninspected and a system used by millions was becoming a danger to them. He thought about a class action suit against the transit system and he was going to lean over and tell Nicki about this, but the train was so noisy that he could not lecture her properly.

Nicki was looking at him and hoping that he was an

animal. Then she stared at the graffiti and imagined how much work it would be to rub it all off. She stared at the faces around her. All were Puerto Rican. Turning her head, she found she was the only white on the packed train. The men all were small and dark and had mustaches and sideburns clipped so that they would resemble as close as possible Barbary pirates. The women had tired eyes, except for a group of younger ones who were laughing in a corner of the car. One of them, a white sweater around her shoulders, smoked a joint. She took a long drag and then talked happily in Spanish as the smoke came out of her mouth. Nicki's eyes rose to Maximo's face.

He looked like a fucking movie star.

As Maximo led her up the stairs to his apartment on Pinto Avenue, the odor of stewed pork filled the hallway. Remembering the smell from the Puerto Rican apartments in East Harlem, she automatically regarded it as bad.

When Maximo got to his door, the dog began barking. *"¡Para!"* Maximo called as he turned the locks. The dog kept barking. *"¡Para!"* Maximo called in a louder voice. The barking stopped and was replaced by an anxious squeal.

As the door opened, the dog came leaping, tongue out, against Maximo's chest.

"Bájate."

The dog would not get down.

"¡Bájate!" Maximo snapped.

The dog got down and loped back into the apartment.

"Come here, boy," Nicki said, as she stepped into the apartment. The dog did not move.

"¡Chévere!" Maximo said.

The dog bounded over to him and Maximo grabbed the furry neck and tousled it. *"Chévere,"* he said again. A few moments later, he said to the dog, *"¡Adentro!"* The dog looked at him. *"¡Adentro!"* Maximo yelled. The dog trotted into the small kitchen.

"I never saw a bilingual dog before," Nicki said.

"He isn't bilingual, he didn't understand one word of

English, didn't you know that? He only understands Spanish.''

"That's what I said. He's bilingual," Nicki said. Nicki turned and pretended to be inspecting the room. Bilingual, she said to herself, all bilingual means is Spic, doesn't it?

"Don't call him," Nicki said, "I'm not here to pet dogs."

Her eyes drew his face to her and as they kissed, she reacted first, controlling the kiss, her body moving, and when his hand ran over her body her arms tightened around his neck.

He took her by the hand into the bedroom, which had no window. As Maximo reached for the lamp, Nicki covered his hand. "No lights," she said. She dropped her clothes on the floor and got into bed with her panties on, threw herself atop his chest and kissed him, then moved her legs in irritation when her knee prevented him from pulling the panties off immediately. As quickly as possible, she wanted him inside her, which, she knew, was all she was there for.

Always her husband had told her that he was the best in the world in bed, told her with this half smile that goes with permanent ownership, and she thought this to be true. But now as Maximo's warmth flooded into her, she sounded and stretched in a long, lovely release, the most delicious, she was sure, of her young years.

Maximo had his head in the crook of her arm and she ran a hand through his hair and thought for a moment of her husband's boast. And I believed him, she said to herself.

He walked her downstairs and they stood at a phone booth on the night-empty street and Nicki went into the booth and called Angela and asked to be picked up. She gave Angela the address.

"You're crazy," Angela said.

"No, I'm not," Nicki said. "Anybody who didn't come here tonight is the crazy one."

"Get inside! You'll get raped!" Angela said.

"Oh, do you think so?" Nicki said.

They held hands and stood by the phone booth waiting for Angela. Across the street, two small boys came out of the door leading to the apartment over the sandwich shop. Immediately, a window flew open and a woman's head came out.

"¡Aqui!"

The kids looked up and complained and the woman shouted again. Reluctantly, the kids went back inside the house.

"I feel sorry for them, they can't come out," Maximo said. "That's how it was with me. If I was out of the house after five o'clock, my father went crazy."

"I have to ask you something," Nicki said.

"What?"

"Say the truth."

"I will."

"Can someone like you, even if you have thin lips, have a nigger baby?"

"I don't think so," Maximo said.

Her hand reached out and touched Maximo's lip. "Open your mouth."

"What for?"

"Never mind. Just open your mouth. Wider. Let me see your teeth. Like I'm a dentist."

Maximo gritted his teeth. Using the light from the fluorescent bulb on the outdoor telephone, Nicki looked closely at Maximo's gums to see if they were purple. She was relieved to see that Maximo's gums were pink.

"What did you see?" Maximo said.

"No nigger babies."

"Is that all you have on your mind?"

"Not now," she said.

"What do you have on your mind?"

"The next time I'm going to see you," she said.

"You will," Maximo said.

"Right away," Nicki said. "I want more of this right away." She began to dance in the light from the outdoor telephone.

"I'll call you," Maximo said.

"Not at home," Nicki said. "Just do it the same way you did it this time."

"What if I want to see you on the spur of the moment?"

"So call Angela on the spur of the moment. If you call my house you'll get killed on the spur of the moment."

When Angela arrived, Nicki gave Maximo a long kiss and then jumped into the car.

"Soon you'll be with niggers," Angela said as she drove the car.

At Nicki's house, Louis Mariani sat at the kitchen table in bathrobe and pajamas. "Where the hell have you been?" he said.

Angela grabbed her midsection. "Oh, I'm so hungry!" She opened the refrigerator, which was the best way to distract Mariani, who always dived for the box the moment he saw its light. The tactic was unneeded this time, for it was obvious that Mariani, staring at the phone, had concerns other than Nicki's arrival time.

"What are you doing up?" Nicki said to her father.

"Send a moron out, you get what you deserve," Mariani said, more to himself. He stood up and inspected the refrigerator. "Used to be, you said that the guy was so dumb he couldn't find a Jew in the Bronx. Now we got guys who can't find a Puerto Rican in the Bronx." He reached in for his favorite, cold spaghetti. "That's worse than when you couldn't find a Jew in the Bronx. How could you miss finding a Puerto Rican?"

....Chapter 12

....

Myles walked out of Martin's office and went to his desk, where Chita Gonzalez, her hair pulled tight against her scalp and into a long ponytail, sat smoking a cigarette.

"All right," Myles said, sitting down. "You were present in the Myruggia the night Gigi and Victor were killed?"

"I see nobody killed."

"We know that. They were killed after they left. But you were in the place when they were in the place."

"This I don't know. I don't remember seeing them."

"You were seen there at the time they were there."

"I just came in that place for ten minutes. I was just looking for my boyfriend."

"Who did you see in the bar?"

"I don't know who I saw."

"You didn't happen to see Teenager there, did you?"

Chita put the cigarette in her mouth, shook her head no and took a long drag.

"Somebody told us that you said hello to Teenager in the bar."

Chita blew smoke up at the ceiling.

"Teenager in jail."

"Now you know he's out."

"How do I know he's out when I just tell you he is in jail?"

"You didn't see him that night?"

"Why are you asking me all this?"

"Chita, this is just between us. You're helping me out. This is no legal matter or anything like that. You're just doing me a personal favor. Nobody will ever know you were here. I won't tell anybody I even saw you."

"You want to talk to me, I bring a lawyer and you can talk to me."

"Get all the lawyers in the world, Chita. You know in your heart that you saw Teenager in the bar that night with Gigi and Victor."

"Who told you that?"

"Never mind. I know and you know."

"I go home now."

"Come on, Chita, do me a favor."

"Want me to talk to you some more?"

"Yes."

"Arrest me."

"Chita."

"No, you arrest me. If you don't I walk out of here."

Myles laughed. "Come on, Chita."

Her chair scraped on the floor as she stood up. "Unless you arrest me, I'm going."

"Hey, I'm not going to arrest you. We're friends."

"Bullshit."

Chita Gonzalez walked to the door, pushed it open with her hip and was gone.

"I'll call you later," Myles said to Martin. He went out after Chita Gonzalez.

On the sidewalk outside, Chita Gonzalez threw her cigarette away and looked up the street.

"You waiting for somebody?" Myles said.

"I'm looking for a taxi," Chita said.

"You won't get one here," Myles said.

He walked to his car and got in. Chita remained on the sidewalk. Myles got out of the car and called to her, "Say, can I take you to a cab?"

She looked up the block once more, shrugged and walked to Myles' car.

"Where do you go?" Myles said.

"To a cab."

"I was just wondering. It might be on my way."

"Take me to Westchester Avenue?"

"Fine."

He said nothing at first. She lit a cigarette and looked straight ahead.

"You work?" Myles said.

She nodded.

"Where?"

"A big office building."

"Oh, that's good. Where?"

"Downtown."

"What do you do?"

"Secretary to a vice-president."

"Pretty good."

She said nothing.

Ahead were the rusting yellow pillars of the El tracks on Westchester Avenue.

"Which way do I turn?"

"I get out at the corner."

"Tell me which way you're going and I turn."

"Are you arresting me?"

"Of course not."

"Then stop the car here and I get out."

Myles pulled up to the corner. Chita pushed open the door and stepped out.

"Aren't you going to thank me?" Myles said.

"Thank you."

She slammed the door and walked out into the street with her arm up, looking for a cab. Myles turned in the opposite direction and started home.

Across the street, in the bar called The Palm, Santos Rivera, one of Teenager's pushers, looked out the window.

"What is she doing riding in the car with this rat cop?"

He watched as Chita got into a gypsy cab and Myles drove off in the opposite direction.

Santos went back to his drink.

"Want some smoke?" Santos Rivera said.

"I have cigarettes," Chita Gonzalez said. She went into her jacket pocket for Winstons.

"Just a few minutes more," Santos said.

"My whole night is gone," Chita, irritated, said.

She had intended to go to Manhattan, to Barney Googles' on 86th Street, but as she left her apartment house at 8:30, Rivera had been at the curb in his Torino and he promised her something important, much money for a simple delivery. Chita had jumped into his car elated. In the hours since, however, all he had done was take her to three bars. Now he had her sitting on a park bench, and she still hadn't earned a quarter.

"He isn't even coming," she said.

"I swear he'll be here," Santos said.

"What would he come here for?" she said.

"Because this is where he said."

"And I will make money with this man?"

"Yes."

The park was a quiet lake in the midst of noisy stone hills. There were about two dozen people, the males in basketball shorts mainly, and the women in jeans or terry-cloth beach outfits that barely stretched across any place important. One street lamp, the only unbroken one in the park, gave a pale light to one end of the basketball court. A high school kid who lived across the street from the park was taking shots. Johnny Benitez, smoking a joint and drinking from a quart bottle of Miller High Life, sat on the broken bench at the edge of the court. Benitez derided the kid for not going mugging downtown with him the night before. "Old Jews got money, man," he said. The kid shook his head and ran through the dim light to the basket.

Chita Gonzalez, sitting with Rivera at the far end of the bench, scuffed her feet on the cement walk. Whole night gone doing nothing, she complained to herself.

"Aha!"

Teenager swaggered into the park with Fernando Lebron and Benny. Double-parked in the street was Teenager's Mercedes car. Somebody was at the wheel.

"I told you he would be here," Rivera said to Chita Gonzalez.

"You didn't tell me who it was that would be here," she said.

"I am the surprise man," Teenager said.

"I don't see you, where have you been?" Chita said.

"Busy," Teenager said.

Chita dropped the cigarette as Teenager took her hands and brought her to her feet and then drew her body flat against him. Immediately, he began humming a tune and dancing with Chita.

"We have just been married," Teenager said.

"This is a wedding," Fernando Lebron called out.

"Toast the bride and groom."

"My wife is beautiful," Teenager said.

Laughing, they stopped dancing.

"I love you," he said.

"I love you more if you give me some business to do," Chita said.

"Business, lots of business," Teenager said.

"When?" Chita said.

"First I wanted to ask you," Teenager said.

"Yes?"

"Remember the night I saw you in the Myruggia?"

"I never saw you in the Myruggia in a long time, since before you went to jail." Chita was remembering how she opened a button on her red blouse the night she had seen Teenager in the Myruggia.

"You're sure?"

"How could I see you in the Myruggia when I have not been in this place in months and months?"

"You were in there with me tonight," Rivera said.

"But that was with you. I haven't been there by myself in months and months."

Teenager watched her without reacting to what she was saying. Once, his eyes moved to show skepticism.

"Has anyone come to you and asked you if you saw me in this bar on that night?"

"Who?"

"Some cop."

"I don't speak to cop," Chita said.

"You sure?"

"Why do you ask me all this?"

"Because I ask," Teenager said.

"Then ask yourself before you ask me. I don't speak

to no cop. I wish some bad girl gives all the cops syphilis.''

Teenager's eyes squinted and he began to chuckle. He ended the tension. Maybe she is all right, Teenager thought.

"Aha!" he said. He put his arms around Chita and began to dance with her again. "We are married!" he called out.

The ones with him, Rivera, Lebron and Benny, lost some of the grimness in their faces. Rivera even smiled.

"Where do I go for my honeymoon?" Chita said.

"No honeymoon tonight," Teenager said. "Tonight your new husband has big business."

"If I don't have a honeymoon with you, then you must give me money to have fun with," Chita said.

"There will be plenty of money for you," Teenager said.

"I do a business for you," Chita said.

"I will pay you plenty of money for it," Teenager said. He smiled, then let her go. "I will see you soon. We all must go someplace on business now."

"Are you taking me home?" Chita said to Santos.

"You cannot come with Santos. Santos must come with us," Teenager said.

"Santos, you said you would drive me tonight. What about my cab money?"

Santos took out money and Chita, dancing with Teenager, took her hand off his shoulder and reached for the money.

A car door slammed and two patrolmen walked into the park. In Teenager's arms, Chita stiffened. She suddenly buried her face into his chest. Her feet did not move. By pushing her, Teenager got her dancing again as the cops walked up to them. Chita's face pressed harder against Teenager's chest. Her body trembled. He looked at her hair as he danced with her. His sleepy eyes were open.

"Oh, man," Johnny Benitez' voice called out.

"Don't try and run or you'll get hurt," one of the cops called to Benitez. His hand was on the gun.

The patrolmen went past Teenager's group and fell on

Johnny Benitez. They handcuffed him behind the back and, each holding an arm, led him out of the park.

As the patrolmen brought Benitez past Teenager, Chita's face remained pressed into Teenager's chest. Her body shook even more. Why does this female get so scared of police, Teenager thought. The patrolmen walked Benitez out of the park. At the curb, a crowd had collected and an old woman began to shout at the patrolmen for arresting such a young man. One patrolman pushed Benitez' head down so it wouldn't bump as Benitez got into the back seat of the car. The patrolman said over his shoulder, "I'm sorry, lady, but this kid is under arrest for killing an old woman just like you."

Teenager pushed Chita's chin up. "What's the matter with you? They gone."

"I don't like them," she said.

"Come on, I think now that I take you home myself."

"I have cab money to get home. Santos gave me."

"I take you home myself," Teenager repeated.

She saw a strange face at the driver's wheel. Chita and Teenager got in the back. As the car got to the corner, she asked them to stop.

"I want to call up and tell them I'm coming home," she said.

"Don't tell them who you're with," Teenager said.

She glared at him. "I never say anything to nobody."

Chita went to the outdoor booth and Teenager walked with her. He stood alongside her as she made the call. Then he walked her back to the car. Chita put her head back and relaxed as the driver sent the Mercedes off with a squeal. She loved big cars.

"Where are we going?" she asked.

"That's all right," Teenager said.

Occurrence
Time: 0355 *Date:* 9/30/76 *Location:* 135th Street and Exterior Avenue
Name: Unidentified F/H/20
Crime: Homicide: At T/P/O one female was found lying face up in street with two bullet wounds in back.

Pronounced DOA by attendant White at Lincoln Hospital.
Description of Perpetrators: Unknown.

At time and date mentioned above the deceased described below was found lying in the gutter, face up, shot approximately three times.

Female/Hispanic Apx 20, 5'3", 100 lbs, black hair, brown eyes, light skin, green velvet pants and jacket, yellow T-shirt with red rose picture on it, brown shoes, knee-high stockings, 2 yellow metal rings on right hand, three thin yellow metal bracelets on right wrist, wedding type band on left hand, two 1½ inch earrings, one on her left ear, one found at scene.
Evidence: 9M/M shell casing voucher #865013/29th Homicide.

The following evidence was recovered and tagged and brought to this Headquarters:

1 pair of hose
1 panties
1 shirt
1 pair of shoes
1 pack of Winston cigarettes
1 pack of matches with the name King Edward written on it
1 pack of Wrigley's chewing gum
Autopsy: 9/31/76 by Dr. Frank Picco
Evidence: Three (3) .38 caliber bullets. To be picked up by Ballistics.
Cause of Death: Multiple bullet wounds (7) of head, back, neck, mouth, subclavian artery: Internal hemorrhage: homicide.

Ptl. M. Crofton, 29th Hom.

....**Chapter 13**

....

At the red light at Greenside, six miles from his house, Myles let his bladder direct him to a tavern that sat between gas stations on the opposite side of the road. For a moment, he couldn't understand why he had to use the bathroom again; this was his second stop on the way home. As he walked through the bar to the men's room, he thought the yogurt was to blame. His wife had given it to him for lunch. Can't take yogurt and expect to drink like a regular man. Stuff must be like a strainer. If you're going to drink, Myles reminded himself, you need tuna fish and mayonnaise, greasy enough to seal the bottom of a boat. But as Myles stood at the urinal, he knew what was the matter with his insides. In shock. When Myles came out of the men's room, he could not walk past the taps and slid onto a stool and first ordered a beer, then a Scotch. Then another right away. He thought of Chita Gonzalez getting out of the car on Westchester Avenue. The whiskey could not drown the anguish inside: You got the broad killed, he told himself again.

When Myles had walked into the precinct that morning and had seen the new file with the block lettering, "GON-ZALEZ, CHITA," a deadness had spread through his body. There had been no nervousness, nor had he felt sick to his stomach. Only a listlessness that prevented him even from sitting down.

165

He took Hansen into a small office and told him what
had happened.

"You drove her to exactly where?" Hansen asked.

"Westchester Avenue."

"She got out of your car there?"

"That's right."

Hansen took out his pipe and looked out the window
as he filled it.

"A broad like this, it could have come from anywhere," Myles said.

"Maybe," Hansen said.

"I mean, who knows who kills who up here?"

"You got a point," Hansen said.

"Should I tell Martin?"

"Why would you do that?" Hansen said.

"Because I tell the truth."

"That's fine. But I don't know why you're even telling
me," Hansen said.

"You think so?" Myles said.

"All I said is, I don't know why you're even telling
me."

Myles was clinging to the approbation in Hansen's
tone. In so many words, Myles assured himself, Hansen
was telling him that it was all right, that he was making
too much of it. Yes, Chita Gonzalez probably had been
shot by some boyfriend, and it had nothing to do with the
day Myles let her out of the car.

"However," Hansen said.

"What?"

"That wasn't what you call a competent way to handle
a witness."

Hansen began lighting his pipe and Myles, insides
wincing, walked back to his desk and sat down.

Now, sitting in the bar on the way home, he glanced at
the clock and noticed that it was 7:00 P.M. already. He
swallowed the last of the beer and left. Outside the bar,
he took a deep breath and let the alcohol in him speak.
You get the broad killed, then you go out and get the guy
killed her. "Fuck you, now it's personal," he said out
loud.

He rushed the car home, dropped his jacket on the

dining room table and walked into the kitchen, where his wife and three children were eating dinner.

"Nobody waits for me?" he said.

"What'd you do today?" he said to the sixteen-year-old son, Eddie.

"Went to school."

"What'd you do after it?"

"Came home, hung out."

"Dad, can I go to the movies tonight?" the fifteen-year-old daughter, Tara, said.

"What's your mother say?"

"She said it was all right."

"So then go."

"I need money."

"How much money?"

"Five dollars."

"Where's the movie, in Cincinnati?"

"Nope. The Suffolk Quartet. Right in the mall."

"And it costs five dollars?"

"Three fifty. Then fifty for a slice of pizza. A Coke costs a quarter. I'll bring you the change."

He looked at Eddie, the sixteen-year-old boy. "You're going out too?"

"It's Friday night."

"So you'll do what?"

"I don't know."

"No idea?"

"Nope."

"If a movie costs five dollars, then what will something unplanned cost me, a hundred?"

"Not yet."

Myles' wife sighed. "It will someday. You ought to see what I did on my way home from Alice's house this afternoon. I stopped in the store and bought nothing and it cost sixteen dollars. Nothing. Dried lima beans, two large yogurts, cottage cheese, a box of pastina. Myles, I mean nothing. Sixteen dollars. You see old people buying one can of soup. They check all the shelves to see which can of soup is the cheapest."

Myles took his money, eighteen dollars in crumpled bills and some change, and placed it on the table.

"Oh, thanks," the daughter said. She took five.

"Best I can do for you," Myles said to his son Eddie.

"We're probably just going to one of the fellas' houses," the son said. He took five.

"I'm staying home," the youngest, the eleven-year-old boy said.

"You said it," Myles said.

Myles picked up a pork chop.

"I gave you a knife and fork," his wife said.

Myles sank his teeth into the pork chop. He was alone at the table now and the phone rang. He heard his daughter, with a whoop, run into the playroom to answer it.

"Who is it?" Myles called out.

His daughter yelled up. "It's for me." The playroom door slammed shut. Immediately, Myles picked up the extension on the kitchen wall.

On the phone, his daughter's voice said, "Is somebody on the phone?"

Myles said, "Oh, I thought it was for me."

The daughter said, "I've got it."

Myles said, "All right."

His daughter said to the caller, "Laura, what time are we meeting?"

Laura said, "Whatever time you wan—"

"—Daddy, I said I've got the phone."

Myles said, "You've got it all right?"

His daughter said, "I told you. I've got it."

Myles hung up the phone, unscrewed the mouthpiece and picked up the phone again. He bit his tongue and listened to his daughter talk to her friend.

"Billy's supposed to meet us."

"Tara, is somebody on the phone again?"

"I think so, Laura."

"There must be. I heard another click. For once, it isn't in my house, either."

At the kitchen table, Myles' wife whispered to him, "I think this is despicable."

Myles closed his eyes and shook his head. He was concentrating on the voices on the phone, one of which, his daughter's, suddenly lost its innocent tone.

"Laura, I got the greatest place to go tonight."

"Where?"

"To this place where we were last night. It's a place all by itself at the end of the mall. It actually isn't in the mall. It's the next thing from the mall. The name of the place is the Mona Lisa and it's the greatest, Laura. They don't proof you. Last night we stayed with the bartender and he said he wouldn't proof us if we came in again tonight. He says as long as kids look eighteen, he doesn't proof them. He's a good guy and boy, did I get wrecked with him last night."

"Last night?"

"Yup. Drinking beers."

"Wow."

"That isn't all, Laura."

"What?"

"I was with Billy Monks."

"Tara!"

"Every time he'd give me a joint, I'd go to the back door of the bar with him and we'd stand outside and smoke the joints."

"How many?"

"You won't believe it, Laura."

"Tell me how many."

"Guess. Guess how many joints I smoked last night."

"Two."

"I wish that's all."

"More than that?"

"Nine joints. I smoked nine joints and had beers."

"Tara!"

"Boy, did I get wrecked. And that's nothing compared to what we're doing tonight, Laura."

"I thought you told me we were going to the movies," Laura said.

"Laura, say you're going to the movies and when you get out of the house put on eye makeup and meet me by the Mona Lisa. Laura, you'll have the best time. We'll get loose joints from Billy Monks and have beers at the bar."

"I don't have enough money, Tara."

"You only need money for the joints. Then you go to the bar and all these men buy you beers."

"Are they all old men with dark beards on their faces? I hate that. Every time they put their face up to mine, I get all scratched."

"Laura, we'll get so wrecked you won't feel anything. I mean, *really* wrecked. Then you know what we'll do, we'll get Billy Monks and we'll go out in the park and have outdoor sex."

In the kitchen, Myles' stomach collapsed.

On the phone, Myles' daughter giggled. "I'm a little high now from smoking joints with Billy Monks in his garage after school."

"You were with Billy Monks today?"

"I just told you. Smoking joints in the garage."

"Is that all?"

"That's for tonight, Laura. We'll get stoned out of our minds, get really wrecked like, and then we'll have the greatest outdoor sex with Billy Monks. We'll get so stoned we won't even know if it's summer or winter out."

"Tara, you're crazy."

"I'm leaving right this minute. Later for you, Laura."

The phone hung up, the playroom door opened, Tara shouted "See ya!" and was at the back door before Myles could react, could leap down the stairs into the playroom and prevent her leaving.

Myles' wife called out calmly, "Have fun, dear."

The back door closed. Myles shuddered.

"How could you listen to her like that?" his wife said.

"I don't even want to talk about it," Myles said.

"You deserve what you get, you listen in on the phone," his wife said.

Myles squirmed in the house for a half hour and then drove to the shopping mall. Swirls of young people were under the marquee of the Suffolk Quartet theater. The anxiety in Myles subsided quickly as he saw a girl he was certain was his daughter, but upon a second look was just another of the masses of young girls who resemble their surroundings. Myles drove to the end of the mall, where the Mona Lisa bar sat by itself, a one-story cement hut, with the charm of a dry cleaning store, separated by an alley from the darkened Suffolk drive-in bank.

Inside, three men in their thirties, wearing jackets from the Long Island Edison Light Company, played shuffleboard under the bored gaze of the bartender, an immense man with sparse gray hair, thick eyeglasses, a chin that hung like a sack and a beltline of at least sixty inches. A juke box played country music and a game show was on television.

"Help you, Mac?" the bartender said.

"Beer," Myles said.

The bartender reached for a beer glass in front of him, stopped, turned around for a bottle of whiskey, poured himself a shot and, downing it, returned his attention to the beer glass for Myles.

Myles checked the bar, saw there were three sets of change, cigarettes and plastic lighters to match the three guys playing shuffleboard, then walked over to the ladies' room door and pulled it open. It was empty.

"Wrong one, Johnny," the bartender called.

"I'm getting punchy," Myles said. He walked into the men's room, saw it was empty, as he expected, came out and stepped out a back door of the bar and into the alley running alongside the bank. His breath caught as he heard voices at the end of the alley. Putting his feet down soundlessly, Myles went to the end of the alley, then suddenly stepped out into a parking lot where four boys, about twelve, played Frisbee under a streetlight.

"I thought you died," the bartender said when Myles came back.

"I was just checking," Myles said.

"Checking it out, eh?" the bartender said. He reached behind him and brought out the whiskey bottle. He poured a double shot, stared at it, sighed and then threw it down.

Myles held out his badge. "I'd like to talk to you."

"Sure, Mac. What department is that, anyway?"

"New York."

"Yeah, but we're here in Suffolk County."

"This is different," Myles said. "I'm part of a state-wide drug task force."

"Yeah?" the bartender said.

"Do you get young girls in here?" Myles said.

The bartender began to laugh. "Twelve year olds," he said.

Myles froze.

"Hey, fellas," the bartender called out, "do we get a lot of young girls in here?"

"Thousands," one of them called back.

"We get young girls in here, all right," the bartender said.

"How old?" Myles said.

"We get Betsy Ross in here," the bartender said. He reached for the whiskey.

"Well, I want to tell you something," Myles said.

"What's that, Mac?"

"I'm part of a state team fighting drugs," Myles said. "I might as well tell you. What we're doing, we're sending very young girls around to bars and if people give them beer and dope, these young girls report to us and then we bust the joint. State Police, State Liquor Authority, federal drug agents. We got a statewide team working this. Young girls come in a bar underage and get beer and dope and then old men look to take advantage of them. Know what I mean?"

"No," the bartender said.

"You don't?"

"No."

Myles stared at him. "You will if some young girl comes in here and you load her up and try and take advantage of her. You'll know what it is then. Because you'll be in the can."

Myles grabbed his change and went to the door.

"How do you like him?" the bartender called out to the three guys at the pool table. "Twenty fucking years of whiskey later, I got cirrhosis. Now he calls me a junkie." He patted his belly. "I haven't seen my prick in the last ten years and he says I'm playing with little girls. I wish the fuck I was."

Myles went out the door with the light company guys laughing at him.

He stayed in the shopping mall for another hour and a half, until nearly ten o'clock. Each time he went to the parking lot behind the bank, he found it empty. He drove past a small park on the far side of the parking lot and found that empty at all times. Finally, he went home, where his wife sat in the playroom watching television.

"She went to the movies," his wife said.

"That's not what I heard."

"I told you, don't listen."

"Do you ever talk to this kid?" Myles asked.

His wife exhaled.

"Do you ever *talk* to her?"

"She's fifteen years old," his wife said slowly. "What would she want to talk to me for?"

"Then how do we know what she's up to?"

"We'll find out in a few years. It's better to hear when it's in the past. She'll do as she pleases anyway."

"What she pleases has me worried," Myles said.

"You worry and she'll have fun. I don't think what she does is as bad or as interesting as you think."

At 11:15, Myles was putting on his coat to go out on another patrol when he heard noise in front of the house. He ran to the door and saw his daughter waving good-bye to a car driven by her girlfriend Laura's father. Tara ran past Myles into the house and in a moment was sitting happily alongside her mother in the playroom.

"What'd you see?" her mother asked.

"*Trial of Billy Jack*. It was great."

Myles opened a can of beer at the kitchen table; he was on his fourth when his wife and daughter went to bed. He sat at the table until 1:00 A.M., drinking beer and smoking cigarettes. As he exhaled, he followed the smoke until it wreathed itself about the face of Chita Gonzalez, her hair pulled back tightly.

Chapter 14

The matter was very simple, the other lawyer said. His voice rose as he arrived at his point. He stopped talking when the judge spun sideways, held out his glasses to the light and tipped so far back in his chair that his head, the color of dust, almost dropped out of sight. Long, dry hands methodically polished the glasses.

"Your Honor," the lawyer said.

"Go on," the judge said.

"Your Honor, this tenant hasn't paid rent since March first. We are now in the fifth month of nonpayment."

"He lie, man," Albert Flores said.

The judge's head popped up. He snapped, "Yes?"

"He lie, man."

Maximo put a hand on Flores' thigh. "Let me do the talking, Mr. Flores."

"You let him lie, man, and don't say nothing to him. Every time he lie, I say something."

Maximo sat in a stable. Officially, the place was Part IX, Bronx Landlord-Tenant Court, but it was located in deepest municipal squalor, a basement room of the Bronx County courthouse. This was the only court in which Maximo was allowed to appear until he had passed the bar, and it was the first time he even had done this. He had on his only suit, blue denim, and a solid dark blue tie that he felt was conservative enough to appease the judge. The lawyer across from him, Maximo's papers

showed, was named Goldblatt. He represented landlord
Theodore Caras, the owner of 1120 Maxwell Street, the
building in which Maximo's client, Flores, existed. Goldblatt, a tall shambles of a man, wore a tan suit which
already, in this sticky July morning, was showing dark
circles under the arms. At the table with Goldblatt was
the building owner, Caras, a squat man with a square face
who wore a yellow shirt with an eyeglass case and pens
jammed in the pocket.

"If I can continue," Goldblatt said. "There's nothing
to discuss here that I can see. The man owes the money
and refuses to pay the money. We want the money and
we want the tenant dispossessed." At each mention of
money, the landlord Caras' body jerked forward, as if
copulating.

"You lie, man," Flores said. He was trying to stand
up and Maximo had to grasp him by the elbow to keep
him on the chair.

"I don't lie about money," Goldblatt said, as Caras
came again.

Anguish sounded in Flores' throat. He could not remain still. He had been in turmoil for many days as he
prepared himself mentally for the court appearance. He
had practiced answers in front of the bathroom mirror.
"The babies suffer, your Honor," he kept saying. Today,
he was up at 4:00 A.M., smoking cigarettes in the kitchen.
He dressed in his best suit, a light green, and with it wore
a red and yellow flowered shirt and a blue polka-dot bow
tie which he felt was particularly appropriate for court.
Now, in this smelly room in the basement of the courthouse, with about one hundred people sitting on benches
and awaiting their turn, Flores, who had trained so hard
for this fight, suddenly was told, right at the bell, to remove his gloves.

"Your Honor," Maximo said. "I've seen the living
conditions in this apartment. For the months of December and January there was no heat in the building. In
February, there was no water. Throughout the entire
month this man and a family of six people, including two
grandchildren, babies, had to exist in an apartment with
no heat and no water. To get water, this family had to go

outside and fill a bucket with snow and bring it up to the house and boil it.''

"Dog piss all over the snow," Flores said.

"Mr. Flores," the judge said.

"What about shit?" Flores said. "No toilet. Shit in the lot!"

"Mr. Flores."

Maximo put a hand on Flores' shoulder and continued. "Beginning March first, when again there was no water, Mr. Flores withheld his checks from the landlord. He placed the money each month into a special banking account which he still maintains—"

"—Your Honor, if there's money here we don't have to go any further," Goldblatt said. "If I get a little something here today—"

Flores was on his feet. "I shit in the lot, man. My grandson shits in the lot, man. This guy wants money?"

"Judge," Goldblatt said, "if we just get a little something for my client here today, I'm sure we can take it from there. Right, counselor?"

Goldblatt turned to Maximo, but instead here was Flores, elbows flailing to keep Maximo away.

"You ever shit in a lot?" Flores shouted. His voice rose and his arms cut through the air. "You use to the warm bathroom. Try it no water in the house you go outside. In the winter. You shit in the lot, you freeze your ass!" Flores' eyes bulged like a trout. His mouth gulped for air. His body trembled.

"Sit down," the judge said.

"What is that you say to me?" Flores said.

"I said be seated," the judge said.

"You say this to me!" Flores shouted. His voice turned into a gargling sound and he pitched forward onto his face on the table in front of the bench.

The court officer stepped over and helped Maximo get Flores onto the floor. Maximo loosened Flores' collar and belt, his eyes darting for a minute to the front of the room, where a clerk sat at a desk with a phone. The clerk was motionless. Maximo said to Flores, "Just a little accident, Mr. Flores. Don't move now, and you'll be all right in a minute."

The court officer helping Maximo said, "Heart!" He jumped up and signaled to the back of the room, where another officer stood.

"Heart!" he called loudly to the officer in the back.

Flores was breathing heavily and Maximo was ready to fall upon him and give mouth-to-mouth resuscitation.

"Heart!" the court officer shouted again. This caused Flores' eyes to roll like pebbles. Maximo threw another glance at the desk in the front. The clerk had pushed the phone out of the way and was opening a sandwich.

"If he has trouble, you start the mouth-to-mouth," Maximo told the court officer.

"I'm here, counselor," the court officer said.

A leg brushed against Maximo's head. Another lawyer was stepping around him to get in front of the judge. Maximo sprang up and dived for the desk with the phone.

"Watch it," the clerk said, pulling away the wax paper on which sat a tuna fish sandwich.

"What do I dial?" Maximo said.

"Well, who do you want to call?" the clerk said.

"An ambulance," Maximo said.

"There's a court doctor, you know," the clerk said.

"Where?"

"Well, let me look." The clerk took out a booklet and began to go through it.

"Do I dial nine to get out?" Maximo said.

"Just let me see if we can get you the court doctor."

Maximo dialed nine, got a dial tone and called 911. He spoke slowly and enunciated carefully.

"Tell them to use the Walton Avenue entrance," the court officer with Flores called to him.

Maximo said this loudly and repeated it. Then he hung up. As he started back to Flores, he found the space in front of the judge crowded.

A small lawyer with a bow tie, standing with his feet about a foot from Flores' head, said, "Your Honor, I have to be upstairs in front of Judge Dubin at eleven-thirty. My matter will take only five minutes. Could I please present it to you now? I just have to get a little something here today."

"Your Honor, I'm still appearing before you," Gold-

blatt said. Caras, the landlord, was now standing up.
Maximo dropped to his knees alongside Flores. Goldblatt
bent over. "How is he?" Goldblatt said.

"I hope," Maximo said.

"He'll be all right in a minute," Goldblatt said.

"I hope," Maximo said.

"Can I talk to you for a moment?" Goldblatt said.

Maximo didn't answer. Out of the corner of his eye he
saw Caras, the landlord, tugging at Goldblatt's jacket.

"If my client can just get a little something," Goldblatt
said.

"What?" Maximo snapped.

"Just talk to me for a minute," Goldblatt said. "This
can all be eased if I can just get even two hundred dollars
as a show of faith to my client. Just a little something."

At the mention of money, Flores' chest heaved. A thud
sounded in his chest.

"Will you stop talking?" Maximo said. "You're exciting this man and you're going to kill him."

Now up the aisle came a cordon of court officers, two
of whom were unstrapping a stretcher.

"We got it, counselor," one of them said to Maximo.
They rolled Flores onto the stretcher. "We called the
ambulance but they told us they already had the call."
They lifted Flores.

The judge, arguing with three lawyers who now
crammed the area in front of the bench, looked up.

"Is he leaving?" he said.

"Yes, Your Honor," one of the court officers said.

"I see," the judge said. He began to go through a sheaf
of papers.

Caras, the landlord, put a pudgy hand onto Goldblatt's
back and shoved the lawyer up against the bench.

"Just a minute, Your Honor," Goldblatt said.

"Yes?"

"Your Honor, before the man goes can't I get a little
something?"

Maximo followed the officers out of the building,
where a squad car pulled up and then an ambulance with
paramedics, who took over. On the way to the hospital,

a paramedic said to Maximo, "Did he have a shock in there?"

"To his sense of fairness."

"He must have an attack every day," the paramedic said.

At the hospital, Maximo called Flores' wife and waited an hour until she arrived in the emergency room. A Pakistani doctor tried to explain Flores' condition, but did not know enough English words to do so.

"He'll live," a black nurse called out. "Got him sedated for the day."

Maximo walked back to his office as if he had just finished a football game. It wasn't until three o'clock that his energy returned, and then he worked slowly for the rest of the afternoon merely shuffling papers.

Later, when he was about to leave the office to ride the train downtown to the bar review course, Maximo called Nicki at her office.

"Where have you been?" she said.

"Many things," Maximo said. "In the office, in court."

"What court?"

"Landlord-tenant."

"Oh, I thought you had something in real court."

"Landlord-tenant is a real court."

"The only real court is criminal court," she said.

"You wouldn't think so if you saw what happened today."

"You can tell me about it when you see me."

"When?" Maximo asked.

"Tonight."

"I've got that course until nine."

"Say the truth. You don't have to go to it."

"Yes, I do."

"Then I'll just see you after it."

"Want dinner?" Maximo said.

"That would be fine."

"I've got a terrific place. Real Puerto Rican food."

"I don't eat Puerto Rican."

"You'll love this place."

"I said I don't eat it. That kind of food is all right for Spics, but not for me."

"Well what am I supposed to be?" Maximo asked.

"A Spic."

"Do you really mean that?"

"Darling, you are a Spic. I don't care what goes on here with us, but let's not fool ourselves. You are a Spic."

After three years of white women in Cambridge stumbling over the word Hispanic while their eyes said Spic, this woman, open as the sea, was a unique joy.

"Where will we eat then?"

"I'll bring it to your home," Nicki said. "Tonight's a suicide squad anyway, I'll get home so late."

She said that she would go to her girlfriend Angela's house and then meet Maximo at his place at 9:30. When Maximo hung up, the girl who typed legal briefs in his office stood in the doorway. Her name was Haydee and she wore a green T-shirt and Levi's. She was quite pretty and very dark.

"I feel like a drink," she said.

"I've got to run to my course," he said.

"Can't you have one before you go?"

"I'm late now," Maximo said.

"All right, then." She walked back to her desk. Immediately, Maximo felt that he had burned a part of his insides and left a small pile of ashes. Of course there was time for a drink, he even felt like one, but his reaction without thinking had been to say no, for he had something that excited him and attracted all his sexual energy, a white girl, and better than just any white girl, the most distant of all white girls, an Italian girl. Haydee was a dark girl, far darker than Maximo. His reaction had been to turn toward something lighter, and as he realized this, he despised himself for it. He had allowed the craving of a sugar-field worker to seep into the base of his body. How could he, Maximo, who intended to wage war throughout his life against the weaknesses that slowed his people, allow his prick to think for him, even for an instant? He decided he would take Haydee for a drink. When he looked out of his office, she was gone.

Later, at the bar review course, Maximo stopped berating himself and began to think of Nicki. The review course that night was on the rules of evidence and as it droned on, Nicki's voice was in his ear. She was calling him a Spic, and he loved it. He knew the evidence lecture almost as well as he knew the Our Father, and he heard the lecturer's voice and Nicki's voice at the same time and he dealt with both and it made the course most pleasant.

At twenty to five, when Nicki came back from the ladies' room, her phone was ringing and Galligan, the heavy guy who worked at the desk nearest hers, didn't touch it. This made Nicki mad. When she had first taken up with Maximo, she had instructed Galligan never to touch her phone and he did as he was told, but now as she walked to her desk, her sense of having everything exactly her own way was offended by Galligan's refusal to answer her phone. It was clear that Maximo was not calling, so why then didn't Galligan do her the favor of picking up the phone? When Nicki picked up the phone, the call was gone. She glared at Galligan. If I only had him on final, she said to herself.

Of the hundred and twenty-five people in Nicki's department, she had seven on final, which was what she liked the most about the job. In the personnel department steps to firing a person, the informal warning was first, then a formal written warning and then came final, which meant the employee had been warned enough and now any infraction at any time meant that the supervisor on the scene could terminate employment by verbal command. As Nicki was the supervisor with this power, she spent at least part of her time perfecting the verbal command that she was entitled to use. The last time, with some gay named Conrad, she had said, "Leave," and he had sat there looking at her. Then she said, "Die!" This he understood. So Nicki decided that this was to be her official verbal command from now on. "Die," she said to herself as she looked at Galligan. But he was only on formal warning and there were at least six months to go before she could get enough on him to place him on final.

She glanced over the room and saw Crowley in the back. He was on informal now, and she would have him on formal in a week, she decided. Final? This smelly little bum would be the fastest final the bank had seen in some time. She would see to that.

She called home to tell her mother that she was going out with Angela.

"For a drink? What is this drink?" her mother said.

"We just want to sit and talk over a drink."

"Where?"

"In a bar."

"Angela don't do things like that."

"She does once in a while."

"No, she doesn't. Neither do you. If your father catches you sitting in a bar . . ."

"I won't be late."

"I don't know what you're doing, Nicki."

"Ma."

"All right. But I'm just telling you."

At Angela's house, she and Nicki drank coffee and smoked cigarettes while the lasagna baked.

"What has this fellow got?" Angela said.

"That's one of those things you'd have to find out for yourself."

"Is all that stuff about Spics true?"

"Every word."

"So they're really six inches when they're born."

"I said, every word."

"Niggers are supposed to be even bigger," Angela said.

Nicki wrapped the dinner in the same kind of tray covered by aluminum foil that she used for bringing food to prison. Angela tore a slip of paper from a pad at the telephone, wrote the date on it, and put it atop the foil.

"I don't want you to feel strange, carrying food with no number on it," Angela said.

"There's enough here to feed a prison," Nicki said.

"Does he eat like a savage?" Angela said.

"No. And he doesn't have a freezer, either. How long can this last if he just leaves it in the refrigerator?"

"I don't know," Angela said.

"Half the time he doesn't get home till late and he doesn't eat. What if he just leaves it there?"

"What's the difference?" Angela said. "Leave it out for three days. He wouldn't know the difference. He'd think it was Puerto Rican food. Then maybe it'll poison him. That would be good."

They arrived at Pinto Avenue at 9:25. Nicki sat in the car and looked up the street for Maximo. She was not getting out of the car until he was within three yards of it.

"You got to be careful," Angela said.

"I can't have an abortion with this guy," Nicki said.

"You know it," Angela said.

"The doctor would see that it's a nigger baby."

Angela began to hum to the car radio. "I hope something good's on television tonight. You'll have me staying up till I'm cross-eyed."

"It won't be that late, I promise," Nicki said.

"Don't worry. Just call and I'll pick you up."

By implied agreement, biology was an accepted excuse between them for any transgression, for the idea of young bodies resisting old urges for protracted blocks of time was alien. After this, however, Nicki had another feeling, one of unaccustomed enjoyment at the chance to set new limits to her serfdom. The moment she made an arrangement to see Maximo, she assured herself that it was for physical reasons, but she then immediately found herself eager for the change, to come out of the suffocation of her world and be set free, even for mere hours of a clock, to walk about Maximo's world. Maximo was a Puerto Rican, but also he was a person who brought to her no ancient chains to ensure the rites of proper conduct when a husband is in prison. And then there was another part of her that was becoming more and more proud of Maximo's qualifications. Several times on the bus ride home —home to be defeated by another night—Maximo's position became vivid and comforting. Say the truth, she would tell herself, doesn't it feel good to know that you could go with a lawyer from Harvard?

All of which was immediately lost now as she saw Maximo coming down the block, his thin frame—all

movie stars are thin—swinging with this marvelous ease,
his head as high as an aristocrat's, the beard giving power
to his gaze. She could not wait for his body to be upon
her.

As Maximo walked up to the car, a door slammed across the street and David Robles came out into the night
in a Civil War cap and sweatshirt. Over the sandwich
shop, a window opened and the mother, Maria Robles,
looked out.

"Ven aquí," she called, telling him to return.

David paused. Under the streetlight at the next corner
three other young kids could be seen.

"*Yo* Chino!" David called.

"*Yo* Davey!" one of the kids called back.

"¡Ven aquí!" the mother called from the window.

David turned and walked back into his building.

Maximo stopped watching him, for in front of him was
Nicki, in a red jersey dress, her long legs gracefully fidgeting as she waited for him.

Upstairs, Maximo settled the dog in a corner while
Nicki stood in the small kitchen and unwrapped the lasagna. She was uncomfortable in the presence of un-
washed dishes in the sink.

"Drink?" Maximo said.

"Aren't we going to eat?"

"Let's relax and have a drink first. I had a tough day."

A drink? Nicki thought. If I wanted to drink I could go
to a bar. "The food will get cold."

"Put it in the oven."

Nicki shuddered. She looked at the old heavy oven
door. It was closed, but she knew what was inside.
Grease. She knew just the smell would kill her. She began
to rewrap the tinfoil about the lasagna.

"Use the oven," Maximo said.

Nicki continued to rewrap the lasagna.

"Here, that's silly, give it to me," Maximo said. He
took the tray and opened the oven. Nicki held her breath
and turned her head.

"What do you want with the drink?" Maximo said.

"Water and ice."

"Sorry, but I've got no ice."

"Then just a little water," she told Maximo.

"With rum? You don't want orange juice?"

"I drink Scotch."

"I'm working only four weeks. I got rum."

"Then give me rum and orange juice."

He handed her the glass and they walked into the living room. He sat in a chair that had books piled on the floor around it. Nicki sat across from him on the couch. She didn't like the look of the books to begin with, almost none of them had the neat, bright dust jackets she associated with good books. When her own copy of *The Godfather* had a tear in the dust jacket, she went into a bookstore on her way from work and grabbed a new one; if there was anything she disliked more than a ripped dust jacket on a book, it was books with no dust jackets. After that came grease.

"You're supposed to have shelves for these," she said.

"My emphasis now is on getting through the day. The esthetics can be taken care of later. Here's to you." He held up his glass.

"All those law books?" Nicki said.

"There are all the books that my family has had. A couple of my father's. The rest are mine from college and law school.

Oh, stop with this talk, she said to herself. Just sit down next to me and we'll take it from there.

As if reading her thoughts, he leaned over and kissed her.

"I like that better," Nicki said.

He walked her downstairs at 12:30 and she was equally as certain, in the light of the phone booth, as she had been in the darkness of bed, that he was the finest thing the jungle ever had produced. She looked up and down the street. "A mess," she said.

"Sure is," Maximo said.

"All on welfare here, I'm sure," she said.

"They're on welfare just like your father would be if he didn't sell heroin," Maximo said.

"Well," Nicki said coolly, "you ought to know. Or have you forgotten the wonderful person you were with when I met you?"

Maximo winced inside. "I don't see that fellow any-more."

When Angela pulled up, Nicki gave Maximo a quick kiss. "You'll call?"

"Don't worry. It was a lovely night."

"Say the truth. Wasn't it?"

"But we didn't eat," he said.

"It's in your oven, dear," Nicki said. She slipped into the car.

There was the noise of a car pulling up sharply at the corner, a few yards away. Out of the back window of a Mercedes, Teenager's head appeared.

"Maximo!"

Maximo turned. Inside Angela's car, Nicki dropped her head under the dashboard.

"Maximo, we're going out. Dancing girls!" Teenager roared.

"Maximo's going to bed," Maximo said. He waved.

Angela's car drove off.

"Maximo is tired from the woman," Teenager said. "Who was that woman who just went away?"

Maximo waved and was gone. Teenager's car didn't move for a moment, waiting for Maximo to reappear. When he didn't the car pulled away.

A blue Oldsmobile came up and stopped at the corner. The man in the back ran his hand over his face.

"I got enough of looking for tonight," Corky, Louis Mariani's man, said.

"You don't want to go around after him no more to-night?" the driver, a young guy in a blue zipper jacket, said.

"No, I just want to get his habits down and I done enough tonight. He talked to the guy in that building," Corky said, pointing at Maximo's.

"Young guy," another zipper jacket in the front seat said.

"The broad got into a car," the driver said.

"It got Jersey plates," the other one in the front said.

"Imagine we got Spics living in Jersey now," Corky said.

"I couldn't see too good from back there, but she didn't look like a Spic to me," the driver said.

"They fool you," Corky said. "Sometimes they look the same as the whites, the dirty bastards."

"I'm sure she was an all-white broad," the driver said.

"If she was, the guy living there must be one of Teenager's top guys," Corky said. "No white broad going to go with a Spic unless he got big bucks for her."

......**Chapter 15**

......

The police car rocked to a stop in front of Ana's bar. Martin stood in the street, pulled his pants up over his belly and walked first into the bar with Myles and Hansen behind him.

Luisa Maria watched as the red-haired cop went to the back of the bar and looked around. The second cop, Myles, who remained in the doorway, did not look as mean to her. But she reminded herself that just because this one does not look as if he wants to do something to you, there is no reason you should trust him. For still he must be bad; he is a cop.

When Hansen walked in, Luisa Maria was outraged. A dirty black nigger. Oh, he has to be a cop, he is with the others, you can see that. And, there, you can see the gun under his jacket. A dirty black cop.

In the back of the bar, Martin opened the men's room door to make sure it was empty, tried the door to what appeared to be a storage room, found it locked, stepped around the small pool table, saw no threat anywhere, then stood with hands on hips and ran his eyes over the barroom once more. There were only two at the bar, Benny Velez and Santos Rivera. The presence of police, particularly at an unpredictable hour, late of an afternoon, caused them discomfort; an indictment ran across Rivera's face.

"We're clear," Martin called out. For Martin, checking the back of a saloon in a black or Latin neighborhood was a ritual, a basketball team taking layups when it first appears on the court.

Myles and Hansen stepped to the empty part of the bar by the window and Martin rolled in alongside them. "Give us a beer," Martin called out.

"*¿Qué marca de tipo?*" Luisa Maria said.

"Beer."

"She want to know the brand," Benny said.

"Schaefer."

"*No tengo ese tipo.*"

"She doesn't have that brand," Santos said.

"Then Piel's."

Luisa Maria put out two bottles of beer and small plastic glasses.

"They don't bother me, man," Benny said quietly. He had a pillbox of cocaine in his shirt pocket, but he saw nothing wrong in this, as long as he did not insult the police by using the cocaine in front of them. Rivera, who had two ounces of heroin in a plastic bag in his pocket, decided he needed some sort of protection. He put on large black sunglasses.

Martin gulped the beer as if in fear it would evaporate. He sucked at the cigarette in the right corner of his mouth and talked to Myles and Hansen out of the other.

"Scummers," he said.

"I think they were in here the same day as me, but I can't be sure," Myles said. "The two I remember aren't in here now. I'd know them anywhere. But these guys here, the trouble is they all look alike to me."

"If that's what you say," Hansen said.

Martin ordered a beer, then Hansen bought one and when Myles pushed a five-dollar bill out, he said to Luisa Maria, "Have one too."

Luisa Maria seemed not to know what was going on until Santos Rivera spoke to her in Spanish. Smiling, she put up three bottles of beer and then said, "*Yo tengo también.*" She poured herself a shot of Scotch, then opened up a bottle of beer for herself. She took the money from Myles, held up the Scotch, threw it down, smiled and walked away holding the bottle of beer.

Martin sat with his hands folded in his lap, cigarette dangling, eyes squinting in the smoke. "Smartass," he muttered. He called out to Luisa Maria, "What does Teenager drink when he's in here?"

Luisa Maria glanced at Benny and spoke to him in Spanish.

"She does not know this person Teenager from this bar," Benny said. "She is new here."

"Then you know what he drinks," Martin said to Benny.

"Teenager," Benny said. His eyebrows came together as if he were in the midst of medical boards. "I try to think, but I do not know this person."

"You live with him, scummer," Martin said. He pointed at Luisa Maria. "You probably sleep with him."

Benny told this to Luisa Maria and she shook her head emphatically. "She says she doesn't know this Teenager," Benny said.

"She's a liar," Martin said.

"Fuck you," Luisa Maria said.

"She doesn't know English!" Martin said.

"I know cop. I know fuck you," Luisa Maria said.

Martin roared and threw down his beer, got off the stool and walked to the men's room.

Hansen gripped his pipe between his teeth and said quietly, "I sure wish we'd go someplace else."

"I like it, I want to try something," Myles said.

Hansen shook his head. "I sure wish we'd do this thing more businesslike. You don't do a job properly when you're messing around like this." He made a face. "Personal jibes."

Myles motioned to Luisa Maria. "Have another."

Luisa Maria, fuming, poured herself another drink. She threw it down and then poured a second, placed the shot glass on the bar and brought up another bottle of beer for Myles.

"Good luck," Myles said.

Luisa Maria threw a glance at the men's room. "I no like him."

"Well, then have a drink with me."

"You a nice fella, but I no like him."

"I'll keep him in line."

"Fuck him. He makes me mad."

"Well, what can I do to make you happy?"

"You carry a gun?"

"Right here."

"Then you shoot him for me."

Myles laughed. Maybe, Myles told himself, that by his warm demeanor he had made an implied agreement with Luisa Maria that they would be able to speak to each other without admitting that they actually were doing so. He took the picture of Chita Gonzalez out of the envelope and put it on the bar.

"Do you know this girl?" he said.

Luisa Maria stared at the picture but did not touch it. "I don't think I know her. I know her face, maybe. I don't know. If I see her sometime, then maybe I know her."

"You won't be able to see her anymore."

"So then I won't know her."

"Would Teenager know her?"

"When this Teenager that you know comes here then you ask him," she said.

"I got a better idea," Myles said. He pushed the picture of Chita Gonzalez across the bar at her. "Take this picture to that friend of yours and tell him I know. Tell him I know and he knows and this picture knows."

Luisa Maria's eyes became agates. She walked away and began looking for things under the bar. Hansen watched her, took the pipe out of his mouth, held it up, examined it and said quietly, "That sure doesn't take us anywhere."

"Well, she'll let that Teenager know," Myles said.

"Why should he know what you got on your mind?" Hansen said.

"Because this is personal."

Hansen put the pipe back in his mouth and said nothing.

Martin came back from the men's room bawling, "I had it in here. Let's go someplace where we belong. Like Sheridan's or something." He rolled out of the bar. Myles left the picture of Chita Gonzalez on the bar. Then he dug into the envelope and brought out three more and left these, too. "Pass them around," he said as he left.

Outside, Martin looked for McGuire and the car. "He said he might go for gas," Martin said. "The way the man drives he'll be gone for a week."

Standing on the sidewalk in front of the bar, they were three men waiting for a lift. As seen from the laundromat across the street, the three were fortifications that no one could dare approach. Corky stood in the back of the laundromat and muttered, "Too hot."

A woman stuffing clothes into the machine alongside him said, "That water must be hot for these things." She held up a greasy T-shirt.

"Wash it clean," Corky said.

He walked out the back door and went down a narrow alley that was covered with garbage. He waved a hand in front of his face against the flies. On the street, out of view from the bar and the sidewalk in front of the bar, the two thugs who traveled with Corky were double-parked in a blue Lincoln.

"Back it up," Corky said as he got in.

"No good?" the thug in the front seat said.

"Law," Corky said.

"Are they there to help him?" the driver said.

"I don't know, but they're there," Corky said.

"We could forget about that joint," the driver said.

"There's other places he's got to go to," Corky said.

"All right. What do you want me to do, take you home?" the driver said.

"Might as well," Corky said.

"Can I just do one thing on the way out of here?" the driver said.

"Go ahead," Corky said.

The driver went through sidestreets and swung around trucks and then turned onto the emptiness of Maximo's block. The car stopped short of the corner and the driver studied the sidewalk and the building. A woman was on the outdoor phone. Maximo's building was lifeless in the late afternoon. Across the street, at a window one flight over the *bodega,* a woman stared down at her kid, who rode a bike on the sidewalk.

"Who could he be, living here?" Corky said.

"You can never tell; they all live like pigs," the driver said.

"But this is really nothing. This guy got to be only a runner," Corky said.

"I think he has to be in with them pretty good. I still say that was a white broad I saw coming out of there," the driver said.

He started the car off to Jersey.

It was not until the next evening that Teenager arrived at the bar. Before entering, he had Albertito, one of his gunmen, drive him around the block three times while he looked at any strange face as if it were a land mine. When he had watched Mama shake the shells, rub them and roll them onto the straw mat as if they were dice, he had not been surprised to hear her say the shells spoke of danger. When she said that the shells warned that the danger was from an American, he said, "Police."

Mama held a shell to her ear and closed her eyes and chanted in Yorubic.

"Yes, police. They want to put you in many jails. Changó says there is a more powerful enemy. A man who is not a policeman. An American man you know. He wants to kill you this day."

"Mariani," Teenager said.

Mama held the shells. "Yes, that is the man. He is going to try and kill you."

"Where would he do it?" Teenager asked.

Mama listened to several shells. "In a door," she said.

"Where is this door?"

Mama squeezed her eyes shut. She took an immense breath and the room was soundless as she listened to the shell. She put the shell down. "Changó is not there anymore. I don't know which door. I think it is a metal door with a broken window. But look out for all doors."

Now, as Teenager got out of the car by the side door to Ana's, he would not walk to the door until he saw Benny Velez standing in it. With Albertito covering his back, Teenager then sauntered into the bar. He laughed as he greeted Luisa Maria, for he knew she had to be angry at him; he had not seen her or called her for two days. His laugh died as Luisa Maria told him of the visit by the cops. The cop leaving the picture of Chita Gonzalez particularly irritated him. What were they bothering about a female like that? Chita was a bad female, man. Why don't they leave me alone? He walked to the front window and looked out at the street. The trucks from the firehouse up the block had just returned from a run. Two firemen stood in the middle of the street and held up the cars until the trucks had backed into the firehouse. Boots flopping, the firemen ran after the trucks as they backed into the house. Teenager smoked his cigarette and stared at the street with sleepy eyes.

"The cop that was here was the same one who hassled us about his battery," Benny said.

"Then he wasn't in here about a battery," Teenager said.

"He was being cute, man," Benny said.

Teenager smoked his cigarette down slowly, lazily. Why do they bother to come here like this, he said to himself. Changó says I have trouble with Mariani. So police should not come here to bother me. I am only home from jail for a little while. Let them bother somebody else. Teenager flicked the butt out the open door. His right elbow smashed into the frame and caused white wood to sprout like a broken bone through the many coats of red paint.

It took several brandies before Benny thought that Teenager had calmed down enough to be spoken to. Benny spilled cocaine out of his pillbox onto the bar. With a single-edged razor he divided the white crystals into ten stubby lines. He rolled up a new fifty-dollar bill and, without talking, handed it to Teenager, who held it to his right nostril, bent over and sniffed. The bill became a pleasant vacuum cleaner and brought the first five lines into the nostril. He put the bill to his left nostril and sniffed up the next five lines.

"Party!" Teenager shouted.

Benny picked his head up from doing his own lines, clapped his hands and then bent over to finish his cocaine.

Luisa Maria said, "It's about time you took me some-place."

"You must stay here," Teenager said. "Money comes here tonight."

"Then I will keep all the fucking money," Luisa Maria said.

"You just take the money and keep it for me," Teen-ager said.

After a few happy shouts, Teenager followed Albertito out the back door and into his Mercedes. Tires sounding, they pulled away from the bar and headed for Watson Avenue, which was Teenager's public gardens. Teenager felt good now. He was dressed to cause even the night air to pay attention. He had on a brown silk body shirt that was open to the chest, allowing everyone to see the great medallion of his saint, Changó. It was, after a sec-ond Mercedes, the first thing Teenager had bought after coming onto the streets and making money. It was made for him by an Hasidic Jew who had a gold jewelry busi-ness behind thick steel doors on the eleventh floor of a building on West 48th in Manhattan. The medallion cost fifteen thousand dollars, and on the day Teenager paid for it he was embarrassed because it had left him penni-less, and also because he wanted a larger medallion. This one was inlaid with red and white stones and hung from his neck on a heavy gold chain. On his left wrist was a yellow bracelet and this, too, embarrassed him because there were no diamonds in it. When he became like Rockefeller and was in charge of all the drugs, he would have diamonds in his eyes, he told himself.

Teenager's medallion blazed in the streetlights as he got out of the car in front of the Casa, on Watson Avenue. He swung around so that the medallion would be noticed by the crowd sitting on car fenders and hanging from the windows of the old apartment buildings that lined the street. Teenager stood while Benny went to the door of the Casa and checked it. Nearly all those watching Teen-ager were people who were up each morning to work at factory jobs, making wallets and belts and dresses, and they spent evenings screeching out windows at the chil-dren on the sidewalk below. They were the members of the underclass who did not steal, tried to have their kids keep pace in school, despised dope and were terrified at the idea of the word jail, but who, at times such as this, when Teenager emerged from his car with his jewelry afire in the streetlights, always paused in their honesty and allowed the delicious thoughts to run through them that they, too, were a part of this.

"Aha!" Teenager announced as he walked into the bar.

A girl named Ramonita, who had been standing at the juke box absently selecting records, suddenly threw her hips into motion. Her head rocked back and forth and her eyes danced as they met Teenager's. He took her by the wrist and drew her to the bar.

"You are with me for the whole week," he said.

As Ramonita giggled, Teenager snapped his fingers. "Money!"

Standing behind Teenager, Santos Rivera dug into a pocket and first brought out the roll of worn bills, then shoved them back in his pocket and brought out a thick wafer of new hundred-dollar bills he had picked up at the bank for Teenager.

"Santos carries my money," Teenager said. He stood away from the bar and patted his tan slacks. "I own so much money that it ruins the look of my pants. I have many people carry my money for me." Underneath his bravado was irritation: tonight he only had eleven hundred dollars. Someday, he would carry thirty thousand, he promised himself.

Around him, a semicircle of people laughed.

"Brandy!" Teenager called out.

"Brandy!" the semicircle called out.

"Aha!" Teenager said. "We are all drinking brandy." Many hands reached out for the honor of handing Teenager his brandy when it came. A couple, particularly the wife of Junior Mendez, a pusher, gagged when they had to drink the brandy, which was not drowned in the sugar and fruit juice they liked, but as this was a business meeting, they sought with each motion to please the president of the firm.

Ramonita leaned over and kissed Teenager on the neck.

"You must behave," Teenager said.

"I do not like this behaving," Ramonita said.

"Luisa Maria will find out that you are kissing me and she will be mad," Teenager said.

"I will beat up Luisa Maria," Ramonita said. She made a fist of her right hand and threw a punch into the smoky air.

"Luisa Maria is very tough," Teenager said.

"Then I will shoot her," Ramonita said.

"If you shoot her, then I will have no woman friend," Teenager said.

"I will be your new woman," Ramonita said.

"When you shoot Luisa Maria, then I will come with you," Teenager said.

"You would not care?"

"I will cry at Luisa Maria's funeral and then I will take you out to watch racing horses," Teenager said. He laughed and threw a hundred on the bar, crisp and unfolded. "For the drinks!" Ramonita looked at the money and did not smile.

"I will shoot Luisa Maria with a shotgun," Ramonita said.

The barmaid's name was Ada and she was from Colombia, as was Luisa Maria, and Ada did not like people from Puerto Rico saying that they were going to kill people from her country.

As she rang up the drinks, she told herself that she would call Luisa Maria the next day and tell her that this Teenager had decided that he wanted to have Luisa Maria killed.

When Teenager had the excitement around him in the bar so high that it had a sound of its own, a strange tune coming out of one of the radios out on the windowsills, perhaps, he threw ten dollars down for Ada the barmaid and ordered his party to walk across the street to the La Barca. He moved as if he were touring a fallen city; medals flashing in the streetlights, an arm about Ramonita's waist, people jostling with each other to walk alongside him. Albertito and Junior Mendez, the pusher, stood in

the doorway first, and then Teenager paraded into the La
Barca and let out his shout. "Aha!"

An hour later, he was dancing with Ramonita, his
hands pressed against the small of her back, his thoughts
considering an announcement to everyone that the place
would have to be emptied so he could dance alone with
Ramonita and perhaps throw her atop the pool table. A
pusher named Tato approached him, then remained in
silence a couple of steps away, a grisly altar boy waiting
to be summoned to the tabernacle.

"I am in love," Teenager said, dancing with his face
buried in Ramonita's mane.

"There are two cops sitting in the car up the block,"
Tato said.

"They are hiding so the sergeant doesn't see them,"
Teenager said.

"These are detectives," Tato said.

At three in the morning, Teenager stood in the street,
glanced up at the Plymouth Fury parked in the shadows
between streetlights on the next block; got in the car for
a moment, stepped out to confuse the cops, then immediately slipped back in and sent the Mercedes rocketing
down the street. He made a left, went to an avenue under
an El, turned right and went into the lane that runs between pillars directly under the El tracks. A bus lumber-
ing toward Teenager's car wanted the entire lane and
Teenager had to swing out into the narrow lane between
the El pillars and curb. In doing this, he smacked the
fender of a car parked in front of a nightclub. Teenager
let out a happy shout as the bus reached a point where it
had the detective's car trapped against a pillar. The bus
yielded no territory and took the doorhandles off the detective's car. Teenager now slowed enough for the car to
catch up with him. With Ramonita sitting in front with
him, and Benny and Albertito in back, Teenager drove
up to 183rd Street, establishing a pace that made it difficult for the detectives to follow him as they wanted to,
keeping another car between them and Teenager in order
to disguise their presence. Going up a hill on 183rd, Teenager caused his machine to crawl; the detective car behind him had no choice but to come close. The light on

the Concourse turned red, and Teenager sat in his Mercedes, looked into the rear-view mirror and, seeing Myles driving, spit words out of a mouth that was suddenly filled with acid. "This mother-fucker!" His body wanted to get out of the car and walk back and yank Myles out of the car and the black nigger with him. His mind told him to try it another way. Teenager pointed back so Ramonita, Benny and Albertito would turn and look at Myles and Hansen. The car burst into laughter as Teenager shot the red light and raced out onto the Grand Concourse. Myles and Hansen did not follow. Myles' fingers drummed on the wheel. Hansen put his head back and closed his eyes. "We got all the time in the world. We get paid for the ride."

Teenager appeared at Ana's Bar at four the next afternoon, found it closed and had to open it himself. He was alone in the place with Benny, and they sat for two hours in the smell of filled ashtrays and stale alcohol. Who is she not to be in this bar when I come, he fumed. When Luisa Maria finally arrived, she took a fat envelope of money out of her purse, threw it on the bar and began to clean the place without bothering to look at Teenager.

"Where the hell have you been?" he said.

"Where were you all night when I was sitting here with this filthy animal? He gives me the money for you and then he says that we should make a bed out of the pool table while I was waiting for you."

The money had been left by a man named Alex from Avenue B on the downtown East Side. Counting it, eleven thousand dollars in small bills, exactly the amount promised, Teenager said to himself that a man who lives up to his word in business like this could say anything he wants to a female, even my female. He put the eleven thousand into both back pockets, buttoning the flaps over them. In the front two pockets he had thirteen thousand more, giving him twenty-four thousand, the light twenty-five thousand that he was to give Mariani's people later in the evening for another half kilo of Marseilles white.

"Why did you count the money twice?" Luisa Maria said. "Don't you trust me?"

"I just count to make sure."

"Count once to make sure once. But the second time you do it to see if I am a thief."

"I didn't say that."

"I should steal your money. You let me stay here all night with this filthy animal."

As the bickering progressed, Teenager slammed the table, causing the ashtray to bounce on the floor. Still, Luisa Maria's complaining filled the bar. Abruptly, Teenager stood up, told Benny to watch the bar and stormed out of the place with Luisa Maria; he would shut her up with a drink after he delivered his money. As he pulled away from the bar, he inspected the rear-view mirror, made a left turn and saw that a red gypsy taxicab and a white panel truck were behind him. At the first corner, he made a left and saw the red cab and the white panel truck disappear. An old blue Falcon now was behind Teenager. At the first corner, Teenager made a left. The blue Falcon went straight. Teenager drove up the block with no one trailing. Detectives, he thought, bother you the way kids do. One moment they are all about you, causing you to keep pushing them away, and then they suddenly run to someplace else and leave you alone with your hand still pushing them and they are not there.

He double-parked on the Grand Concourse at Echo Place where a Wop would be in the rear first-floor apartment with his hand out for money; in his schooling in his trade, Teenager had learned that foreign trade and foreign relations are entirely separate disciplines. The saints had spoken through the shells to Mama and told her that a man, undoubtedly Mariani, wanted to do away with him. But the saints had said nothing so far about this animosity superseding the need for Teenager and Mariani to do business together.

"How long will you leave me sitting here?" Luisa Maria said as Teenager left the car.

"Just a minute."

"A minute like last night?" Luisa Maria said.

A black man in a raincoat and his girlfriend in a zipper jacket were passing by and they smiled as they heard the tone in Luisa Maria's voice. Teenager closed his eyes and exhaled. I should turn around, he told himself, and go back and slap this bitch in the face to teach her not to yell at a man anytime. And to yell at a man in front of a black nigger and his girlfriend, that is the worst thing a woman can do. Instead of following his fury and going back to the car, Teenager walked around the corner, the air hissing from his mouth, and came onto Echo Place. A man in the outdoor phone booth turned his face quickly. Is he trying to hide from me, or is he just turning because he thought of something as he was talking, Teenager said to himself. His anger at Luisa Maria distracted him and he walked the few steps past the phone booth and up to the entrance of the musty six-story apartment building. The streetlight bathed the aluminum frame and the badly cracked glass of the door. As the entranceway inside was dark, the cracked glass window reflected the street behind Teenager who, as he dumbly pushed in the door with his right hand, saw for an instant in the glass the reflection of the man in the phone booth dropping to the floor. Teenager had the aluminum frame door pushed in and the darkness in front of him and he flung himself to the left as the *fu-wa fu-wa fu-wa* of three shotgun explosions filled the hallway. Buckshot tore apart the entranceway inside and stormed on the sidewalk and street like angry sleet. Flat on his stomach, Teenager felt the shoe missing on his right foot and the heel of the foot stinging. He pulled himself into a sitting position with his back against the wall of the building, directly alongside the entranceway. His hand went to his belt, as if reaching for a gun. Because so many police followed him, he had been moving around without a gun. He cursed the police now. A figure scrambled out of the phone booth and into the gutter and then suddenly was off and running between cars. Teenager got on his feet, flattened against the wall and waited for anything to come through the doorway. No sound was being made inside. Teenager got away from the doorway with the stocking foot paining him now.

"What is it?" Luisa Maria said.

"Your fault," Teenager said. He drove hastily for several blocks up the Grand Concourse, went left, made two more lefts, then satisfied no one was trailing him, pulled the car to the curb, leaned over and brought the palm of his right hand hard against Luisa Maria's face.

He went home to his wife that night for the first time in several weeks. She sat on the edge of the bed and removed the buckshot from his heel with a hot knife. His five-year-old son stood in the doorway and watched. Between winces, Teenager thought about how good it would be to have a baby with Luisa Maria and to let his wife raise the child.

When he left the house the next day, he tried to reach any of Mariani's couriers to determine if there had been, by some odd chance, a mistake. Teenager was met with radio silence, a prime indicator that the attack had been quite real. Then early of a Saturday evening, he was confronted with Primo's wife. Primo was one of Teenager's runners. On the night Teenager was to deliver the cash, Primo went to the drive-in movie alongside the Bruckner Expressway for the transfer of the dope for which Teenager was paying. Primo thus far had failed to return.

His wife, Rosie, dark-faced and with long, unruly hair, sat by the juke box, smoked cigarettes and kept shifting impatiently while complaining to Teenager about Primo's absence.

"Primo goes somewhere for you with a girlfriend?" she said.

"He didn't take his girlfriend with him," Teenager said.

"Primo never called you up?" she said.

"Not once."

"Then where is Primo?"

"I told you I don't know."

"Somebody must," she said.

"Why don't you ask the police where Primo is?" Teenager said.

"I can't do that. Primo told me only to talk to police to tell them the name of the man the policeman's wife sleeps with."

"Then what do you want me to do?" Teenager said.

"Pay me money if Primo does not come back."

Teenager paced in anger. He tried Mama three times,

then drove with Benny over to her new apartment, but she was not home. Noticing that he was not being followed, Teenager then went out for a night of social clubs and bars. In the morning, he again could not find Mama, so he drove over to Maximo's and leaned on the horn until Maximo's head came out the window.

"Have you spoken to Mama?" Teenager called up.

"Not in a while. I know where she is, though."

"Where?"

"The concert. Don't you know that?"

Teenager was angry at himself for forgetting. A weekend of big *Santeria* concerts was being held in honor of the saints of love, Ochun and Yemawa, at a movie house on 137th Street and Broadway.

"I bought tickets and I forget about it," Teenager said.

"That's where she is," Maximo said.

"Get dressed and come with me," Teenager said.

"I've got work to do."

"What does it matter if you come for an hour? I never see you. Why do you stay so far away from me? You have time for girls at night? Why don't you ever see me?"

Trapped, Maximo started to say something, knew it would have the quality of a cracked note and be received as such, and so reluctantly held up a finger that told Teenager to wait. A few minutes later, Maximo sat uncomfortably alongside Teenager as he double-parked in front of the theater on Broadway. The act of getting out of the car with Teenager on a street, and having these two in back bouncing out at the same time caused him to grimace. The thought that his presence was in disregard of Nicki's warning produced an accompanying sense of depression. Dope peddlers shot on street.

The concert was listed to start at two and it was now two forty-five and the crowd standing under the marquee indicated that there would be the usual lag of about an hour between advertised time and performance time. Mama appeared out of the crowd, dressed in a red pants suit and white shirt of Changó's colors, despite the fact that the gods being honored by the concert, Ochun and Yemawa, stood for Love and Health, whose colors ran to white and yellow. Mama's red and white, giving the illusion of a warship on an otherwise peaceful sea, took on more dramatic meaning when Teenager stepped up and embraced her. Those who knew moved away, for their belief in their religion formed a sword poised at the evil in front of them. A lanky, somber man stepped through the crowd and entered the theater, thus removing himself from the sight of Mama and Teenager. From Mama, Maximo knew the man was the Oba, a rank equivalent to cardinal or king, and thus the foremost member of the *Santeria* religion in New York.

Mama, seeing Maximo, disengaged herself from Teenager's hug, took Maximo by the arm, noticed his unease and walked him up the sidewalk away from the crowd.

"You don't like being here?" she said.

"Not because of you," Maximo said.

"No, but I can tell. This person in the other world told you to stay away and now you are nervous that you are here."

"What kind of another world can it be if I just got an apartment on Pinto Avenue?"

"I told you, being in two worlds only makes it harder for you."

"And I told you, I barely see the person."

"You will see more of her."

"I don't know that I will."

"Once the man touches white skin, he cannot keep his hands off it. He thinks it makes him white, too. He thinks it rubs off."

"I have no trouble with that," Maximo said.

"In the man's head he might say, oh, I know what I am doing with this white woman. To me, she is just a *gringo*. I love my people. But then this man's body says to him that there are diamonds in the hair of the white woman."

"I promise I won't put a finger to anybody's hair."

"This he believes over what his head says to him."

"Maybe somebody else. Not me."

"I hope so. You take a big tree in the rain forest, it is used to all this water and being where the air is warm. You take this same tree and put it in a place where there is not so much rain and the air is cold, this tree becomes a little bush. Some person comes along and steps on the bush. Poof! Now the bush is dead. You never see it again."

"I know who I am," Maximo said firmly. There was a comfortable feeling to the conversation, a sense of security that always was present when he spoke to Mama, even in short bursts such as this. Her mythology was closer to what he was than all the subclauses with which he spent nearly all his time. He felt close enough to her to assume the lectern himself.

"I hope that you know what you're doing," he said to Mama, indicating Teenager. The moral advantage that caused these words to be spoken evaporated in her steady gaze, one that did not permit a fleck of concern to appear in the eyes.

"The spirits tell me what I must do. You do not want to hear them, so you must go try to live by what you think yourself. That is very hard."

Teenager came over to them and Maximo said he didn't feel like going inside for the show and would leave them to talk. Teenager was too intent on speaking to Mama to mind that Maximo, whom he had practically ordered to appear, now was walking away to the subway.

"There goes the fresh bastard," Myles said, watching Maximo.

"I don't know him," Hansen said. "Told you about the woman. She's Teenager's voodoo woman. Don't know the kid at all."

"I got half a mind to take a ride with him and see who he is," Myles said.

"The main chance is here," Hansen said, his eyes on Teenager, who stood under the movie marquee with Mama. Hansen and Myles were in the rear of a hot dog counter directly across the street. On the counter under his elbow Myles had a manila envelope filled with pictures of Chita Gonzalez; the tools of an inexperienced but willing picador.

"Junkie woman in a religion for junkies," Myles said. Earlier, as they had dawdled through the morning until the hour was proper for Teenager to appear on the streets, Myles had attended mass at St. Raymond's Church in Parkchester while Hansen remained in the car with the newspapers. Sitting with a crowd filled with sad oval Irish faces, Myles felt the safety and superiority of people residing in a holy fortress; the idea of this refuse across the street at the movie house considering itself members of a religion infuriated him.

"A real dope religion," Myles said.

"Don't know about that," Hansen said. "I don't pass on any man's way of praying."

"You're not saying that's a real religion?" Myles said.

"To me, they all get kind of real," Hansen said.

Myles was starting to say something else when Hansen pointed to the assemblage moving into the theater across the street.

"I'm going in there," Myles said.

He walked over to the theater alone, carrying the envelope of Chita Gonzalez pictures. A short man in a brown suit and yellow shirt open at the collar peered out of the doorway behind the ticket-taker and waved his hand at the woman selling tickets. "It's a pleasure to see you, Officer," he called out, holding the door for Myles, who stepped inside and slipped into a seat in the last row. On stage, three men in African dress walked out into soft red light and began to pound their long hands on high drums. In the darkness, Myles could see bodies in the rows about him rocking and swaying to the bare hands pounding on the drums. As Myles became used to the darkness he began to look around for Teenager and Mama, but could see neither.

They were sitting on a couch covered with cracked brown leather that was against the stucco wall of a corridor that ran the length of the far side of the theater.

"The saint says that Teenager should only be with Spanish people," Mama said.

"That is easy for the saint to say. The Guineas own everything."

"You must listen to the saint or he will not help you anymore," Mama said.

"What am I going to do if I can't do a business with the Guineas?"

"Where do you buy cocaine from?" Mama asked.

"From everybody in Jackson Heights. Ramirez. This guy Dominguen."

"They are Spanish."

"All Colombians. But they have no heroin like I need."

"The saint says you are to get the heroin only from Spanish people," Mama said.

"Where do I do this? Go to San Pedro and buy from Ralphie Gomez? He gets it from the Guineas too."

"Spanish," Mama said again.

"Mexico is Spanish. All they have is brown rocks. They sell it all over in Los Angeles. It is weak dope. You step on it five or six times and it is dead."

"The saint will say that brown rocks that are not so strong are better than white dope from the Guinea."

"You know he will say this?" Teenager said.

"He has said it many times. He spoke to me that you will make many millions by staying only with the Spanish people. The saint says only the Spanish can make you very rich. Spanish are not like the Guineas, who think you are dirt in a field."

For a mind geared to the formation of conspiracies to get a can of tuna fish into a prison, Teenager was uncomfortable with the simplicity of Mama's program. Also the necessity of going to Los Angeles, going to Mexico, to Tampico, probably, where Gonzales from Ponce stayed, sold dope nice, everybody said, or to some other places in Mexico, Culiacán for sure, bothered Teenager. How could it be that he lived in the Bronx, sold dope in the Bronx, did so many favors for people in the Bronx and still he had to go away? How could this man Mariani, whose nephew he had helped so much in jail, not only try to kill him, but now make the matter serious by cutting off his dope? This was unheard of, a big shot not wanting to sell dope to someone reliable. Usually, nearly all time in the dope business was spent trying to find new customers to replace the old ones who were killed for nonpay-

ment. Not to sell to someone because you didn't like
him? Only a crazy man would do that.

For a moment, Teenager thought of Paulie and his new
capped teeth. How could anybody get so mad about such
a bad guy? As he continued brooding, he realized that he
had no alternative except to listen to the saints. He could
keep doing business for only a little while longer before
somebody, Pedro Torres, would simply replace him on
the matter of supply and demand alone. Teenager could
hustle dope from Jackson Heights and some from San
Pedro and rob and kill for it in other places. At the end,
however, Pedro Torres and his good white would take
over everything.

Teenager then thought that while he despised the idea
of having to go elsewhere, a trip to Mexico could be the
path that would take him up to a high plateau where he
could stroll across sloping grass and peer down at a river
below and, off at one edge of the field, see another man
strolling and this of course would be Rockefeller. With
Mexican dope, Teenager thought, he surely could be like
Rockefeller, who had the oil and the place to turn it into
gasoline. He, Teenager, would have the poppy and the
place to turn it into dope.

He took Mama's hand and told her, "I do just what the
saints say."

As they stepped out of the corridor, the theater manager walked toward them, waving something in his hand.

"The cop just gave it to me," he said. He handed
Teenager a picture of Chita Gonzalez.

"Which cop?"

"The white cop sitting in the last row there."

"Why are you showing this picture to me?" Teenager
said.

"The cop told me to," the manager said.

"That's all right," Teenager said.

Teenager retreated into the corridor, went out through
a fire exit and asked a boy on the side street to go around
to Broadway and tell the two men in the double-parked
Mercedes to come and get him.

On the stage in the theater, men bare to the waist stood
in the red light, chanting in Yorubic and waving spears.

As they shook their legs, small bells attached to their white pants sounded over the thumping of the drums behind them. The audience first chanted with the dancers and now writhed with them, causing the tired seats to squeak loudly, as if all in the theater were aboard an old wooden ship. Myles, sitting in the last row, was uneasy to the point of fear: all these dark bastards jumping themselves into such excitement that they might turn, maybe all of them had spears under the seats, and pounce on Myles. He was sorry that he had given the theater manager the picture of Chita Gonzalez; it could wind up as a match thrown into oil.

He turned his head and looked into the darkness for Teenager. Suddenly, a woman with long dark hair hanging halfway down the back of a blue dress ran barefooted down the aisle and onto the stage. Eyes closed, arms out, she swayed to Yorubic chants. A hand reached out of the wings and placed a large candle, shoulder high, in a red holder, on the stage. A towering man, bare-chested, strings of red and white beads around his neck, wearing long white satin pants with red strings hanging from them, came out and stood alongside the candle and chanted to the woman, who danced furiously. The flame in the candle was steady and held Myles' eyes for a moment. The woman in blue, hair flying, legs flashing, yelped and ripped open the top of her dress. She danced in a white bra and then pulled that off, shook the dress from her hips and soon was dancing as naked as she was ecstatic. The candle flame now came over the top of the holder. The drums quickened and the bare brown woman's body tried to keep pace with the hands thumping on the drums. The woman convulsed and screamed. Myles saw the candle flame come high out of the holder, three feet high, he was certain, and grow fat; he was afraid it would touch the curtain and set it afire. The audience groaned and shouted. The bare woman ran off the stage and threw herself on the floor in front of the cardinal, who leaned forward in his seat and placed his hands on her head. The candle flame on the stage immediately dropped back inside the red holder.

Myles jumped as a hand touched him.

"The button," Mama said.

"What button?" Myles said nervously.

"This one." She touched a button that was hanging from the cuff of his checked polyester jacket.

Myles looked down at it. "Oh, that one."

"Can I fix it for you?" Mama said.

Black face shining, eyes unblinking, red and white beads around her neck, the dark people everywhere about him shrieking. When Myles did not answer or move, Mama reached for the button.

"I fix this button," she said. Her fingers pulled the button off the jacket. She stared directly into his eyes as one hand went into a straw purse and brought out a black cloth. She held the cloth in the palm of one hand and muttered a prayer in African. She dropped the button onto the cloth, then her hand closed on the cloth and placed it back into the straw bag. Her chin came up in a gesture of triumph.

"I take this button and fix it in the cemetery."

She turned and walked down the aisle between the rows of writhing, chanting dark people.

.... Chapter 16

The day flight from New York arrived at midafternoon in Mexico City, where Gonzales, whom Teenager knew from the whorehouse in Belgica, the black section of Ponce, picked him up in a yellow BMW. As there is a 100 percent tax on imported cars in Mexico, Gonzales could not be a figure of importance unless he drove such a car for all to see and immediately respect. It was one of three he owned, the others being kept in Tampico, a tough dock town on the Gulf of Mexico where he did most of his trading business, and Culiacán, the city in the mountains of the West Coast where farmers could see no difference between growing poppy and cauliflower. Both required the same bent back, except that poppy was more valuable and therefore until such time as cauliflower similarly excited purchasers, the farmer's landscapes, hidden in ravines, would consist of as much poppy as the earth could hold.

At the section of Mexico City to which Gonzales drove Teenager, Zona Rosa, there was an outdoor cafe amidst the splendor of the Calle Genoa where a man of perhaps an inch over five feet directed a dancing bear through what seemed like a cheerful routine. On hind legs, the bear was at least two feet higher than the master, who held the bear by chain with one hand and poked a short heavy stick into the bear's body with the other. Alongside the animal, the man looked like an active tree stump.

"*Jabéalo*," young men at tables called. The short man sunk the stick into the bear's flank. The pain caused the bear to grunt and sway his hips. The young men at the tables laughed and called for more.

The bear should eat the little man in front of these *maricónes* at the table, Teenager thought. He found his next thought more important: The realization that this was the first time in his life he had been with Hispanic people when they were customers of a place such as this, sitting in indolence, being as obnoxious as any white person with money, not chasing around as busboys. There were blinding white tablecloths and a sidewalk of dark pink lava stone, and art galleries and silver shops lined the cosmopolitan street, whose traffic consisted mainly of BMW's and Mercedes cars.

In Ponce, there had been rich families, the Serralles, Mayorales, Carbones and Vassallos, but never once had Teenager been in the same place with them. Here in Mexico City, everyone spoke Spanish and had skin of color and most had high cheekbones, but because they were of some wealth they were seated at tables with expensive drinks and demanding that the short man jab the bear with his stick.

We do not have to live like dogs in the Bronx, either, Teenager told himself. Someday, all my people in the Bronx will be living like this, with waiters who bow because there will be much tips if they provide the feeling of importance. My business will accomplish all this; the only reason they try to stop me from doing my business is that I pay no taxes. Someday, they will realize that all the people want dope and someone has to sell it to them, so the government might as well collect taxes. Then I will pay them taxes and sit at any table in New York City, with rich white women at the very next table, and I will be treated better than the white women because the waiter knows where the best tip comes from.

On his second drink, when he felt lazy enough to sleep at the table, he shook himself and said to Gonzales, "Tell me, brother, what do we do?"

"Fly to Culiacán on the seven o'clock plane. It only takes an hour and forty-five minutes."

"Who do we see there?"

"The man I do business with."

"Will he do a business with me?"

"Yes."

"Why should he do this when he doesn't know me?"

"Because of me," Gonzales said.

"I haven't seen you in years," Teenager said.

"You have a city," Gonzales said. "If I don't see you for a century, I want to do a business with you immediately because you come from a city."

At Culiacán, a shabby pastel city surrounded by dark mountains, they were met at the airport by a man introduced as El Manillo who was about twenty-five and had sullen lips and a thin neck laden with enough gold chains to approximate a medical brace. He drove a Mercedes that had no license plates. Beside El Manillo on the front seat was a fourteen-shot Browning .9 millimeter High-Power pistol. El Manillo, saying nothing, drove to a parking lot across the street from the side entrance to the Hotel Ejecutivo, then led Teenager and Gonzales into the bar, where he slid into a booth alongside an older man who sat heavy-eyed, a bottle of beer in his hands.

"Wake up," El Manillo said to the man.

"The beer puts him to sleep," Teenager said.

"He is to farm . . . he is a farmer," El Manillo said. "Arizmendi, say hello."

When Arizmendi only nodded, Teenager said, "Wake up. We must wake up Arizmendi. Here, Arizmendi, something to drink for Arizmendi. Two, brandy."

"Ah, enough, ah, I don't need anything," Arizmendi said.

"He's all right," El Manillo said. He looked hard at Teenager. "My friend here," he said, touching Gonzales, "says that you are from a city. What city?"

"All the cities," Teenager said.

"Detroit City?"

"Just one city. Soon I will live in all the cities in America."

"But you live now in New York City?"

"Why do you ask if you know?" Teenager said.

"Because Gonzales tells me. I just wanted to see what you told me."

"Do you know where Detroit City is?" Teenager asked.

"No. They make cars, that's all I know."

Teenager laughed. "Someday I will own New York City and Detroit. I will be like Rockefeller."

"The best poppy is in his ground," El Manillo said, indicating Arizmendi.

"This will make me Rockefeller," Teenager said.

"I know this name," El Manillo said.

"This is the man who owns my city," Teenager said. "Maybe he owns this city of yours too. What we are discussing from now on, brother, is exactly how Rockefeller started. All the storybooks tell this to you. The grandfather of Rockefeller brought in opium. The government yelled at him. It was too late, man. The grandfather had all the money. He was bringing opium in, stepping on it himself, selling it himself. Top to bottom, man. Just what I'm going to do. It was easy for the grandfather to go into oil. He had all the money from dope, brother."

"With a farm you could do this?" El Manillo said.

"I have to try to do it all by myself. Rockefeller will try to put me in jail for all of my life. He knows that I am starting just the way he did. He is afraid that I will become as big as he is. I will have all this money. I am not a white man. The Arabs will like me. If I have money they will give me some of Rockefeller's oil. Then I will be as important as Rockefeller."

As Arizmendi now was asleep, El Manillo said they would meet at noon the next day in the hotel. Teenager and Gonzales remained in the bar for an hour and then took rooms for the night. The next day, El Manillo called and said he could not be there because of a birthday party for the aunt of his wife. He reset the date for the following day, at which time he arrived with a wide-awake Arizmendi. El Manillo also had five thousand grams of brown heroin as a sample of the quality of the farmer's crop. Teenager reached into the bag El Manillo had on the chair alongside him and put some of the heroin on the tip of his tongue. He looked upward as he judged the bitterness.

"I will have to try this in New York," he said.

"I used to use some of it for food," Arizmendi said. "The seeds are very good for children."

"All the people eat the seeds," El Manillo said.

"Because of the good oil," Arizmendi said.

"Not this year," Teenager said.

"This year I take the rubber from every plant," Arizmendi said.

"Good rubber. Dope rubber," El Manillo said.

El Manillo paid the check and took the group out to a black vinyl-top red Ford LTD. As they were getting into the car, a man in a yellow shirt walked over and started talking to El Manillo.

"We are going for a ride," El Manillo said.

"I want to do a business," the yellow shirt said.

"Get in," El Manillo said.

El Manillo drove to a rundown section called Tierra Blanca, which had narrow streets, one of which was blocked by a man riding a barebacked farm horse. They stopped at a two-story green wood building that had been cut up into apartments. El Manillo opened a first-floor apartment that had two stained mattresses on the floor and a table and a couple of broken chairs.

Teenager put twenty-nine thousand dollars in fives, tens and twentys on the table as payment for part ownership in Arizmendi's poppy farm. When it was counted, it was El Manillo who took the money.

"Do you want to see the farm?" Teenager's friend Gonzales said.

"Of course."

El Manillo and Arizmendi sat in the front seat and Teenager, Gonzales and the man in the yellow shirt sat in the back. As the car drove out of Culiacán, the man in the yellow shirt asked Teenager, "What is your name again?"

"Teenager."

"*Joven*," the yellow shirt said to himself, in Spanish, in order to help memorize the name.

"And you are from New York City?"

"Yes," Teenager said. He said it uneasily, and he was
sure that he was going to get the yellow shirt alone sometime during the day and choke him and ask him why he
asked so many questions. Just then, El Manillo said to
the yellow shirt, "Why did you want to come on this ride
with us?"

"I just want to do a business with you. I have nothing
else to do."

El Manillo nodded. He drove on Federal Highway 6
and then to Autopista de Culiacán Litoral. After an hour
on the highway, he drove up to a restaurant called the
Barba Azul. He said that from this point on, the drive
was into the mountains and could only be made with a
four-wheel-drive jeep. Sometime in the next few hours,
he said, a man from Arizmendi's farm would come to the
restaurant in such a vehicle.

El Manillo took Teenager off to the side. "This guy
with us, I don't like him," he said. The man in the yellow
shirt sat and drank beer with Arizmendi.

"Why do you keep him with you?" Teenager said.

"So he won't be around to bother me some other day,"
El Manillo said.

"Do what you have to do, brother," Teenager said.

"I wish we didn't have to wait here all day," El Manillo said.

"So we won't wait," Teenager said.

"It's just a farm," Teenager's friend Gonzales said.
"It grows from the ground, brother, I guarantee you
that."

Teenager shook hands with Arizmendi and said he
couldn't wait for the trip to the farm.

A shadow of disappointment appeared on yellow
shirt's eyes and just as quickly went away. Yellow shirt
got into the front seat with El Manillo and they drove
back to Culiacán. El Manillo drove the car onto an empty
street and stopped in front of the church of Nuestra Se-
ñora de Guadalupe.

"You get out now," he told yellow shirt.

"Why?"

"Because we are going someplace and you cannot
come."

As the man got out of the car, El Manillo shot him four times in the back of the yellow shirt, pulled the car door shut and drove back to the Tierra Blanca, where Teenager and Gonzales left in a taxicab for the airport and the evening plane back to Mexico City.

The dead man in the yellow shirt was identified later as Rafael Torres-Cruz, Mexican Federal Judicial Police informant number 7–376–4532. He became the 976th homicide in Culiacán from the period, 1 January 1977 until 14 August 1977. The local police, State of Sinaola Police Department, announced that it would investigate the death. The Mexican Federal Judicial Police in charge said that his investigation was hampered because any legitimate inquiry would have to be done in the area known as Tierra Blanca, and no police agents of any sort were allowed in that section by the people who reside there.

Back in Mexico City, watching the dancing bear at night, Teenager felt highly prosperous.

He no longer had to beg for dope, he reminded himself. Now he grew it.

....**Chapter 17**

....

When she heard her mother caterwauling somewhere in the back of the house, Nicki called from the kitchen.

"You better," her mother shrieked.

"Better what?"

"You just better." Her mother was in the hallway.

"You better tell me what these are doing in your closet," the mother said, carrying in the three boxes of towels that Nicki had bought for Maximo.

Nicki's answer was to sip her coffee.

The top of her mother's blue quilted housecoat expanded as she took a deep, angry breath. A wind shear came from her mouth. "I'm looking for a place on your shelf to put your pocketbook and I find these boxes and I say, 'What the hell is this?' So I open them up and look what I find. We got no orange towels in this house. We got every color in the world, we got no orange towels in this house." She took the top off a box to show good, heavy Martex orange towels.

"They're a shower gift," Nicki said.

"Yeah? For who?"

Nicki looked up from her fingernails and into her mother's eyes. There was no way that she could lie to the woman; the mother felt that anyone who could state an untruth to her was insulting her very being. How could she, the mother made it plain, who in her own life kept truth in captivity and regarded a lie as a statement of

218

strength and superiority over the person being spoken to, allow herself to be manipulated by the lie of another? And for her own daughter to attempt even elementary deceit was utter betrayal.

"For nobody," Nicki said.

"Well," the mother said, putting the boxes on the table.

"Ma, it was either this or go crazy."

"But you go to see him."

"Ma."

"I guess so. But you were so good for so long."

"And I've been going crazy for so long."

"He'll get paroled."

"Ma, this got nothing to do with him. The minute he comes out, I live my life out to the end with him. This thing now has got to do with me. I can't last anymore."

"Only to the parole," the mother said.

"The minute I hear he's getting out."

"This guy now, he's not Italian," the mother said.

"Of course not," Nicki said. "Then the whole world would know."

"Swear on God."

"I swear."

"Oh, if your father ever knew. That would be the end of everything."

"Don't I know that! Ma, he'll never know anything."

"Does that mean this guy is Irish?"

"No."

"At least I could be thankful for that."

"He's Puerto Rican."

The mother gathered the boxes and stood up. "Don't make no jokes with me. You're playing with our lives here."

"It's the truth, Ma."

The mother, paying no attention to this, said, "There's ways that these things are supposed to be done. The women have to wait for the men. So all right. A little something goes on that nobody has to know about. But don't make no jokes about it. Because if we ever got caught, believe me, it would be no joke."

"What do you mean *we* got caught?"

"Because even if I don't want to know nothing more about it, which I don't, I'll still get blamed for it."

"By Ronnie?"

"Ronnie. He better not say anything to me about anything or I'll slap him like a fag. Your father is the one I'm worried about. He'll blame me."

"Ma, he'll never know."

"He better not."

The mother left the kitchen with the towel boxes and Nicki sat with coffee and thought of how Maximo would look with the bright orange towel wrapped around his waist. Standing in the bedroom, the towel knotted at the side and hanging up on its own because the waist was so beautifully proportioned. Looking for something on the bureau. While I'm in his bed looking at his back, Nicki thought.

She had made a date to bring the towels to his house on a Saturday, a day Maximo had spent in the red brick library on Southern Boulevard, a small building that sat amid the ruins that ran for so many blocks that to concentrate on them was to strain the vision. Bleached by the sun, the ruins took on the quality of a desert, the library becoming a French outpost in the sand. Two dogs, outcasts from an Arab alley, were on the sidewalk in front of the library, gnawing at fleas on their flanks. When the library closed at four o'clock, Maximo walked past the dogs, along with the only two people who had been in the reading room with him, an old woman, who had gone through a book on Thomas Jefferson, and a boy of about twelve, whose afternoon had been spent taking notes from a picture-and-text book about iron forging in Colonial times.

As Maximo walked home, he at first felt depressed that he was passing up a study group at somebody's house that night in Riverdale; the Protestant ethic, even vaccinated into tan skins, takes. Then he thought of seeing Nicki, of talking to her and adoring her body and impressing her with his conversation, which would delight her because he was probably the only one she had ever

known who used his head for something more complicated than butting down doors.

As Maximo reached his corner, he heard a high wail
and he turned and saw David Robles walking swiftly
down the block, calling into the air. With him was a taller
kid named Pedro.

David half ran and half loped, his body spilling in many
directions.

"*Yo*, Maximo," David called.

Maximo looked at him carefully. David's face and the
front of his hair was covered with scum.

"Fucked up," Pedro said.

"*Yo*, Maximo, fist fight," David said. He began flailing
the air, first leading with his right hand and then turning
around and leading with his left hand and then stopping
in the middle of a punch and putting the right hand in
front.

"Which hand are you supposed to hold out?" Maximo
said to him. "Are you right-handed or left-handed?"

David shrugged.

"Which hand do you eat with?" Maximo said.

David looked at his hands for a moment, let a scream
come out of his mouth and ran across the street to his
doorway, an uncontrolled screech coming from him.

"Fucked up on glue, man," Pedro said.

Maximo shook his head.

"He didn't do it by himself," Pedro said.

"What did he do, catch it like it's a cold?" Maximo
said.

"These older dudes come and they say, '*Yo*, Pedro.
Yo, David. Come over here.' I was afraid to go over with
them, because they bad dudes. David, he goes over to
them and they take him and put his head in this bag and
tell him to breathe or they kick his ass. He doesn't know
what he's doing. They made him do it, man."

Maximo first thought about going over to David's
house, but then he decided he would let the mother handle it this time, although he would have to talk to her
very soon about the boy's hand confusion. If the boy
didn't know his right from a left in a fist fight, then surely
he could not tell a "d" from a "b" in school, and proba-

bly had greater difficulties than that. He decided to pursue this at another time. He went up to the apartment and brought the dog down. Unleashed, the dog lunged into the free air and tore down the empty street, a tan blur. Maximo sat on the curb and each time the dog came racing back, Maximo waved him off. He wanted the dog tired for the night, so no paw would be scratching his door.

When he opened the door for her, Nicki brushed past him, her arms wrapped about a package, and when his hand came after her, she shook her head.

"I have to do something right away. Before we get all involved."

"Do what?"

"This," she said, opening the package and pulling out one of the orange towels.

"Are they for here?"

"How could you ask? With the rags you use, you think you don't need new towels?"

She put a couple in the bathroom and then began walking around, looking for a closet.

"The only closet I have is in here," Maximo said, walking into the bedroom.

She followed him in, dropped the towels on the bed and reached up onto the closet shelf.

"Fil*thy*," she said. "I got to do something about that." She walked out to the kitchen, and Maximo looked out the window to see if by some chance David was back out on the street.

"I can't put new towels into a filthy place like this," she said when she returned. Standing on her toes, she wiped the closet shelf. "What are you looking for?" she said as she dusted.

"The boy across the street. He was obliterated when he was around before."

"Has he become your little charge?" she asked.

"No. But he does live across the street from me."

"Stay out of it," she said.

"What should I do? Make believe I didn't see him? Woman's trying to raise him by herself."

"If you let one account tie you up, you won't get the whole job done," she said. "You could spend your lifetime on one kid. Concentrate on getting someplace. And taking care of me."

He approached her from the back and put his arms on her shoulders and she leaned into him and craned her neck as he kissed it.

"You walked in here without even a 'hello,' " he said.

"I want to get these towels fixed. Besides, you got your little friend across the street on your mind."

"No, I don't," he said, kissing her again.

She turned around and held up a finger. "Speaking of friends. You're doing what I told you about the other one."

"Who?"

"Who. You know who. Your marvelous friend with the beard."

"Teenager? I haven't seen him in so long I forgot who you were talking about."

"You better," she said. "Because I like what I see when I come here. And I don't want to see you dead."

She smiled and then kissed him and, controlling the kiss, moved with him to a bed which became sweet.

Teenager's business now started in Mexico and came to the streets of the Bronx by methods as complicated and eventful as a bus ride. His partner in Mexico, El Manillo, collected black ovals of poppy gum from Arizmendi, the farmer outside Culiacán. El Manillo drove up the federal highway to the border with the black ovals of poppy gum, double-wrapped in plastic, stuffed into the front housing of a four-wheel drive. The trip took nine hours and El Manillo drove through the border station without taking a deep breath, for he crossed only during those times when his personal American border guard, a man who believed in supplemental income, was on duty. While tourists had cameras taken apart and college students were searched internally, El Manillo and his pounds of dope were waved on. In the backyard of a grocery store in the Boyle Heights section of Los Angeles, he was met, on schedule, by Benny or Albertito. El

Manillo usually had stuffed into the front of his four-wheel drive some twenty rubbery ovals, each weighing a kilogram, or 2.2 pounds. They were placed into an attaché case, sprinkled with perfume to smother any possible scent that an airport search dog might catch, and then hand-carried on a domestic commercial flight to New York. El Manillo, with twenty-five thousand dollars for himself, the farmer Arizmendi and others in the Culiacán economy, slid back into his jeep and headed for home.

In the Bronx, the drugs were taken to a garage between factory buildings on Bruckner Boulevard, a few blocks away from Ana's Bar. Gilberto Dones, his face covered by a surgical mask, wearing only undershorts, worked on the material under blazing arc lights and in the noise of old exhaust fans. He turned the black ovals of gum from Culiacán into heroin for the streets of the Bronx. Gilberto worked from a recipe on the wall of his garage. As Gilberto did not understand what he was doing, he did not go one breath past the recipe. He had heard about the Italians using chemists to make their heroin, which puzzled Dones for he found the process required not as much ability as baking pizzas. Dones used large drums, cheesecloth filters, hydrochloric acid and acetic anhydrite. To Dones, the chemicals he used might as well have been baking powder. But in continually filtering his mixtures through cheesecloth and drying the crystals under the arc lights, Dones was able to take twenty kilograms of black poppy gum from Culiacán and turn it into two kilograms of 90 percent pure heroin. At the completion of the day's work, Dones, cockeyed from heroin fumes, walked around the garage and told himself that he was in a Spanish castle.

The drugs were stored in a hundred and ninety-five dollar a month apartment on Strathmore Avenue, twenty-five blocks from Ana's Bar. Living in the apartment was Junior Mendez, his wife Mirta, their baby Ramon, and three Doberman pinschers who were fed just enough to keep their black coats stretched across rangy bones. Each dog had a scar on his throat from an operation that removed the voice box, this to make certain that the dogs could give no warning of their presence to an invader. A bark, a growl of anticipation, an angry whine could alert such a person and provide time for shooting the dogs, who were kept in a small windowless room with the heroin, which was in suitcases. The floor was covered with newspapers that served the same purpose as straw in a horse's stall. When acute hunger caused the dogs to gnaw at the suitcases and thump against the door, Junior Mendez opened the door slightly and pushed in paper plates of dog food and a bucket of water.

Junior and his wife slept on a mattress on the living room floor, a shotgun beside the mattress. The baby was in a cardboard box. The only other furniture in the apartment was a large table and a television set that Junior stared at day and night. Under the terms of his employment, he was not allowed to leave the house when dope was in it. On the few days that there was no dope, Junior would feed the dogs enough to calm them, clean out their room and take them out for silent runs through Crotona Park.

Teenager and Benny Velez came to the apartment in the middle of the morning to work on the drugs. Using a window pole, Junior slid the suitcases out of the dogs' room. On the table in the living room Teenager stacked packages of quinine, which he had bought for five hundred dollars a pound. Measuring with a gram scale, he put together two packages, each containing an eighth of a kilo of the 90 percent heroin. These were for customers willing to pay six thousand dollars for each eighth. He also measured several one-ounce bags of pure heroin that would be sold in bars in the grisly nights. Teenager took the remaining heroin, spilled it onto the table, and doubled its size by adding quinine. Then he and Benny, using tin quarter-inch pastry spoons, measured six spoons of quinine to each of heroin, packaged the mixture—got it "decked up"—in envelopes that were of the same size and paper as used for postage stamps. These envelopes were the spinal cord of the drug trade and at this time, 1976, could be bought for two dollars a bag from one of Teenager's dealers.

* * *

"It is very good," Teenager said to one of his dealers, Indio, at the bar in the afternoon.

"Let me find out," Indio said.

"Give it to everyone to see that it is the best," Teenager said.

Indio went to the back of the place and stood at a door alongside the one to the men's room. Luisa Maria reached under the bar, pressed a buzzer and the door unlocked. Indio went up a short flight of stairs to a heavy metal door that had a two-way mirror as a window. A slot in the door opened. "What did he say?" Benny Velez' voice called out.

"Enough to test it with everyone on the street."

Benny stuck five bags through the slot. Indio took them with him to St. Anselm's Avenue.

"Shake hands with me," he said to Chino, who stood by the newsstand. Chino's face brightened as he felt the heroin decks.

"Share with your friends," Indio said.

Indio stood by the newsstand and read the Spanish paper, *El Diario*.

Twenty minutes later, Chino walked back to the newsstand. He was yawning, his hands clawing the sides of his face.

"Where did you cop?" a guy asked him.

"Indio."

"That's good stuff, man," the guy said. "Where is Indio?"

Chino gave a great yawn and pointed to Indio.

"Indio," the guy said.

"You come later," Indio said.

Indio went back to the bar and told Teenager he would handle the new dope from Mexico. He asked for forty half loads—"half los." A half lo is a set of fifteen packets that cost Indio twenty dollars to buy from Teenager and which, sold on the streets for two dollars each, would give Indio a profit of ten dollars. Indio's order of forty half loads, six hundred doses of heroin for street junkies, would bring Teenager eight hundred dollars and Indio four hundred dollars, if all money was faithfully paid.

"Write it down," Teenager said to Albertito, who sat at the bar.

"Give me a pencil," Albertito said.

"I have none," Teenager said.

Luisa Maria looked around the bar and found a ball-point pen.

"Now give me paper," Albertito said.

Luisa went through her purse and came out with a bill from a boutique. Albertito made a note on the back of it.

"Indio has four days to pay for the forty half los," Teenager said.

"I pay in two days," Indio said. "Then I want forty more half los."

"That's all right," Teenager said.

At eight o'clock the next morning, Indio heard knocking on his door. Through his peephole he saw two junkies.

"What?"

"A half lo."

"You got to be crazy."

"We got some dudes waitin'." He ran a hand over a pockmarked face.

"Show me the money," Indio said.

The pockmarked face held a fist up to the peephole and opened it. Indio looked at the crumpled bills.

"How much is there?"

"Twenty-four dollar, man."

"A half lo is thirty dollar."

"I promise you on my mother I be back at eleven-thirty with the money. Then I bring you even more business."

"Let me see the money again."

The hand held the money up to the peephole. Sixteen, Indio said to himself.

A door opened at the end of the hall and the junkies, startled, looked at it. The door at the end of the hall closed. The girl, Indio thought.

He went to his bedroom, which was a room without doors between the kitchen and the living room. His wife and boys, both under ten, sat in pajamas on the living room couch and watched the Flintstone cartoon. Indio reached under his shirts in the dresser and brought out nine bags of heroin. They want a half lo, they must think my brain died, he thought. He went back to the door, which was spangled with locks and draped with chains. Indio took a .357 Magnum out of his belt, held it in his right hand and opened the door with his left. The three chains allowed the door to open just wide enough for the fingertips of a hand to stick through.

"Money," Indio said.

The hand came in and Indio snatched the money, then passed out the nine bags of heroin.

"All right, man," the pockmark said. "If it's good we tell everybody we know."

In the apartment at the end of the hallway, Francisca Perez leaned against the door she had just closed.

"Didn't you leave?" her sister called from the bedroom.

"I'm still here," Francisca said.

"You'll be late for your job."

"I cannot help this."

"They will take out of your pay."

"I won't go out while those bad men are standing there."

"They are just buying dope. That is none of your business." Her sister, body bulging with an imminent child, shuffled out of the bedroom. "Just walk past them and go to work."

Francisca shut her eyes and did not move. She was fourteen. The sister, Gloria, was eighteen. In June, Francisca came to New York from Santurce because her sister, who had been in New York for three years, had promised to find her a good high school for science. Francisca came to New York on a Sunday night to find her sister pregnant and without a husband. On Monday morning, the sister took Francisca to the top floor of a factory building on Bruckner Boulevard. The sister told the foreman that she was quitting and that Francisca would take her place. Gloria went home to bed and Francisca sat at a sewing machine and worked on quilted robes for a salary of seventy dollars and fifty cents a week, thirty dollars under the federal minimum wage. The factory windows were kept closed for the summer, and there were no fans inside, because any breeze would disturb the material on the sewing machines. Francisca cried as she worked. In September, when it was time for Francisca to go to school, the sister still would call out from the bedroom each morning, "Time to go to work."

At fourteen, Francisca became a sparrow surrounded by iron, and as the first fall chill came through her summer clothes and caused her body to flinch, she realized that she no longer could comply with the rules of her life. Now, as she leaned against the door in the morning and waited for the junkies to leave the hallway, she once again tried to think of reasons that would make her suicide acceptable to God.

Three days later, Indio was in the hallway when Francisca passed. He smiled. When she got home from work, he was standing outside the apartment for a rare breath of air. He smiled and held the door for her. "Thank you," she said. The next morning, when Francisca gloomily left her apartment to go to work, Indio was in the hallway.

"You like your job?"

"I hate it."

"How much do you make?"

"Seventy-nine dollar."

"I pay you a hundred and fifty to stay in my apartment."

"Sex?" Francisca said.

"How could you ask me such a thing when you know that I am the father of children who live in the house with me? I just want you to stay in my house and give out dope at the door."

Under this new arrangement, with Francisca at home, Indio could go outside his apartment and enlarge his business through personal contacts. In Bronx County jail he had become known as the humorist of 6W, a prominent wing of the jail. He once fashioned a dummy in Gilberto Perez' bed by using a black cap, overcoat and shoes. He then ran into the dayroom and told Perez, "There's some big colored guy in your bed." Perez went into his shoe for a shiv and tip-toed up to the bed and attacked the dummy. Because of stories such as these, junkies smiled when they saw Indio. His trade grew even larger as he showed a persistence rarely seen: he would sell a "bundle" of ten bags for fifteen dollars to a junkie and then stand outside an abandoned building until the junkie had gone into the shooting gallery, sold everything and came out with the fifteen dollars.

.... **Chapter 18**

....

Christmas Eve, which supersedes Christmas Day in religious and family significance to Puerto Ricans, fell on a Thursday that year. On Monday of that week, Teenager was aggravated to find himself in the same defensive circumstances as some *pendejito* sent out to the store by his wife. He knew of his situation immediately that morning, when he arose to find his wife moving briskly about a kitchen whose surfaces were covered with the white yucca vegetable and plantains that would be formed into *pasteles,* meat pies, for the Christmas Eve feast. Usually, Teenager's appearances at home were sporadic, with arrivals and departures made without as much as a nod to the kitchen. This time, arising into eleven o'clock activity rather than midafternoon emptiness, he was attracted and then trapped by his wife's preparations.

"My aunt and my cousins are coming for Christmas Eve," Lydia said.

"That's good," Teenager said. He was wrapped in a deep blue velour robe that allowed his thick, shaped calves to be displayed.

"Who are you telling to come?" Lydia said.

"All my friends."

Lydia's face, which usually had the character of wallpaper in Teenager's presence, now showed great displeasure. "I don't like your friends. Somebody nice must come."

A conversation such as this at any other time would be terminated with a snarl, a slap perhaps, a spinning around and exiting. Yet the most disoriented of Puerto Rican marriages became as formal as a high court during any holiday season, when relatives arrive to eat and peer and carry back to the family networks the precise estimates of the worth of the relationship they have observed. For the highest principle of all, form on a holiday, Lydia suddenly had her husband, for all his evil, pushed into a corner.

"Mama is coming too," Teenager said.

Lydia rocked her head from side to side in skepticism. "Mama is always somewhere in this house. Is that all we have coming? Mama and these people I don't like?"

"Oh, no," Teenager said. "Maximo and his mother are coming too. I asked them and they said they would be here."

Lydia's head turned quickly enough to show excitement and pleasure. She immediately tempered it with suspicion. "You asked them?" she said.

"Just the other day."

"Which other day?"

"Two, three days ago. I told them, 'You're coming Christmas Eve.' They both were very happy."

"I love Maximo's mother. I love Maximo," Lydia said.

"He is going to be an important man," Teenager said.

"Oh, yes. Everybody says that. What time did you tell Maximo and his mother to come?"

"At eight o'clock."

Lydia nodded in satisfaction as her hands resumed stuffing the plantain leaves with yucca.

Teenager drank grapefruit juice, then dressed and left for Ana's. A half hour later, as he walked into the bar, Luisa Maria said to him, "I have to go out shopping for some things."

"What things?"

"I have to get coconuts and buy good rum, not this rum you have here. I make *coquito* for you on Christmas Eve."

"Just for me?" Teenager said.

"Oh, no, I am having my brother and my brother's wife and all my nephews and my girlfriend. And you and Benny."

She looked at him through narrowed eyes. "You are coming to my house on Christmas Eve?"

"Certainly," Teenager said.

"What time will you be there?"

"Ten o'clock, eleven o'clock," Teenager said.

"You will be there," Luisa Maria said, with the same firmness exhibited by Lydia only a short time before.

Through the rest of the day, as he drove to collect money, Teenager planned his Christmas Eve. Because he had been in prison, he had not been obliged to do this for some time, but it was the usage of time by a Puerto Rican man on Christmas Eve, and then on New Year's Eve, that determined the condition of his sexual arrangements for the remainder of the year. On Christmas Eve, Teenager thought, if he could ease out of the big party at his own house, using a pretext that satisfied the wife, he then could rush to the house of Luisa Maria, remaining there just long enough to give her the satisfaction of his presence. He then would return to his own house and somewhere in the early hours of Christmas Day he would measure the situation and decide that he had made a great success of the night, that he had pleased both his wife and his girlfriend.

Following this, on New Year's Eve, he would have to be with Luisa Maria at the start of the evening, glancing at the clock as if working in a knitting mill, waiting until he could kiss her, promise to return before the night dissolved, and then whip out of her house and get home with only minutes left, perhaps five, before the most important moment of the year to a Puerto Rican, the moment of twelve, at which point he would have Lydia nestled comfortably in his arms and thus lulled for the year to come; as would, elsewhere, Luisa Maria, who understood that Teenager's promise to return on this night was a lie, but one that still showed that Teenager cared enough about her to make such a promise. Luisa Maria's view, Teenager knew, then would be that the man had spent so much of the evening with her as to make the moment of twelve a meaningless one for the stupid lazy sonofabitch who carried the title, Wife.

In order for him to carry out such exquisite timing, Teenager knew, the presence of Maximo in his house on Christmas Eve was crucial. Maximo was the only legitimate person Teenager knew, and it gave him a feeling of power to be able to say to Maximo, here, ride in the car with me and we will talk; here, meet my wife's cousin. Why hasn't Maximo been around for him to do this? Teenager also knew that Maximo's presence would impress Lydia's relatives so much that it immediately would reflect on Teenager to such a point that Lydia's family could overlook their distaste for him for what he did. With Maximo in his house, Teenager in the midst of the night could motion to Lydia and she would place her head to his lips and he would mumble that he had to leave for something important, that it would only take a short time, and Lydia would kiss him and say, you must return quickly or I will lock the door so that you never can get back in. She would say this mildly, however, and Teenager would translate the amount of acquiescence in her voice, as against the measure of hardness, into almost the exact amount of time he could spend with Luisa Maria.

At five-thirty on Monday night, December 21, Teenager drove up to Maximo's, went immediately upstairs to look for Maximo's mother, was annoyed to find that she had not returned from work, pounded down the stairs and drove over to Maximo's apartment where, again, there was no answer. He rang the doorbell downstairs and a square-faced woman answered.

"Do you know Maximo upstairs?"

"The new guy?"

"That's right. When you hear him come home, tell him that Teenager wants him. It is very important."

"Teenager?" the woman said.

"Tell him Teenager. He'll know."

"That's the name?" the woman said.

"You never heard of him?" Teenager said.

The woman's face not only was blank, but indicated lack of interest. Teenager's face flushed, as if the woman had just slapped him. He looked at her in disdain. Fat stupid Indian.

"Just tell Maximo Teenager."

He left, but was so annoyed by the woman that he had to go immediately to Mi Corazón, which was on Broadway and 138th Street, where the western edge of Harlem becomes Hispanic, and where the barmaid, Lucy, threw up her hands when he walked in and announced: "Here is the strongest man in New York City!" She ran down the bar and kissed him on the cheek. It was after eleven when he remembered that he had to find Maximo. Instead, he drove to Luisa Maria's apartment, remaining there until seven on Tuesday morning. When he arrived home, he went to bed without speaking.

When he got up at two that afternoon, he found Lydia in the kitchen chopping coconuts. "*Coquito*," she said.

"I will drink a tub of it," Teenager said.

"You spoke to Maximo?" Lydia said.

"I told you I did that before."

"Just making sure."

His son came in from playing in the apartment next door and Teenager swung him up to the ceiling. "Santa Claus will bring you a present that will make everybody jealous of you."

He was annoyed again that afternoon to walk into the bar and find that there was no word from Maximo or his mother despite his message. He decided to find Maximo by himself, but he did not know the exact name of the place where Maximo worked, and neither did anybody else around him. He then started for Westchester Avenue to look for Luis Jimenez' office, but on the way there remembered that he had to meet Albertito at four-thirty at the Carolina Social Club on 154th Street.

At six, with Albertito riding shotgun, he drove to the Soundview Projects, where three men sat in a basement apartment with shotguns and thirty-six thousand dollars in fives, tens and twenties. Teenager and Benny stepped in with drawn guns. Albertito held a kilo of heroin. The exchange was made and Benny and Teenager drove off with their money, then stopped five blocks away at a social club where a barmaid named Rosa sat alone in the early evening and promptly locked the door as she saw that the two wanted to do lines and were including her in. When Rosa got off at nine o'clock, they went to her apartment and spent the night.

On Wednesday, nervous and drinking and doing lines, Teenager walked around with his pockets filled with money until eight o'clock, when he went to LaRoche Motors, in Yonkers, which specialized in cars for pimps and dope dealers. He bought a Mercedes 220 for $23,000, which the salesman counted out in the locked office, then drove the new car home while Benny followed in his old Mercedes. In the trunk of the old Mercedes Teenager had a moped which he had bought from a junkie for two hundred dollars.

At five o'clock, with a finger on his lips, he lugged the moped into his bedroom.

"I am Santa Claus," he said.

Lydia looked at him crossly. "He is too young for such a thing."

"That's all right," Teenager said.

"What does he do with it?" she said.

Teenager closed his fist around the keys to the new Mercedes and held the fist in the air. "Inside my hand is your present from Santa Claus."

Lydia's eyes opened quite wide. "What is it?"

"Tomorrow night I give it to you," he said.

She dropped her head back on the pillow. "Tomorrow is today. You better hide it very good, because I will be cleaning the whole house for the company." Her head came off the pillow again. "Maximo and his mother are coming?"

"Of course," Teenager said, taking off his shirt. His hands stopped at the last button as he realized that not even the new car would make up for his loss of face and romance if Maximo was not present.

At eleven o'clock on Christmas Eve morning, Teenager arrived at Ana's, holding a hand in the air to prevent Luisa Maria from speaking first.

"I will be at your house this night," he said.

"What time?" she demanded.

"Nine o'clock, ten o'clock."

"And you are staying?"

"I will party all night with you."

Teenager felt his nerves rustling. At any other time, he thought again, he would slap his wife and slap this female. But the meaning of holidays to women had left him tied with a thousand ropes. And the simplest task, getting Maximo, had eluded him.

Teenager went around to Indio's apartment, where Francisca stood on the stoop with two other women. The two women held large cans of Spaghetti-Os that had steam coming out of them. Their children, playing on the sidewalk, would run up the stoop, receive a spoonful of the canned spaghetti and, lips orange, return to playing. Francisca stood on the bottom step and mechanically pushed a stroller back and forth in an attempt to rock her sister's baby, four months old now, to sleep. The baby wore a red snowsuit and sucked on a plastic bottle filled with grape soda. When the baby threw the bottle down, Francisca picked it up, took a tablespoon full of Spaghetti-Os from one of the women, mashed the spaghetti with a finger and wedged the spoon into the baby's mouth.

"Teenager approached her and said, "Who is upstairs?"

"Indio. He lets me stay here to take care of my sister's baby. She is sleeping."

"Do you know Maximo?"

"Yes."

"Do you know where you can find him?"

She looked down the block. "One of the women went to see him for help at some office someplace. I could ask her."

"Find him. And tell him that he must be at my house at eight o'clock tonight. Tell Maximo he must call me on the telephone at the bar and I will tell him about tonight myself."

Maximo had spent most of the afternoon at two basement parties held by block associations with whom he worked. Arriving back at his office he found himself in the midst of a wine and rum party that was to close out the day.

"One woman was here with a baby to see you," the woman in the next cubicle, Haydee, told him.

"What did she need?" Maximo asked.

"I don't know. From the looks of it, probably welfare trouble. She left her name and a phone number." On the slip Haydee handed him, Maximo saw the names of Francisca and Teenager and the familiar phone number for Ana's Bar. "That wasn't welfare," he said, more to himself.

"It wasn't?" Haydee said.

"No."

He called Nicki at her office, but her detached voice, with the office party noise in the background, told him that she didn't want to talk.

"I'll be leaving soon," she said.

"Meet you?"

"You know I can't today. I have to get home and help my mother."

"What are you up to all weekend?"

"Family."

He said nothing.

"Family all weekend," she said.

When he still said nothing, she said, "Angela got family all weekend too. So what can I tell you? I might like it to be different. I think I really would. But I can't. Merry Christmas and talk to you Monday." There was laughter close to her now. "Got to go," she said.

After he hung up, Maximo had a few drinks and talked too long in the office and he was the last to leave, walking out into the end of a dark afternoon. It was after four-thirty when Maximo stepped off the subway at 138th Street. The platform was filled with music from the social club that was behind a door a few feet away from the turnstiles.

Maximo came up the stairs on the other side of the street from Ana's Bar and started down the hill to Eddie Hernandez' store. He was going to buy two shirts, or a sweater, for his uncle in Brooklyn, his mother's favorite brother. He had just enough rum in him to make it casual and enough cash in his pocket to buy himself out of as much pain as possible in this first visit.

He also had more confidence when he faced Eddie, because he had been able to keep Teenager almost completely out of his life. On Monday night, when Maximo returned from the airport after putting his mother on the plane to San Pedro, the woman downstairs had delivered Maximo the message from Teenager. As the woman and her husband had since gone to Brooklyn for the holidays, Maximo now could take the position that he never received a message. The same would apply to the girl, Francisca, who had shown up at the office: I never was there.

Maximo's apprehension rose as he reached Eddie Hernandez' store. Eddie was busy with two women buying men's underwear; Weinstein sat on a chair smoking a cigarette and watching the street, his usual activity in the few minutes between the close of his shop and the start of his ride home.

"This is the first time Eddie's business has thinned out all day," Weinstein said proudly.

"That's good," Maximo said.

Eddie Hernandez looked past the women, saw Maximo and called out, in a voice that was overly familiar, "What can I do for you?"

"Shirts, when you're finished there," Maximo said.

Eddie nodded and went back to the women. Finishing with them, he gestured for Maximo to come to the counter. Maximo told him who the shirts were for, and the size, and Eddie got up on a stepladder, reached for a box and brought down the shirts.

"Good enough," Maximo said, looking at them. Bright plaids. The uncle would wear them proudly.

"Do you want them gift wrapped?" Eddie said.

"I don't know," Maximo said.

"When are you going to give them to him?"

"Tonight. I'm going over to Brooklyn on the subway now."

"Then you get them wrapped," Eddie said. He reached for paper.

"Maximo."

Maximo turned around to Weinstein. "Your fan club," Weinstein said. In the doorway to the store, Francisca had the stroller tilted to get over the one step up. Weinstein opened the door for her and she walked in behind a wailing baby.

"Yes?" Maximo said.

"I need to talk to you," Francisca said.

"What about?" Maximo said.

"Teenager says you and your mother must come to his house tonight."

"My mother is in Puerto Rico."

"Then I guess he means that you must come."

"Tell him I have to go to my uncle's house in Brooklyn."

Francisca frowned. She was not used to people saying they would not obey Teenager. She reached down, put a pacifier in the baby's mouth and then stood looking steadily at Maximo.

"Tell him that I thank him very much for his invitation and that I will try my best to be there. I first have to go to my uncle's house in Brooklyn. Tell him I promised my mother I would do that. But then after my uncle's house, I will try my best to get to see Teenager at his house."

"Does that mean I should tell him you are coming?" Francisca said.

"It means I will try."

"He will be angry," she said. She looked at the phone on the wall behind Eddie. Eddie shook his head. "Not on this one, darling."

"I'll just go outside," Francisca said.

"I'm going now," Maximo said.

"Wait until I call Teenager," she said.

She left the baby in the store and went outside to the phone booth.

"Do you do what she says all the time?" Weinstein said.

Maximo pretended not to hear. He took his time paying Eddie for the shirts and then pretended to be thinking of something else he had to buy; anything but let them see that he could not leave the store because Francisca, on behalf of Teenager, had told him to wait. She was back quickly, her attitude telling Maximo that she had been quite correct in ordering him to wait.

"He is coming right down here to get you," she said.

"I thought you were going to Brooklyn," Eddie Hernandez said. Before Maximo could by word or body motion find a way to evade the question, a man came in and Eddie had to wait on him.

"Why don't you go ahead?" Maximo quietly said to Francisca. "I'll wait for him."

She made a face and did not move.

"Don't worry. I'll be right outside when he comes."

Weinstein half rose from his chair to flick his cigarette in an ashstand. "I thought you were the smart one," he said to Maximo.

"Who knows," Maximo said.

"I guess nobody does," Weinstein said. "If somebody like you works for that dirt up the street."

"I don't work for him," Maximo said sharply.

"She mentions his name and you're afraid to move," Weinstein said.

"I'm only doing it so she won't get in trouble," Maximo said.

"Sure," Weinstein said.

Out of some yearning for protection, for cover, Maximo held the gift-wrapped boxes in front of him, but he was stung too badly and had to do something more; he simply could not walk out of the store and leave Weinstein and Eddie to talk to each other about him.

"Whose baby is this?" Maximo quickly asked Francisca.

"My sister."

"Where is she?"

"She was home sleeping."

"Are you still in the same building?"

"Ah hah."

"Do you still work by Indio?"

She nodded yes.

"How old are you?"

"Fourteen."

"Do you think you should sell dope?"

"I don't sell it. I only give it out."

"Well, do you think you should give it out? Would you like someone giving out dope to this baby someday?"

"The baby wouldn't take dope."

"How do you know?"

"Because I would stop it."

"Would you like to stop it for others too?"

"Maybe."

"Why only 'maybe'?"

"My sister has no job. I must get the money."

"Does your sister receive welfare?"

"She doesn't go yet."

"If she got welfare, then you wouldn't need the money from Indio."

Francisca thought. "What if Teenager got very mad at me?"

"We could fix that," Maximo said.

"How do you do that?" Francisca asked.

"Because I can," Maximo said.

"You can?" she said.

"Yes."

She was a ridiculous little girl, standing here in front of him in a blue schoolgirl's parka that had strings hanging from the hood and tangled black hair and one small hand on the handle of the stroller containing her sister's baby, a child with a chance to go nowhere. And now her free hand reached up and smoothed the front of Maximo's hair. Reached up with a woman's confidence, and eyes that told him that a young body inside schoolgirl's clothes was restless.

"I'd like that," she said.

"Then I'll do it," Maximo said. For a moment, between the rum and her eyes, he felt his prick stirring. Crazy, he said to himself. No, he said. He could see that she knew exactly what she was doing.

A screech and sudden horn blaring outside ended the mood. Inside the Mercedes, Teenager motioned for Maximo. Maximo did not move for a moment. Teenager opened the door and stood out in the street, his bearded face looking across the top of the car, his shout coming through the glass windows and door to fill Eddie Hernandez' store.

"*Yo*, Maximo!"

Without speaking, Maximo left the store, went out to the car and got in. Francisca walked out behind him and acknowledged her reward, a wave from Teenager as he got back into his Mercedes.

Watching from the counter, Eddie Hernandez pursed his lips in thought. "At least he says something to the girl."

"What? He shows off for us," Weinstein said.

"At least he put it in her mind," Eddie said.

"And the second that dirt shows up in his big car he runs out like a punk. What is she supposed to think? She thinks the same thing I do. There's something the matter with him. You're sure he's not in with this dirt?"

"No, he just doesn't know how to get away from the guy," Eddie said.

"Gutless," Weinstein said.

"Who knows how a guy thinks," Eddie said.

That night, at eleven o'clock on Christmas Eve, Teenager had three pillows propped under his head in his bed, a dish of brown rice and pork balanced on his chest and a glass of *coquito,* thick and white, strong with rum, on the night table next to him. Benny and Santos Rivera sat on the floor, eating.

"Maximo!" Teenager called out.

Maximo, leaning in the doorway, took another large sip of *coquito.* By now he had enough to feel comfortable in the crowded apartment.

Teenager took the plate from his chest and swung out of bed. He picked up his leather coat.

"Tell Lydia that I just had to go someplace for a little while. Tell her it was very important. It was to do some good, to help somebody. She will believe you."

As Maximo went into the kitchen to speak to Lydia, Teenager, swallowing his drink, went out the door and started for Luisa Maria's. He did not even have to face his wife, he exulted; Maximo did everything.

The rum made Maximo think it was all humorous. He put an earnest look on his face as he approached Lydia, who smiled proudly that Maximo was in her kitchen.

* * *

Also at this time, in the Christmas rush of 1976, there
appeared in the middle of a long customs line at Kennedy
Airport one Gaetano Ricci, forty, who had just stepped
off TWA flight 75 from Rome. His ticket indicated that
his trip had originated at Palermo, Sicily. At five-foot-six
and weighing one hundred forty-two pounds, Gaetano
was not imposing, but one physical attribute did make
him stand out in the crowded hall: he had a square chest.

Sweating lightly, he placed two old leather suitcases in
front of a customs man. Gaetano had his overcoat buttoned, and he kept one hand spread across his chest, as
if giving the oath of allegiance to this new country. The
customs man carefully went through his bags, smiled and
handed Gaetano the customs slip.

"Just hand it to the guard on your way out," the customs man said.

Gaetano picked up the bags and walked toward the
guard who stood in front of swinging doors that would
take Gaetano out of the customs area and to the street,
to the blue Mercedes of his cousin out in parking field
two. Gaetano walked up to the customs man, dropped
one of the bags and held out the marked slip.

"Thank you," the guard said.

Gaetano picked up the suitcase.

"Excuse me," the guard said, his arm out like a gate.
"Would you mind stepping over to that room?"

"Non pozzo parrare le paroli Americani," Gaetano
said.

Gaetano glanced about and saw that he was being
watched by a group of young men with severe faces and
three-piece business suits.

In the airport offices of the Drug Enforcement Agency,
Gaetano, asked in Sicilian to remove his coat and shirt,
sighed and unbuttoned himself and revealed ten pounds
of heroin strapped to his upper torso.

"Trovaio sut'll letto," Gaetano said.

"He says he found it under the bed," one of the drug
agents said.

The others in the room nodded. For six weeks they had
been monitoring this particular TWA flight, along with
two Alitalia runs, for single passengers who appeared

nervous or, like Gaetano, deformed. Gaetano was the seventh to be caught with heroin.

Two days after Gaetano's arrest, a licensed customs broker named Guiliani, with offices in the overseas freight terminal at Kennedy Airport, reported to drug agents that a shipment of Italian provincial furniture was on hand. Guiliani called because he had been told that failure to do so would cost him his license and perhaps his freedom. The drug agents were concerned with Guiliani's daily business, for he was the only top customs broker at Kennedy with an Italian name and was the one to whom Italian exporters went automatically. This time, agents found the legs of the dining room table were hollow and stuffed with one hundred fifteen pounds of heroin. When agents delivered the furniture to a house at Randall Avenue in the Bronx, two men let the agents, dressed in coveralls, lug in the furniture. The two men remained inside the house long enough to twist off the table top and discover that bags of talcum had been stuffed into the table legs. Both went crashing out the back door and into the arms of agents.

Such arrests produced another of the momentary, bothersome interruptions in the drug peddling being done by the gangster family of Louis Mariani. The dope, of course, would reappear shortly; a few cars riding into New York from Canada would rectify everything. But this particular lapse caused trouble in the Bronx, where Pedro Torres sat in his club and did not have enough white heroin, while everywhere in his area the streets were coated with this new brown heroin being sold by Teenager. Teenager's pushers were boasting, "This is Spanish from the ground where it is grown all the way into your arm. The Wop has nothing to do with this."

Reluctantly, Mariani allowed Torres to have a cup of coffee with him on the matter. Mariani did not feel that he, a man of honor and stature, should be required to speak to a Spic, and Torres would make the second such person, a person as low as a dog, with whom he had sat. The first one, Teenager, was supposed to be part of a cemetery by now. How could Corky miss him like he did? Then this Teenager disappeared and Corky was

going around saying that he had scared the Spic away.
Scared him like you scare a tractor trailer. Wherever
Teenager had gone, he sure was back now. Torres was a
Spic, Mariani thought, who lived with all these Spics.
Maybe he could get a close shot.

When Mariani arrived at the coffee shop of the Mirror
Motel, on the approach to the Whitestone Bridge, he
found Torres at a center table, the morning sunlight ex-
ploding off the rows of heavy gold chains around his
neck. Mariani, who wore a four-carat pinky ring, became
uneasy; the eyes of all were supposed to be attracted to
this ring, to the hand of a man of honor, not to the neck
of some filthy Spic. Mariani immediately suggested they
sit in the back, by the kitchen door, so that he could
pretend that the Spic sitting with him was merely a busboy whom he was graciously allowing to relax.

"Have coffee?" Mariani said.

"I'm just drinking a juice," Torres said.

"Coffee," Mariani said.

"I don't drink coffee."

"Have coffee."

"All right."

"Want Danish?"

"No."

"Have Danish."

"I don't feel like eating."

"Sure you do. Have Danish."

Torres was irritated that Mariani had to show his control in such a way, but as he needed something, he ac-
quiesced.

Mariani yawned over his coffee. "I'm exhausted. Wife
got me crazy last night. Soon's Johnny Carson's over I
always go right off. Like I'm hit on the head. Last night
my wife gets up and goes down and sits in the kitchen.
She's still there at two o'clock in the morning. I yell
down to her, 'Hey, are you thinking up some way to get
rid of me?' She says, 'I'm waiting for Nicki.' That's my
daughter. She's out somewhere. So I says to my wife,
'You could wait in bed just as good as you could in the
kitchen.' Not my wife. Three o'clock she sits there until.
Finally my daughter comes home and the wife comes up

to bed. I want to get up and strangle my daughter. Got me awake all these hours. What does the wife say to me? 'Go back to sleep.' What sleep? I didn't catch a minute. Her and that daughter. Don't let my wife hear one word from anyone else about her daughter."

"That is the mother for you," Torres said.

"Don't get me wrong, my daughter don't do nothing wrong. Any daughter of mine does it right. You know that. If the guy goes away, the wife stays in the house until the day he comes home. And that's it. Anybody don't do that, don't deserve to live. My daughter does it the right way, don't worry about her. Last night, you know what she did? Went to a late movie with a girl-friend. A girl we know. You should've seen my daughter this morning. Up and singing at seven o'clock. I says to her, 'Hey, let an old man sleep.' I could hardly freaking move. That's when you get old."

Mariani gulped coffee, took a bite of the Danish and, mouth full, asked, "What's your problem?"

"So many people are making business and I don't have enough to sell."

"Two days, three days, everything will be all right," Mariani said.

"Excuse me, but your man said this to me last week."

"Wait a couple more days."

"The good pushers go to Teenager because he gives them brown rocks to sell."

"Anybody leaves you, then you got to do what you got to do," Mariani said.

"I know. I have to take a pusher off the count if he leaves me."

Mariani gulped the rest of his coffee and looked out the restaurant door at the parking lot. Standing up, he reached across the table and tugged at Torres' cheek. "Take a pusher off the count and then take the other guy, too."

"Teenager?"

"He's the guy taking the business away from you."

Mariani looked out at the parking lot again. Then he reached for Torres' cheek again. "I know you'll do this right, sweetheart. Let me tell you what I'll do for you.

You know Corky? Sure you do. He's my man. I'll tell Corky to come around give you three thousand. That's for expenses. All right, sweetheart? Anything else? I'm counting on you.''

Mariani left. Let these Spics kill each other, the way they're supposed to, he told himself.

Torres followed slowly. He had come to Mariani for help, and he wound up carrying a contract on Teenager.

"Excuse me," the cashier said.

"Yes?" Torres said.

"The check," she said. "The gentleman walked out before you said you'd pay."

As Torres paid the check, he saw Mariani slip into the passenger seat of a blue Cadillac and be driven away.

At noon on Friday, Haydee looked into Maximo's cubicle and asked if he would be around later and Maximo
quickly said yes, without asking what it was about, for
never again was he going to allow himself to gash his
insides by refusing her. This time, Haydee wanted Maximo not for his company over a drink, but for his assistance at a Bronx Democratic Party meeting where judges
were to be selected. The meeting was to start at three-
thirty and be over at five.

"Whole idea of these things is to hold them when nobody can get there but the politicians," Haydee said.
"They'd die if they had the public in there watching them
make up judges."

"What happens when they see us?" Maximo said.

"Nigger like me walks in? A riot."

After lunch, Maximo called Nicki.

"I want to have an early dinner with you."

"I can't."

"Why?"

"Because it's Friday and I have to go home. By the
time I get to your house and then Angela picks me up,
it's too late. I'm starting to get asked a lot of questions at
home. Next thing, they'll put a timelock on the door."

"I don't want you to come to my house. I want to go
out someplace with you."

"I don't want to do that," Nicki said.

249

"Why not?"

"I don't want to waste a night in a restaurant. If I wanted to do that, I'd go be a waitress."

"I'll be through at five. I have no bar course tonight. I can meet you for a drink and have a nice dinner. You can get home early. I just want to see you."

"To do what?"

"To sit down like civilized people and have a decent conversation over a meal."

"If you lived in a civilized place, I'd go up and let myself in and we could have some real conversation," she said. "Oh, freak it! Look at this. I just spilled all over. I'm trying to polish my nails and talk at the same time."

"Dinner," Maximo said.

"Well, I'd love to see you. But I have to be home early."

"So have dinner and go home."

"That isn't what I want, but, all right, I'll take it."

He made a date for five at La Casa Wong, a Chinese-Latin restaurant on Fordham Road, three blocks from the building where the meeting about judges was being held.

At three o'clock, Haydee appeared in Maximo's cubicle doorway with a Puerto Rican who was quite dark, had a shaved head and was so thin he appeared starved. A small gold earring was speared through the right earlobe. A T-shirt made from a flag of Puerto Rico hung on his bony frame. Haydee introduced him as Ron Seguera and said he was the chairman of the Bronx Hispanic Judicial Coalition.

"The only thing Ron knows about the law is to plead guilty," Haydee added.

They took the subway to Fordham Road and arrived at a quarter past three at the office building where the Democratic headquarters was located. Maximo removed his tie and rolled up his shirtsleeves in order to comply as much as possible with the Third World dress of Ron with his earring, and Haydee who wore a yellow T-shirt and black pants. They took the elevator to the fourth floor, where at the end of the narrow hallway, mail still stuck in the discolored slot under the lettering on the frosted glass door that said "Democratic Executive Committee of Bronx County."

Haydee pulled the mail out of the slot and walked in. At a desk in a large room there was a woman in her fifties, champagne hair as pale as a stone under the ceiling lights, who immediately looked up from her typewriter.

"Got your mail," Haydee said.

"Junk mail. Must have just come. We got all the good mail," the woman said.

"Here it is, anyway," Haydee said. She dropped the envelopes on the woman's desk.

"Can I help you?" the woman said.

"We're here for the meeting," Haydee said.

"Which meeting?"

"The judicial convention."

"Oh, you can't go to that."

"Of course we can," Haydee said.

"No, you can't go into that. Nobody's allowed into that."

"I'm sorry, but we can."

"No, you can't. They pick the judges today. You can't go in there. That's private."

"That's why we're here," Haydee said. "We're from the Bronx Hispanic Coalition."

Relief brightened the woman's face. "Oh. Then you have the wrong place. This is the Bronx Democratic organization."

Seguera said, "This is the place for us, all right."

"I said this is the Democratic Party," the woman said.

"We all registered Democrats," Seguera said.

There was a sound and a man rushed past them with his arms held out like a lineman and he fell onto a man and woman who had just entered the office.

"Arthur!" Murray bawled.

"Love you, Murray."

"Rose!"

"Murray, darling."

The woman, obviously Irish, had on a grey fedora with the brim down. She had red hair pulled straight back. Her face was thin, suggesting an upbringing with porcelain on the mantelpiece, rather than a cement truck in the side-

yard. A double-breasted dark blue pin-striped suit hung
sternly from her thin frame. The man with her, who
seemed to be her husband, was in a dark brown three-
piece suit whose front needed a heavy metal buckle,
rather than a mere button, to keep fastened over a pot
belly. Much of his face was obscured by eyeglasses that
were as large and thick as the bottom of a Coke bottle.
The front of his head was covered by a black wig.

"We've been waiting for you," Murray said.

"By the time I left work and went up to Larchmont to
get her," Arthur said.

"I wouldn't leave until the kids got home from school,
I wanted them to see me leave," the woman said.

"That's a good enough reason to keep us waiting,"
Murray said.

"Murray. Can you imagine it!" Rose said.

"Sure, I can. You *deserve* it," Murray said. "Come
on, let's get in there now. We're all waiting for you."

Murray walked the two to the door and he pulled it
open for them and they walked in to the sound of applause. Murray shut the door and turned to face Maximo.

"Now, can I help you?" he said.

"Yes, if that's the judicial meeting, you can let us in."

"You can't go in there. This is for the judges," Murray
said.

"Then that's just the place for us," Maximo said.
"We're all going to be judges."

"I going to give out twenty-year sentences," Seguera
said.

Maximo stepped past Murray and pulled the door
open. He made sure that Haydee and Seguera got inside
with him. Then he noticed that he was in a long, narrow,
paneled room that was filled with about seventy-five people, middle-aged men mostly, who sat in rows on folding
chairs. At the front of the room there was a table and an
American flag. Rose and her husband were at the table,
being greeted by a man with sparse hair and rounded
shoulders. The man's eyebrows went up as he saw Maximo, Haydee and Seguera.

"Help you?" the man said.

From the doorway, Murray called out, "They claim they're from some Hispanic group."

"We don't claim to be anything," Maximo said. "We *are* the Bronx Hispanic Judicial Coalition."

"Who says so?" the man at the table said. He looked at the middle of the room.

"Luis?"

The man with brilliant black hair and skin that was quite pale stood up.

"You know these people?"

"I don't," Luis said. No wonder he doesn't remember me, Maximo thought. The last time I was near him, he was under a chair because Teenager shot his gun.

"Then if Luis Jimenez doesn't know who you are, perhaps you're misrepresenting yourselves," the man at the table said.

"If you'll excuse me," Maximo said. "It seems to me that Mr. Jimenez has spent so much time hiding his head under a parasol that he hasn't seen another Hispanic in the last twenty years."

Jimenez was embarrassed and he sat down.

"We happen to be citizens who have a slight personal interest in who becomes a judge," Maximo said.

"But you're intruding on regular Democratic Party business," the man at the table said.

"Isn't party registration all that is needed to become a member of the party?" Maximo said. "Or is there some secret initiation that we seem to be in ignorance of?"

In the front of the room, a stubby man popped up and began whispering. The round-shouldered man sneered and shook his head emphatically. The stubby man sat down and the one with round shoulders called out, "If everyone will please be seated, we'll begin our program." He waved at Maximo, Haydee and Seguera. "If you'll just be seated."

"Why, thank you for having us," Seguera said. His sarcasm produced a series of grunts from the men in the room.

"All right," the man in the front said, "my name is Henry McCafferty and I am the Bronx County Democratic leader." The people clapped and McCafferty held up his hands. "I'd like to keep the traditions of this organization intact. Please do not clap until I tell you to. In fact, we have had county leaders in the past who did not permit you to breathe unless given permission. The late and great Charley Buckley—"

At this, there was loud applause.

"—Mr. Buckley raised horses and he appointed seven of them to the executive committee and he held the meeting in a barn. He said it was the best meeting the Bronx Democratic organization ever had because the horses didn't talk back to him."

As the crowd laughed, McCafferty allowed the suggestion of a smile to seep onto his straight, dry face.

"All right, what is our business here today?" he said. "Our business is the most important business, in fact it is the *only* business of this political organization. Today, we are going to vote for our candidate for a State Supreme Court nomination. This is the most solemn duty you will ever have as members of the Bronx Democratic organization. A State Supreme Court judge earns fifty-one thousand five hundred dollars a year." He was interrupted by applause. "A State Supreme Court judge serves a term of fourteen years and never in my time in this city has a State Supreme Court judge failed to win reelection for a second fourteen-year term." This time, McCafferty had to fight to be heard over the applause. "Only God in His wisdom can remove a State Supreme Court judge once we put him in! Only a fatal heart attack can get one of our judges off the bench!"

This was met with such great enthusiasm that McCafferty had to pause for many moments. Then his voice lowered and his expression became dour as he outlined the specific problem the Bronx County Regular Democratic organization faced. He reminded them that under the usual deal with Republicans, the Democrat who got his party's nomination would automatically get the Republican line on the ballot. This way there would never be an accident on election day, when the public became involved, he reminded them. However, this still left them with one painful obstacle. Because the Bronx had lost so much population, the choosing of a judge had been com-

bined with Manhattan Democrats. The Bronx Democrats
first had to agree today, and then go downtown on the
next Monday to a joint meeting of Bronx and Manhattan
Democrats and attempt to get the entire group to support
the Bronx candidate. Someday, he said, control would be
given back to the Bronx, but for now they must live in
conflict.

"You know what's going to be at that meeting,"
McCafferty said.

A white-haired man in the center of the room called
out, "Liberals!"

"Reformers!"

"The element from Harlem!"

McCafferty, a pleased teacher, nodded his head.
"We're going down there and we're not going to deal
with these other people," he said. "We're going to deal
with Manhattan Regular Democrats. The old guys. The
good guys. We're going to put this judgeship across without the help of any of this element that caused a lot of
decent people to move out of this county because of the
way this same element burned this place down until it
looks like Dresden. So you see we live in serious times,"
McCafferty said. "And we have serious business to conduct here today. Let's get with it."

Everybody in the room clapped.

"All right. Now we'll hear from the candidates for the
Bronx County backing for the State Supreme Court."
There was applause. McCafferty smiled. "Actually,
there's only one candidate. You know her and I know her
for a long time. I first met Rose Keogh in the Sharkey-
Melito primary at the Chippewa Club. That was so long
ago that Rose Keogh and I both will deny being there.
But over all the years, she has served this party well.
And now she is going to put the lie to all those liberals
and reformers. She is going to show that Bronx County
is modern. She is going to be the first woman to be named
to the State Supreme Court."

McCafferty began clapping and Rose Keogh, in her
pin-striped suit, stood up. She smiled at the audience and
gave little waves to people she knew.

"I will make this brief because I know you all have

places to be. I want to thank Henry McCafferty for what he has done for me. He is the greatest political leader in this city.'' Applause. ''I want to thank the various organizations that support me, particularly the Riverdale Jewish Women's Club, the Kingsbridge Gaelic Society and, of course, my home political club, the Adlai Stevenson Club in Riverdale.''

She spoke with her hands clasped. ''I want to tell you that the State Supreme Court is the greatest thing that can happen to a human being. A fourteen-year term. Oh, I can't believe it!'' She shivered in delight and the audience applauded lustily. ''Now some of you might ask my qualifications. Well, I graduated from Manhattan Law School and went to work for the State Liquor Authority. That appointment was given to me by Henry McCafferty and I want to say that publicly. I remained with the SLA for twelve years. I also was very active in the Bronx Women's Bar Association. And as all of you know, I was the chairlady of the Bronx Democratic county dinner on three occasions. And if you ask Henry McCafferty, he will tell you. We never sold more tickets or more ads in the journal than we did at the dinners I was in charge of. As Henry pointed out, the first time he met me was in the Sharkey-Melito primary. That's, of course, only one of the campaigns I've been in. I have devoted my life to the Bronx County Democratic organization and I am thankful to this organization for the great honor you bestow on me. I promise that I will attend the Bronx-Manhattan judicial convention and return to this room to say to you all, as a member of the State Supreme Court, thank you. I love you.''

''Any questions?'' Henry McCafferty called out.

The stubby man in front popped up. ''If you get the nomination, who will you name as your law secretary? That job pays twenty-five thousand.''

Rose Keogh nodded and smiled. She looked at Henry McCafferty. McCafferty said nothing.

''He hasn't told me yet,'' Rose Keogh said.

Maximo stood up. ''What is your position on capital punishment?'' he asked.

Rose Keogh smiled at him and said nothing. McCafferty stood up. ''Well, I don't see what we're going to accomplish by making a candidate go on the record with what she's going to do on sentencing. That's what a judge is for. To make up his, or in this case her, mind at the appropriate time.''

Maximo said, ''I'd also be interested to hear some of the cases she has tried in a courtroom. Other than State Liquor Authority matters.''

McCafferty looked over the audience. ''Let's give someone else a chance here. Henry, you've got a question?''

A man rose. ''I'd like to ask one thing. Rose, who replaces you at the State Liquor Authority? That's a real good job there.''

''It's a Bronx job,'' she said. ''I know this county keeps the job. But if you want to know the particular person that gets the job, I refer you again to our county leader.''

McCafferty said, ''I can answer that one. Walter Halloran of the Parkchester club is going to get Rose's State Liquor Authority job.''

The answer made the man who asked the question become agitated. ''Isn't he Pat Walsh's cousin?''

''I believe he is,'' McCafferty said.

''Then that makes two cousins that Pat Walsh has on the state payroll.''

A man against the wall stood up. ''I'm Pat Walsh and I'll answer that charge myself. That statement is a lie. I do not have two cousins on the state payroll. I have *three* cousins on the state payroll!''

Maximo, Haydee and Seguera laughed and clapped their hands, and then Maximo looked around and saw that they were the only ones who found the remark amusing. The others in the room glared at them.

''I think I can anticipate one important question you're going to ask,'' Rose Keogh said. ''Since I am leaving my job at the SLA, what happens to me if somehow I am not nominated at the Bronx-Manhattan meeting on Monday night? Does it mean Rose Keogh after all these years is out on the street? No, it doesn't. Henry McCafferty has a fallback job for me. I can have an appointment to the Criminal Court bench. This is not an elected post, as you

know. It is the city court, not the state, so the Mayor
appoints you. Henry says I can have an appointment
Tuesday morning if, bite your tongue, anything goes
wrong on Monday night. The only Criminal Court opening this time is for an eighteen-month term. The pay is,
well, what can I tell you? Thirty thousand. You work in
the most abominable conditions. Really crummy. You
don't have chambers. And what kind of a pension can
you get from an eighteen-month term? Just as important
to this gathering, a Criminal Court judge gets no secretary.''

She finished saying this with a sweet smile that went
off her face as Seguera, in his flag of Puerto Rico, stood
up and said, ''When you walked in here today, I heard
you and your husband talking about Larchmont. That's
up in Westchester. What you doing being a judge in the
Bronx with the poor people?''

''I have a voting address in the Bronx, therefore I am
a Bronx resident.''

''You got kids?'' Seguera said.

''Three.''

''Where do they go to school?''

Rose Keogh's facial composure fell apart. Her eyes
were embarrassed and her throat was working.

Seguera yelled. ''Where do your kids go to school?
With all the nice white suburban kids? Sure they do.
Cause you live there too. You a suburban lady. What
right you got to come in here and rule over people from
the Bronx when you don't even like us enough to live
with us?''

McCafferty stepped alongside Rose Keogh. ''I think
that should do it now. When questions become personal,
it's time we went home.''

Maximo stood up. ''I think we ought to get more personal. I have a personal question I'd be quite interested
in having answered.''

''There are no more questions for our judicial candidate,'' McCafferty said.

''The personal question is to you,'' Maximo said.

McCafferty pretended to be arranging papers on the
table.

"With all due respect to this woman, I am sure that she is a lovely woman and a fine mother, but in all due respect, she doesn't appear to be much more qualified than a typist. I wonder how she has gained such stature in this organization that you are willing to fight to make her a State Supreme Court judge? Could it be that the reason she is your choice is that she has paid you more money than all the other people in the Bronx who aspire to the bench?"

McCafferty's chin came up in anger. Rose Keogh's eyes became filled with poison.

"Sergeant at arms!" McCafferty said. "These people are out of order. Remove them from the room."

Haydee's finger poked into Maximo's side. Her other hand pushed Seguera. The three went out the door, past the woman in the outer office without looking at her, out into the hallway and onto the staircase. Haydee said she wanted to get out of the way quickly and not be standing around at the elevator doors. "I don't want anybody figuring out where we work," she said to Maximo. "We'll blow our jobs. I don't know about you, but I *need* mine." One flight down, she stopped and stamped her feet and began to laugh.

"Did you see that white bitch's face?"

Laughing, they went down to the street to La Casa Wong.

She was walking with happy strides and thinking about his face. I like everything about his face, she told herself. Then she remembered the letters in her purse. Scowling now, she walked over to the mailbox in the lobby of her office building and dropped in the two letters, one to her husband, the other, the one that irritated, the car payment to the Citicorp Bank. All those months later, she still was making payments on the car, three hundred twenty-five dollars a month, and the car was sitting in a government motor pool someplace, to be used by drug agents when they rode around impersonating peddlers. Meanwhile, Nicki reminded herself, she had to work for the money to pay for the car while her husband played basketball in jail. No, not basketball, she corrected herself. He stays in jail lifting weights. Lifting weights and sleeping. Then he complains, she thought. When she first was without the car, she was so mad at her husband that she did not visit him in jail for the first three months. Now, making another payment, she slammed the mailbox lid and, for an instant, its clanging sound caused her to think of a barbell dropping on her husband's feet.

At the top of the subway stairs, she took off her large gold earrings. Some black savage rip them off my ears in front of everybody. People stand there, let him get away with it. As it was still before five o'clock, it took only usual pushing for her to get a seat. She was surprised to find that not only was she sitting next to a white man, but that there were several on the train. When she got off at Fordham Road, she lit a cigarette, put a stick of gum in her mouth and, humming, walked up the street to La Casa Wong. She paused outside to put on her gold earrings, Chiquita Banana earrings she called them, for they were large and splashy enough to please a Spic. Head rocking slightly, so that the earrings would flash and be pleasing to Maximo, she walked into the restaurant. In front of her as she entered was Maximo at the bar talking to this black bitch in a T-shirt and this ridiculous black wearing a flag. Some element.

"You had a bad day," Maximo said.

"No, I didn't," Nicki said.

"You've got exasperation all over your face," he said.

"Maybe it's because I just had to mail my car payment."

"That's enough to make anybody grouchy," Haydee said. She held a large glass, almost a basin, with orange slices sticking up.

Who drinks like this? Now Nicki saw that Maximo had something in his drink. Something long and white and when the drink moved the white thing revealed itself against the side of the glass, it looked like something— Nicki wouldn't even say to herself what it looked like that Maximo was sticking in his mouth.

"What are you drinking?" she asked him.

"Rum and banana. See? They crush the bananas, but this time he left one in, like a celery stalk."

"What is this, when you drink you mix a bar and a vegetable store? I'll have a Scotch and water."

"This is Nicki," Maximo said to the others. He turned and ordered her drink.

"I'm Haydee Fernandez."

"Pleased," Nicki said.

"And I'm Ron Seguera."

"Pleased," Nicki said. She looked unhappy.

When Nicki's drink came, she became silent and looked at her glass carefully.

"Your earrings are fantastic," Haydee said.

"Oh, thank you," Nicki said, brightening immediately. "I'm glad you like them. These are my favorites." She turned to Maximo. "Don't you like them?"

"They're quite attractive." In the smoky late afternoon light of the bar, the gold had an age and richness to it.

"Where would I go to get a pair like that?" Maximo asked her.

"Snatch them off somebody's ears downtown on the street," Haydee said.

Maximo fingered a charm that hung from a thin gold bracelet on her right wrist.

"What does it stand for?" he asked.

"The hands are for friendship, the heart is for love and the crown is for loyalty."

"What about sex?"

"That doesn't go on a bracelet. You need money. Then you get sex. The two go together."

To Maximo, her meaning was quite unmistakable; while she might find his career and concerns interesting, the general topic of poverty was alien to her. You have to be something, Maximo told himself proudly, to overcome this kind of materialism.

Ron Seguera stood up and began to dance and clap his hands. "Oh, did you see those faces today!"

Maximo watched Nicki's eyes as she stared at this dancing flag of Puerto Rico. Maximo never had seen great fighting bulls, but he had read of them, and he was certain that not even the greatest bull, a bull bred to fight a dozen swords at once, became as agitated at the show of a cape as Nicki was by the Puerto Rican flag wrapped around Ron's moving body.

The three, with Nicki as outsider, went into a clipped, name-filled discussion of what they had just attended and what they thought would happen next, and after several minutes, Haydee said to Nicki, "This must be awfully boring to you."

"It's all about getting to be a judge," Maximo said. "If I had time, I'd explain it to you."

"Oh, I think you'd find it boring," Haydee said.

Nicki's eyes widened and her lips parted slightly in a look that, for part of an instant, Maximo thought could be purposely dumb, but he dismissed this, for his own eye contact with her was too sexually warm for him to feel that she was anything but captured by his style and knowledge. She just didn't understand Haydee, but she will when I explain it to her, he told himself. Nicki kept looking at Haydee with a face that gave nothing away.

Haydee said to Seguera that she would see him the next day, at another meeting, this one a meeting of those in favor of keeping bilingual education.

"They're sure trying to do away with us," Haydee said.

"Do away with what?" Nicki asked.

"Teaching in Spanish to children in school," Haydee said.

"Why would they do that?" Nicki asked.

"If you force a child from a Hispanic household to learn everything in English, then you're asking him to handle two unknowns at once. Learning in a new school, and learning in a strange language."

"What's strange about English?" Nicki asked.

"You work into it," Haydee said.

"How?" Nicki asked.

"Let me tell you," Haydee said firmly. "While they are being taught English, this new language, it makes no sense to have them miss out on arithmetic and history because they don't know enough English yet. So you teach these things to them in Spanish. Then day by day, little by little, you teach them English."

Maximo said, "It's like—"

"—Let me explain it to her," Haydee said. She lectured directly into Nicki's eyes and parted lips. "Let me tell you how it works. While the children are being taught their new language, English, each day, it makes no sense for them to miss out on arithmetic and history simply because they don't know enough English words. So you teach them English. Then, while they're learning English, you keep them up in the other courses by teaching them in Spanish. It seems to go slowly for a while but you get up to the seventh grade and it all comes together. But you teach many things in Spanish for a while."

"I don't know about that," Nicki said.

"What don't you know?" Haydee said.

"Who says the teachers are so good they can teach in Spanish and English both?" Nicki said.

"We have Hispanic teachers who can handle this," Haydee said.

"They could speak in Spanish and you couldn't understand a word they say in English," Nicki said.

Maximo cut in. "We are dealing here with—"

"—Not me. You are, darling. My people speak English." Nicki's eyes were not so wide now.

"We're speaking of children from homes where no one speaks English," Haydee said.

"Both my grandfathers couldn't speak English when they got here," Nicki said. "Nobody gave them this— what do you call it?"

"Bilingual education," Haydee said.

"That's for Spanish. What's the word for Italian?" Nicki said.

"Bilingual," Haydee said.

"Bilingual is your kind, not my kind," Nicki said.

"So whatever," Haydee said.

"Yeah, well, whatever it is, they didn't do it for my grandparents. They had to learn English or else."

"It's quite difficult for these children to start English right away," Haydee said.

"Oh, is it?" Nicki said.

"Sure is."

"Well, they don't have any trouble learning how to say, 'Stick 'em up.' "

Haydee shrieked so loudly that the Chinese sitting in the back of the empty restaurant were startled. "That's wonderful!" Haydee said. She and Seguera finished their drinks and left with a laugh. At the bar, Maximo was still wondering whether it was a simple case of openness or something a bit more stealthy, a trap carefully covered with leaves.

When they sat down to eat, Maximo saw her staring at the menu, which was printed in Spanish.

"Do you know what you want?" he asked her.

"I can't even read the thing," she said.

"Do you trust me?"

"Dear, I trust nobody."

"Then I won't order."

"No, go ahead. I'll just watch you careful."

He ordered in Spanish to the old Chinese waiter. When the waiter arrived with the first course, a soup, Nicki asked suspiciously, "What is this?"

"Caldo gallepago," Maximo said.

She held the spoon hesitantly over the dish. "And?"

"It's a soup named after Galicia, which is a province in Spain."

Oh, good, Nicki told herself, a Spaniard from Spain soup. Happily, her spoon went into the soup.

"Tell me something," she said.

"What?"

"How can these Chinks have Spanish restaurants? You don't see a Chink with an Italian restaurant, I'll tell you that."

"If the Chinese had an opium addict in the family they used to send him away on a freighter," Maximo said. "Make him an outcast. A lot of them wound up in Cuba, Peru, Mexico, places like that. Then when they came up here, they had Spanish mixed with their Chinese cooking."

"The guy who owns this place is a junkie?" Nicki said.

"Nope. But I'll bet his grandfather or father was."

"Well all your people should feel right at home here," she said.

"So should your father," Maximo said.

"And your friend," she said.

"I don't see my friend anymore. You see your father every day."

Her eyes were narrowing and she was about to say something when the waiter reached past her and began placing bowls on the table.

"Now what's all this?" she said suspiciously.

"*Ropa vieja*," Maximo said, placing some on Nicki's plate.

"It looks like meat."

"It's shredded beef."

"Oh. All right. And what's all this black stuff?"

"Black beans."

The waiter put a couple of more dishes on the table. "Here, give me your plate," Maximo said. He gave her what appeared to be large potato chips.

"What are these?" Nicki said.

"*Tostones.*"

He then put fried black fingers on her plate. Her spinal column went up against the back of the chair as he put the dish in front of her.

"*Plátanos maduros*," Maximo said, indicating the black fingers.

Her fork touched the food as if it were about to detonate.

"Try it, you'll love it," Maximo said.

She picked at the black finger and put a small amount against her tongue. She frowned as she tried to place the taste.

"What is that in real language?"

"Fried bananas."

She thought of pushing the bananas onto the butter plate and demanding they be taken away. Monkey food. Then for some reason, looking at Maximo, she took a forkful of fried bananas and ate it.

"I thought I could meet you Saturday afternoon," Maximo said.

"You can't. I got to go to Paramus Mall."

"I'll come with you."

"To the Paramus Mall with me? Never. The whole state of New Jersey is off limits to you."

"I'll meet you after you go shopping."

"That sounds very nice," she said. "You'll call Angela about four, five o'clock and I'll get back to you. But early, please. Otherwise I just can't, you know, walk out. I got my mother there and my aunts come over and all of a sudden at eight o'clock or something I say I got to meet Angela. Then I don't come home until three in the morning. If you call Angela early, I can get out at a decent hour. I could meet you seven o'clock someplace for a real dinner. Not some monkey jungle like this place. But I can't meet you any earlier. I got to shop Saturday."

"What do you have to get?"

"I need collar shirts."

"You're wearing a collar shirt right now." She was wearing a raspberry cotton shirt with a flat round collar.

"I need a cotton shirt with ombre stripes. Ombre! What's the matter with you? You should know what that means. Ombre stripes!"

"¿Hombre?" Maximo said.

"Ombre. You don't know what it is? The stripe that starts up here. It's mauve up here. Then it gets darker as it comes down." Her long fingernails traced a wavering line across the front of her shirt. "It goes to tan and then you get further down and it becomes dark brown."

"I don't know what it looks like," Maximo said. "When you wear it for me, I'll see it and I'll like it."

"Oh, you will," she said. "That's what I've got to do tomorrow. Go shopping for a collar shirt with ombre stripes."

"For the entire day?"

"It takes time."

"That's something I can't do," Maximo said.

"You never feel like just going out and buying something?"

"What for?"

"Just to have things."

"What things?"

"Things that you could have."

"I'd like to have a painting," Maximo said. "I'd live in a shack the rest of my life if it had paintings on the wall."

"Not me. I like nice houses. Right now I don't need a

painting. I need a collar shirt with ombre stripes. After that, I need a car and some nice big diamonds."

"You got the wrong person for diamonds," Maximo said. "You ought to get your father to buy you diamonds."

"How are your towels?" Nicki said.

"Every day when I wrap one around me I think of you."

"That's nice."

"I keep thinking it's the same towel that was around you."

"No!"

"Yes, don't you like that?"

"I'd like it better if you washed the towels once in a while. Use Tide. I like it better than Cheer."

"I wash them when I get a chance."

"How could you wash if you're wrapping the same towel around you that I used a week ago?"

"Is it a week? That's too long."

"An hour is too long for a dirty towel."

Maximo shrugged his shoulders. What was she getting so excited about towels for? Maximo didn't share this mania for cleanliness.

"You were off on Wednesday?" he asked.

"Yes."

"Then I called you Thursday and you still weren't around."

"Thursday? What time Thursday?"

"Two o'clock."

"Oh, I went out to lunch with Galligan and we had such a good time that we said, freak it, we go back to the office when we feel like it. We got back late."

"Who's Galligan?"

"The nice big guy in the office. He's my friend. I told you about him."

"What were you doing out to lunch with him all afternoon?"

"Because I was out with him."

"I don't want you to go to lunch with him."

"What?"

"I don't want you to."

"You can't tell me that."

"I don't want you going out to lunch with Galligan or anybody else."

She absently toyed with the spoon in front of her.

"Is that how you feel?" she said. Her eyes were wide and the lips parted slightly.

Maximo spoke into this face he saw as open, vulnerable as if he were a commander. "That's exactly how I feel."

Her fingers spread and covered the rest of the silverware. My husband sits in prison and sends out orders and I'm supposed to run for him. Then I go see him and he looks at me like I'm one of his new sweatshirts. Now look at you, just because you're a movie star you think you own me too? She picked up the silverware and threw it onto the table and a couple of pieces bounced off the table and onto the tile floor. They made a noise in the empty restaurant.

Nicki stood up and walked to the ladies' room. She fumed in front of the mirror. Giving me orders and he's not responsible for me and I'm not responsible for him. He's got it wrong. As she redid her eyes, rubbing a thumb over the part of the blue that needed more tone, she decided that she would punish Maximo for this.

Maximo had paid the check and was waiting at the door. He said nothing and walked her toward the subway.

"I want a cab," she said.

He stepped off the curb and hailed a gypsy cab. The cab, dented and with no company name, was driven by a Puerto Rican in a black T-shirt, sounded as if there were men hidden under the hood who were swinging sledge hammers.

"I don't get in a cab like that," Nicki said.

Maximo waved the gypsy cab on. "Too messy for you?"

"You know it, darling."

A yellow metered cab stopped for a red light a block away and when Maximo waved, put on a directional. When Nicki stepped out with her hand up, the cab jumped the light and pulled up.

"It's only seven-thirty," Maximo said.

"That's good. We said it would be an early night."

"Why don't you change your plans and come home with me for a little while?"

"I told you, I can't."

"It's still early."

"I have to get up early. I have to go to the Paramus Mall and buy a collar shirt with ombre stripes. Ombre! You know ombre."

Maximo held the door. Nicki paused as she was about to get in.

"Tomorrow?" she said.

"I guess so," Maximo said.

"Don't guess. Don't leave me hanging home all night."

"All right."

"Call Angela. Call her early tomorrow." She kissed him on the cheek and slipped into the cab.

Nicki took the cab over to the bus terminal on Broadway and 165th Street where the commuter buses leave for New Jersey. Before she got on her bus she called Angela and asked her not to answer the phone all weekend. Angela said, yes, that she would love to do a thing like this for Nicki.

.... Chapter 20

Maximo tried Nicki at her office twice during the week, was told each time that she was at a meeting, never received a call back and found himself, at dusk on Saturday, with a great restlessness through the insides of his thighs. He went down to the phone booth to call Angela and tell her that he was waiting at the booth number, 263–2090. This would, of course, produce a callback from Nicki, who then could save herself from a night of sitting at home with her mother and aunts. Maximo knew that Nicki would say to him that it had to be early, and he knew exactly what he would say to her: leave right now.

He felt Nicki's body against his, and he saw her face vividly. She dug her teeth into the left side of her lower lip just before coming, and while it was a confirmation of the pleasure within herself, Maximo preferred to regard it as dramatic proof of his ability to screw until it hurts. As he dialed Angela, he marveled at the speed with which he could arrange his sex life. One call now, a few words to Angela, hang up, stand here and wait and within, oh, five minutes, she would be on the phone saying, yes, she would be there quickly, her body prepared to reveal all its secrets. Maximo dialed Angela and after eight rings, hung up. He went upstairs for a half hour and then came down. Maximo dialed Angela again. The first ring became another and the phone settled down to ring to eternity. He went back upstairs and dropped onto the bed for a few minutes. He awoke at midnight. On Sunday afternoon, stretching, he felt need welling up again. This time Angela's phone rang ten times without an answer.

He did not call her again until Wednesday. In the cubicle next door, Haydee was busy talking about the Manhattan judicial conference that was being held later in the night. Maximo told himself to mention this to Nicki, and then change the subject; let her know that he was going to be within blocks of her and then let the matter be sheared off. Even up, he told himself.

She was on the phone immediately. "You! Where have you been?" she said.

"Working."

"When am I going to see you?"

"Tonight."

"Where?"

"At the Hotel Marlborough."

"The what?"

"On 46th Street."

"Are you crazy? I don't go into a hotel like that."

"I'm going there for that business with the judges."

"Oh, that's as bad as what I thought you meant. All right. What time?"

"Nine o'clock. I'm going to leave the lecture early so I can be there."

"How long do we have to stay?"

"It won't take that long."

"All right. Because I don't want to waste a night there. I've got better things to do."

That night, he saw her from the dingy balcony that ran along one wall of the hotel lobby. She sat in an old leather chair alongside the doorway, smoking a cigarette and talking to a bellhop who stood with his hands on his hips and looked out into the summer night onto the bruised sidestreet.

"It's lucky you got here, I was ready to leave," she said when she saw Maximo coming down the stairs.

"I've been upstairs for an hour," Maximo said.

"You expected me to go upstairs in this place?"

"Just up those steps to the ballroom."

"For what?"

"They're going to vote in about a half hour and then we'll go."

"As if I have all night."

"Just a half hour."

Through the doorway stepped a woman whose legs struggled to move in a shiny red sheath. She wore a black wig that added a half foot to her height, and a fall that went halfway down her substantial back.

"Hiya, Jackie," the bellhop said.

The woman nodded regally and walked to a doorway over which grimy blue neon advertised a cocktail lounge.

"That's Jackie Onassis," the bellhop said. "That's the name she uses. Know her girlfriend's name? Mary Tyler Moore."

"I can tell you this Jackie Onassis no woman," Nicki said.

"That's right, she's a prostitute," the bellhop said.

"I wasn't referring to that," Nicki said. "I mean she's not a woman, period. Jackie is a guy."

"Oh, sure," the bellhop said. "You know what I did once? Just to kid around, I asked her what she ate so she could keep the weight down. Being a guy, it's tough to get that skinny to fit into a dress. I don't know, I asked her. Know what she told me she eats? Said it right out loud, front of the whole place here. She says to me, she eats—"

"—I don't want to hear," Nicki said. She stood up to leave.

"Oh, you're going upstairs?" the bellhop said. "Speaking of whores, that's some bunch you got up there. Politicians. This is turnin' into some place. Whores in the lobby, whores in the bar, whores up in the rooms, now you got the whole grand ballroom full of whores. Place getting to be a regular whorehouse."

Maximo led her up the flight of stairs to the grand ballroom, whose old radiators had sprayed rust onto large areas of the gray walls. There were about three hundred people in the room, some dawdling among the rows of folding chairs and others milling along the walls. This was the Bronx-Manhattan Judicial Convention, Maximo explained to Nicki, with two candidates running and the one receiving 100 of the 199 delegate votes would die and enter heaven, a Supreme Court judgeship. A cardboard sign over a doorway in the front of the room said, "Meet Rose Keogh over Coffee." Standing under the sign was Rose Keogh's husband, who attacked the hand of each person he could reach. On the far side of the room, Maximo pointed out, was the one Rose Keogh had to beat, a man named Goldenberg, who was the favorite of the liberals, blacks and Hispanics. A woman in jeans, her rear end as big as a rail worker's, ushered people into Goldenberg's room.

"I see where you're going," Nicki said. She pointed with her chin to a crowd of blacks and Puerto Ricans who stood in a doorway that had a fire exit sign over it. They seemed to be listening intently to something going on out on the staircase.

"That's a caucus," Maximo said.

"That isn't what I call them," Nicki said.

She took a seat in the last row. Maximo went into Rose Keogh's room, reveling in the stares he received, and filled a container of coffee. Rose Keogh was hugging a white-haired man. She made a point of not looking at Maximo; therefore, it did not matter whether or not she remembered his face from the Bronx meeting. He brought the coffee to Nicki and she took it and lit a cigarette and stared about the room as Maximo ran to the crowd under the fire exit sign.

The stairway was filled with people who listened to a chunky black man with wavy hair who said that until a day ago, there appeared to have been enough people associating with each other to compile enough votes to get Goldenberg, the liberal, the nomination. Since then, the black man explained, a leader on the lower East Side of Manhattan, who controlled six of the voting delegates, suddenly had announced his intentions to support Keogh. This swift turn of current left several delegates clinging to barrels and indications now were that their fingers were becoming fatigued and they were about ready to let go and allow the current to carry them. This would give the judgeship to Rose Keogh. At the moment, Goldenberg, who was in the room next door, was catatonic and unable to rescue his own cause.

A black woman on the stairs called out, "We sure don't want that woman. She don't even want to talk to us. According to her, we just people from the forest."

The chunky black man said, "That's not the point. Nobody is ever going to do us any favors. The point of this election is that Goldenberg is going to give the law secretary job to the black and Hispanic caucus. Don't spend your time fretting over who's good and who's bad. Tell me about who's giving out the jobs to us."

A man called out, "You say 'us.' But then when this job come through, I hear you goin' give it to your own wife."

"I'm not going to give it to her," the speaker said. "She's just going to reach out and take it right out of my hands. After twenty years in Harlem politics, do you think she's about to play fair?"

He shot his finger into the laughter. "And the next time we win something and a job comes out, it could be *your* turn. If we win now, and my wife takes this job because she's earned it, then next time the job that comes up could be *yours!*"

He began to pace back and forth, his hands in his pockets. "Don't know what to tell you about those votes we're losing right now. I can't imagine why Feinstein would vote for Keogh." A small, loser's smile came on his lips.

"People getting paid," Ron Seguera's voice called out.

"Right in the pocket," Haydee said.

The man running the meeting shrugged. "Don't know how I can say that."

"We can," Seguera said. His arms began to wave, causing his flag of Puerto Rico T-shirt to jump.

At this, Luis Jimenez, the pale one, obviously present as an agent for the regulars outside, stood and pointed a finger at Seguera. "You tried that last time and what did it get you? People like you make it harder for Hispanics. We're trying to work in order, and you walk into rooms and look to bust them up."

He was drowned out by yells from several people, including Maximo, who tasted rage in his throat as the man called Jimenez spoke. When the have-nots become reasonable, Maximo thought, they become servants of the influential.

"What are you doing here?" Maximo said. "You belong outside with the regulars. The whites."

The tall fair Puerto Rican sneered through the applause for this.

"I've been in this business for twenty years now," he said. "And who are you and how long have you been around?"

"What have you done in your twenty years?" Maximo asked.

"Survive," the tall one said.

When Maximo did not answer, the tall one said, "And that's more than you're going to do."

Maximo glanced out at the ballroom and saw the student he knew from Harvard, Woolcott. He wore a dark blue suit and vest and stood in the aisle with his father, a sleek real estate man whose name was frequently in newspaper stories about Democratic politics. When the older Woolcott moved two steps to shake hands with somebody, the son moved two steps. When the father stepped into a row to shake hands with a delegate, the son remained six inches behind. When the father smiled, Woolcott smiled. As he watched Woolcott, Maximo felt even more comfortable with this crowd of outcasts listening to a lunatic dressed in a Puerto Rican flag.

Out in the ballroom, Nicki looked around for a place to put out her cigarette, saw none and dropped it into her coffee container. Now she had to find a place to put the container; she would not be like everybody else in the place and throw it on the floor. All slobs. She walked to a trashcan in a corner of the ballroom. The trashcan was placed at the door to the ladies' room. As long as she was up, Nicki decided, she would go to the bathroom. Under ordinary circumstances she would not dare use such a place as this for a facility, but she thought of sitting in this ballroom for another half hour, perhaps an hour, and then the train ride all the way up to Maximo's house.

"Door's locked, you got to go downstairs," a woman said to her.

Nicki walked down to the lobby and the bellhop directed her to the ladies' room. As Nicki started over to it, the red sheath with Jacqueline Onassis inside it walked out of the cocktail lounge and into the ladies' room.

"I'm not going in there," Nicki said.

"Come here," the bellhop said to her.

"Come where?"

"I'll take care of you." He led her to the other side of the lobby and pushed open the men's room door.

"I'll stay right here and keep everybody out until you come out yourself," the bellhop said.

"You better," Nicki said.

"Rely on me," the bellhop said.

As Nicki walked in, she glanced at herself in the mirror over the sink and was disgusted to find her hair matted from the ballroom heat. Then she walked over to the stalls which sat in dimness under a ceiling light that had burned out. No sooner had she settled her thin cotton pants about her legs when the door opened and two men walked up to the urinals alongside the sinks. At least if they look, they'll see pants, Nicki told herself. She peered through the crack in the door and saw a man with a drawn face, the hair slicked straight back, talking to a chubby man with thick glasses. The man with the drawn face was at the urinal and the one with thick glasses was splashing water on his face. Nicki dropped her face into her hands and sat motionless. If anybody looks in on me, I'll scream.

"It's all right," Rose Keogh's husband said.

"Just," McCafferty said.

"What was the figure?" Keogh said.

"Ten."

"Ten? Henry, we're putting up one year's salary for the job. It isn't fair to ask us to come up with ten more. A whole year's salary. Do you know anybody who'd pledge that?"

"Not this year. That's why you're getting the nomination in the first place."

"But now it's ten more?"

"Did I ask you for it yet? I said, I promised him ten. That doesn't mean he'll ever see it."

"Henry, what if he doesn't get it and he yells?"

"How's Feinstein going to yell? He's going to do the same thing as Wolf did last time. We promised him more than ten and after the vote we wouldn't even take his phone calls. You know what happened? He was very mad at me. He pouted. Until he needed something, and then he came around to me one night as if nothing had happened. We made a lamb out of Wolfie. Same thing will happen here. Who the hell is this guy to get ten thousand for a half dozen votes?"

McCafferty stepped to the sink.

Just don't come *near* me, Nicki said to herself. She squeezed her face with her hands. I'm so *embarrassed,* she thought.

The bellhop was not in the lobby when Nicki came out of the men's room, causing her to become even more angry. She regarded betrayal as a personal possession; when practiced by others, even at the lowest form, it became a sacrilege. She glanced at the clock over the room clerk and saw that it was after eight o'clock already, which would make it impossible for her to spend time with Maximo and still get home at an hour other than one so late as to cause certain detection. At the same time, she told herself that she deserved a night with the body of her choice. She looked around the decrepit hotel lobby, saw a phone and called her friend Angela and informed her that as far as anyone was concerned, she, Nicki, was staying with her tonight. Then Nicki called her mother and said that she was going to be out late shopping with Angela and it would be easier to stay over night with her.

"What shopping?" the mother said. "You went shopping Saturday."

"Just some things I want to get with Angela."

"Lately, you're starting to live in the wind," the mother said, her voice trying to lead Nicki into the reaction, overly loud protest, the least stammer or traceable falsehood that would expose the evil she suspected.

"Ma," Nicki said evenly, "are you telling me I can't

spend one night with a girlfriend, go home and wash my hair with her?''

"I never said a thing like that," the mother said.

"I'll call you from work in the morning," Nicki said. "Unless you want to call me at Angela's tonight and check up on me."

The sarcasm hit her mother, who backed off and said, no, she would never do such a thing as check on her daughter. Let her try, Nicki thought; Angela would declare that there was no way to wake up anybody sleeping this soundly, and persuasion would not move her from this.

Nicki went upstairs where she found Maximo looking about the room bleakly. Seeing her, a smile came onto his face that caused Nicki to touch him before she spoke.

"I have something important to tell you," she said.

Maximo's eyebrows went up.

Oh, I like his eyes so much. I like his whole face.

"I'm staying with you tonight," she said gaily.

He answered with his eyes.

She squeezed his hand. "Unless you don't want me."

"As long as everything is all right at home. I don't want your father crawling through my window at four in the morning."

"He doesn't know you exist, dear," she said.

"How much longer is all this going to take here," she said, indicating the crowd now milling about the ballroom at a more excited rate.

"Not long now," Maximo said. "But it's all right. We've got a lot of time ton—"

Nicki suddenly dropped her forehead on his shoulder.

"Oh, please. I don't want that man to see me. I'm so *embarrassed*."

"Which man?"

Nicki's eyes peered over Maximo's shoulder as if it were a parapet. "The man over there. In the brown suit."

Maximo turned his head and saw McCafferty and Rose Keogh's husband talking in the middle aisle.

"Do you know him?" Maximo said.

"The one in the brown suit," she said.

"From where?"

"From no place. I went down to the ladies' room before and the greasy bellhop, oh, I never should have *trusted* him; anyway, he told me to use the men's room. Said he'd be right there to keep people out. I'm not inside there twenty seconds and these two men, the man in the brown suit and somebody else, walk right in on me and start peeing. Oh, I wanted to *die*."

"Right in front of you?"

"Oh, I was in one of the booths. They didn't even notice I was there. At least, I hope. I could see through the crack in the door and I saw him, all right, the one in the brown suit."

"He didn't say anything to you?"

"No, he didn't know I was there. I told you. He was talking to the man with him. Do you know him?"

"I've seen him," Maximo said.

"Not much to get excited about."

"I know that," Maximo said.

"He's a thief, too."

"That goes without saying."

"Oh, this man said it. What a rat this one is. He said he promised some man ten thousand and he wasn't going to pay it in a million years."

"Promised who?"

"Who else? Some Jew. Who could know the name? I know he said he did the same thing to some guy Wolf last year. I remember that name because he said he made a lamb out of him."

Maximo led Nicki to her chair, sat alongside her for a moment and then walked along the side of the room to where the head of the black and Hispanic caucus was standing. The chunky black man cocked his head and made a dubious face as Maximo spoke to him. Then the chunky black man walked slowly around the room until he saw Feinstein, the leader whose six votes were going to Keogh. Feinstein dropped his chin on his chest and listened. Then the chunky black man walked away and Feinstein stood for a moment, then his head rose and he prowled the center aisle. He beckoned to a man who sat in the middle of a row. The man got up and followed

Feinstein out to the staircase. A lapel badge said his name was Wolf.

The head of the black and Hispanic caucus stood along the wall with Maximo. Then Feinstein and Wolf came out of the staircase with their faces showing boredom. The head of the black and Hispanic caucus spread his hands to Maximo to indicate that now it surely was over; the vote was lost.

Maximo walked back and sat with Nicki.

"What did you just do?" she asked.

"I told that man what you just told me."

"How could you?"

"What?"

"You made a stool pigeon out of me. I don't tell you for someone else to know. I don't even know what I told you means, but whatever it was, I told it to you. I can't trust you."

"I didn't say you were the one who told me."

"But I know I told."

"Well, anyway, nobody knows if it was true or not."

"Of course it was. I say the truth."

"He doesn't know that. I was giving him third party hearsay. All he did was tell the guy who's supposed to be getting paid this year. It didn't look like anything happened."

Two blacks in business suits and an emaciated white woman, hair straggly and arms filled with notebooks and leaflets, pushed past them into the row. The black man nearest Nicki immediately was wracked with a cigarette cough. He dropped his cigarette onto the floor, heaved once more and then, with a strangling sound, spit phlegm into a tissue in his hand. He crumpled the tissue, looked around for someplace to put it, saw none and dropped the tissue on the floor.

Nicki stood up. "That's it for me, dear."

"We're going in a minute," Maximo said.

"Sooner than that," she said.

As he followed her to the back of the room, toward the stairway to the lobby, reaching for her arm, there was a banging sound at the front of the ballroom and an old nasal voice sounded through a loudspeaker whose crack-

ling accompanied each word. Maximo touched Nicki.
"This should take only a few minutes," he said.

He stood with her in the back and watched the old
woman in the front of the room adjust her glasses, then
make some comment that caused all the important-look-
ing men around her to laugh uncontrollably; the generals,
having pretended to turn the army over to a private, now
enjoyed the scene. The woman now began to call out
names, and in the seats a delegate would stand and call
out his vote. Everyone was bent over keeping tally. She
had called about thirty names and the votes were cast
without causing any stir and then she called out, "George
Feinstein."

Feinstein half-rose. He called out a name so softly that
it could not be heard in most parts of the room. But those
able to hear it turned their heads in sudden interest.

The old nasal voice in the front of the room said,
"Would you please repeat your vote."

Feinstein half-rose again. "Goldenberg," he said in a
clear voice.

Henry McCafferty's head snapped from Feinstein to
Rose Keogh's husband, who was standing in complete
stillness in the doorway of the room where his wife sat.

McCafferty placed his elbow on the back of his folding
chair and dropped his cheek onto it. He stared at Feinstein as the next five names were called, names of people
who sat in the same row with Feinstein. Each person who
stood called out, "Goldenberg." McCafferty's cheek lin-
gered on his fist for several moments after the six votes
had been recorded and the entire room broke into excited
conversation. Then McCafferty picked up his head, removed his elbow from the back of the chair, returned his
body to its normal sitting position and stared at the front
of the room, a spectator at an autopsy of his own greed.

Maximo had a glimpse of the Keogh woman. She was
standing in the doorway with her husband, waiting for
the room to clear so that they could leave without further
mortification. The winner, Goldenberg, had such a crowd
of hand-reachers about him, including several blacks and
Hispanics, that there was no way to get past them. Rose
Keogh pretended not to be looking, but her eyes slowly

ran over the crowd and that was when Maximo saw her, and he thought at first that she was seeing nothing and then he saw her eyes move almost unnoticeably and fall on Ron Seguera's flag of Puerto Rico.

In the subway train on the way home, Maximo balanced himself in the middle of the car so he would not have to hold onto anything. He wanted to speak with gestures, for now he saw clearly great possibilities for the life he had chosen, and he was immensely pleased to see that Nicki's eyes shone with excitement over what he was saying to her. When the powerless organize, he told her, in the eyes of others they become powerful and this immediately makes the powerless powerful. It can be all so simple, he enthused. Merely people with the same problem associating with each other and remaining with each other long enough to attain the power to change their lives and the lives of their children. Think what can be done, he said to Nicki. He exulted in the lighted eyes that acknowledged him.

Nicki, clinging to a post, not hearing a word Maximo said over the train's noise, studied his beard and the slope of his neck onto his shoulders. She could not wait to have his body pressed against hers. *A fucking movie star!* she said to herself. And he's mine.

.... **Chapter 21**

....

When Francisca arrived for work, she was let into Indio's apartment by his wife, who said he still was out from the night before. Francisca found only twenty bags of heroin under the shirts and half of them were gone after only a few knocks on the door. At 10:30, Indio, his eyes red from the night, walked in. His business sense was offended when Francisca told him there was no merchandise left, but his body was unable to react. He gave Francisca six hundred dollars and instructed her to go to Ana's Bar, ask for Teenager or Benny, hand them the money and say that Indio was in bed, that he was tired, that he needed forty half los.

"Buy a loaf of bread at the store that is long, so that it sticks out of the bag and people can see that you were to the store," Indio told her. "Then put the half los in the bag."

Indio, still in his clothes, climbed into bed, stretched his legs under the sheet and yawned. He never felt his eyelids come down.

The gun poking the right side of Indio's head woke him up. When he jerked his head away from the gun, his left temple hit the other gun held to his head. He saw his wife standing at the foot of the bed while a short man in a Yankee baseball cap pressed a sawed-off shotgun against her head. Two or three others were in the apartment, and

283

Indio saw one of them start out of the living room with a television set in his arms. One of Indio's kids jumped off the couch and tried to stop the guy. Someone else, in a black shirt, threw Indio's kid onto the floor. Indio bolted, and everything became dark pain as a gun came down on his head.

"You better kill me," Indio said.

"That is no trouble for me, man," one of them next to him said. He wore a brown shirt and a truck driver's cap. Out of a corner of his eye Indio could see that the man in the brown shirt had a .357 Magnum.

At the foot of the bed, the one in the Yankee baseball cap said, "Where is the dope?"

Indio pointed to the dresser. "Under the shirts."

The guy with the shotgun pushed Indio's wife onto the bed, held the gun on her and ran a hand through the dresser, found the decks of heroin, put the shotgun atop the dresser and scooped up the heroin with both hands.

"This is all?" he said.

"I have to get more later," Indio said.

"You will get more now," he said.

He held up the heroin decks for the others in the room to see.

"This is for you, Jamie," he called out.

One of the junkies grinned. "Angel copped!" he called out.

Jamie, Indio repeated to himself. He would remember that name. Angel, he repeated to himself. He would remember that name too. Indio counted six of them in the room. They didn't care how much noise they made either.

Out in the hallway, the junkies struggled with the couch. Francisca was coming up the stairs with a loaf of bread sticking out of the top of the bag of heroin decks. She turned around as if she forgot something and went back down the stairs.

When the junkies came back into the apartment after taking the couch someplace, they went into the bathroom with Angel. Several minutes later, Angel looked out and motioned. The man still holding the Magnum to Indio's head used it as a prod and brought Indio into the bathroom. Two of the junkies were sitting on the edge of the bathtub. Burned matches and used syringes were on the sink. Angel ran water in the bathtub until it was nearly full. Then he grabbed Indio by the hair and forced his head down toward the water. Indio gripped the side of the tub and kept his face in the air, but then the junkies grabbed his arms and locked hands on Indio's neck and Indio's face splashed into the water and the water covered his ears. For a moment, Indio opened his eyes in the water, but he thought that meant he was accepting what was happening and he closed them and tried to shake his head and fight for his life. The first place it hurt him was in the stomach, then at the bottom of his throat. He screamed inside. Now the pain was everywhere.

Angel pulled the head out of the water. "You will get Teenager for us or we will drown you in this water," Angel said. The silence that followed was interrupted by a slight noise that caused Angel to pause in his work.

"What is this you are doing, giving Indio a bath?" Teenager said. He stood in the bathroom doorway, eyes narrow, mouth in a cold smile.

Angel jumped up and his hand went straight out so that the sawed-off shotgun was directly in Teenager's face.

"That's all right," Teenager said.

"We want your dope or I will blow your face away," Angel said.

"That's all right," Teenager said.

He turned and walked out of the bathroom. Angel, embarrassed that someone would walk away from him in such a way, ran behind Teenager and stuck the shotgun barrel against the back of Teenager's neck. Teenager kept walking, with steps so long that Angel had to put himself out to be able to keep the shotgun against the back of Teenager's neck.

The one holding the Magnum pushed Indio after them. When Teenager went out into the hall, the man with the Magnum pushed Indio out, too. The others stayed in the apartment with Indio's wife and children.

Teenager climbed the apartment house stairs to the fifth floor, and walked to the apartment at the end of the hall. The staircase leading up to the roof was a couple of paces to the right of the door.

"All my dope in this apartment," Teenager said.

"If you knock on this door and it is the wrong place, then we blow your head right here in this hallway," Angel said.

"That's all right," Teenager said.

Teenager knocked sharply on the door. When Indio heard a squeak inside the apartment, he closed his eyes and prepared to die. A stranger would open the door and the guns would go off. Nobody came to the door. Teenager knocked again. When the door still did not open, Teenager banged his fist. He had won his gamble, that the apartment would be empty.

He stepped past Angel and sat down on the cracked stone staircase leading to the roof.

"He is just gone for a minute," Teenager said. "Soon he will come back. He has all my dope in his apartment. You cannot get in there because he has so many locks. Soon he will come back."

Teenager went into the pocket of his green silk shirt and took out cigarettes.

"Indio, you look tired. Sit with me, Indio."

Indio was afraid to move. Teenager got up and took Indio by the arm and brought him to the staircase. The one holding the Magnum jumped.

"That's all right," Teenager said.

He put Indio alongside him on the staircase.

"Smoke, Indio," Teenager said. "We must wait." He gave Indio a cigarette. He held out the pack to Angel and the one with the Magnum, but they were afraid of Teenager's hand and moved away. Teenager shrugged, put the cigarettes back into his shirt pocket and sat on the staircase and smoked. They were there for nearly fifteen minutes, Teenager and Indio on the staircase and the two gunmen a couple of steps away, in front of the apartment house door at the end of the fifth floor hallway, which exploded.

The one with the Magnum pitched onto the back of his head. Angel, terrified, faced where the shot had come from, from the top of the staircase leading to the fifth floor from the fourth floor. Teenager boiled off the steps to the roof and his feet kicked out and crashed into the side of Angel's head. The shotgun went out of Angel's hands and Angel dropped to his knees. Teenager's foot came into his face and knocked Angel onto his back. Teenager jumped in the air and his Cuban heels came down on Angel's face. He danced on Angel's face until he lost interest.

Albertito and Benny Velez stood in the hallway. "One shot I take," Benny said.

"You can take what your shot did to this guy and throw him in the furnace where he belongs," Teenager said.

He reached down and grabbed Angel under the arm and pulled him up. He wrapped an arm around Angel and carried him like a sack of rice. Angel's feet dragged on the hallway floor.

"This man is injured and I must help him," Teenager said. He bent down and kissed Angel on the cheek. "That's all right," Teenager said.

Each time Angel started to fall off the bar stool, Teenager grabbed him under the arm and boosted him.

"Another drink for Angel!" Teenager called.

Luisa Maria poured more Bacardi into a glass and Teenager held it to Angel's mouth.

"Drink, Angel, this will make you strong again." He tipped the glass and Angel's mouth dropped and the tan rum ran off Angel's bottom lip and dripped onto his polo shirt, which stuck to him, wet and dark, from the blood from his face.

"A beer for Angel," Teenager said.

Luisa Maria opened a nip and handed it to Teenager.

"Cold beer, Angel!" Teenager said. He put the bottle into Angel's mouth and when he tipped it, the liquid again ran out of Angel's mouth. Teenager held the bottle up and emptied it over Angel's head.

"Wake up, Angel, you have been drinking too much!" Benny sat at the bar clicking a set of pliers.

"Angel," Teenager said, "Torres sends you, right?"

"Yes," Angel said.

"These ones with you, who are they?"

Angel shook his head. "Torres told them," he mumbled.

"I know who told them, but their names I want," Teenager said. "I want to send them invitations to a big party."

Angel was silent.

Teenager waved at the juke box.

"Give Angel some music!"

Luisa Maria put a dollar into the machine and punched C–11 four times.

As she walked back to the bar, the music began.

> *Toro mata ahí*
> *Toro*
> *mata . . .*

Teenager's hand began to wave. "Louder," he said.

Behind the bar, Luisa Maria turned the key that caused the juke box to become louder.

> *Toro viejo se murió . . .*

"Much louder," Teenager called.

Luisa Maria turned the key all the way and now the trumpets on the record vibrated in the barroom as loud as a rock band.

Teenager whispered in Angel's ear and then cocked his head so that his ear was very close to Angel, so he could hear anything Angel said. Angel said nothing. Teenager gently took Angel's wrist and brought the hand out.

When Luisa Maria saw Benny get off the bar stool with the pliers she covered her face with both hands, then spread her fingers so that she could see through them. Benny looked at Angel's cracked, dirty fingers, selected one nail, on the right middle finger, and put the pliers to it. Angel tried to pull his hand back, but Teenager's hand remained locked on the wrist. He kept his ear to Angel's mouth. Luisa Maria yelped as she saw Benny yank the pliers. Angel's middle fingernail sat in the plier's jaws. In

Teenager's ear there was a scream that started in Angel's stomach and rose to a sudden pitch.

He let go of Angel's wrist, and Angel stuck the finger into his mouth. Teenager took the wrist again and forced the finger out of the mouth. He whispered into Angel's ear. Angel, crying, shook his head no. Teenager forced the hand out again. Benny opened the pliers and let the old nail drop to the floor and then he inspected Angel's hand again, selected the thumb, gripped it with the pliers and pulled the dirty thumbnail out of the hand.

On the juke box, the trumpets came to a high pitch to mark the end of the record. Teenager slapped a hand across Angel's mouth and held it there as the record changed. As the first notes of its second play started, Teenager removed his hand from Angel's mouth and again put his ear to it.

Teenager began nodding and yanking on Angel's wrist as a threat, and then Teenager looked up with a great smile. He motioned to Luisa Maria to cut the juke box down, and she turned the key and made the music so low she could hardly hear the words of the song.

"Angel has told me who it was that was with him at Indio's house," Teenager said. He called it, ticking off a finger at a time as he mentioned a name.

"This fellow Pedro."

Benny nodded. At the door, Albertito said, "Who is this Pedro?"

"Little Ralph's brother, Pedro," Teenager said.

"Oh," Albertito said.

"And Little Ralph," Teenager said.

"Aha," Benny said.

"NeNe," Teenager said.

"I hate NeNe the worst," Albertito said.

"Jamie," Teenager said.

"How could he do such a thing?" Benny said. "I just give him fifty dollar the other day."

"The main one is Torres," Teenager said. "Torres paid them to get me." He patted Angel on the shoulder. "I told Angel we would let him leave here if he would tell us. And now I am going to live up to my word."

He told Luisa Maria to turn up the juke box. Teenager began singing with it, *"Toro mata ahí."*

He lifted Angel off the stool and half pushed, half carried Angel to the back of the room. As Teenager passed Benny, he held a hand out. Benny went into his waistband and brought out a nickel-plated Colt Detective Special. Luisa Maria sucked in her breath.

She clapped her hands over her face again. Through the fingers she could see Teenager put the barrel of the gun to Angel's head. Teenager waited until the trumpets of *"¡Toro Mata!"* were at their highest and then he roared out, *"Toro torito . . ."*

The juke box almost completely drowned out the sound of the gun as it went off against Angel's head.

Luisa Maria, peering through her hands, screeched.

At the bar, Benny went into his shirt pocket and brought out his cocaine.

....Chapter 22

....

The number five IRT subway train came out of the tunnel and onto the iron bridge crossing the Harlem River. Standing between the third and fourth cars, the wind blowing his hair, Maximo watched the lights of a tugboat glancing across the top of the black water.

"Fixtures are chattels so affixed to land or buildings as to lose their identity as chattels and become part of the land or buildings," he recited to himself, like an incantation.

It wandered into his mind like a thought about drinking water or eating dinner. For weeks, Maximo had been going by subway to and from the Statler Hilton in Manhattan, sitting in the faded ballroom with four hundred other students, mostly in blue jeans, and he had just finished the last evening in which the professor would inflict on them his three-hour monotone on the most important subjects to know for the New York State Bar exam, which was to start the next morning. The ballroom was full on this last night because the professor, who had a reputation of being able to predict most of the questions to appear on the bar exam, was, like a horse tout at post time, giving his final selections, the last-minute specials that had earned him fame. Tonight's last words had centered on real property.

"Timing is all important with regard to trade fixtures,"

the professor had said. "If fixtures are not removed in time, they become the property of the landlord."

To prepare Maximo to assist the South Bronx, the professor with the sure-shot questions had droned, "A bathroom cabinet attached to the surface of a wall does not evidence the same intent as does one installed flush against the wall." The words remained in Maximo's ears as he rode the train.

The train pulled into the first station in the Bronx. "No riding between cars," a cop standing in the station shouted to Maximo. Maximo went into the car. The cop came into the same car. A kid of high school age, toothpick hanging from the corner of his mouth, turned on the portable cassette player he had on his lap. Salsa music blared.

"Turn that thing off," the cop said. The young man pushed up the lever on the side of the cassette player. The volume doubled.

"I said to turn that thing off," the cop said.

With a simple motion, he scooped up the cassette player and threw it out the window over the schoolboy's head. The schoolboy started to rise from the seat to take on the cop. The cop's right hand banged into the kid's left ear. Not enough punch to stun and harm and cause people throughout the car to erupt, but enough for the kid to get the message.

Five stops later, Maximo stepped off the train and went through the turnstile and down the stairs leading from the elevated station to the street. He walked along Southern Boulevard and turned into Pinto Avenue. Through the truck fumes, through the smell of fish frying in stands whose glass was too smeared for vision, and all through the tar heat of the street, Maximo could smell her neck. If he could be with her for just a few minutes, make it an hour, an hour would be lovely, and feel her body against his, perhaps he could get the ownership of bathroom fixtures out of his mind for the night.

At the corner on Pinto, four men were sitting on milk crates, playing dominoes on a piece of plywood propped on a cardboard box. One of them swiveled and called across the street. David Robles' mother looked out the window. *"Espera!"* Maximo stopped. Her head disappeared from the window, and in a few moments the street door flew open and David came running into the street. He handed Maximo a folded sheet of paper. Then David went into his shirt pocket and took out a dollar bill. "For doing my job," he said proudly. He ran back to his door. Maximo climbed the stairs, pushed the dog aside when he opened the door and leaned against the living room wall and read the note under the ceiling light.

M—

I am going to Novena tonight so you will pass your exam. I will prove how sure I am of you. The Novena is not to St. Jude. It is to St. Ann. I am not worried about your passing. I am going to Novena so that you will get the highest mark and be the richest lawyer in New York.

You are nice.
N.

Maximo read the note several times. While he was proud that she understood both the importance of the exams and the extent of his smartness, the line that he kept rereading was the one where she said he was nice. When he took the dog out for his nightly run, Maximo kept thinking of the line. It was the close of a short note and he saw it as great poetry.

The wolf whistle was the overt act that caused her to think differently of her life with her husband for the first time since the night she had sat on the park bench and looked at the East River and agreed to go out with no other man. The wolf whistle came from this stupid moron who was leaning on a rake inside the prison's outer fence, a high storm fence. Nicki and her husband were in the conjugal visit trailer parked on the grass outside the storm fence. At four o'clock that afternoon, Nicki and her husband looked out and waved at the guard at the main gate, who nodded and then wrote on his clipboard that prisoner Schiavone, housed for this day in the fuck truck, was present at the afternoon head count. At first,

Nicki and her husband were smiling as they waved at the guard, but then as this stupid moron behind the fence kept whistling, Nicki's husband broke into a giggle. He hopped from the trailer and stood out on the grass and began pounding his chest like an ape. The moron behind the storm fence shook with laughter. Nicki's husband now made ape sounds. The guy behind the fence fell on the grass, his legs kicking in the air. The guard with the clipboard yelled something and the moron rolled onto his feet and walked off with the rake. But now from an upper floor in the main building there came more wolf whistles and shouts from men pressed against barred windows.

"Eat your hearts out," Nicki's husband yelled.

Nicki quickly ducked inside the trailer, for she knew what the retorts from the window would be. The sounds of voices calling from the prison caused her to cringe. The trailer was neat, and the bed was covered with her own sheets and pillowcases and blankets, but she now imagined the place smelled faintly of a place where dogs had lain. Each day of the month, different bodies were on this bed, black nigger bodies mostly, thick lips smacking, big long cow tongues lapping, the bodies rolling around on the mattress, probably with some used sheet on it, not even tucked in, the heels finally kicking the sheet onto the floor and making everything the way they were used to it, bareass on dirty mattresses. Because some schedule in a guard's office said it now was the turn of #327C19 Schiavone, into this fuck truck she came, seamy with semen, a place that made a motel whorehouse seem as fresh as new grass. Here was her husband validating her feeling as he hooted back at the men behind the bars. Above all, he knew that she liked sex in the dark, where she could surrender her privacy with murmurs. Now he was taking her privacy and spilling it across the floor of a cellblock.

When her husband stepped into the trailer, he walked up behind her and locked his arm under her chin. He made an animal sound.

"Please, I need a minute," Nicki said. The arm released and she walked to the kitchenette and began washing plates that were already clean. The next time I have to come here, I will have my period, she told herself.

Later, they decided to finish the last bottle of red wine before leaving the trailer.

"So it looks good," her husband said.

"What looks good?" Nicki said.

"Me getting out of here," he said. "I told you."

"When?"

"I just told you before."

"Oh, well, you've been telling me all day."

"They said when I meet the board in February, I got a shot."

"That's good," she said.

"Good? It's my whole life."

"When could you get out?"

"If they give me a date in February, I could be in a halfway house by March."

"Uh huh."

"We'd be back where we were." He drained the wine, stood up and bent down to kiss her. She responded, but then when he began to press his body on hers, she held up a hand.

"Too late," she said. "We have to be out of here."

She felt better when he stepped back.

Driving home in her father's car, Nicki wondered about the rules of her life. If she was breaking them already by seeing Maximo now and then, perhaps someday she would break nearly all the rest of the rules and live according to her desires, and not by some ancient code that her people followed. In the beginning, nothing mattered except to be with her husband. When he worked construction the first year that they were married, she went to a job on Lexington Avenue, a twenty-five-story apartment building, and she waited by the cement trucks for two hours, and then he finally came down and they kissed in the hot sun and then he turned around and went right back up, and she would have waited far longer, for the thought of him made time and comfort meaningless. Prison was something else. There had been a forlornness to her life that she tried not to think about, but now this wolf whistle from this stupid moron had brought it all to the surface: her husband had been away too long and she no longer could handle it.

She stopped for coffee at a Hot Shoppe on the Thruway, took a piece of paper from the cashier and wrote the note to Maximo. She gave it to David Robles on Pinto Avenue and then drove to New Jersey in time to go to novena with her mother and aunts. This she had to do; one of the few things you could not lie about was making a novena for a person. If you said you were going, you had to go.

She prayed by rote, using her white rosary beads, thinking of what Maximo looked like when he read a book to her. When she thought of the wolf whistle, she closed her eyes and said the rosary louder to rid herself of the scene in the trailer. At home, the mother and aunts sat in the kitchen. Aunt Philomena brought out the Polaroid shots of her nephew, who was in Lewisburg.

"You got your pictures?" the aunt said to Nicki.

"Somewhere," Nicki said.

"Let me see. I want to see what he looks like these days."

"I'll look around for them," Nicki said.

She went down into the playroom and put Donna Summer on the stereo. She flicked one switch, the one that turned on only the ceiling lights, miniature spotlights that were imbedded in the ceiling. She stood in one beam of light and swayed to the music. She thought of the trailer and the wolf whistle again—why does this freaking thing *bother* me now?—and wondered what other things time had done to her husband. He knew what she was like, yet he had pranced in front of the trailer and proclaimed that she was some hot bitch to be dog-jumped in the sunlight, with the whole village watching. Maximo, she had never spent a crude moment with that one. He allowed her lust to spill from her when she wanted it. Maximo had a quality that she never before had experienced, understatement. He knew that the lights were to be out, that her feelings for what she was doing were to be protected.

When she was around him, she felt a confidence in herself that was unique. She did not realize how she felt at the time, but at several odd moments, at the desk in the office, on the bus on the way home, she remembered the night in the hotel with the judges. It wasn't the kind of life she ever would feel comfortable around, she felt, but for the one night, even though she didn't realize it until much later, there was an excitement to her life that centered on something that was considered out of her class. Maximo. Oh, he is so courteous. You could see he went to a high-class school.

When the song "Bad Girl" came on the stereo, Nicki picked up a stirrer from a glass on the bar, held it to her lips like a microphone, and began to hum along with Donna Summer. Nicki started to sing softly, then louder, and she danced under the spotlights. Her head rocked and she sang "Bad Girl" into the stirrer and she swept her hand out, as if shaking the microphone wire from about her feet, and she danced and sang on, at first pretending to be in a Las Vegas nightclub, in a top lounge, and then she no longer was pretending; singing as high and loud as possible, wailing really, head back, body swaying, she sang into the microphone in her hand in this nightclub. She saw Maximo by himself at a table by the wall.

The next day, she felt that somewhere inside her a feeling that she thought had been anchored began to move. She knew this in the morning, when the exhaust from the bus clung to the pine tree branches like paste and yet she noticed only the color of the pine. She stood on line at the bus stop and thought of Maximo brushing his hair to start his morning.

On the bus to Manhattan, she stared out the window and saw Maximo taking his exams. At work, she saw for the first time that there was perhaps more to her computer terminal than words and figures that swam under the glass surface like baitfish. Suddenly the computer terminal, once a machine with a strange tongue, now became a wise, familiar voice. The computer dealt with only one universe at a time, and then only at those moments for which it had been programmed. Sitting at the computer, she suddenly knew that it was important for her to deal with one subject in one place and in one soli-

tary time frame. Just as her computer worked only with
the information given to it, so would she call up her life
one screen at a time. Her heritage was to control every
moment of her life; in dealing with another person, the
only consideration was the amount of good the other person could accomplish for you before reaching the point
where he had to be betrayed. True affection was reserved
for possessions. Until today, she loved most the diamond
trinket hanging on a gold chain about her neck. The trinket had diamonds set tastefully and richly. It was not a
glaring diamond, but it was her most costly piece of jewelry and it made her feel superior, which to her was all-
important.

She came from a body of people who believed, whether
indeed it ever had happened or not, that their family
names called for brother to kill brother if one was found
to be treasonous. Control of emotions and relationships
was everything. And now, of this morning, from the moment she looked at the leaves on the bus stop, she understood that her usual staying hand was not quick enough,
the palm spread not wide enough, to suppress what was
happening. Therefore, she said to herself at her computer, if she was falling in love with Maximo Escobar—
falling? Say the truth: you want to scream—then she
would make sure to contain the romance on one screen
of her life. When she wanted to deal with Maximo, it
would be only at those times when she was actually with
him or had to think of him. Otherwise, she would log him
off. When it was time for her to deal with her husband in
jail, she would either be visiting him or on the phone with
him or standing at the stove and wrapping tinfoil about
food for him. She would keep everything on separate
screens.

In a reaction to her emotions wandering, Nicki's eyes
became mean whips as they went across those names she
called up on her "ST" file, or skip-tracing. She became
personally infuriated with each name. Who were these
people not to be paying their bills, and not paying them
to *her?* For an hour, Nicki studied the work productivity
sheets on skip-tracing and then settled on one screen that
showed a man named Carpenter had lived in Cleveland,

moved to Akron without notifying the credit-card company and had run up bills of $1,753.27. At midmorning, Nicki indicated on the computer that the administrator was checking on the case. She went to the Akron cross-directory—a phone book listed by streets—and found a family with a phone who lived next door to Carpenter. She called the neighbor and said she was from the Akron Edison Company and because of a misunderstanding the power to Carpenter's house would have to be shut off by five o'clock, unless Carpenter called and cleared up the misunderstanding. Nicki left her 800 number.

At three o'clock that afternoon, Nicki's phone rang.

"This is Mrs. Carpenter," an annoyed voice said. "We paid you."

"You didn't pay me," Nicki said.

"We did so. We paid our deposit to Akron Edison."

"But you didn't pay me. You didn't pay your credit card."

"What's that got to do with the electric lights?"

"It's got to do with your husband's credit-card bill."

"You're not from the electric company?"

"No, I'm worse. I'm the place your husband owes one thousand seven hundred fifty-three dollars and twenty-seven cents."

"Oh, I don't know anything about that."

"You don't know he has a credit card, Mrs. Carpenter?"

"I know he has it, but that's his business."

"You mean your husband doesn't tell you about the things he charges and never pays for?" Nicki said. Her eyes ran over the list of places and amounts on the computer screen. "You mean your husband didn't tell you that on March 4, he rented a room at the Jade East Motel at Cleveland Airport and that the charge for the room was thirty-two dollars? That was the night rate. Did he tell you that on March 16, he rented another room at the Jade East Motel and the charge for the room was eighteen dollars? That sounds like the rate for one of those afternoon quickies. That's that airport element."

"Where are you getting this from?" the woman on the phone said.

"Right from your husband's signed receipts. I have them right on the screen in front of me. Your husband's life is on a computer, Mrs. Carpenter."

"I don't believe you."

"It doesn't matter whether you believe me or not. Your husband used all these motels and he doesn't want to pay for them."

"Well, I'm sure I don't know anything about this."

"Oh, you weren't in the motels with him?"

"You'll get in trouble for speaking like this," Mrs. Carpenter said.

"Does this mean, Mrs. Carpenter, that you don't know that your husband spent the weekend of April first and second at the Holiday Inn at New Trier? Or—"

"—Dorothy!"

"Excuse me, Mrs. Carpenter?"

"He was in New Trier?"

"For two nights in the Holiday Inn, plus restaurant and bar, your husband ran up a bill of two hundred and seventy-six dollars and forty-eight cents at the Holiday Inn at New Tri—"

"—He was with Dorothy!"

"Excuse me, Mrs. Carpenter?"

"He was with Dorothy in New Trier," the woman moaned. "That bastard!"

Nicki spoke forcefully, to raise her voice over the woman's shrieking. "Mrs. Carpenter, I don't care who he was in the motel with. But you just tell your husband that if he wants to run around with women, do it on his own money. Don't expect this bank to pay for his sex. Just tell him, you pay to play in this league, darling. Good afternoon, Mrs. Carpenter."

She went into the kitchen with one of the sheets wrapped around her, sipped from a can of Coke and then stood in the bedroom door and examined her legs.

"I almost have Irish legs," she said.

"What are they?" Maximo asked from the bed.

"You don't know Irish legs? Burned at the knees and the feet. I'm out in the sun one day and I almost got Irish legs. That's not me, you know. I'm Italian. I tan."

"You like being tan?" Maximo said.

"Oh, I love it. Wait'll you see me once I start going to the beach. I'm Sicilian. I get so dark. I make you look like skimmed milk."

"You know what Puerto Ricans use for suntan lotion?" Maximo said.

"What?"

"The shade."

"They don't like sun?" Nicki said.

"Nobody wants to get any darker than he is," Maximo said.

"But they live in the sun, near the beach and everything."

"And they stay in doorways."

She held out a leg and examined it. "That's all from doing my father's car. I had on shorts. I did my father's car four hours today. Took me hours. When I do something, I don't pass it off. I do the trunk, the floors, the works. Vacuum the floor, shine all the leather. I was working so long my brother felt sorry for me and he came out and washed the tires. Look what I got from being out in the sun all those hours. Look at the knees. Look at my feet. How do you like them? Irish legs."

She slipped into bed and Maximo nuzzled his face into the crook of her neck.

"What made you stay home and not go to work today?" he said.

"Because you had me so freaked up thinking of this test you took that I could go to work yesterday, but then when I got up this morning I couldn't do it. Whoever heard of a test taking two days?"

"You were worried about me?" Maximo said.

"Not worried that you wouldn't pass or anything. But you've made such a big thing of this, it got to me."

"That's nice," he said. He kissed her.

"Besides, I thought I'd make my father feel good by doing the car for him. That way he won't be asking any questions about me not coming home tonight. I keep him thinking all good things about me." She turned her face and kissed him on the forehead.

"This is the best thing that could have happened," Maximo said.

"Is it?"

"The minute everybody finished the test, they wanted to run out and party. 'Let's go here, let's go there. Let's get really wrecked.' I said, no, I'm too tired. I just want to go home."

"You were tired, all right. You attacked me like it was a war."

"I ran twenty blocks, and the only reason I didn't run another two hundred was that I knew I had to meet you, so I jumped on the subway."

"I would've waited for you," she said. "I would've had coffee for hours waiting for you to pick me up."

"Why should I waste time running when I could be with you? I wanted to walk out of the test in the middle of it and call you up just to speak to you."

"That would've been silly."

"Never," he said. He kissed her neck. "I love you."

He said it first, Nicki told herself. No matter how crazy I get, maybe now I never have to say anything. He said it first.

"I love you," he said again.

She kissed him. "That's nice."

"Do you love me?" he asked.

"How do you say 'I love you' in Puerto Rican?" she asked.

"*Te quiero.*"

"Oh."

"Say it," Maximo said.

"Say what?"

"Tell me, '*Te quiero.*' "

"Oh, I just wanted to know how you say it in Spanish. So now you told me."

"I want you to say it."

She tried to divert him with a small kiss, but he collected her to him and said fiercely, "I want you to say '*te quiero*' to me and then I want you to come and live with me and marry me. I love you."

Wide eyes looked up at Maximo from his chest. "Are you crazy?"

"No, I love you."

"Don't you think about your life?"

"Yes, I do. I think my life out. I know what I want out of my work. And I am going to get it. I am going to do exactly what I want to do in my life. I think it out. Then I do it. I'm smart. And I know what I want with you. I want to love you and live with you. Because I love you."

"I have to tell you the same thing I've been telling you all along."

"Just tell me you love me. Say, '*Te quiero.*' "

"I'll tell you that if my father ever found out that you so much as touched me, you'd be a dead man."

"Stop talking nonsense."

"It's not nonsense. It would happen."

"That's your stupid Guinea movies," Maximo said.

"No, it's my Guinea guns."

"I said I love you and I want you to say that you love me."

"Maximo, I'm married."

"To whom? To a number in jail? You're not married. You're here with me."

"My husband might be coming home."

"When?"

"In a few months."

"What difference does it make?"

"A lot to me, darling."

"You've got nothing left with this guy."

"Who told you?"

"All I have to do is look. You're with me."

"This is only a little disgrace to my life. When he comes home, I'll still be his wife."

"You have nothing with him right now. What do you think you'll have in a few months from now?"

"A husband."

"Yes, you will have a husband. I'll be your husband."

She looked at him and ran a hand through his hair and down his face. She traced the ridge of his nose and then brought her fingers down to his lips. Maximo began kissing them.

"A movie star," she said.

"I'm more than that," he said.

"To me, you're a movie star," she said.

They kissed and Maximo pressed full against her and he was mad at himself that his breath came so quickly and his words sounded desperate.

"Tell me."

"Please, don't talk. Just love me," Nicki said.

"Tell me."

"I don't want to make speeches. Just make love."

"Tell me."

Physically, she was moving, stretching, caressing, feeling. Then everything inside her began to slide, a ship tilting suddenly and things falling off the table, and here she was trying to catch them, but her hands were too slow, her fingers too short. She thought she said something to Maximo and she became alarmed. Then she realized that it was only a moan and that the words had remained inside her. But now nothing inside her would stop and she arranged her body against this man who was causing her to fall into something of which she knew nothing and then she remembered exactly what to do. Her computer screen. Call up one thing at a time and in one time frame.

"I love you today," she said to Maximo.

Who then whispered, *"Te quiero,"* and Nicki drew from his body a sunburst.

Chapter 23

Teenager lived with an oil fire inside him after he killed Angel, and he prowled the streets looking for the others who were with Angel in the raid on Indio's apartment. In the midst of this anger, however, he had to conduct business, including the sale of one kilo of brown heroin to a man named Hector the Buzzard for forty thousand dollars. Hector drove down from Holyoke, Massachusetts, with his ten-year-old son along to throw off any police. Hector arrived at Ana's Bar with twenty thousand dollars and the knowledge that the balance was to be paid within twelve selling days or mayhem would flourish. Teenager took the money, kept in cake boxes tied with red and white bakery string, to the room upstairs from the bar and stood behind the two-way mirror and counted it. He then came down to the bar and called Junior Mendez, who had the heroin stored in his apartment, the voiceless Dobermans pacing back and forth around the plastic bags of heroin.

"Where is your baby?" Teenager said.

"With me in the house," Junior said.

"It is too nice a day for that," Teenager said. "Take your baby out walking. Take him for a big walk."

A half hour later, Teenager got into his Mercedes and had Hector the Buzzard follow. He drove to the Aguaserra, a *cuchifritos* stand with window lights shining on greasy pans in the front window. Next door to it was a

bar with music screeching out the open door and into the
crowded night. As Teenager stepped out of his car, he
waved an arm in the air. Across the street, in a first floor
apartment, a man named Pancha picked up a phone.
Either Pancha or his wife always were on duty at the
window, as if at the periscope of a submarine. Pancha
dialed the Aguaserra. The pay phone on the wall was
picked up by a waitress. Then there was the sound of an
extension being picked up. The extension was in the
basement.

On the extension, Junior Mendez' voice said to the
waitress on the pay phone, *"Cuelga."* The waitress hung
up. Pancha told Junior that it was all right to open the
trap door, that Teenager and people were coming. Junior
Mendez crept up a flight of iron stairs and pulled back the
heavy bolt that prevented anyone upstairs from pulling
the trap door up and coming down unannounced. Teenager's rule was that no one could unlock the trapdoor
unless Pancha first had inspected the people from his window and called in.

Teenager walked Hector the Buzzard into the front of
the *cuchifritos* stand and then stopped. Hector went
alone to the rear, picked up the trap door and went down
the iron stairs to the basement where Junior Mendez sat
with a kilo of brown heroin. By the time Hector came
back up into the *cuchifritos* stand, his ten-year-old son
was chewing on *cuchifritos,* pork skin deep-fried in fat,
and Teenager was driving away in his car.

At Ana's Bar that night, Teenager counted out twelve
hundred dollars and placed it on the bar.

"Do you know my special tailor?" he said to Luisa
Maria.

"I do not know this guy."

"Mel Sharf, the name of this guy is. Go see him tomorrow morning and give him this money and tell him that I
am going to a wedding on Saturday and Benny is going to
this wedding too and we need suits for this wedding. Mel
Sharf has the measurements. Just tell him to work all the
time and make the suits by Saturday."

The next morning, Luisa Maria began to think hard of
the money in her purse. She stopped for coffee at the

stand across from Eddie Hernandez' clothing shop, and she drank her coffee slowly and watched Eddie Hernandez wash his show windows. She thought of the money in her purse some more.

"I need two wedding suits, one with very big shoulders," she explained to Eddie Hernandez a few minutes later.

"How big?" Eddie said.

"Teenager."

"Then it must be very big."

"And one for Benny."

"Teenager and Benny are going to a wedding?" Eddie Hernandez said.

"They go to one Saturday," Luisa Maria said.

"The suits I can get for you will cost two hundred each," Eddie said.

"That is very good," Luisa Maria said.

She gave Eddie Hernandez the four hundred and walked out of the store cooing to the eight hundred dollars left in her purse.

On Saturday morning, Teenager and Benny were so concerned with drinking brandy in preparation for the wedding that they took little notice of the clothes Luisa Maria delivered to them. There were blue velvet jackets, the brand-new name ripped out as neatly as Luisa Maria could do it, and black pants; there was no way that Eddie Hernandez could put together a suit that would cover Teenager's fifty-two-inch shoulders and thirty-inch waist.

At four that afternoon, at Diego's ballroom on Westchester Avenue, Gumersindo Torres, known as NeNe, swallowed rum at the bar and, smiling, proud of the big carnation in his lapel, he decided to promenade. He immediately bumped into another wedding guest, who pressed a gun into his stomach.

"Let's go to the men's room together," Teenager said.

He directed NeNe down a passageway that went past the men's room and through a door to the parking lot, where Benny Velez sat in the car with a nickel-plated .357 Magnum.

"You sit and keep Benny company," Teenager said to NeNe.

Inside, Pedro Torres was dancing with a girl when he felt a hand on his shoulder.

"I am dancing," Torres said.

"I want to dance too."

"So get a girl and dance."

"No, I want to dance with you." Teenager leaned into Torres, and when Torres felt the gun his knees became weak.

"We will go outside for dancing," Teenager said.

NeNe and Torres, handcuffed and staring at the nickel-plated .357 Magnum in Benny's hand, sat in the back seat of the Mercedes with Benny while Teenager, a cigar in his mouth, drove along Southern Boulevard, thinking, staring at factory buildings and then, happening to glance to his right, seeing the Mayaguez Express Company. Teenager made a sudden turn, causing his passengers to rock forward. He pulled up at the warehouse, where a man dozed in the sun in a chair that was covered with plastic and had labels on it saying it was to be sent to Calle Marie 7, Santo Domingo, Dominican Republic. On the ground next to the chair was a large statue of a black Virgin Mary.

"What if it break?" the man in the chair asked a warehouse attendant.

"We wrap everything carefully."

"I work my whole life to get this for my mother," the man in the chair said. "If the chair breaks, the Virgin Mary breaks, my whole life breaks."

Inside, Teenager had to wait until a woman with an electric can opener spoke to the warehouse manager.

"Is this all you're sending?" he said.

She nodded.

"It'll cost you forty dollars just to ship this one thing to Santo Domingo," the manager said. "Why don't you wait till you get a lot of other stuff together and then ship it? Or find somebody sending a whole package. Why pay for the one thing?"

The woman shrugged. "For my sister," she said.

"Does your sister ever have any cans to open?" the man said.

"Sometimes she has."

"Let me ask you another thing. Does your sister have electricity?"

"Sometimes she does."

Teenager decided he didn't want to wait any longer. He walked over to a stack of Mayaguez boxes, brown cartons that can hold as much as one hundred and fifty pounds of clothes and are known as Puerto Rican moving vans.

Teenager took three of the boxes. "I am just going to load them up," he said to the manager.

"Who are you going to put in there, the bride?" the manager said, looking at Teenager's wedding clothes.

"They both go on the honeymoon this way," Teenager said, laughing.

He put the boxes in the car trunk and then drove up to the corner, where a pusher named Nesterline was standing in the afternoon shade in front of the bar. Nesterline was dressed in a powder-blue suit and a yellow flowered shirt and red tie.

"Come with us, Nesterline," Teenager called out the car window. "We are going to a baptism."

"To the baptism?" Nesterline said, looking at their wedding clothes.

"Yes, the baptism is now," Teenager said. "First the wedding and now the baptism. The bride had her baby at the wedding party."

He pulled the car around the corner and parked it facing the wrong way. Benny opened the rear door and pushed NeNe and Torres out onto the sidewalk and down the basement stairs.

"Carry the boxes, Nesterline," Teenager said.

He opened the trunk for Nesterline and then went down the basement stairs.

Nesterline carried the Mayaguez boxes down the steps and along a damp cement hallway and into a room with sweating pipes running across a low ceiling. A single light bulb hung on a long cord. A Ping-Pong table sat under the light. Benny stood on the far side of the Ping-Pong

table. He had a power chain saw in his hands. NeNe tried
to step backward. Teenager pushed NeNe against the
table. Torres began to tremble. Benny's eyes gleamed.

"This is a baptism?" Nesterline said.

"Yes," Teenager said.

At midday, a woman leaned out the third-floor window
of her building on Whittier Street to hang out wash. Immediately, a smell reached her that caused her to close
the window. She waited for an hour, opened the window
again, recoiled, shut the window and went out to the
phone on the street. Some time later a patrolman, hand
clamped to his mouth, trudged through the garbage in the
lot and stopped several yards away from three Mayaguez
boxes that baked in the sun. The policeman went back
out to the street, for he felt that this was a matter for a
supervisor. By late afternoon Myles, working the four-
to-midnight shift, appeared on the lot, covered his face
with a handkerchief and waited for the emergency service
squad. When they arrived, a red-headed man in baseball
cap and coveralls came up, sniffed and said to Myles,
"You caught the case."

"Looks like it."

"Good luck."

Myles had arrived with Hansen, who wore a leather
coat, an olive drab suit that did not have a wrinkle in it
and polished brown shoes with thick shoe-repair-shop
soles. Hansen took a couple of resigned steps over to the
boxes, ripped the top off one and began poking inside.
Myles, holding the handkerchief to his face, went up to
the box and reached past Hansen. Myles brought out a
black plastic bag, inside of which was a foot. He dropped
the foot back into the box and began to breathe evenly so
he would not gag.

Initial Investigation
At about 0810 hours the undersigned responded to rear
yard of 747 Whittier Avenue Bronx due to a report of
bodies in a bag. Upon arriving, the undersigned observed 3 boxes which upon examination were found to
contain 2 bodies. Box #1 contained the body of Gu-

mersindo Torres, aka NeNe, which had been cut up in the following fashion: the head had been severed as had the legs from the torso apparently to make it easier to put it in the bag. It was also observed that his genitals had been cut off and there were apparent gunshot wounds in the face. Body #2, that of Pedro Torres, was severed at the belt line and the lower torso was placed in bag #2 and the upper torso was placed in bag #3. All of the aforementioned bodies were first placed in black plastic bags and then placed in cardboard boxes which were taped and tied. The boxes bore the name of the Mayaguez Express Company, 311 Bruckner Blvd. 261–5300. Box size 18 x 18 x 30.

Ptl. M. Crofton

In the precinct, there were now files for eight fresh homicides and it took no particular poring over them by Martin to decide that they were probably related and undoubtedly motivated by drugs. Even the most immoral woman he ever had heard of, and he had heard of many, could not cause this much carnage in so short a time, he declared. While these people of grease always will fight one battle over a woman, Martin believed they could not possibly have enough sperm boiling inside them to conduct a full war. And today's homicides, Martin snarled, bodies left cut up like chops, was the worst he ever had seen in his career. For his listeners in the squad room he recalled a case he once had on the West Side, where he arrived to find a man who had cut up his wife. The man was standing placidly in the kitchen, cooking his wife's vagina in a frying pan. "Cooking up her thing," Martin said. Of course Martin had not looked at the frying vagina, but remembered instead the man standing there and pouring frying oil into the frying pan and the pale yellow oil dripping off the oil bottle spout.

On the day they found the cut-up bodies, Myles and Hansen worked until 1:00 A.M. At 11:30 P.M., they drove up to Whittier Street to interview a man who said he had seen a couple of men carrying Mayaguez boxes into the lot behind the apartments.

"One of them was dressed up in a wedding suit," the man said.

"What do you mean, wedding suit?"

The man's wife cut in. "Oh, yes, I see this man dressed like this. A very beautiful blue jacket and black pants. He was carrying this big box."

The detectives' work chart had Myles and Hansen starting a day tour at 8:00 A.M. the next morning. Eyes flecked with red, they drove to the Mayaguez offices and the manager who had been on duty when Teenager arrived to take the boxes said that he could not possibly remember any single person in wedding clothes on any Saturday because there were so many people going to weddings in the Bronx who stopped at his place to send presents to Puerto Rico.

"If the wedding is in the Bronx, then why are they sending presents to Puerto Rico?" Myles asked.

"Because that is what they do," the manager said.

The manager rode with them to the precinct, where a pile of pictures was placed on a desk. As each picture of a known Puerto Rican killer in the Bronx was shown to the warehouse manager, he took a great amount of time with the picture, biting his lip in an attempt to remember, then sorrowfully handing the picture back to Myles and Hansen. The manager took exactly the same amount of time with the picture of Teenager as he did with the others. He did not allow his blood pressure to rise even a point as he stared at Teenager's face, bit his lip, and then gave this picture, too, to Crofton. The manager's hand went out for the next picture.

In the afternoon, Myles and Hansen pulled up across the street from Ana's Bar. Luisa Maria stepped out of the bar once, wearing a low-cut summer dress and high heels. When she saw Myles and Hansen, she then went inside quickly.

"Right to the phone," Hansen said.

Twenty minutes later, Santos Rivera walked along the street, looked at Myles' car and kept going.

"Now they got two witnesses say we're here," Hansen said.

"I feel like going inside," Myles said.

"Sitting here bothers them enough," Hansen said.

They were off for seventy-two hours. On the first day back, Hansen had to go to the firing range and Myles was drawn for special duty at the United Nations, where a demonstration in support of the Palestine Liberation Organization took place. It wasn't until the following Saturday at 1:00 A.M. that their tour resumed. They drove immediately to Ana's and saw only three people sitting listlessly at the bar.

"Out partying someplace," Hansen said. He put the car into motion.

────────── ....**Chapter 24** ....

At 1:30, Teenager stepped out of his car in front of the Aguaserra, waved his arm for Pancha to see him from the apartment across the street and walked past the window shining with grease and into the stand.

A girl in a tight black blouse and flowered apron stood behind the counter, smoking a cigarette and listening to the juke box.

"Who are you?" Teenager said.

"Doris. I am here only five days." She took a deep breath so that her already large chest would become as pronounced as possible.

"That is too long for you to be here," Teenager said. "You are too beautiful for this place."

He walked to the end of the counter, stepped through an opening and picked up the last tray of yellow rice on the steam table. Under it was a .38 Ruger with a black barrel and brown handle. He took the gun and went to the rear of the store, pulled open the trap door, by now unlocked for him, and went down the metal steps into the cellar. A thin man in a rainhat and Flex-a-Lite mask stood at a small table and cut brown heroin with mannite.

"Junior told me to do this here," the one in the rainhat said. "Someone is to pick it up. Junior said he was going out to have fun."

The table was alongside a generator that served the Aguaserra's refrigerators. The generator was covered with thick grease. The guy in the rainhat brushed his elbow against the generator, placing a large black grease smear on his elbow. He rubbed the grease off his elbow with his hand, wiped the hand on his pants and resumed cutting the heroin.

Teenager stepped through a door into a long narrow room where Benny Velez sprawled in a chair and Nesterline, still in his best powder blue suit, and two young guys who had wisps of hair on their chins sat on the edge of a studio bed. A television set was at one end of the room, a statue of a black Madonna at the other.

"I am busy," Teenager said. "Be fast."

"They owe thirty-five hundred," Nesterline said.

"So give me thirty-five hundred," Teenager said.

"They only gave me seventeen hundred," Nesterline said.

"What am I supposed to do?" Teenager said. "I want my money. If I do not get it, I will shoot you first and then these two with you."

Nesterline stood up in disbelief. "How could you say this fucking thing about me, man?"

"Because you don't pay, why should he care about you?" Benny asked.

"Shoot them," Teenager said. He handed Benny the .38 Ruger.

"You're wrong, man!" Nesterline yelled. Benny was standing up with the gun pointed at Nesterline and the two on the couch.

"You don't give us the money," Benny said.

"Give me everything you have," Teenager said.

He looked at the watch Nesterline was wearing.

"Give it to me," he said.

"It's nothing, man," Nesterline said.

"Give it to me," Teenager said.

Nesterline handed him the watch, a four hundred dollar Rolex steel watch. Teenager looked at it, then handed it to Benny. "This is yours," he said. Benny dropped it into his pocket.

"You wear my watch?" Nesterline said.

"Later I will," Benny said, "when you're dead under this basement."

Nesterline looked at Teenager. "You just made me do a whole baptism for you."

I should shoot Nesterline right now, Teenager said to himself, for even *mentioning* this baptism that nobody should ever think of. But if he shot Nesterline right away, then he never would have a chance to get the money. The thought of lost money caused Teenager's eyes to crinkle and his insides to boil.

"It is not our fault that we owe this money," Nesterline said. "We give these half los to this guy down the street and we go to get the money and he said to us yesterday, "Oh, I went to Benny and I said to him that here is the money I owe.' We said, 'All right, if you give this money to Benny then Benny has it and everything is all right. We believe this guy. Then we come here tonight and we say, well, we owe Benny seventeen hundred and we have our money with us. I say to Benny, here, and Benny says to me he wants all the money. He says we must pay to him the money this guy down the street lied to us about."

"What does this guy have to do with me?" Teenager asked. "I do not even know this guy. I just know thirty-five hundred dollars you owe me. You go over to this guy down the street and show him what happens for money he does not pay."

Teenager threw the .38 Ruger on the daybed. Nesterline, the sweat causing fresh dark circles under the arms of his red sweatshirt, picked up the gun as if it were a religious object.

"Is it a good gun?" Nesterline asked.

"If I give it to you, it is good," Teenager said.

Nesterline aimed the pistol at the wall over the statue of the black Madonna. When he fired, the two young guys on the daybed jumped. The slug caused another hole in the pattern of holes in the wall over the statue.

"If you do not get the other eighteen hundred, then you take the guy down the street off the count," Teenager said. "If you do not do that, then I will come back here and take the three of you off the count tonight."

Teenager left the room, climbed the basement stairs and went out into the night to his Mercedes, which catapulted down the street toward his playground. This time, he felt properly dressed: a new medallion, Santa Barbara on one side, Changó on the other, was inlaid with red and white stones and had cost twenty-two thousand dollars. On his left wrist, the yellow bracelet now had "Teenager" inlaid in diamonds. He wore two rings, a gold wedding band with diamonds, and on his right hand, the largest ring in the South Bronx, gold studded with diamonds, a ring as heavy as a paperweight.

He went to the La Barca first. After two drinks he went into the kitchen and did up lines of cocaine on the table and snorted them up. Twenty minutes later, he picked up the phone in the bar and found the Aguaserra line was busy. He dialed continuously until he got through.

The countergirl at the Aguaserra answered. Teenager could hear that Benny had picked up the extension downstairs.

"I want Benny," Teenager said. The countergirl hung up.

"Why is this phone so busy?" Teenager said.

"Because many people are calling here," Benny said.

"Girls call you," Teenager said.

"What should I do, tell them not to call me?" Benny said.

"I do not care about them. I want to know about those three. Did they bring you money yet?"

"I am waiting for them," Benny said.

"I thought they said this guy lives just around the corner."

"I am waiting," Benny said.

"If they don't bring you the money, or they don't shoot this guy, then I will come back and they will get a banking lesson. Nesterline will learn that you pay your banker on time or your banker will get mad at you."

For an hour, as Teenager drank in the bar and Benny waited in the Aguaserra cellar, Nesterline and the two young guys with him had been sitting in the dark in the apartment of the guy who owed eighteen hundred dollars. He lived on the third floor of a six-story attached building on Faile Street, a morose block which began outside the

locked back door of the Aguaserra and, alongside, the
open back door of Flores' bar, and then ran perpendicu-
larly into the darkness. Most of the buildings on Faile
Street had windows covered with tin and insides shelled
by fire. Nesterline and the two had entered the guy's
three-room apartment by breaking the window at the fire
escape. Nesterline sat on a chair facing the door, listening
to footsteps out in the hall. One set of footsteps stopped
at the apartment door. Keys jangled. Nesterline held out
the gun.

"Don't move your hands," Nesterline said as the guy
walked into the apartment.

"What do you have that for?" the guy said, sneering
at the gun.

"You lie to us," Nesterline said. "You say to us that
you pay Benny eighteen hundred dollar and you never
give to Benny anything."

"I swear to you that I pay Benny," the guy said.

"When?"

"I just saw him this afternoon and gave to him the
money."

"Who was Benny with?"

"With Teenager. Teenager kissed me for giving the
money. They said they will do a big business with me."

"Give me the money now," Nesterline said.

"I told you I gave the money to Benny and Teenager
already."

"They just told me that you never pay them," Nesterline said.

"They tell you lies," he said. "They just want to collect twice."

"Give me eighteen hundred," Nesterline said.

"I have no money. I gave it to Benny and Teen—"

Nesterline started shooting. They were all standing so
close in the living room that the blood got over Nesterline
and the two with him. When the gun was empty, Nesterline stood for a moment in awe of what he had done.
Then there was a shout on the night street outside the
building. Nesterline and the two scrambled out the window and went down the fire escape.

* * *

In the 43rd Precinct, there was a report of shots fired at 1155 Faile Street.

"We ought to take a look," Hansen said, as it came over the radio.

Myles put his hand on the horn and Hansen had the roof light attached and blinking as they went under the Bruckner Expressway, careened onto Southern Boulevard, dived into the darkness of the street running behind the Aguaserra and stopped at the crowd in front of the apartment building on Faile Street.

A patrolman was upstairs already, looking down at the body of a guy, who was on his back with the front of his yellow shirt covered with blood. His eyes were fixed in a cringe.

A squat man in a baseball cap stood in the doorway with a woman.

"She see them go away."

"When?" Myles said.

"Five minutes," the man said.

"Where did they go?" Myles said.

The woman chattered in Spanish.

"She say they go straight up the block to the back of the bar. Three of them."

Myles and Hansen left the patrolman and backed the car up the street until they nearly were inside Flore's Bar. The barred windows of the back of the Aguaserra were next to the open back door of the bar. Myles and Hansen walked into the bar, which was crowded. At the front of the bar, by the door to the street, the owner sat on a high stool. He looked straight ahead and chewed gum and jiggled a baseball bat between his knees. Without seeming to notice Myles and Hansen, the owner's thumb jerked in the direction of the Aguaserra, next door.

Myles had his gun out as he wheeled into the grease smell of the Aguaserra's front door. Three frightened faces looked at him. The fronts of their jackets were covered with blood.

"Police! Freeze!" Myles said.

Hansen was behind him.

"He did the shooting," one of them said, his head indicating Nesterline.

"I kill you too," Nesterline said to the one.

Myles said nothing. He couldn't wait to get handcuffs on them so he could write down in his pad what he had just heard.

It was two in the morning before Benny felt safe to climb out of the cellar of the Aguaserra and look for Teenager. He found him at the La Barca.

"Pancha saw them coming out," Benny told Teenager. "He says one of the cops is the same guy was around before. He says it is the cop with the long face."

"And he arrested Nesterline and those other two?"

"I just told you yes."

Teenager slapped Benny in the face. "Don't talk to me like that when I'm thinking." He was thinking of Nesterline and the baptism. He wondered if there was a way that he could kill Nesterline in the police station.

"You are sure that this cop is the same guy?" he said finally.

"Pancha saw him from the window. Pancha can tell Americans from each other," Benny said.

"Why does this one cop bother us so much?" Teenager said. "This guy tonight was a bad guy that lied about business. Why should the cops care about him? Why should they bother us? I am only doing business. I don't hurt anybody legitimate. Let them worry about these niggers mugging legitimate people."

Q. I am Patrolman Myles Crofton, badge number 76324. Would you state your name for the record, please?

A. Herman Carvallo.

Q. Are you known by any other name?

A. Nesterline.

Q. How old are you?

A. Twenty-six.

Q. Have you been a resident of Bronx County?

A. Yes.

Q. And you realize that you have been arrested for the crime of homicide in Bronx County?

A. Yes.

Q. You are talking to me of your own free will, is that correct?

A. Yes.

Q. Have you been advised that you could have a lawyer?

A. Yes.

Q. And you still wish to talk to me?

A. Yes.

Q. Did I do anything to force you into talking to me?

A. No.

Q. Did I promise you anything?

A. Yes.

Q. What did I promise you?

A. You said you would tell the DA that I help you out.

Q. Is that the only promise you heard from me, that I would tell the district attorney that you are cooperating in the investigation of these two homicides?

A. Yes.

Q. Did I tell you what good this would do?

A. You told me you didn't know.

Q. Then we understand each other.

A. Sure.

Q. Do you know an individual whose street name is NeNe?

A. Yes, sir.

Q. How long have you known him?

A. I met NeNe in jail and I know him for about a year.

Q. When was the last time you saw NeNe?

A. The last time that I saw him I was on the street on 138th Street and I was talking to this guy Benny and I was invited to a baptism.

Q. When you say you were invited to a baptism, what did that mean to you?

A. A baptism to us means that they're going to kill somebody, that somebody wasn't doing too good, he was going to be killed.

Q. Now Benny said this to you?

A. Yes.

Q. Did he tell you where to go, where to come for this baptism?

A. Yes.

Q. Where did he say to come?

A. In the basement where he lived.

Q. Now describe what you saw after you went inside.

A. Benny opened the door, when I walked downstairs they opened the room, in one of the rooms they were cutting up a person.

Q. When you say cutting up a person, did you see what they were cutting up that person with?

A. With a chain saw.

Q. Now you said they opened the room for you. Who are they?

A. I don't know them.

Q. If I show you pictures of people would you be able to pick any of them out?

A. I'll try.

Q. All right, what did you see inside the room?

A. NeNe and somebody else who was tied up and another person they were cutting up.

Q. The person that was tied up, was that male or female?

A. A male.

Q. Now, you say you saw NeNe in there?

A. Yes.

Q. What was he doing?

A. Not good.

Q. What do you mean by that?

A. He was sitting down in a chair with his hands tied behind his back.

Q. Did you see what was being done with the body that was being cut up?

A. They were cutting up the body and they were putting it in a plastic bag.

Q. Was anyone speaking to NeNe at this time?

A. Benny asked him who put out the contract on somebody.

Q. Who is this somebody?

A. I don't know.

Q. Was his name Teenager?

A. I don't know this name.

Q. You don't know?

A. No.

Q. Wasn't Teenager there?

A. I don't know this name.

Q. How come you knew Benny and you don't know Teenager?

A. I don't like Benny.

Q. All right. Now they wanted to know something from NeNe.

A. They say to him if you say who was this person we're going to give you your freedom.

Q. Who was doing the cutting up of the other body when you came in?

A. Benny was helping.

Q. Now did you see anything happen to NeNe at that point?

A. NeNe knew that anyway whether he would talk or not he was going to get killed.

Q. Did you hear NeNe say anything when he was being questioned?

A. He was denying he was involved in this. One of the persons in the group said that NeNe was one of the ones who came into the apartment that they were mad about.

Q. Who was the person who said NeNe was in the apartment, do you remember?

A. Benny.

Q. As best you can remember, how long did they question NeNe?

A. For about five, ten minutes.

Q. Did anybody do anything to NeNe?

A. They were mistreating him, hitting him so hard with a gun that he couldn't talk.

Q. Then what did they do?

A. They got mad at NeNe and put him on the table.

Q. Do you recall what happened after that, after they put NeNe on the table?

A. Yeah, the first thing I saw was when they cut his member.

Q. When he was on the table, was he alive?

A. Yeah, he was alive.

Q. What did they cut him with?

A. With a knife.

Q. Did they do anything else to him that you saw?

A. They put the saw to his belly, the chain saw, and they started cutting him up. Then Benny shot him with a forty-five twice.

Q. Shot NeNe?

A. Sure.

Q. Was NeNe alive at that time, was he alive when they were sawing him or were the bullets already in him?

A. Half and half. He was real alive when they cut up his belly with the electric buzz saw and then they shoot him in the head before they cut off his arms and legs.

Q. Mr. Carvallo, do you know why they told you to come to this baptism?

A. I was working for Benny. I'm a drug addict and was using two hundred a day so I had to do whatever Benny said for money. When I came there that night I stayed forty-five, fifty minutes and then they sent me out to pick up some drugs for them.

Q. Who are they?

A. Benny.

Q. You saw people cutting up other people and you didn't know one of these criminals by name?

A. Only Benny. He did everything. He let me in, he shot NeNe, then he cut up NeNe and the other one too.

Teenager got out of the car carrying a supermarket carton tied with rope. Inside it was about sixty-five thousand dollars, nearly all of it in small bills. He walked it to the front door of the Rincon Social Club, a storefront whose windows and door were painted a tired red. The door, operated by a buzzer, was opened for him and he stepped into a room lit by Christmas tree bulbs hanging on cords along the walls. Benny Velez sat at the small bar. His wife, Carmen, plump and expressionless, sat on a chair alongside the juke box, one hand in the pocket of her crimson baseball jacket, the other held out, the edict of a bored mediator, to separate her children, Letty, eight, and Wanda, nine, who fought with each other for the juke box. At Carmen's feet were two large bags of groceries.

"I go shopping in the store and I buy all this food and I am just coming out with all these packages in my arms," Carmen said, "and Albertito comes running up to me. 'You cannot go home. All the police is there.' "

"Benny was with you?" Teenager said.

"Benny was not with me. Benny never carries a package for me in his whole life."

"I was on 140th Street," Benny said.

"Well, they're just sitting at the corner waiting for you," Teenager said.

"Just for me?" Benny said.

"Only for you."

"They don't want you?"

"No. You're their man."

"Who told them to look for me and not for you?"

"Nesterline got busted," Teenager said.

"Why would Nesterline want to be a rat on me?" Benny asked. "I never did anything to Nesterline."

"Because he's a real bad guy, this Nesterline."

"Nesterline must get taken off the count," Benny said.

"They got him hid away," Teenager said. "I ask somebody who goes to the Bronx County jail and this guy says to me, 'Nesterline isn't in the place. They took him where no one can see him.' "

"What do I do?" Benny said.

"Go away," Teenager said.

Benny stiffened. His fear passed when Teenager held out the carton tied with rope.

"You go away to Ponce and give this to my mother. She will take care of it for me. I cannot put it in a bank. They might check on me and take all my money. You just give this to my mother and stay in PR until all this is over."

"How long will this take?" Benny asked.

"Four, five months," Teenager said. "They will get tired of this Nesterline. They will see he is a real bad guy. They will throw him out into the street and then we will take him right off the count."

Benny nodded. "So, four or five months in San Pedro. That I could take."

Teenager shook his head. "Not San Pedro. In San Pedro they would look for you. The cops love to go to San Pedro to look for people. The police in San Pedro meet them at the plane and take them out with girls. You go where you belong. To Salinas. No cop would ever go to Salinas to find anything."

"I love this," Carmen said. She got up and hugged the children at the juke box. "We are going to see Grandma," she said.

The two little girls began to jump about. "Grandma!"

Benny Velez looked at the floor. In Salinas, he had grown up sitting on the road running between fields of sugar cane, with his front teeth pulling the skin off the hard white center of the cane and chewing it down until it could be sucked. When he was twelve, his uncle wanted him to go fishing with him. Benny knew that the uncle went on a small boat and spent the first night sleeping in the boat at La Playa de Ponce and then for the next three days he sat in the sun on the water and caught fish, took them to La Playa de Ponce to sell and then went back out onto the water. The night before he was to go fishing with his uncle, Benny ran away. A month later, his mother left his father and took him to the Bronx. The mother got a job in a factory, and at the end of work one day she came home and was unable to find Benny until ten o'clock that night. He was on the sidewalk in front of a candy store that sold drugs. When the mother announced that she was sending him to his grandmother's in Salinas, Benny ran away and lived in basements and pushed drugs. Through the years, particularly since he had married Carmen, he had returned to Salinas for visits. Always, he found the place lonely and could not wait to get back to the Bronx. He now was being told that he had to live in Salinas for a period of months. This he did not like.

"I am not responsible for the money when it gets to your mother's house," Benny said.

"That's all right," Teenager said.

Teenager had arrived in a light-blue two-door Continental driven by Albertito. He told Benny and his wife and kids to go out to the car, and Albertito would take them to Kennedy Airport for the 5:50 P.M. flight to Puerto Rico.

"What if the police are by the plane?" Benny said.

Teenager sneered. "It takes them a day to do a thing like this, to go to the airport. First they must sit by your house all day. They expect you to walk into the bar any minute now. You go to the airport. Nobody will be there."

Both children, realizing they were leaving without stopping at home, began to cry and mention things they absolutely had to have in order to survive.

"Buy them new anything they need," Teenager said.

"Do I use this?" Benny said, holding up the carton.

"That's all right," Teenager said.

The car taking Benny and his family to the airport raced along the Bruckner Expressway, passing two blocks away from the bar on the corner, where Myles Crofton and his partner Hansen sat. Myles held a Coke and Hansen the typed warrant for the arrest of Benny Velez for the crime of killing other people.

"You got a gun?" Luisa Maria said to Myles.

"I guess so."

"You better not guess. You must have a gun if Benny comes in here."

"He thinks he's tough?" Myles said.

"He wants to kill you because you are such bad police. You big and strong. He wants to kill you."

"That's good to know," Myles said.

Hansen, looking out the window, said, "No man ever died from talk."

"Benny does not talk. Benny will shoot."

"What about his friend?" Myles said.

"Who's friend?"

"His friend Teenager."

"Which Teenager? Little Teenager or Big Teenager? Lot of guys here called Teenager."

"There's only one that you know and I know," Myles said.

Luisa Maria watched as Hansen walked to the back door and surveyed the sidestreet.

"I ask you something," Luisa Maria said.

"What?"

"You like fresh sexy movies?"

"What's that supposed to mean?"

"Fresh sexy movies. *Oooh. Pardonnez moi.* They fun. What's the matter with you? Fresh sexy movies."

"Yeah, so?" Myles said.

"So you come with me and watch fresh sexy movies."

"Lady, I'm just here working."

Hansen now walked from the back door to the front door. Luisa Maria turned her back and began rearranging bottles on the back bar. She wanted them to leave, because she wanted to get somebody to watch the bar for her while she went up to Watson Avenue to talk to Ada, who came from her country, Colombia. Over the phone, Ada had told her that Teenager had said to this bitch girl Ramonita that he would let Ramonita shoot her with a shotgun. Maybe, she told herself, she would do something to Teenager first if Ada was right. Do something very bad to Teenager. He likes to have everyone killed but himself. He will not have me killed before he is killed, Luisa Maria said. For something this important she would have to see Ada in person. All she knew now was what Ada had told her over the phone. But if it was right, and Ada never would lie because she was from my country, Colombia, Luisa Maria knew she would do something to Teenager first. Do what? She thought about the detectives behind her. They could be very good for her.

"I love French movies," Myles said.

Hansen, looking out the front window, said, "I don't get to see many myself." He had his back turned and he did not see Luisa Maria turn around and smile at Myles.

"Some day we will all go to movie maybe," she said.
"Then we talk."

Myles and Hansen sat in the bar, and the two unmarked cars, one on the main street and one on the sidestreet, remained on duty until 1:00 A.M. They were relieved and went out into the Bronx night and drove to
their homes. By that same hour, Benny Velez stood at
the black grillwork covering the front porch of the house
of Teenager's mother in Ponce, a new ranch house. In
the driveway was a gold Cadillac, whose front appeared
to have run into a group of redwood trees. Alongside it
was a red Lincoln Mark IV. Suddenly, the dark porch
was flooded with light and Teenager's mother stood in a
long housecoat and peered out.

"Who?"

"Benny."

A delighted squeal came from inside the house. Teenager's sister Wanda, with at once the largest pair of
breasts and hips imaginable, came trotting onto the porch
in nightgown and bare feet. She opened the grillwork
door, kissed Benny and grabbed the carton.

"Look at my car," she said to Benny. "Some bad guy
hit my car up."

"My daughter needs a car," Teenager's mother said.

"She don't let me drive hers," the daughter said.

"If she takes my car to drive, then that means I need a
car," the mother said.

The daughter Wanda took the carton from Teenager
and hopped into the house with it. Teenager's mother
said good-bye and closed and locked the black grillwork
door.

"Why do you have this thing?" Benny asked, tapping
the grillwork.

"Drug addicts try to rob these houses."

Benny walked in the darkness out to the car where his
children slept in the back and his wife sat with a paper
bag full of money on her lap.

Benny took the highway that ran along the sea and at
the first lights of Salinas he felt like he was standing in a
vacant room. Beside him, Carmen called excitedly to the

kids to wake up and watch for their grandmother's house, which was in a *caserío*, public housing almost forty years old, that sat at the foot of the exit from the highway. Carmen's mother lived in apartment number one and when she banged on the door, the mother answered with the door open a crack and a thick safety chain showing. She howled when she saw her daughter and fumbled with the chain in her excitement. The mother and daughter fell into each other's arms when the door finally opened.

As Benny stepped in, the mother pointed to the chain. "Drug addicts."

At bedtime, the two daughters were put in one bed in a bedroom and then Carmen pointed to the other bed in the room, kissed her husband on the cheek and went in and slept with her mother. The next day, Benny arose and found his wife singing while she cleaned a fish at the kitchen sink. He had not seen her this happy in a long time. He sat around the house and then took a walk to the plaza, where a cluster of men sat in a place called La Tablita.

"Clemente picked his pitchers," a man at a table said.

The owner, lounging behind the bar, became erect. "How do you say this thing?"

"That's right," the man at the table said. "If Steve Loring is pitching for the Dodgers, Clemente comes to the game early. He knows he can hit Loring. But if Tommy John is pitching, here is Clemente. 'Oh, I cannot play today. I have this bad flu.' That is how Clemente had such a great batting average. He picked his pitchers."

"That's a lie, man," the owner said.

"That's the truth, man," the guy at the table said.

The owner looked at Benny. "What do you think of what he just said?"

Fuck this Clemente, Benny said to himself. I never made any money with him. What does he matter to me?

To the owner, Benny said, "I don't know."

After dinner that night, Benny went for another walk to the plaza. In the La Tablita, the same man sat at the same table.

"I can prove to you that Roberto Clemente picked his pitchers," he was saying.

Benny left. He walked around the town and saw the stores all had gates on them.

"I'll go home and have sex with my wife," he said to himself.

When he got home, he found his wife already had gone to bed in her mother's room. The door was shut. Benny sat in the living room and stared at Kojak speaking Spanish. He did not like what was going on; if all of his stay in Salinas was to be like these first two nights, then he would go crazy.

Oscar Ocascio, nineteen, and his friend Ralphie, twenty, celebrated a robbery of a hundred and twenty-six dollars and a pearl necklace. The party was a good one. It started with quart bottles of beer and joints in an empty flat on the top floor of a building on 138th Street. At eight o'clock in the morning, the friend went down and bought some wine, met Melody Martinez on the street and brought her back with him. She sat on the floor next to Oscar Ocascio and drank wine. The friend fell asleep. Oscar put his arm around her and said, "Do you want a pretty necklace?"

"I want everything pretty."

Oscar held up the pearl beads.

"Oh, I want them," Melody said.

"What will you do to get this?"

"Don't worry," Melody said. Her hand went to his fly. When she felt the metal barrel of the pistol she looked up. "I do not make love to that." Oscar took the .45 Colt Commander out of his belt and put it on the floor and sighed as Melody went down on him.

Afterward, Oscar draped the pearl necklace around her neck and the two went up on the roof to drink wine and watch the traffic on the street. Oscar had his left arm about Melody's waist. The .45 Colt Commander was back in his belt. He had taken it from under the pillow of a man sleeping as Ralphie burgled a Queens house. He took a large swallow of the wine, leaned unsteadily against Melody and looked down. A black Plymouth

Fury pulled up to Ana's Bar. A black detective got out of the passenger's side and walked into the bar. The driver, white, got out, then reached in for something, then stepped out and walked around the front of the car.

"Look at this guy," Oscar said.

"Who?" Melody said.

"This guy." Oscar put down the bottle of wine, went into his belt for the Colt Commander and then aimed it at the white detective's head. The detective was a step away from the doorway of the bar when Oscar Ocascio fired the .45 Colt Commander. Melody now was running across the roof to jump the divider to the next building and Oscar stuffed the gun into his belt, grabbed the wine, and ran unsteadily after her.

Across the street, Myles and Hansen were crouched inside the bar, guns drawn, peering through the saloon window, which had a large bullet hole in it.

"You set us up!" Myles said.

"I did not," Luisa Maria screamed. "I did not even know you were coming."

"Just call 911 and say '1013,' that police officers are being shot at and give the address," Hansen said.

Late that afternoon, nine detectives, wearing bullet-proof vests and carrying shotguns, crashed into Ana's Bar, where two delivery boys drank beer and Luisa Maria listened to the juke box. Lieutenant Robert Martin stepped behind the bar and began smashing bottles with his shotgun barrel. Two other detectives drove shotgun butts into the juke box.

"You know I had nothing to do with it," Luisa Maria said. She pointed to Myles. "You tell them."

"No. You tell Teenager that when we see him we're going to get him," Myles said.

After they left, the door in the back of the bar opened and Albertito, who had been upstairs with the drugs, looked out.

"Somebody shot at them this morning and they're mad," Luisa Maria said.

"We didn't shoot at them," Albertito said. "Why should they be mad at us?"

"The shot misses them anyway," Luisa Maria said.

* * *

The shotgun barrels moved like iron locusts through Teenager's territory. First to the Aguaserra, where the glass counters splintered and greasy pigs' ears rolled to the floor. Then to the La Barca, where bottles smashed loudly. Then across the street to the Casa, where Ada, the barmaid, ran into the kitchen as the detectives wrecked the place. There were six people in the Casa, sitting at tables, and they remained there as the detectives swung the guns at anything glass.

Myles stepped into the Casa's kitchen and brought the shotgun barrel down on a stack of plates. He wheeled around and saw Ada cowering against a counter. Alongside her was a pestle and mortar that was decorated as if it were an expensive beer mug.

"What's that for?" Myles said.

"For the garlic bread," Ada said.

"Where's the garlic?" Myles said.

Ada pushed two cloves that were on the counter behind her. Myles put the garlic into the mortar and carried it outside. He rested the shotgun against the bar and took out his .38. He looked at the sullen faces at the tables.

"Watch this," he said.

He held up a clove of garlic and then began to rub it inside the mortar. He emptied the bullets from the gun cylinder onto the bar and then dropped them one by one into the mortar. He took the pestle and ran it around the inside of the mortar. The bullets clinked on the sides as he stirred them. He spilled the bullets out of the mortar and with deliberate motions inserted them back into the cylinder. He shoved the gun into the holster on his hip.

"Tell him that I will shoot him with one of these bullets. That's what I think of him. I'll shoot him with garlic-bullets."

Satisfied with himself, Myles followed the others out of the bar. That was a good thing, he told himself, thought it up just while I was standing there. The Guineas are supposed to shoot garlic bullets when they're mad. Or at least Myles thought he had heard that someplace.

He had not noticed the sudden fear that came over a couple of the faces when he dropped the bullets in with the garlic. Later, when Teenager was told of what had happened, he sneered until the garlic bullets were mentioned. Then he left immediately for Mama's house.

"If he shoots me with a garlic bullet, the soul dies too," Teenager said.

Mama nodded.

"I must get protection from the saint," Teenager said.

"The saint doesn't talk to me today yet," Mama said.

"Then I must kill this cop or he will kill my soul," Teenager said.

Mama shook her head. "The one cop is like the teeth in a shell. There are many, many cops. One does not matter. If you kill him, you will make a hero of him. If the cop you kill wanted to put garlic bullets into you, then all the other cops will come to avenge him. They will shoot many garlic bullets into you."

"What should I do?" Teenager said.

Mama showed him the button from Myles' jacket, which sat on a black cloth with a yellow sulphur powder spread over the button and cloth. A small reptile's tongue was alongside the button.

"Soon I will take this and bury it in the cemetery and the cop will die," Mama said.

"What do I do until he dies?" Teenager said.

"You must go away."

"This I cannot do."

"You should go away until this is in the ground and the cop dies," Mama said again.

Teenager left her, went out the cellar door of the building and drove to his own apartment. "Get these kids out of the way," he told his wife. He went into the bedroom and called Benny in Puerto Rico.

"I am dying here," Benny said.

"I was thinking that I should come down," Teenager said.

"You will die here," Benny said. "For me they have a warrant. I have to die here. You, they have nothing to arrest you for. Why should you come here?"

"I don't know. I'm thinking."

"Why don't you ask the lawyer what you should do?" Benny said.

"Fuck the lawyer. He will tell me I am in such trouble I must pay him thousands," Teenager said.

"Then ask Maximo. Maybe he could tell you," Benny said.

"I think I will do that," Teenager said. He hung up and wondered where Maximo was. With all these police around, he couldn't go directly to Maximo's house. He would send somebody.

.....**Chapter 25**

At twelve-thirty, when Nicki was sitting at the desk and thinking about going out for her usual lunch of coffee and cigarettes, the phone rang.

"Nicki?"

"Who else?"

"I want to meet you. Early. Very early."

"All right, I guess," she said.

"You guess? What's the matter?"

"I'm just thinking of how I have to push my way onto the subway again."

"We won't have to. I want to meet you by your office right after work. I have to be someplace at nine-thirty."

"Some more freaking politics?"

"No. I just have one thing I have to see in Times Square. At nine-thirty. Then I'll get you to the bus terminal."

"This doesn't sound like much of a night to me."

"It's the best I can offer. Unless after, you wan—"

"—I can't tonight. I'll just get the bus home."

"So I'll meet you at five," Maximo said.

"Fine."

Stepping from the elevator after work, she picked his beard out of the crowd and walked to him boldly, almost not caring if anybody she worked with happened to notice them together. She took him by the hand and led him

336

down to the bank, which was at the far end of the lobby and which remained open until six o'clock each night. They walked casually, she leading him by the hand, as if dragging a wagon, and he laughing and asking where she was taking him, and they were walking with their bodies apart, arms extended, walking jauntily, sportily, and yet the mere holding of hands sent a tremor through her that almost had the strength of sex.

Oh, what's to *do* with you? she said to herself.

Inside the bank, she released his hand and went to a line with her check and bankbook. She did not want him to stand with her, for now she was dealing with another universe and would be unable to do it if her insides stirred with his touch. There was no deposit slip to be made out, of course, for that had been done in the morning, the moment her check was placed on her desk. The weekly salary check amounted to three hundred and thirty-nine dollars and sixty-seven cents, of which she was depositing two hundred and fifty. On a week such as this, when she intended to buy nothing for herself, she needed only carfare and coffee and cigarette money.

While waiting on line, she glanced back at Maximo. She sighed.

Two nights before, the moment she heard her husband's voice, she took a deep breath. It was Monday, a night he was not due to call—his regular time was each Thursday at eight o'clock—and immediately she felt this heavy robe fall over her, a robe of beautiful, costly material, but so thick and heavy that she could walk only as far as the door before the material became so heavy to carry that her legs could go no more.

"I saw the board today," her husband had said.

"Today? It wasn't supposed to be for a month?"

"Don't ask me how it happened, Nicki. The lieutenant just came and said, 'Come on, they're here today and let's get you over with.' "

"What did they say?"

"You know them, they don't say nothing. But the lieutenant come up to me later and said he thought it was all right. He said they're going to give me a date."

"Ronnie!"

"Isn't that something?"

"When?"

"Well, if it goes the way he says it's going, these joints are so filled with the other kind that they don't like to keep whites around. All kinds of trouble starts on account of us being under the same roof with this other element. So he says that if things stay the way they are, I'll get a date in February."

"Ronnie!"

"I know. I can't believe it, either."

"What am I supposed to do?" she said.

"Just get ready."

"Ronnie, could we do one thing?"

"Anything."

"The minute you get it all official and we know the date, then could we forget about the next time in the trailer?"

"Are you crazy?"

"No. I want to drive myself crazy. I want to make such a buildup for you coming home that I'll explode."

"Honey, whatever you say."

"Let's just wait and drive each other crazy."

"Whatever you say."

"When are you going to know official?"

"What could it take? Two days, three days. But the lieutenant knows what he's talking about. He says he thinks they'll give me a release date for February sometime."

When she had hung up, her mother, sitting at the kitchen table, grunted. "You know what you should do?"

"What, Ma?"

"Get those towels of yours, wherever you put them and wherever you use them, and burn them up in a fire. While you're at it, burn up whoever the son of a bitch is right with the towels. Get rid of everything you've been doing all at once. Get it out of your mind. You got your husband coming home and you got a whole life to get back to now."

* * *

Now, standing at the teller's window, she inspected the book when it was handed back to her. The balance was thirteen thousand, six hundred and ten dollars. To her, the progress of her life was marked by the numbers on the pages: I lived and was able to save this much money, she told herself proudly. For an instant, she regarded the numbers as the cables on a bridge that would take her to her own life. When you have money, she told herself, you can choose any night and hide yourself in it and walk across the bridge to anywhere forever. Iowa, she thought. Nobody ever would think of looking for you if you simply picked up and went to Iowa. You could live and die in Iowa and nobody would even know who to notify when they found the body. She saw herself walking on a farm, walking on her toes so as not to disturb the dirt, going down an aisle between furrows of high corn that ran for so far into the distance that if you tried to look for the end of the lane you became disoriented. Pale green leaves tightly bound around the corn and only these blades of green, flopping out from somewhere at the base of the corn, able to touch her. She saw herself taking a step and on both sides of her the long green leaves reaching out to touch her sides and arms. For each time in her life that something had reached out, a hand, a look that demanded compliance, a custom that caused her to concede and remain inside the circle in which she had been born and raised and taught that she never would be able to leave, she could in Iowa walk past a thousand corn stalks, feeling the long green leaves brushing off her arms as she moved as she pleased.

However, now, standing beside the teller's window, the numbers in the bankbook suddenly represented something more realistic: figures to impress a parole officer—a record of money honestly earned over a long period—and also numbers to offer a husband as proof of virtue and loyalty during all the desolate months of his absence. Numbers that signaled that this great beautiful housecoat was about to fall upon her and prevent her from walking about life every bit as much as would a pair of broken legs.

The manner in which the teller had placed the change

inside the bankbook irritated Nicki. There was only
eighty-four dollars, but the teller had the tens mixed up,
a couple of wrong sides facing up, and even if it were
only two dollars, Nicki wanted her money always to be
as neat as she kept her bedspread.

She straightened the money, put the bankbook into her
bag and walked up to Maximo and took his hand. Happily, she walked with him on the crowded sidewalks to a
restaurant on East 58th Street where a woman in a white
smock sat in the window and made pasta. Nicki immediately withdrew; what are we going to do, walk into a
place where somebody will run to the phone and get us
killed? Then through the windows she could see that
among those at the bar were at least several blacks. This
eased her fear; there could be no one in this place who
would know her or her family.

The bar was crowded and she opened her coat and
leaned on a ledge against the wall as Maximo, in a black
coat with toggle buttons, picked his way through shoulders and brought her back a Scotch and water. In his
other hand he held a screwdriver, which to her was a
ridiculous drink because she knew the bartender put only
a hint of liquor in such a drink.

She took some of the Scotch, then stared at the glass.
When, she thought, do I talk to him? Here in this crowd?
What if he became mad. No, this is no way to get anything done. I'm melting in my coat in this place. She
thought about taking off the coat, but then, as she
watched the blacks moving to and from the bar, brushing
against the chests of white women, she decided to keep
it on, no matter how uncomfortable.

"How's the job?" she heard Maximo ask.

"It's fine." He never had asked her about the job before this.

"Where do you think you're headed for?" he asked.

"With the job?"

"Yes."

"I don't know. I'll keep the job until it's time to stay
home and have a baby." She poked a finger into his
chest. "And don't you misunderstand what I'm saying. I

said 'have a baby' and that means a real baby. I take no chances on kinky hair.''

"Who says I want to have a child who looks like Lucky Luciano?'' Maximo said.

"Then both of us have nothing to be afraid about,'' she said.

"Is that your ambition, just to go home and have children someday?''

"I think I've done pretty well to get as far as I have at work,'' she said.

"I'm not saying that. I'm wondering how much farther you can go.''

"Banks like men,'' she said.

"They seem to like you so far.''

"Anything above my job is a man with college,'' Nicki said. "I'm a woman with high school.''

"Then go to college.''

"And do what for a living, steal cars?''

"No, you keep working. Go to school at night. Probably you won't have to go all the way through. The minute they hear at the bank that you're in college, they'll look at you differently. And I'll be around to help you.''

At 7:15, they left the bar and walked up to a theater on 59th Street that was showing a three-hour movie about beleaguered gays in France. Nicki waved a hand. "I can't sit through that,'' she said, "I thought we had to go to the West Side for something.''

"Not until 10,'' he said.

"Where on the West Side?''

"Broadway and 43rd.''

"What's so important there?''

"I have to be there for five minutes, but I have to be there.''

"If it's so important,'' she said.

"It is.''

"Then we'll go,'' she said.

They walked over to Broadway and went past car showrooms and faded Chinese restaurants, and the sidewalks soon were filled with freaks hanging out under marquees advertising sex shows and on the crossstreets the traffic was solid with theater people, thin wrists sticking

out of fur coats, chatting in limousines taking them to
plays. Now there were several large movie houses, but
nothing appealed to Maximo, and Nicki liked only *Rocky,*
which she already had seen twice. At 42nd Street, the
Amsterdam was showing an old James Bond double-
header, which Maximo thought was perfect for wasting
an hour or so.

At nine fifty they came out into the crowds of street
whores in short imitation fur jackets and fake leather
boots and pimps in big hats hanging around pinball machines in games arcades. Maximo led her to 43rd Street
to the *New York Times* building. Its editors sit upstairs
and debate American policy toward Nambia, while on the
street in front of the building a pimp cuts his whore's
cheek because she held out twenty dollars. At the *Times*
on this night, there was a crowd of young men and
women pushing excitedly through the revolving doors
and into a lobby that was a tangle of young people, many
of whom were waving to a battery of lights set up for
television cameras.

"What is this?" Nicki said.

Distaste showed on Maximo's lips. "Let's get out of
here," he said.

They went back to Broadway and 42nd and stepped
into a Nedick's, which was on the corner with the newsstand. They sat at the empty end of the counter and had
coffee.

"Tell me what we're supposed to be doing here,"
Nicki said.

"You'll see," Maximo said.

Two pimps came in and sat alongside them. "Got his
hands cut all up," one of them said, "just like he was out
picking up old garbage cans."

"Teach him to *be*have," the other said.

Maximo discarded the conversation as it was being
held. He kept watching the newsstand outside. At a few
minutes after ten, a *Times* truck pulled up and the door
was pulled back and the driver's helper carried out two
bundles of papers. The helper had to push through jos-
tlers and whores to drop the papers on the newsstand.

The coffee cup in Maximo's hand came down, and he

pushed change across the counter and took Nicki by the hand and led her out to the newsstand. The dealer was cutting the wires on the papers and arranging them to sell. The *Times* was placed alongside the *Daily News* on one side, and on the other, a magazine whose title was *Girls! Girls! Girls!* Maximo picked up a paper. He stepped into the light coming from the Nedick's stand and flipped the paper to the first page of the second section. He looked at the index and then quickly, rattling the pages, went through the paper, stopped, eyes scanning rapidly, then riveting on a story.

"Here you are," he said, handing the folded paper to Nicki. His finger tapped a story. Nicki read it. The story said simply that the results of the State Bar Examination had been released. Underneath, in agate type, was a long list of names. Nicki's eyes raced down to the E's. "Escobar, Maximo, 252 Pinto Avenue, the Bronx."

Her body told her to throw her arms around his neck, grab the back of his hair, press herself against him, kiss him in front of everybody on the street and then scream to the night sky. She remained motionless while continuing to study the newspaper. She had been raised, as had all of her blood for all of the years they had been present on the crust of the earth, to conceal emotion as if it were a wound in the middle of a fight. A stranger should know! Yet this time there was so much wonder and craving inside her that only the most pain-causing effort kept the feeling private, prevented a shriek from leaving her mouth. With his eyes, smile, beard, his wonderful sloping neck, he had gone out and done something that nobody she ever knew could do. Look at the paper and see how smart he is. A movie star who is a genius. Oh, am I falling in love with him? Stop that. You can't even think of things like that. A Puerto Rican!

Maximo brushed against her. He had a Latin roar inside him, a crowd in the sun in the stands, but he could not afford to release any of this while he stood with this strange woman, a woman who did not feel enough to put her arms around him. To protect himself against this woman, Maximo concentrated on maintaining a stolid face. He started to walk into Nedick's ahead of her.

"Come back here," she said.

She stood with her head turned, the cheek waiting to be kissed.

Maximo walked up to her and kissed her on the cheek.

"That's very good," she said.

"Is that all?" he said.

"I want a cup of coffee and then I have to go home," she said.

"Home?"

"I told you today when you called me."

"That was before this," he said, taking the paper from her.

"Well, I didn't know then. And all I know now is I have to be home."

"Call."

"I can't."

He looked at her for a moment. "Then I'll get you to the bus."

"I said I'd have a cup of coffee."

Maximo shook his head. "No, I'll get you to the bus."

She started down the street with him in silence. They had gone four or five doorways like this when she decided that she was the one who had to start the talk.

"The other people we saw waiting at the newspaper office, were they there for this?" she said, indicating the paper under his arm.

"I guess so."

"Did they want this for a souvenir or is this how you find out if you pass?"

"Find out."

"How much sooner did they see the paper than you did?"

"Fifteen, twenty minutes. Standing there like beggars. If this is how they act now, imagine what they're willing to do for money on a case."

"But that's going to be their business," she said.

"What?"

"Stealing money."

"That's not what I want," he said.

"What else is there but money?"

"Accomplishing something."

"A big diamond, that's a real accomplishment."

"What about a big help to people?"

"I like possessions. They don't bother you."

"Then you've got the wrong man."

"Oh, I know that."

She told herself again that she had to remain in one universe at a time. He's not money, she reminded herself, he's a movie star. Lawyer. The only lawyers she ever met were Jews, and she never had known anybody who could compete with Jews when it came to books. Yet, here was Maximo, a marvelous savage in bed, just like the Puerto Ricans are supposed to be, and he still could get up and sit down at a desk like he was a Jew. Nicki found this thought stunning. She looked at him and wanted to throw her arms around him.

They walked down 42nd Street toward the terminal for the New Jersey buses, which was at the end of the street. Maximo had one hand on Nicki's elbow, protectively, for they were passing clusters of winos and doorway loungers. The newspaper was folded under the other arm. At the end of the block they stood in front of a peep show that had a twirling red light over the entrance. He walked over to a trashcan to throw the paper away.

"Give me that," Nicki said. She grabbed for the paper.

"You won't come home with me?" Maximo said.

"I can't," she said. The avenue was filled with yellow cabs. Wave your arm for one, she told herself, and go to the Bronx with him in a cab for once. She could feel herself with him in his bed. Go ahead, hold up a hand and wave, she told herself. Get in a cab with him and never come back.

She held out her cheek again. "Kiss me goodbye."

"I'll walk you to the bus."

"So half of Jersey could see me with you? They'd all swear I picked you up at the bus terminal. Kiss."

"Forget it," Maximo said. "Go home."

He held the paper up to the red light from the peep show. "I guess we've seen enough of this, then." He dropped the paper in the trashcan, where it sat with dented soda cans and Kentucky Fried Chicken boxes. "So long," Maximo said.

That's a nice baby, she thought, watching him disappear, feeling the ache in her gut. I love you today.

She turned and walked across Eighth Avenue toward the bus terminal and Maximo walked up 42nd Street toward the subway. When Nicki crossed the avenue and got in front of the bus terminal, she stopped and lit a cigarette. On the second inhale, she walked back across Eighth Avenue and came past pimps and junkies and into the twirling light and the blare of music for blacks and, nose crinkled against the slime she was certain she had to touch, she held her hand out and walked up to the trashcan, in which there now was no *New York Times* newspaper.

"Why that son of a bitch," she said. She saw Maximo nowhere on the street, but as she walked back to the bus terminal she now felt pleased that she had it on him, for he most certainly had doubled back and grabbed the paper, and at the same time there was this tenderness deep inside her as she thought of Maximo standing in the subway train and looking at his name in the paper.

At the bus terminal, Nicki bought a *Times* and turned it to the page and looked at it during the bus ride home.

Oh, what's to *do* about you? she said to herself.

In the morning, when Nicki's mother came into the room to wake her up, the mother said, "What the hell is this?" The mother poked the copy of the newspaper that was on a chair.

"I bought it for the ride home," Nicki said.

"What's in it?" the mother said, apprehension causing her voice to rise. "Your father's upstairs, so it can't be anybody here."

"Nothing."

"How could it be nothing? You don't buy a paper unless there's something you got to know about."

"It's nothing, Ma."

"This new boyfriend of yours, he got himself in some big bust that made the papers?"

"Ma."

"What'd he do, shoot somebody?"

"Ma."

"Well, he must've done something big to make the

newspaper. This here newspaper don't print a lot of cheap crime. When they got you on something big you get in this newspaper. Is it drugs?''

"Ma, it's nothing.''

"A swindler? A conspiracy. That's a bad charge. Everybody gets sent away on conspiracy.''

"I promise you there's nothing," Nicki said.

"I'll bet," the mother said.

When the mother left, Nicki got out of bed and looked at the paper again. "Escobar, Maximo." She brought the paper to her mouth and kissed it. Suddenly, she shook her head. That was yesterday, baby, she said to herself. Today is different. Today I don't know what's going to be.

.... **Chapter 26**

It was a Friday and with the office open until 9:00 P.M., Maximo went to the San Juan coffee shop for dinner and then came back and saw people. The first was a slender man of twenty, who explained that he was a transsexual. As a girl of seventeen, the transsexual had been married to an impotent old man and the transsexual left him and went for an operation to change into a man.

"How did you get the money to go to Sweden for an operation like that?" Maximo said.

"I didn't go to Sweden. I went to Johns Hopkins. Hardly had the carfare to Baltimore."

"And they did it there?"

"Of course. I told you. I'm a transsexual, not a transvestite. I was born with two sets of organs. I had a vagina and then I had my prick tied up in my intestines."

"So what can I do for you?"

"Well, I got married last year to this dirty bitch who's running around on me. She says my prick is no good even if it did come from my intestines."

"Did you obtain a legal divorce from the first marriage?"

"I walk out on that useless old man, I never look back."

"You're telling me that you never went to court?"

"Never."

"If you're telling me the truth, then it makes the case

348

easy. You are still legally married to the man. Therefore, this marriage you now have to the young woman is not legal. You don't have to divorce her. It's the old man that you have to divorce."

"How do I do that?"

"Get me all your papers, the marriage license, something to prove that you earn less than five thousand dollars a year and be back here on Monday."

When the transsexual left, Maximo was depressed. I didn't come to work for marginal concerns, he told himself. He even thought, for the first time, of leaving the job.

A tall woman with huge lips and a left eye that was reduced to a slit by a bulging, red-black lump, walked into his office.

"You the lawyer?" she said.

"Yes, I am," Maximo said.

"That's right, you are."

The woman had on a black cap, which she took off to show thick bandages wrapped around her head.

"We tried having a meeting two weeks ago and this is what happened," she said. "They sent those rotten kids in here beatin' on us with baseball bats."

"They won't do that again," Maximo said.

"I know they won't," the woman said. She reached for an old handbag that was on the table, opened it and pulled out a nickel-plated .25.

Maximo pretended not to notice the gun and sat down at the table. The woman was from the home-aid program, a program for poverty areas, which hired neighborhood women to care for those who, by age or infirmity, were unable to care for themselves in the housing project. Maximo had helped work on the case for the last two months. A poverty community corporation, run by a man named Anders, received the government grants and hired and paid the workers, women such as this one. They were paid two-fifty an hour by Anders, and research by Maximo showed that Anders was reimbursed by Medicare at the rate of four dollars and fifty cents an hour for each worker. Administrative expenses, Anders claimed, when the women complained individually.

Maximo opened a manila envelope and took out records and papers pertaining to the program. As he looked at the papers, his level of annoyance rose. Anders, running the community corporation, was making a profit center out of the women home-aid workers. In doing this he merely was following what every landlord in New York did: charge tenants so much for maintenance and cleaning people that a clear profit was made off the back of every porter and scrubwoman. A midtown landlord, whose last Cadillac came from the brows of forty porters, would, upon inspecting the books of the poverty organization, scream that the director, Anders, be placed in leg irons. Trouble was, Maximo thought, Anders was not only taking money from his own people, he also was taking it from the federal government. Yet Maximo knew that if this woman were given her money, she would be the first to demand that Anders be given a medal for stealing from the federal government.

"We're having a meeting on Sunday night," she said.

"I'll see you there," Maximo said.

"Will the other woman be there too?"

"Haydee," Maximo said.

"That's the one. She's good."

"Yes, she is."

"Nobody talked as nice to us as you people did."

"That's nice of you."

"That ain't being nice. That's just what things is."

"Thank you," Maximo said.

When he reached Southern Boulevard, he began thinking of her. She had a new schedule for him, she had told him on the phone. Starting tomorrow, she had said, she would be around on Saturday. Through the truck fumes, through the grease smell of fish frying in stores with windows too smeared to see through, Maximo could smell her neck. At the first corner on Pinto, four men were sitting on milk crates, playing dominoes on a piece of plywood propped on a cardboard box.

"Maximo," one of the men said, "David's mother is looking for you, man."

"What for?"

"Trouble, man."

On the next corner, David's mother stood by the phone booth, her head down, the hands fidgeting with a piece of folded paper. When she saw Maximo, she did not pick up her head.

"What's the matter?" Maximo said.

A sob caused her body to move.

"What is it?" Maximo said again.

She handed him the folded paper. It was a birth certificate made out to David Robles, born May 19, 1964, in District Number 13, Caguas, Puerto Rico.

"The police take him," the mother said. She was crying, but did not lose her small, embarrassed voice.

"For what?"

"The police say he make a fire that killed two people."

"When was this?"

"They say the fire was last night. They take him tonight. He is only eleven. The police say he is fourteen. They say he is a man."

"Did you get a lawyer?" Maximo asked her.

Her wet face turned away in embarrassment.

"You."

"You mean no lawyer has seen you and your boy?"

She gave him a card from a Legal Aid attorney named Katz.

"He saw your boy?"

She nodded.

"Then he's your lawyer."

Maria Robles said, "He told me that he wouldn't be in court tomorrow. He say another lawyer do that. He has to go away."

"I have a problem," Maximo said. "I'm not supposed to be doing criminal work. I do things like rent and people who should get welfare. I don't do criminal."

Large soft eyes directed him to the ridiculousness of what he had just said.

"Where is he now?" he asked.

"The police."

"And what did they tell you?"

"They tell me come back to the court in the morning."

"In the morning I'll try to help you," Maximo said.

"They put my boy on TV."

"What did he say?"

"He say nothing. But they say about him."

"Say what?"

"That he set a fire to kill people he hates. He does not even know the people in the fire." She unfolded the birth certificate again. "They say he is fourteen, a man. He is not. He is only eleven."

Maximo said, "Tomorrow morning at eight o'clock. I will meet you here."

When he got upstairs, he pushed the dog back. Disappointed that he wouldn't be taken for a run, the dog's claws sounded as he sprawled on the floor. Maximo turned on the television, and at 10:00 P.M. the David Robles story led the news.

"A fourteen-year-old arrested for arson in connection with a Bronx fire that left two dead," the anchorman, a blow-dried blond from Nebraska, said. "District Attorney Robert Garafola says that David Robles will be prosecuted as an adult and he said he expects the grand jury to return a homicide indictment, based on the evidence he intends to present."

The scene shifted to a gutted frame building on Mackey Avenue, two blocks from Maximo's bedroom. While a crowd of children waved at the camera, a television reporter with California asparagus tones clutched a microphone and explained that the suspect had broken into the basement and deliberately set the fire in revenge for some slight perpetrated by the inhabitants of the building.

"The suspect will appear tomorrow in Bronx Criminal Court where a hearing will be held to determine if he should become the youngest person in the history of Bronx County to be tried as an adult on a murder charge."

Maximo took the dog down to the street, watched him race into the darkness, then walked him to the candy store on Southern Boulevard. The *News* was up. On page three was the story about David Robles being held for arraignment on homicide charges. He took the paper home, read it and then lay awake with his fingernails tapping his chest as he thought of what he could do. He decided that he had no idea, that all he was certain of was that he would be in court with Maria Robles in the morning.

The next day, at 7:15 A.M., Nicki walked out of the New Jersey bus terminal at Washington Heights and looked around the street, the stores silent, and then got into a yellow cab. As she slid in and saw the white driver, she became flustered.

"What are you going there for?" he asked her when she gave the address.

"I own a building there and I have to clean it," she said.

"What's in the building?"

"People."

He held his hand on the flag. "You're going over there to clean up after those people?"

"My mother told me I had to."

He pushed the flag down. "I guess you know what you're doing." Wispy gray hair grew like weeds out of a wrinkled neck. "How old are you?" he asked.

"Twenty-six."

"You got a lot of guts your age, going to Pinto Avenue."

Nicki lit a cigarette and looked out both windows for a store. In the shopping bag with her she had the basis for all good cleaning, houserags, cut-up old winter pajamas with the buttons removed and strips of old bed sheets. In her mother's pile of cleaning rags home in the basement there was cut-up old underwear, which of course Nicki left. Imagine if I'm standing there doing the kitchen sink with my mother's underwear? Even the things Nicki had been raised to hate, Handi Wipes, would be better than that.

She saw a woman walking into a *bodega* on 163rd Street and she told the cab driver to pull over. "You're not gettin' nothin' to eat in there?" he said.

"No, just some cleaning stuff."

The *bodega* had Spic 'n Span next to the bread. It was a dollar two a gallon and the idea of paying thirteen cents more than charged by the Gristedes in Swiftbrook irritated Nicki. She then bought clear ammonia, Clorox, Ajax, Kirkman's yellow soap, Noxon and vinegar. She resented paying the higher ghetto prices, but consoled herself with the thought that she would clean like an animal. When she cleaned a house as furiously as she intended to today, it always gave her a sense of doing penance and at the end of the day her soul was scrubbed nearly as clean as the kitchen. She had to do this today, she knew, perhaps more than any other day in her times this far.

In front of Maximo's house, the cab driver said, "You all right now?"

"Positive."

"Broad daylight don't mean nothing to these people."

"I know."

"I read a story in the *Post* where they raped a girl five to seven in the morning."

"Don't worry."

"All right, then. But I told you."

Upstairs, her knocking brought the dog first and then Maximo to the door. He stood in his underwear and reached for the shopping bag, which she held away from him as she stepped past him and headed directly for the kitchen.

"At least say hello," Maximo said.

"Later."

She draped her coat over a chair and began emptying her treasure on the kitchen table. Last out were her great prizes, the cleaning rags, which she laid out as if they were a weapons display. She selected the arm of her father's former winter pajamas and decided to commit it against the major enemies she hated the most, two rust marks on the kitchen sink. One was a long vertical patch under the faucet, and the second was a large splotch on the sink bottom. The sight or thought of each mark had caused her to choke each time she had a glass of water in the house.

Maximo took a container of orange juice out of the refrigerator and took a long swallow.

"I'm not going to be here this morning," he said.

"I'm not leaving here until this is finished," Nicki said. "And I'm certainly not staying here alone. So whatever you're going to do will have to wait."

"It can't. I have to go to court."

"I'm sure that's your business," she said.

"I have to go for the kid across the street."

"David? What happened to him? The mother's always watching him." As she was talking, she was mixing ammonia and Clorox in a bowl so she could do the rust marks in the sink. She once had read where this mixture was a chemical disaster and that in cleaning the rust off the sink it took all the enamel with it, leaving a surface that caused a glass of tea spilled into the sink to leave a wider mark than the one before. But she continued to mix the ammonia and Clorox because this was how she had been taught to clean by her mother and aunts, who too had been raised to clean this way and tolerated no deviation. She concentrated on her mixture because the moment she heard the word court, and that the little boy across the street was involved, she searched for a sound or a scene that would instruct her what to do and she could find none and she knew immediately that whatever it was that Maximo was talking about had to be kept out of her life on this day.

He left the kitchen for a moment and brought in the *Daily News*. He put it on the kitchen table with the paper open to the story on page three. As she glanced at the story, her insides cringed. "I don't want to know anymore," she said, pushing the paper aside.

"What do you mean?"

"Just that."

Maximo shook his head. "I know, it's horrible. I can't even think about it. They have this little kid on a hom—"

"—You don't understand me. I don't care. Today I do the sink."

When Maximo didn't answer, Nicki said, "I go to court for myself. I don't want to know about it if other people are involved."

"I'm talking about a little kid from right across the street," Maximo said.

"If he's outside playing in the street, then I'll be nice to him and play with him," she said. "But if he's in court, then he's in court, and I don't want to know about it. I stay here."

"Stop the nonsense. You're not that cold."

She dropped the rag in the bowl of ammonia and Clorox, wrung it out, sprinkled Ajax on the rust marks and began to rub directly under the faucet.

"You get paid for today?" she said.

"How can I get paid?"

"They don't have any relatives?"

"I don't know what they have. What do I care? Her boy is in trouble."

"She has no relatives she can ask for something?"

"For what?"

"They don't have a car around?"

"You see how she lives."

"I mean a relative might have a car. Let them sell the car."

"Come on," Maximo said.

He watched her rub furiously at the rust mark under the faucet, then went into his bedroom. One thing about living with my husband, Nicki thought as she rubbed, there would be no rust marks anyplace in any house where he lived. She exhaled in despair. She rubbed at the rust spot with her father's pajama arm wet and gritty from the ammonia and Ajax. She concentrated on this task. This one computer screen of her life.

She remembered being woken up on Thursdays by the squeaking of her mother's rag on the bedroom window in East Harlem. The window looked out on an alley that appeared to be in a state of festival with washlines drooping with sheets and nightwear. When rain came, the empty washlines slapped against the chipped, uneven bricks of the old building walls. Yet Nicki's bedroom window had to sparkle at all times, for this was the way the windows in her grandmother's house were kept, and so would all the windows of all her mother's houses, from the East Harlem apartment until the present, the big yellow brick house in Swiftbrook whose windows looked over a golf course. In whatever houses Nicki would live

her life, each Thursday there would be vinegar and water
on the windows, for this was what a woman was taught
to do as a girl and was expected to do until her hands
were stilled by death or arthritis.

As she rubbed the sink, she could feel her arm out in
front of her as she slipped through the cornfield in Iowa.
The leaves brushing off her arm, then coming back to
brush off her body. If there was someplace, she thought,
where she could build a life that was her own, and one
that came from what she felt and saw and worked for,
and not what she was told and taught and stumbled into.
For a time, she reminded herself, it seemed like Maximo
was building his life in a way that did not make him a
Spic. Some chance of that. So here he was going out with
some derelict kid—that's just what he is, say the truth
now, don't start thinking he's cute; he's just another derelict on the streets—and Maximo was doing it under the
most unforgivable of circumstances, without profit. Oh,
no, baby. No, thank you. She bit her lower lip and tried
to scrub through the face of the sink. She began to cry
freely and did nothing to stop it.

Maximo came in dressed in his courtroom suit. She
kept her head down. He took another swallow of the
orange juice.

"Want some?" he asked.

"No, thank you."

"Well, I have to leave."

"You can't wait until I finish this?"

"No, I told her I'd pick her up outside at eight
o'clock."

"All right. I'll be right with you."

"You're not staying?"

"Not here."

"Why don't you come with me, then?" he said.

"Me? Go to a courthouse?"

"Well, you could wait in the delicatessen right across
the street from court."

"Not I, dear."

She paused for a moment and looked at the rust. The
spot directly under the faucet had grown smaller. It

needed more time and it would be gone, she thought. She dropped the rag, stepped back, pulled the sleeves of her sweatshirt down, looked directly at him, for the only time in her life not even caring if somebody could see tears, if any were left, and said, "My husband is coming home Tuesday and I won't be seeing you anymore."

She did not wait for a reaction. She took the container of orange juice out of his hand and poured some of it into one of the paper cups he kept stacked on the sink. She handed him the cup. "Here, at least take this downstairs with you while you go to your people." She stepped past him, took her coat from the chair and walked out of the kitchen. As she passed the bathroom, she saw an orange towel on the floor. Wet, trampled on. Another towel was thrown over the side of the bathtub. To her eyes, it was too dirty to be a cleaning rag. He must wash the dog and dry him with the towel, she thought. She grabbed the towels, rolled them up and walked to the front door with the towels in her hand. The dog began yelping and leaping at the door.

"Keep your dog in," she said.

"Give me a minute," Maximo said.

"I'm going."

"I want to talk to you."

"You can talk downstairs. Now keep your dog back and don't spill the juice all over yourself."

"I'll put it down."

"No, I want you to have it."

"What are you doing with the towels?"

"Just hold the dog back," she said.

He held the juice in one hand and grabbed the dog with the other. She opened the door and tripped down the stairs. The door slammed and he caught up with her as she stepped onto the street.

David Robles' mother, Maria Robles, stood in the morning sun wearing a raincoat over her white church dress and red shoes. She held her son's birth certificate in her hands as if it were a note from a saint.

"Take care of her," Nicki said.

"Wait a minute," Maximo said.

"No, I'm going." She glanced at the orange towels she

was holding. "You'll get these back. It'll probably take a week to wash them clean. You're so sloppy."

"You'll bring them back?" Maximo said.

"No. I'll mail them. Take care of her."

She turned her head and melancholy steps took her toward the corner.

Maria Robles handed Maximo the birth certificate. He took it, but his eyes were following Nicki as she went down the street.

"Is she going to be at the court?" Maria Robles said.

"No, she's going home."

"Oh, she will meet us there."

"She won't. She's going home."

Maria Robles seemed surprised. "I thought she would come with you today."

"She just said I won't see her anymore.

"Oh, no. Soon she will be back. She loves Maximo."

"What is she leaving for then?"

"Soon she will be back. I can see that she loves you," Maria said. "Now you will get my son for me?"

"We're going to try," Maximo said gloomily.

——— .... **Chapter 27**

——— ....

"Let's get the bus," Maximo said to Maria Robles.

As they walked to the corner, he said to her, "Now, tell me what happened."

"He is only a child."

"And."

Her eyes on the sidewalk as she walked, Maria Robles said that her boy David had been sleeping in the basement of the building at 998 Mackey Avenue.

"Why wasn't he home?"

"I hit my boy because he hit his sister and he run away."

"How do they say this fire started?"

"He hid in this building. Then he wanted to come home. It was dark and he lit a paper to see. Everybody does this in cellars. But he forgot. He drops the paper. He always forgets. He forget the paper was lit and he comes home."

"Did you tell this to the police?"

"I tell them, and they only say my boy did this fire and he is in big trouble."

The courthouse faced a street of abandoned apartment buildings, black from fire, the rows of windows, covered with tin, staring like unkempt graves. Streaming into the courthouse were the consumers of the Bronx criminal justice system: young blacks in sneakers, smoking cigarettes, who showed up because court is an event, as grad-

uation is for others; Puerto Ricans in gold chains and
flowered shirts protesting loudly—"It's a bullshit case,
man"—as the lawyers, young and Jewish, dressed in the
clothes of old Protestants, vests and watchfobs, told
them of the charges. Maximo led her inside this building,
a monument that had been overrun and left as a barn.
The banister was speckled with spent gum and gashed
with the initials of those who, in the absence of a tree in
a secret place, made permanent their love by carving out
their oaths. Cigarette butts and candy wrappers covered
the steps, one of which creaked so badly on first weight
that Maximo helped Maria Robles to step over it.

Once, there had been transoms of stained glass over
the courtroom doors and now there was cardboard. Maximo read the sheets tacked to the wall and found the right
courtroom. As he held open the door for Maria Robles, a
man's voice in the front of the room called out,
"Ready?"

It was a clerk sitting at a table under the judge's bench.
Stacks of manila folders stuffed with white and yellow
paper were shuffled by the clerk's bored hands.

Immediately Maximo's attention was taken by a court
officer who stood on the left side of the courtroom.

"I guess so," he said to the clerk.

"All right," the clerk said.

The court officer pounded on the door. "Bring him out,
Mike."

Maximo and Maria Robles were sliding into seats,
looking at the door where the court officer stood, and
there could now be heard a clanking of locks and steel
doors. Two court officers stepped into the room. Then,
escorted by another pair of court officers, David Robles
shuffled into the room. He acted as he had been taught to
act in the principal's office. He wore cheap sneakers, the
ten-dollar pairs that a mother buys and are a sign that the
wearer has not learned how to glide through a store and
come back onto the street with real sneakers, great thick
soles and wonderful sides with the name Nike or Puma
printed on them.

"Go up to the bench," one of the court officers said.
David spun around. There was nothing that looked to him

like a bench. The court officer pointed over to the defense table. He walked over to the defense table and stood facing the bench. A court officer tapped David on the shoulder.

"Take your hands out of your pockets," the court officer said. David took his hands out of the pockets of his blue hooded sweatshirt and placed them on the defense table. The fingers tapped the table edge like a piano. David's knee worked back and forth.

"Stop tapping the table," the court officer said. David's hands dropped to his side. The fingers now played with the cuffs of his sweatshirt.

"Can I take off my jacket?" David asked.

"Yes," the court officer said.

David had the jacket halfway off when he changed his mind and yanked it back over his shoulders. He began pulling the zipper up and down.

"All right," the judge, Rose Keogh, said. The clerks began digging into papers with both hands.

Rose Keogh was so slight and the bench about her so large, that she nearly became lost, a pencil mark on gray paper. Even her red hair seemed dulled by the surroundings. To Maximo, her expression suggested infected gums. She sat in a place whose dusty windows were covered with wire grill so that thieves couldn't climb into the place at night. Her surroundings were prostitutes throwing up on the floor in front of her and young muggers bending over to show bloodied heads from a police beating. And now she looked down at this kid in front of her. She screwed her lips and ordered the clerk to start the proceedings.

The clerk picked up a yellow folder. "Docket number X875643, David Robles. Charged with 125.25 and 150.15. Arresting officer, Detective Harold McGahan."

The 125.25 was homicide and the 150.15 meant arson. Maximo sat with his head down. Could the judge, Rose Keogh, have seen him, he wondered, and if she had seen him did she even know who he was? Then he relaxed. Even if she knows me, he said to himself, if I sit here and show nothing, then she will not know what case I am interested in.

"Your Honor."

"Yes?"

"If it please the court, Your Honor." The district attorney of Bronx County himself, not some cheap assistant, arose, tugged at the bottom of his vest, and began talking.

His name was Ben Rossoff. The story about him was so famous that even law students like Maximo knew it: the day in 1969 that he heard Kennedy had gone off the bridge at Chappaquiddick, Rossoff went to the windows of his office, looked out over the Bronx and said, "Why couldn't it have been on the Willis Avenue Bridge?"

As he spoke to the judge, Rossoff used words like "text of affidavit," "inhibiting factor," and "application." Maximo thought he was back at the lectures in the royal ballroom of the Statler Hilton. Looking over at David, Maximo saw the words produced the same narcotic effect on the boy as they do on students at the bar exam class. As if he were a law student two hours into a lecture on torts, David Robles let his eyes droop and then close.

When Rossoff finished, David's Legal Aid lawyer took a step toward the bench.

"On behalf of the defendant Robles, I would point out that this youngster has no place to go if he wanted to," the Legal Aid lawyer said. "He can't take a boat to China. He should be allowed to go home to his mother."

"And what is the people's recommendation?" the judge asked.

"The crime was committed at 4:30 A.M.," the district attorney said. "This gentleman is not a good bail risk."

"This gentleman is a child," the Legal Aid lawyer said.

"If I may continue," the district attorney said. "Your Honor, we ask for high bail because there is a strong possibility of conviction, and also because, may I remind you again, that as for his being home, the crime was committed at 4:30 A.M. Your honor, this is a homicide case and it will be tried as such. The defendant is over the age of fourteen and Bronx County is prepared to display its outrage over this matter. We remind you again,

Your Honor, the crime took place at 4:30 A.M. The defendant was not at home, we assure you of that.''

Maria Robles unfolded the birth certificate and handed it to Maximo.

"You take it up," he said to her.

"Where?" she asked.

Maximo brought his head up and pointed to the Legal Aid lawyer. As he did this, the judge, who had been staring at the light fixtures hanging over the bench, suddenly rocked forward and her eyes fell on Maximo. Then she watched intently as Maria Robles, in her white dress and red shoes, walked haltingly down the aisle.

"What is it?" Rose Keogh said.

Maria Robles stopped. Her paper was held out as an offering.

"Take your seat," Rose Keogh said.

Maximo was out of his seat and up the aisle. "If it please the court," he said. "This woman is the boy's mother." Maximo pointed at David Robles. "And she would like at this time to hand her attorney proof that the boy is not fourteen, as the district attorney says, but is actually eleven."

"You may hand it to the lawyer and then take your seat," she said to Maximo.

"Can I take my boy home?" Maria Robles said.

"Please be seated, madam," Rose Keogh said.

Maximo handed the certificate to the Legal Aid lawyer, who regarded it as a triumph. Maximo went back and sat with Maria Robles as the Legal Aid lawyer presented the birth certificate to the district attorney and the judge. The Legal Aid lawyer said that the presence of the certificate meant that all charges had to be changed to juvenile status. The district attorney said no matter of importance such as this could be settled by a mere piece of paper. There were other records, and the boy's own statement, to show that he was fourteen and thus eligible to be tried as an adult for murder.

Judge Rose Keogh, who had been staring at the light fixture hanging over the bench, rocked forward in her chair and stared down at the defendant.

"I believe it is my duty, and I will do my duty," the judge said. "I will remand the defendant."

One of the court officers tapped David on the shoulder. David's eyes widened and then blinked away the spell of the airless room.

"It's over," the court officer said.

Turning, David walked toward the bench where his mother sat. The mother was halfway out of her seat when the court officer caught David by the elbow. Spinning David around, the court officer led him toward the door on the right of the courtroom and into the detention pens.

"Where they taking him?" the mother asked Maximo.

"They are taking him to Spofford," Maximo said.

"What is Spofford?" the mother asked.

"It is the jail for children," Maximo said.

"In the Bronx?" the woman asked.

"In the Bronx," Maximo said. "You can visit him there."

When Maximo stepped out onto the sidewalk, Rossoff, the district attorney, was already speaking to the television news cameras.

"Most people don't understand the problems we have here in the Bronx," the district attorney told five cameras. "We have 250,000 burned-out apartments in the South Bronx. This is not theory. This is not law school. This is a problem we have to come to grips with. We have had an investigation of massive proportions into this fire. This was a fire that killed two people."

As he spoke, Maximo saw, the district attorney did not look at the reporters. The district attorney looked directly at the cameras.

"That is the man who put my boy in jail?" the mother asked Maximo.

"Yes," Maximo said. "He is called the district attorney. We will go see your boy tomorrow."

At ten o'clock the next morning, Maximo met the mother in front of her building on Pinto Avenue. Once again, the mother was wearing the white dress and the red high-heeled shoes.

Walking under the Bruckner Expressway, Maximo and

the mother walked over to Hunts Point Boulevard. Turning left onto Spofford Avenue, they walked two blocks to the four-story, white brick building called the Spofford Juvenile Detention Facility.

In the driveway, two detectives in an unmarked car honked twice. There was the hum of an electric motor and the metal gate covering the entrance rolled up like a garage door. Maximo and the mother followed the car into the courtyard.

"This one's so small, we almost had to throw it back," one of the detectives shouted to a guard as he reached into the back of the unmarked car. A small foot stuck out of the back door. The five-foot three-inch prisoner stepped out of the car into the courtyard.

"You have to take the handcuffs off," the prisoner said. "The law say when I get here you got to take the handcuffs off."

"He's been here before," the detective said to the guard.

"He's been here three times this month," the guard said.

As he handed the detective a receipt for the prisoner, the guard looked over at Maximo and the mother.

"What're you doing here?" the guard asked.

"We came to visit a boy named David Robles," Maximo said.

"Well, the entrance for the visitors is down at the side," the guard said.

Walking back onto the sidewalk, Maximo and the mother turned right.

"Who you coming to see?" a woman at a table just inside the visitor's entrance asked.

"David Robles," Maximo said.

"When'd he come in?" the woman asked.

"Yesterday," Maximo said.

"Just have a seat over there," the woman said. "We'll fetch him."

Fifteen minutes later, the door at the far end of the room opened and David swiveled his head until he saw his mother. There was no sleep in his eyes now. His eyebrows were knotted and his jaw muscles bulged. His hands were at his side, clenched into fists. He shuffled over to the table, his back arched, his feet moving without leaving the floor. As the mother reached across the table to hug him, David stared straight ahead, his mouth drawn back tight.

"Sit down," the mother said.

The boy shook his head.

"Sit down," the mother said.

Gripping the edge of the table, the boy slowly lowered himself onto the bench.

"Maximo is here now," the mother said. "He is going to help us."

"If you want to help me, get me out of here," the boy said.

"There is nothing that can be done until the bail hearing," Maximo said. "I hope it will not be long before the hearing."

"I have been here one night and that is a long time," the boy said. "If I told what they did to me, it would make them let me out."

"The guards hurt you?" Maximo asked.

"No, not the guards," the boy said.

"The other boys?" Maximo asked. The boy put his hands in his lap. Silent, he rocked back and forth. Maximo studied the boy's face. There were not cuts or bruises.

"They didn't beat you up," Maximo said.

"No," the boy said.

"They did something to you?" Maximo asked.

"A little something," the boy said.

"A sex thing?" Maximo asked.

"A little something," the boy said.

"Are you bleeding?" Maximo asked.

"I was," the boy said. "All night. But not now. I hide under my bed until there is no more blood."

"Who was the boy?" Maximo asked.

"He said he would kill me if I told," the boy said.

"What was his name?"

"Homo."

Reaching across the table, the mother touched the boy's cheek with her fingertips. The boy shook off the touch. The mother pulled back her hand and bit the knuckle of her index finger.

The door at the back of the room opened again and a husky prisoner wearing a denim cap strode into the room.

"*Yo*," the prisoner called to two other teenagers sitting at the far corner of the room.

"*Yo*," the two teenagers called back.

David's eyes nervously followed the husky prisoner, who went to the corner of the room.

"Is that Homo?" Maximo asked. David nodded once.

"Do you want me to tell the police or the guards?" Maximo asked. David shook his head once.

"Are you afraid he will hurt you if I tell?" Maximo asked. David nodded once.

"I will leave you with your mother," Maximo said. Rising from the table, Maximo left the visitor's room and cut over to the main entrance.

"Hey," Maximo shouted to one of the guards. "I want to see the man in charge."

"He's not here," the guard said. "What do you want?"

"I want one of the prisoners arrested," Maximo said.

"If he's a prisoner, he's already been arrested," the guard said.

"But he raped one of the other prisoners," Maximo said.

"Did the boy tell you what would happen to him if he reported it?" the guard asked.

"He said the other boy would kill him."

"Believe him," the guard said.

"He broke the law," Maximo said.

"Everybody in here broke the law," the guard said. "In here, the law been broke."

Walking out of the building and into Maria Robles' alarmed look, Maximo knew that he should have many soft words before the truth, but nothing formed in the hollowness inside him.

"Where is he?" she said.

"Nothing," Maximo said.

"Nothing?" Her eyes became very wide.

"I can't get anything done today."

"You are as wise as a spider. You must do something."

"Not today."

"When can you?"

"I can't tell you anything. I don't know."

Her hand trembled and gripped the front of her coat against the cold. "I will bring a gun and shoot somebody to get my little boy back."

He put his hands into his pockets and started walking away. He called over his shoulder to her, "You might as well come with me."

"I stay here."

"What for?"

"For my son."

He resumed walking down the side of the building along the high cyclone fence with barbed-wire topping that surrounded the white brick building, which reflected both the dreary winter afternoon and the cultures of the two communities it served almost exclusively: *"Nemo Y Linda"* and "I Luv Baby Dee." Words put on the wall by some kid in the night had done more harm to the system than he had been able to do with his ambition, energy, time and the beginnings of knowledge. He had been able to separate himself from his culture and to know more than the average person who was born Puerto Rican, he told himself, but he found that the power that this gave him, to make his own decisions, was not enough to disturb a hierarchy that could hear no crying.

For no reason he thought of, out of animal habit, some small memory of a warm barn, he walked up to 138th Street and moved along a frozen street that was as lonely as a field. When Maximo walked into the bar, Teenager was sitting on the pool table with a cigarette in one hand, a glass of brandy in the other and a sneer on his lips as he spoke to a serf in a blue imitation leather jacket. Seeing Maximo, Teenager called over the serf's head, "I don't see you for months."

Maximo was too tired to answer with anything more than a nod. At the bar were Santos Rivera and Albertito.

"Where is Benny?" Maximo asked.

"Who knows?" Rivera said.

"This is Tatiro," Teenager called out, placing a hand
on the head of the man in the blue jacket. "Tatiro is
saying something to me. Tell Maximo what you just said
to me."

Tatiro turned his head and said to Maximo, "I just took
Pepe off the count for Teenager."

"Is he telling the truth?" Teenager called to Maximo.

Maximo stared at the floor. "I don't want to hear anything," he said.

"Here, show him your evidence," Teenager said to
Tatiro. "Maximo, see the evidence the man brings."

Tatiro turned to face Maximo. He stood with his legs
together. The front of his red basketball pants was
stained with a deeper red. The basketball pants were
worn over gray sweatpants.

"Show him," Teenager said.

Tatiro lifted his right leg to show the inside of this one
leg of the gray sweatpants was splotched with blood.

"Pepe," Tatiro said.

"Aha!" Teenager shouted.

Santos Rivera pushed his rotten teeth into Maximo's
face and shook with laughter.

"It is Pepe," Tatiro said. "I take him off in his cellar.
You could ask anybody who knows Pepe if he didn't get
taken off in his cellar last night."

Teenager's face crinkled with laughter. "He comes
here to show me his evidence. He thinks that on the
street nobody will see the blood on him because it is on
the red trunks."

The others in the bar exploded into laughter. Teenager
put his drink and cigarette on the edge of the pool table
and stood up. "So now he sees he has this blood on the
sweatpants. So he comes over to here by walking like
this." Teenager started to shuffle with his legs clamped
together. While everyone screamed, Maximo looked at
the rotten teeth and inhaled the smell of Luisa Maria's
thick perfume rising from the dust behind the bar, and
here in front of him was this Tatiro with his bloody front
and his eyebrows raised in reasonableness: is it not fair
to say that if I have this man's blood on me, then it was I
who killed him?

Teenager's hand came through the laughter and slammed Maximo on the shoulder.

"What's the matter with you? I don't like people coming in here and not laughing with me."

The slap on the shoulder irritated Maximo. "I don't feel so funny," he said.

"I never can find you. Then you come here and tell me you don't feel funny."

"I've been busy," Maximo said.

"All of a sudden you are too busy for me," Teenager said. "Now you are sad because you see me."

"That isn't it," Maximo said.

"Sure it is," Teenager said. "Here, give Maximo a drink. Make him laugh." Teenager finished his brandy and sniffed loudly as he put the glass down.

"Sounds like you have a cold," Maximo said.

"A very bad cold," Teenager said.

Santos Rivera thrust a hand into his jacket and brought out a gold cigarette case which he opened with a show.

"Medicine for the cold."

"Aha!" Teenager said as he saw the crystals inside. "Do lines."

Maximo stood up. Once too often, he told himself. If once he thought there was comfort and excitement here, with Teenager protecting him like he was a cub and danger that seemed delicious and acceptable because it was present only in the air, then to preserve the illusion he should have remained away forever. For he saw now only rotten teeth and lips covered with spit. In his mind now he saw David Robles cringing in a corner of an empty room in Spofford, with the big black kid stepping in and closing the door behind him. Maximo closed his eyes.

"I'm going," he said.

"You must first have your drink," Teenager said.

"No, I'm going," Maximo said.

Teenager clamped a hand on Maximo's wrist. "You are not leaving."

Maximo yanked his arm back suddenly, breaking Teenager's grip. A tiny dart ran across Teenager's eyes.

His hand went back to Maximo's wrist, clamping more firmly this time.

"What's the matter with you?" Teenager said.

Maximo tried to pull his arm back. This time he could not.

"I said I want to go."

"You never see me and now you want to leave when I tell you to stay?"

"I'm all screwed up with some kid," Maximo said.

"What kid?" Teenager said.

"A kid in Spofford. Let go of my arm."

Teenager's eyes narrowed. "What is this? First I don't see you, then you come here and you tell me some kid and you try to go."

"It's a kid in trouble in Spofford," Maximo said slowly.

"Spofford, everybody is in Spofford," Teenager said.

"This kid is under age. He isn't fourteen. And he's in there getting raped by some big nigger."

"They hit him in the ass," Teenager said.

"Yes." Maximo tried to tug his arm away.

"A little boy like that," Teenager said. With his free hand, he took a long drag on his cigarette. Exhaling, he looked at Maximo with a sneer.

"Is this kid a very good kid?"

"Yes, he is."

"Well, if he was so good, then he would get out and bang somebody in the ass himself instead of stay there and get fucked."

"Somebody ought to do the same thing to you," Maximo said.

"Do what?"

"Bang you in the ass." Maximo did not move and he locked his eyes on Teenager's.

Teenager threw his head back and laughed crazily and this made Maximo quiver with anger and he yanked his arm hard to free it and amid the laugh Teenager was off the bar stool and he hit Maximo as hard as he could on the left side of Maximo's head.

Maximo pitched off the stool and landed on his side, on his arm and shoulder, and then his head banged the floor hard. It was many seconds, a minute perhaps, before Maximo saw where he was. One ear was clogged and ringing. When he moved, pain sprang from the center of his head.

At the bar, Teenager looked down at Maximo. "That's why nobody rapes me," he said. "You say that I should get raped? I should rape you. I should pull down your pants now and throw you on the pool table over there and we all could take turns sticking it up your ass. What would you do about it? What would you do if I bent over now and pulled down your pants?"

Maximo lay in pain and silence.

"Now the great genius has nothing to say," Teenager said. He picked up a paper napkin from the bar. "This is how much backbone you have." He crumpled the napkin in his fist. "This is what happens to you when you have to face the world like a man."

Tatiro stood in his bloody sweatpants and began to laugh. "I come here because I owe you this money and I expect to get beaten and instead this punk walks in and takes the smack for me."

Tatiro laughed and Teenager roared and Rivera's rotten teeth showed and Luisa Maria served drinks and somebody said, do lines, and as Maximo got up, he saw Teenager bent over the bar like a dog sniffing droppings on the street. He walked to the door, veering to one side with this toothache pain in the center of his head, and he went out onto the cold cement and the pain caused the orange skins and flattened soda cans to be burned in his mind forever.

He tried to walk steadily, but missteps caused him to appear to be drunk. He made his way down the hill to the light in Eddie Hernandez' store window.

"What happened to you?" Eddie said.

"Nothing," Maximo mumbled.

"Here, you sit down," Weinstein said, getting up from the chair by the window.

"I'm all right," Maximo said.

"Of course you are," Weinstein said. "Sit down anyway."

Maximo sat down and Weinstein looked at his face.

Eddie Hernandez stepped out from behind the counter, bent over Maximo, nodded and said, "A little cold water won't hurt." He walked into the back of the store and came out with a wet towel, which Maximo rolled into a cold ball and held against his left temple.

"You get mugged?" Weinstein said.

"No, somebody hit me," Maximo said, looking directly at Eddie Hernandez, whose face had the power to issue redemption.

"Teenager," Maximo said.

"What was that about?" Eddie said.

"I told him that somebody should stick it up his ass."

"They should," Eddie Hernandez said.

"It's about time somebody told that gorilla," Weinstein said.

"No matter what happened to you, you did the right thing," Eddie Hernandez said. His tone was of equals addressing each other.

A few minutes later, Maximo got up.

"Where are you going?" Eddie said.

"I want to put your towel back and go home."

"Give me the towel," Eddie said.

"I'll drive you to your door," Weinstein said.

"As long as I'm out, I got one more thing to do," Maximo said. He handed Eddie the towel and walked out into the cold night.

Francisca's sister, still in a robe, answered the door. There was the sound of a man's voice behind her somewhere. Francisca appeared behind her sister.

"Could I see you for a moment?" Maximo said.

Francisca stepped out into the hall. She had on a rose sweater and blue skirt and looked like she belonged with schoolbooks in her arms. Maximo took both of her hands and spoke softly to her, smiling, staring into her eyes.

"Would you get some clothes and come away with me?"

Her eyes widened. She thought for a moment, biting her lip, and then said, "I have to be here Monday."

"Don't worry about Monday," Maximo said.

She went back into the apartment. She returned in a

gray coat, carrying a small suitcase and with her sister's moaning trailing after her. "You must help me with the baby," the sister cried.

Francisca shut the door, slipped an arm through Maximo's and proudly walked down the hall with him.

"Do we go to your apartment?" she said.

"No," Maximo said.

At eight-fifteen that night, Maximo led Francisca into the basement meeting room of the New Bronx Housing Projects, a cluster of twenty-four-story brick buildings whose hallways screeched of pain going on behind closed doors. About ten women, seven blacks, three Hispanics, sat on gray folding chairs at a long picnic table in one corner of the room, which during the day served as a child-care center, evidence of which was the homemade posters on the walls and the stale smell of children.

He and Francisca took chairs and pulled them up behind Haydee who had the folder for the case and was answering questions.

A short woman with a missing front tooth held up her hand. "I axt you one thing?"

"Yes," Haydee said.

"They fire me. You can do something about it?"

"When did they fire you?"

"Fire me Friday."

"Who fired you?"

"The man Anders."

"I told you earlier," Haydee said, "we contacted him Friday and he agreed to stop all such activity. Do you see what happens when people stick together?"

They die together, Maximo said to himself. He touched Haydee's arm. "Have they got any room for somebody to go to work?"

Haydee looked down the table. "Mrs. Earle, did you say you were leaving, right?"

"Sure did. I've had it up to here."

Maximo said to Haydee, "Good. Can you get her in?" He indicated Francisca.

"Suppose so," Haydee said. "The man is talking to us this week."

"Perfect," Maximo said. He leaned over to Francisca. "Now you can get paid for taking care of a baby."

He looked down the table. "Has anybody here got a bed they want to rent to a nice young woman who's going to work around here?"

Three hands went up.

"Take your pick," Maximo said to Francisca. He kissed Haydee on the cheek and stood up. Haydee looked fully at him for the first time.

"What happened to your face?"

"It's an allergy," Maximo said.

"Are you leaving?" Francisca said.

"Yes," Maximo said.

"Then I am coming with you."

"No, you're going to stay here. Unless you want to go back to your sister's and go to jail."

Maximo patted her on the head and waved his hand to the people at the table and left.

His sleep was troubled and when he woke up the next day he was disheartened by the pain that was still fresh in his head. He craved solace and wondered immediately where she would be. At home, certainly, perhaps still asleep; it was only nine o'clock. He dressed and went down to the phone booth and called Angela.

"Where is Nicki?"

Angela said, "I imagine she's home."

"Could you ask her to call me?"

Angela's voice was skeptical. "Didn't she talk to you?"

"Yesterday."

"Are you sure you talked to her?"

"Yes."

"Didn't she say anything to you?"

"About what?"

"Her husband coming home?"

"Yes, she did."

"Then I shouldn't be calling her for you anymore."

"Don't worry about it. Just ask her to call me."

"Where are you?"

"She knows. The phone booth at my corner."

"That's the same booth. Right on your corner?"

"That's right."

"Why don't you move your bed down on the sidewalk next to it? Just in case you get tired waiting for a call."

He leaned against the phone booth and was still there when the dog, bored with sniffing the tires of parked cars, ambled back. And he was still there at twelve-thirty when the phone rang.

As he spoke, he heard the click of the cutoff.

Maximo attempted to pace away the anger, but the feeling of powerlessness caused him to ask questions of himself, the answers to which disturbed him even more. He had thought of himself as a proud, priestly person making individual decisions in a high, icy wind. He had to kick his foot out at that notion. The motion disturbed the dog, who had been asleep on the sidewalk. Maximo knew that he actually was standing at the intersection of different worlds, his feet slipping each time he tried to turn about. He had informed himself grandly that he was challenging established order on behalf of the populace. He had found that he was the only one who knew that he was doing so. For living in such an illusion, he had been thrown down with an admonition that was indirect, but as apparent as flame at night: life is dictated by rules of books that are to be followed with the same purpose that people attend sports events; the tenets are so rigid that a spectator feels there is perfect order to life. And for daring to feel that he had any special rights left in the world to which he had been born, on the streets on which he had grown, he had received a smack in the face.

It had been a short trip; what was it, six months now, or not even that, Maximo thought; but there had been nothing veiled, the conductor had called each stop and held the door open for all to see, and Maximo had stared out and seen only images of a dream. Now, however, he knew. It was not his line. He thought he knew the people sitting with him but they actually were strangers. When he followed them to the street, they prevented him from walking further. Go where you belong, everything told him.

And of course he had allowed his prick to lead him to

the worst avenue of all, one where he surely could not
get over the stones, and this was the part that tormented
him. He could explain the justness of defeat and the
wiseness of recognizing, at age twenty-three, that you
must lose, and perhaps only accomplish harm to others,
by forcing yourself into a kitchen run by devils. But he
could not reason or suppress the sudden emptiness that
Nicki had left inside him. *Hija de puta!* Daughter of a
whore. Tell me you love me, then the next minute you
walk out on me. It probably isn't her fault, she's so evil.
She was born this way. She wasn't a baby pulled out of a
mother's belly; she was a scheme that took a breath.

Later when he went for a walk, there was a family
climbing the steps to the El. The mother carried one child
and the father absently held out his hand for one of walking age, and the kid, rather than take the hand, leaned
over the banister and looked down at the street and Maximo was about to say something when the father, on his
own, reached out and yanked the kid off the banister and
gripped the small hand and led the boy up the steps.
There was a release inside Maximo. It was mingled with
defeat, of course, but still there was the release, as if he
had paid some sort of mortgage. Only Nicki made it un-
livable. Music about a wounded heart came from the
cuchifritos stand under the El, and it bothered Maximo.

......Chapter 28

......

In New Jersey at that hour the music was softer, with Sinatra singing on tape throughout the house, but the subject of the song was the same, being alone at a bar and feeling love lost. Nicki's husband, unsettled by all the people in Mariani's house, sat alone with Nicki on the living room couch and stared at television, which was tuned to channel nine, a station that carries no news during the evening and thus is considered safe to have on.

"Don't you want anything else to eat?" she said to her husband.

"Had too much."

"Don't you want to go talk to the men?"

"I feel like, you know, shy."

"Of course," she said.

He had arrived from the long ride down from prison just two hours ago. Nicki had not gone to pick him up, for she felt it was more important to help clean the house and fix her hair for this coming-home party. She lit a cigarette and sat back, stretching her legs so she could admire the hundred-and-fifty-dollar Italian imported high-heels she was wearing. In honor of her husband being home, she wore the three-carat engagement ring and a set of diamond earrings that her husband had given her as a wedding present. For nearly three years now, she had worn them only at important family functions. She looked at herself in the large mirror across the room, then swung her head slightly to make the earrings blaze in the light. She thought of standing on the number six train going to the Bronx with earrings like these flashing in the subway car. For the old gold earrings I used to wear to work, she thought, the savages would have pulled my ears off. If I got on the train wearing these, they would kill each other for the chance to cut off my head. She giggled to herself.

"What are you smiling at?" her husband asked her.

"The movie."

On television, a doctor was looking through a microscope at a disease.

Her father walked into the corner with his arms held out. "What are you doing in a corner?" he said to Nicki's husband. "Why aren't you eating something?"

"I'm not so hungry," her husband said.

"Fish salad," Mariani said.

"Maybe later."

"Fish salad," Mariani said.

"You think I should eat some?"

"What do you mean, 'think'? "

"Go get me some," the husband said to Nicki.

"Yeah, get the guy something to eat," Mariani said.

She rose to the sound of the order as women in the house had done for years. She began to walk to the kitchen in numb compliance, but this time, the manner in which she had been told to serve, a foot reaching out to clear debris, produced a feeling of squalor. Her mouth and eyes smiled obediently as she walked into the kitchen, but her ribs smarted.

Her father's man, Corky, was walking in the front door. "Hey, you must be happy, good to see you," he said to Nicki.

She smiled vacantly, gave him her hand and walked past him.

Corky went into the living room where his booming voice caused Nicki's husband to jump.

"Look at what you do with your big mouth," Mariani said.

"I'm happy to see the guy," Corky said.

"I wish you'd come and tell me something good soon," Mariani said.

"Hey, we're out there trying. You know how it is. Takes time."

"I want that guy's head on the table for dinner," Mariani said.

"Louis, you know for yourself what it is. All Spics there. They could spot us coming along a hundred miles away."

"Look at what this son of a bitch does to us," Mariani said. "We got to do something back to them people to show that we're alive. Who the hell listens to me, I let a thing like this go on? They kill Paulie. Then they kill Torres. I look like a fag."

"I'll get something done for you if it takes all year," Corky said.

"I don't care who or what or where. I want something," Mariani said.

"You'll get something," Corky said.

In the kitchen, her mother sat with a cigarette and coffee and two of her aunts, Aunt Rose Montano and Aunt Rose Tortice, ladled out food with fanaticism.

"Having a nice time, Nicki?" her mother said.

"Oh, it's lovely."

"Ronnie seems all right," the mother said. "A little quiet, but you know that's the way they all are on the first day."

"It'll take a little time," Nicki said.

"He needs some time and some love," the mother said. "Make sure that's what he gets."

"Certainly."

"He don't need aggravation," the mother said.

"Ma, don't say that. He's my husband."

"See that you remember that."

Aunt Rose Montano looked up from a platter of spaghetti and broccoli she had just wrestled from the oven. "Nicki, when are you going to have a baby?"

"Never," Nicki said. Both aunts laughed. But the word had come out of her without mirth, and before she realized that she had said it. Her mother, however, had caught the tone. "Well, he just got home," Nicki said quickly. "I mean, please."

Her mother's eyes were bowls of suspicion. "The sooner you have a baby, the sooner this will be a happy house."

Aunt Rose Tortice said, "They haven't even been in bed yet and we want the girl to have a baby. First the bed, then the baby. Remember?"

The other aunt said, "Well, what's she doing in the kitchen, then? No beds around this kitchen."

Nicki carried a plate of fish salad back to her husband. Her father smiled at her.

"She's something this girl," he said to her husband. "She doesn't take a quarter off me all the time you're gone."

"I have a job," Nicki said.

"Not no more you won't," the husband said.

"What do you mean?" Nicki said.

"My wife won't work," the husband said.

"Eat," Nicki said. "You're home only two hours and you're changing the world."

"I don't have to be home a half hour to know what's going to be," he said.

"Well," Nicki said lightly, "we're going to need my paycheck for a little while, anyway. We can't live on what you're going to get for dispatching trucks."

"The job is just for a couple of months for the parole officer," the husband said.

"He'll earn bucks soon enough," the father said.

"The first thing I do is get you your own car," the husband said.

"I'll take it," Nicki said.

"You'll have a car exactly four weeks from now," the husband said.

"Why do I have to wait so long?"

"Three weeks," the husband said, looking at her father.

"That's better," Nicki said.

She looked at her earrings in the mirror once more. Pretty good. A car my own way, without having to take it from my father. Oh, he'll have it for me in three weeks. To the day. Death before dishonor.

"And you won't be usin' it to go to work," her husband said.

"Well," Nicki said.

"Well, nothing."

Her father laughed. "He's the boss."

"See what he says?" the husband said. The ownership in his voice brought Nicki's teeth together. What was the word Maximo used out of his freaking law books all the time? Chattel. That's it. Chattel cow. Oh, remember what I did when that Spic tried to pull it on me? Sitting in the restaurant saying he owned me? He didn't do that again. She looked in her mirror at the earrings. This was different. Here, she'd get. I like having things, Nicki told herself. A car. A car is great. It doesn't talk to you and put things on your mind.

In bed that night, in her own room, Nicki lay still while he touched her nipples lightly, causing them to harden. She turned against him and held his prick while he kissed her. There was a hunger in her tissues, but it was then dulled by her husband's satisfaction with himself, as if each time he plunged a curtain rose to permit him to take another bow.

"How do you like it?"

She answered with a small sound.

"Tell me!"

She moaned. At this, his eyes blazed with ego. I get the Academy Award, Nicki thought.

The moment he was off her, she went onto her side and bunched the pillow under her. Long minutes later, when she was certain he was asleep, she propped herself up on an elbow and looked at him. Handsome, all right. Oh, he had to be more handsome than Maximo; after all, he was white. Or was he more handsome? Come on, forget about Maximo. She could not. When she had sex with Maximo she always felt she was drowning within herself. She concentrated on her husband's sleeping face. She wondered if the trouble tonight could all be because of the fuck truck. She put her head back on the pillow and fell asleep,

thinking of the color of the car she would get in three
weeks.

All the next day, her husband's friends came to see
him. They were young, with faces lined only by sneers,
and they moved from seat to seat in the big basement
den, snapping fingers, displaying jewelry, passing gas and
laughing loudly at it, and punching each other on biceps
that had been fashioned by long months in prison gyms.
At ten o'clock at night, Nicki found herself staring from
one of the den couches while her husband's best friend,
Jiggs, walked around the room eating pretzels and then,
ducking down, pretended to throw a punch at her husband's stomach.

"Pow!" Jiggs said. Straightening up, chewing pretzels,
he walked to the bar, grabbed another handful, stuck
them in his mouth and walked up to the husband again,
bent over, pretended to throw a punch and then called
out, "Pow!"

"So how's it going?" Jiggs asked.

"All right. You know," her husband said.

"Yeah, I know just what you mean," Jiggs said.

Pushing pretzels into a crowded mouth, he walked
from the bar to the husband, bent, threw his imaginary
punch, said, "Pow!" and went back to the bar.

As Jiggs started walking again toward Ronnie so he
could throw his punch, Ronnie said, "Hear from
Sonny?"

The change in the conversation pattern caused Jiggs to
stand still and think.

"He was over in Allenwood and he had some bullshit
with a guard. They put him back in Lewisburg," Jiggs
said.

"Yeah," Ronnie said.

"So, how's it going?" Jiggs said.

"All right. You know."

"Yeah. I know just what you mean."

Jiggs, back in sync, started to move again. Then Ronnie said, "You hear from Biffy?" Jiggs had to stop again.

"You know he got fucked."

"Yeah, how?"

"They made an absolute deal with the United States Attorney. He was supposed to cop out for a flat two years. He goes into court and what do you think happens? A pound. A fucking pound they give him."

"What a shame," the husband said.

"Yeah, what a fucking shame. So how's it going?"

"All right. You know."

Jiggs walked over to Ronnie, bent down and threw an imaginary punch at Ronnie's middle. "Pow!" Jiggs said.

Nicki yawned, stretched, smiled at her husband and said she was exhausted. She ruffled his hair and told him to stay with his friend. "I'll see you later," she said, smiling, and in meaningful tones. Up in the bedroom, she closed the door and dialed the outdoor phone booth on Maximo's corner. Maybe he's still out walking the dog, she thought. Of course she never would talk to him if he answered, but she could at least listen to his voice for a moment. The phone rang twelve times without an answer. Disappointed, she went to bed.

When her husband came to bed, she told him that she had just started her period.

"Do you love me?" he said.

"Yes."

"Then what's the difference?"

As his body came toward hers, she put her hands against his chest. "What are you, some kind of a filthy Spic?" she said.

Later, as he slept, she again looked at him in the darkness. For a long time, an hour perhaps. She knew something had died during the time he was in jail.

At seven o'clock the next morning, Thursday, Angela was standing in the kitchen in sweatshirt and jeans when Nicki came in from the bedroom similarly dressed. Her mother and two aunts stood along the long counter in the uniform of their generation, flowered housedresses, bare fleshy arms pouring out the tops, and flat shoes. The five women smoked cigarettes and drank coffee; two crack units awaiting morning formation and the opportunity to smash the enemy most hated, old wax on parquet flooring.

"You got your furniture comin' Saturday," one of the aunts said.

"Why should she lose the weekend?" Nicki's mother asked.

"It costs extra to have it moved on Saturday," the aunt said.

"It's worth it," the mother said. "Let her get in her own house with her own husband and nobody around to bother them. That's putting nature on the job."

"Ma, how can you even talk like this so early in the morning?"

"Because I can talk like this in the night and I can talk like this in the morning. I always got the same story, which means I'm telling the truth. The surest way for a young girl to make absolutely sure that she don't wind up alone is to have a baby."

Nicki placed a hand on her midsection. A baby? Imagine having a baby inside me and having to sit here like this? Pills. One a day. Somebody like me ought to be allowed to take two and three at a time, like aspirin. Upset stomach, try Tums. Like hell. Upset stomach, take cyanide. Because it isn't food poisoning, sister.

Nicki, who had taken two drags on her first cigarette of the day, mashed it into the ashtray.

"I want to go," she said to Angela.

"Say the truth," the mother said. "Don't I know what I'm talking about?"

"Sure," Nicki said. The word had the beginnings of bitterness in it. Angela put down her coffee cup and covered everything with a laugh.

"One step at a time," Angela said. "We'll start by getting her to the stores and then we'll see you at the apartment."

The mother looked at the clock. "Floor waxer comes eight o'clock. We'll get in there, start on the windows before he comes."

Nicki started for the door, but instead went swiftly back to her bedroom in the back of the house. She was standing on tiptoes at her closet, reaching under the shoeboxes, when the bedcovers rustled and her husband picked up his head.

"What are you doin'?" he asked.

"Nothing."

"Then come on back to bed with me."

"Not a chance. I'm up. It's daytime."

"You'd love it in here," he said, patting the bed alongside him.

"You think," she said. She said it lightly, to keep his head on the pillow.

"Come on."

"Nope." She took the folded copy of the *Times* from beneath the boxes of her summer shoes. Nicki held the paper against her, so her husband wouldn't see it.

"I've got to go to the apartment," she said.

"Come here and give me a kiss."

"Later."

"I said, come here."

She held the *Times* behind her back with one hand and took two great strides, stretching out so the arm behind her wouldn't be so noticeable and kissed him on the cheek.

"There. Now I've got to go fix up the apartment."

She whirled away from the bed, bringing the *Times* against her stomach again, and she went down the hallway, past the kitchen, calling out, "Later," and was out of the house with her paper. She imagined the tension that would have assaulted her if she suddenly remembered, while working in her new apartment, that the paper was home and could be thrown out at any moment by somebody packing her things.

"What's in the ads?" Angela asked when Nicki got in the car with the paper.

"Nothing."

"Nothing in there you could buy from?"

"Nope. It isn't even today's. It's old."

"What's in it, then?"

"Never mind. But you're keeping it for me until I get my place straightened out, if I ever do."

"You will."

"You think," Nicki said.

"He's only been home a few nights. Of course it's strange," Angela said.

"I get a car, I'll feel better," Nicki said.

"Sure you will. And he won't stop at a car," Angela said.

"No, he won't," Nicki said. That was one thing, anyway.

As they came to a diner that sat alongside a brake-lining garage, Nicki had Angela stop. They went into a place that was a Greek's pride, Formica and tile, platters of muffins that had been injected with imitation blueberries, an ugly plant atop the cashier's counter.

As she got into a booth, Nicki saw that Angela was not carrying the paper. "Where's my paper?" she said.

"In the car."

"What if the car gets stolen?"

"You'll get another paper."

"No, I won't. I only want this one."

"What's in it, some story saying how great the Spics are?"

"Yes."

"Well, you can forget about them now."

"I guess so," Nicki said.

"Then why do you still want the paper, for whatever the hell is in it?"

"Because I want it."

"What good is it going to do you?"

"None. I want coffee."

"Coffee for me. And an order of rye toast," Angela said.

"I get confused sometimes," Nicki said.

"Nicki, you gave it almost four years already. What's another three or four months? For that matter, what's another year? You're a young girl. You're twenty-six. You've invested all this time. Now just because you wake up one morning a little irritated you want to throw it all away?"

"I wonder why I waited."

"You did. You did because that's what you're supposed to do. That's your life. Now you just have to wait a little longer to get used to it. Let things get settled."

The coffee arrived and Nicki stared at it moodily.

"As for the other thing," Angela said.

Nicki looked up sharply from the coffee.

"It's ridiculous even to think about," Angela said. "Even if you were allowed, and you know you're not allowed, nobody is allowed to leave a husband when he just gets home from jail, but even if you were allowed, you can't just go throwing over a life for somebody you can't even bring home. You can never even introduce him to anyone you know. Forget it."

"I guess," Nicki said.

"You mean you know. You're not allowed to leave your husband, so don't let your mind play games with you. Relax and get your car."

"Give up my job?"

Angela's lips pursed. "Well, he's your husband."

"And have a baby?"

"Well," Angela said.

"Well what?"

"Well, either you're married to him or not."

Nicki held the coffee cup with both hands. The closeness of her wrists reminded her of someone in handcuffs; she almost felt them pinching the flesh over the bones. She realized that throughout all the months of evasion and turmoil over Maximo, through all the nights of writhing, she was playing with a freedom that she never had had before, and she became so accustomed to it that she began to hold it in contempt. She had limited ability to choose, but still she could listen to her own voice debate, at the ring of a phone, whether or not she would go to meet this Maximo. She had come to regard this as being nothing more than opportunity to torture herself. She ignored it and dreamed of true freedom, a cornfield in Iowa. And now her small freedom had been jerked away from her, by heritage, by her husband's sneer and mother's glare, even by her best friend's counsel, and there could now be no small decisions to make, and certainly no more dreams; she was to stroll about a cage made sparkling by cleaning fluid.

As they were leaving in the car, Nicki took the folded *Times* from the dashboard and placed it on the back seat.

"I want it back next week. I can't have it around today," Nicki said.

"Where is he, anyway?"

"Work, I guess."

"Now that you're gone, I might give him a call myself," Angela said. "As long as he's got what you keep giving all these sighs about."

Angela laughed and Nicki did not.

Late Saturday afternoon, when the movers were gone and her mother and aunts were busy in the apartment kitchen, Nicki was alone in the living room, with the lights off, looking out at a sky the color of tree bark that covered the cold river. On the far side of the water, the first lights of night appeared in the old apartment towers of Riverside Drive, the dull tans and reds of the buildings beginning to recede into the dusk.

Her mother came into the entranceway. "It's so beautiful," she said.

Nicki nodded.

"You could get up here in the morning and have your coffee and sit here and relax until you want to go out shopping for something," her mother said.

Nicki nodded.

"Then in the summer, look what you got. Run right over the bridge and you're at the beach in no time. You could spend every day just relaxing in the sun. I'm telling you, you got it beautiful, young girl like you."

The mother went back in the kitchen and Nicki looked at the long couch she had against the wall on her right. As soon as the movers had walked out, she had known that the couch belonged on the opposite wall. She went into the kitchen and picked newspapers that hadn't been crumpled up out of the garbage pail. She carried them inside, placed them on the floor and then, hurriedly, so nobody would come in to help, she sent the couch skidding across the floor on the newspapers.

"What the hell are you doing that all by yourself?" her mother said.

Nicki stepped back and looked at the couch; she liked where it was now, and its look, long and comfortable and new, with the sky and the river right outside the window,

gave her a feeling of great satisfaction. Who knows? she
thought.

"Ma."

"What, dear?"

"When is Ronnie coming?"

"When we finish here. He's sitting home with your
father nice. What do you want the two of them here?
This ain't their work."

"All right," Nicki said. She bent down and began to
pull the newspapers out from under the couch. She
glanced down at one of the sections. It was the leisure
section of the *Bergen County Evening Record*. The small
print at the bottom of one story, a list of people in a
winter charity dance, reminded her of the type in the
Times story: Escobar, Maximo. She crumpled the newspaper up and threw it aside, as if tapping her computer to
clear the screen.

On that Monday morning in the apartment, the husband was gliding around the bedroom at six o'clock, a
towel around his neck, workboots in his hands, enough
cologne seeping through his skin to form groundwater.
He chose the living room to finish dressing for his first
day's work at the trucking company.

"Don't you want coffee?" she called.

"Stay in bed."

She swung out of bed and walked into the living room
in her nightie, glancing out the window at the river in the
morning. For a moment, she could understand how all of
them felt they were saying the truth; it appeared to be a
most attractive reward to awake in the morning to such a
sight as this and have nothing more pressing to think
about than a shopping trip.

"Where do you think you're going today?" he said.

"Work."

"Why?"

"Because."

"You won't be going anymore. Why don't you start
today? Stay home. Don't even call them."

"I have to go this week."

"For what?"

"We'll talk about it."

"What talk?"

"There's all these hospitalizations and insurances. I can't just walk away from that. I get all these benefits. If I stay for such and such a length of time, then I get so many things when I leave to have a baby."

The moment she said this, her breath held; she had, on record, just finished the fifth night of her period, which was about the modern record for female, Bergen County, New Jersey.

"Being that you brought it up," he said.

"Tonight, probably."

"Probably?"

"Tonight."

"Another thing. I don't care what you do all day. When I come home, I get dinner."

"You will."

"Nothing off a silverfoil tray."

"You'll get a regular dinner."

His street smile flashed. "You make it sound like a job," he said. "I know guys would come two hundred miles to eat anything you cooked. Nobody knows how to cook like my wife. One day in the joint, a nigger done me a favor and I tell him, 'Come here, I'll give you something you never had before.' I bring him in and give him some of the spaghetti and crabs you made up. The nigger goes, 'What's this?' I tell him, 'Just eat it.' When he ate it, he wanted to lick my feet. He said to me, 'Is this how white folks eat like?' I told him, 'No, only people lucky enough to have my wife. And there's only one person on earth got that lucky and that's me.' "

He jumped up from lacing his shoes and kissed her on the cheek. "I want you home at night right away because I don't want anybody else even to see you all day."

"Now that you're out of jail, you're putting me in one?"

He laughed. "You got Friday night. Deal? Friday night is yours. You go shopping with Angela or something. I give you the night."

"How much of it?" she said.

"What time do the stores close?"

"Nine."

"If you're not here by nine-fifteen, I get a gun and go out looking for you."

"I thought you promised me a car?"

"You're going to have a car for the day and a car for the night. It don't matter. I'll find you wherever you are."

He laughed, teeth buffed and shining, and then kissed her on the neck. It was the bubbling, arrogant, tender, almost charming way in which he had first sought her and captured her so easily; she had been so overpowered by him that her agreement was almost involuntary. But that seemed to her now to be so long ago as to be part of some other decade. As he kissed her neck, her chin rose and she laughed, jogged by memory as much as manner. She would, she guessed, let this, along with a new car and a few other things, take the place of real love.

She was at her desk at eight o'clock, reading productivity charts on the computer. She made an estimate that she would need fifteen hundred calls made during the day, and with an attendance report showing that three people were listed as being sick, and knowing that two more surely would call in, Nicki figured that she would have to inform her people to cut the number of rings from six to four on calls and then declare "no answer." On a pad, she jotted the words "down time" and made a face. Over the months, the computer at least once a day boiled over as if it were stuck in traffic. Nicki figured the down time on the computer averaged out to ten minutes a day. In what she called the one-bucket category, those accounts that were from five to twenty days delinquent, she usually was able to have one hundred twenty-six calls made each day, ninety of them being "no answer." This was an area where she wanted improvement, meatier answers, more payments. One of her people, Brooks, a slim black woman, had pulled in thirty thousand dollars during the month before. That was the productivity she wanted, yet she had to sit here and worry about losing time because the computer passed out. Somewhere in the offices behind her, she knew, an assistant vice-president, who

had the job because of his pedigree, was back to full time
at his desk after spending the last three weeks helping to
fill in for Nicki. The assistant vice-president was using a
computer to make the same estimates that she had just
made on a scratch pad. She knew that his estimates were
off from the start, for he was basing it on three people
being out sick and she knew, simply from being alive,
that at least two additionals would pick this day to call in
and report nearness of death.

At eight-thirty, the secretary who worked for the assistant vice-president came by and handed Nicki a low pile
of mail and telephone messages. She went through the
messages and stopped at the one she was looking for:
"Mr. Escobar. Re: old account." She looked at the date.
He had called on the first day she was out. So he had to
know when she was returning to work. Returning today.
She put the message aside and began to go through the
mail.

"Good morning, Nicki." Roy breezed in with his quick
little feet sounding and a grin on his undersized mouth.
He had a large coffee and oatmeal cookies on a cardboard
tray.

"Keep the cookies away from me," she said.

"Nicki, what did you have for breakfast?"

"Orange juice."

"Then eat a cookie. You need the energy."

"I need the weight off. I diet, Roy."

"Energy comes first for you, Nicki."

"I've got plenty of energy."

"Oh, but you know you need more. Now with your
husband home, I'll bet you're like a regular steam engine."

"Roy, how could you talk like that to me?"

"Because I just know all you girls. All you must do is
fuck."

"Roy, you're a pig."

"Of course I am. Don't you just love it?"

As she was talking to him, she saw that it was a couple
of minutes after nine o'clock. Of course there had to be a
phone call from Maximo at any moment, and there really
would be nothing wrong with it, for she knew exactly

what she had to say to him. It was simply a matter of getting things out of the way.

For a moment, she felt the excitement that always washed through her, a foaming wave splashing delightfully, as she walked up the short dark staircase on Pinto Avenue. The sounds of the South Bronx were outside, steel beams bouncing on racing flatbed trucks, trailer trucks changing gears, but on the stairs she always heard through her excitement only the purr of music. She would allow herself only this last act, bringing Maximo's screen up on the computer terminal for a final review, closing out an account, and from here there could be no backward look. She would live by rule of flesh and blood, by habit and custom, and if longings had to be suffocated and great emptiness endured, then she would cover her body with clothes and spangles, with her colors, maroons and royal blues and ombre-striped shirts, with chains and bracelets, and she would worry about ovens and aunts and shoeboxes and nieces and, dominating all, the baby of her own.

That, she knew, would cause all of life, all of her yearnings, to fold about her like pleats, while the days and weeks and months would be settled into her arms while she fed her own and, later, into her hand as she walked her own. So for now, she would take this last call from Maximo, certainly it had to come because, of course, she would never call him. Perhaps she would even see him— would that be good? Oh, there could be no harm in coffee or a drink; perhaps it would even become unpleasant, thereby making it all so much easier to leave. There could be no life with him, outside of the walk up the narrow staircase to his door.

She put Maximo alone into her mind, and thought out her alternative to any action he would attempt. She decided that she would speak directly and handle any reaction with coolness. A drag on a cigarette. A sip of a drink. Somehow, keep her eyes from jumping ahead of her and revealing something they shouldn't. My face, I have to stop my face from flushing and letting him notice. She drank her coffee and smoked a cigarette and then, await-

ing her certain call, tried to concentrate on the business
of the day.

Later, at four-thirty, she felt the quiver of anticipation
as the phone rang. She waved to Galligan that she would
take the call herself.

"Mrs. Schiavone."

"I'd like to talk to somebody," a strange voice said.

"Yes, sir. What is it about?"

"That I'm going to sue you by the ass."

"Excuse me. Did you say that somebody was an ass?"

The voice on the other end rose, "I go to the Town
Tavern for lunch, I live in Cleveland, and I'm with three
customers and I go to pay the check with my credit card
and the waiter takes the card right in front of the table
and cuts it in half with a fucking scissors. I'm going to
sue you people by the ass."

"Excuse me. I will turn you over to someone who
might understand what you are talking about when you
tell me, at least that's what I think I heard, that you are
interested in being an ass."

She turned the call over to someone handling the pre-
legal accounts and sat numbly until five o'clock when she
went home and, in furious movements, threw her frustra-
tions about the kitchen.

"You cook like you're playing basketball," her husband said.

"Stay out of here," she said.

At eleven o'clock on Wednesday, Galligan called over
to her, "Personal call on 09." She pressed the button and
heard his voice.

"Hey, what's doing?" Maximo said cheerfully, as if
this were some off-hand call.

"Nothing much," she said, trying to match his uncon-
cern, but she knew that the first word, the "nothing,"
had come out with such hollowness to it that he had to
sense her disorientation.

"When am I going to see you?" he said.

"Oh, I don't know. How have you been?"

"I'll tell you when I see you."

"Oh, I don't know."

"We'll have a drink tonight and I'll tell you all about it."

"I can't tonight."

"Tomorrow then."

"Oh, no, not Thursday. What's the matter with you? Every Thursday is macaroni. I have to be home cooking."

"Friday's the last chance," he said.

"Tell me what you've been doing," she said. Perhaps all this could be done away with right here on the phone. Her blood raced with so many feelings, anxiety and tenderness and, why certainly, lust, that she could not trust herself to be near him. Restrict everything to the phone, she told herself.

"That's a long story. I'll tell you Friday over a drink."

"Tell me now."

"Friday."

"I want to know."

"See you Friday."

Her voice reluctant, she said, "All right. But it has to be early."

"Such as?"

"Well, I can leave here at four if I want to. But then I have to be home."

"By when?"

"By long before you think I do."

He laughed. "Well, I'm going to be uptown at four-thirty."

"Where uptown?"

"I'll be in the place we ate in that time on Fordham Road. La Casa Wong."

"Not with all those people again," she said.

"No, just me. I have one stupid tenants group I have to go up there for."

"Stupid? You never called those wonderful people of yours stupid before."

"That's the way I feel today."

"And that's why I'm always ahead of you, dear. I always thought they were stupid."

The plausible reason for meeting him at the restaurant took the tension out of the conversation.

"So four-thirty," she said. "Then I have to be home early."

"So get home early," he said. "This time don't fall asleep on me and make me wake you up."

"I can have a drink with you," she said, coolly. "Then I have to be home at eight o'clock."

There was a pause on the other end. "See you Friday," Maximo said.

Walking into the restaurant on Friday, she had in her mind a couple of things to say about the food as she remembered it, that jungle food, in order to put a sudden bend, produce a diverting smile, into any conversation she found uncomfortable. The moment she saw Maximo as stranger, his beard gone, smooth chin resting in the cup of his hand, everything else left her mind.

As he saw her face, he knew that whatever way he was moving, and he now was deciding as he went along—he had only decided to shave the beard when he was in the drug-store the night before and, on an impulse, bought shaving cream and a new razor—it was worth it, if only to make her uncertain.

Her mouth was open as she walked up to him, stood with legs apart, rocking from side to side on her high-heels, hands thrust deep into the pockets of the new gray Calvin Klein coat she had bought at the Saks in the Short Hills shopping center.

"What did you do to yourself?"

"What does it matter to you?"

"It does matter; you look so different. Oh! I don't even *know* you anymore."

"Do you like it?"

"Oh, I love it. You look just like a Puerto Rican door-man."

Her right hand came out elegantly and touched his head as she kissed him on the cheek as if he were a relation. She noticed the traces of the bruise Teenager had put on the side of his face.

"What's *that?*"

"Nothing."

"Yes, it is. Tell me."

"Forget about it."

Nicki turned her back to him. "Here, doorman, take my coat, please."

As Maximo helped her out of the coat, she gave the back of her hair a toss, then sat up on the stool, crossing her legs while looking away, not seeming to notice what she was doing, but creating just enough flash of legs, she hoped, to jar Maximo.

"Do they have Harvey's Bristol Cream in a place like this?"

Maximo looked at the bartender, a bored Chinese man, who placed a bottle of Gallo sherry on the bar.

"That's all you have?" Nicki said.

The bartender nodded.

"I suppose so," Nicki said.

"Just give me a glass of club soda," Maximo said.

"You don't want a drink?" Nicki said.

"I have a meeting to go to," Maximo said. "I'll take a drink only if you come home with me. Otherwise, I'll keep my mind clear so I don't fall asleep during the meeting."

Nicki picked up the sherry, took a sip, and said, "All right. So tell me what happened."

"I shaved it off because of you."

"Stop it."

"I did."

"I said, stop it. You make me feel terrible."

"That's what I did."

"How could you do such a thing?"

"With a razor."

"I'm sure you did."

"Do you know what I do next?" He pinched the flesh at the point of his chin. "Right here. I take a razor and cut myself so deeply that the mark is there for the rest of my life. Every morning when I get up, I'll look at the scar and think of you."

"Maximo." Instinctively her hand went out and touched his.

"That's where it stands," he said.

She withdrew her hand before he could start holding it;

that could take her into areas she had drilled herself to stay out.

"I know what I wanted to ask you," she said brightly. "What happened to David? I haven't seen you since the day you went to court with him."

"I know that," Maximo said.

"Yes, but tell me what happened to him. I want to know."

"It made all the papers."

"I never read the papers, you know that."

"I guess I do know that."

Someday, she thought, when neither of us can get hurt, I am going to tell you how often I look at your name in the paper under the shoeboxes. "So tell me," she said.

"Nothing happened. They held him as an adult on a homicide charge. He's in." He touched his bruise. "I got this for it."

"A cop hit you?"

"Teenager."

"I told you to swear to me that you'd stay away from that bum."

"I just saw him to talk about getting the kid out or something. It was stupid."

"You broke your promise to me."

"I was trying to help the kid."

"Oh, I'm so mad at you. I told you to say the truth to me and you lied to me. You did see him. Oh, I wish I could punish you for this."

"I won't be around to give you the chance," he said.

"Don't talk like that."

"What are you going to do for me?"

"Nothing, dear."

"So why care?"

"I do. But I can't change my whole life for you."

"I'd change mine for you," Maximo said.

"You mean leave these wonderful people of yours? Never."

"I'll do it in a day."

"To do what?"

"I'll go downtown in the morning and they'll give me a job for thirty-five thousand dollars and they won't even let me go home for lunch. They'll have me at a desk working before noon."

He had never spoken of anything like this before, and at first she thought it was some kind of bravado to lure her into a trap, but then she sensed that underneath the words this time there was fact.

"When did you start thinking like this?" she said.

"Oh, for some time now," he said.

"Well, I don't know about you. I can't even think of turning my whole life over. I'm not a gypsy like you people."

"But you're a grown woman. You can do whatever you like."

"I've got family, husband and a whole life that I've had all my life. I can't walk out on that."

"What's to hold you? You don't even have children."

"In time."

"But not now."

"How do you know? I'm married, you know."

"Are you sure?"

"Positive."

Maximo leaned toward her, his eyes intensifying, and they commanded hers to look at him directly, which she did, steadily but apprehensively, for she was certain that her face was coated with her feelings.

"Are you married to the man because you have your name on a doorbell or because you want to be married to him?"

"I'm married," Nicki said.

"Tell me how you're married to him," Maximo said.

His voice was demanding and he put his face closer to hers. Nicki took her eyes from him, turned her head to pick up her drink and slowly brought the glass to her lips. "I am married," she said.

For part of an instant, the flesh on his face seemed to shake, as if he'd been punched. Or was it anger? I can never tell with these people, she thought.

"I'm sorry," she said. "But I've told you two hundred times. You're a Spic and you'll always be a Spic."

"I'd take that as a compliment, in view of the way you hurried into bed for this Spic," Maximo said.

"I'll admit to anything you say," Nicki said. "I loved being in bed with you. I even was in love with you, or at least I thought I loved you a couple of times. But you're still a Spic and you'll always be a Spic."

"That's not even funny anymore."

"It never was," she said. "Say the truth. Did I ever once lie to you?"

Maximo, silent, stared at a face that now surrendered nothing.

"All right, then," he said lightly. "We'll have a private drink here and that's it. I'll even have one." He waved to the bartender.

"I don't want another," Nicki said.

"Forget it," Maximo said to the bartender. He put ten dollars on the bar. "Take out, will you?" Maximo stood up and reached for her coat.

"Maximo."

"Yes?"

She sighed. "What could I tell you?"

She slipped into her coat and walked out ahead of him as he picked up the change from the bar. She stood on the sidewalk in the cold shadows, her hands in her pockets, searching the traffic for a cab, then turning to face him. His bare chin gave him a vulnerability she never had noticed before. She smiled and brought her hand up to his face and began to kiss him on the cheek. Maximo put his arm around her and pulled her face to his and his mouth covered hers. Her tongue responded to his and her hand, which had been touching the side of his head lightly, became firmer.

The flow of women shoppers coming out of Alexander's department store turned into creeks running around either side of them. The women walked in shoes that were either plastic or of such cheap leather as to appear plastic, and they looked at the couple kissing, then at one of Nicki's rich maroon shoes as it lifted off the sidewalk and swung behind her other foot while Maximo held the kiss and she did not try to stop it.

Now a couple of kids, walking with long, bouncing strides, reached them. "The *ladies*," one of the kids said.

Nicki, closing her eyes more tightly, losing herself in the kiss on the crowded street, did not care.

Maximo stepped back. He took her hands and his chin jutted out, as strongly as it seemed to when it was protected by a forest.

"I quit you," he said.

"Maximo."

"I just said to you, 'I quit you.' "

"Let's always be friends."

"I quit you."

The words came out of a stony face. Maximo dropped her hands, turned and walked away until he became one of the crowd on the street in the early evening chill.

_____....Chapter
29
_____....

The United States Attorney Civil Rights March 26, 1979
Federal Courthouse
Foley Square
New York City
(This letter written with the aid of interpreter Rita
Acevedo.)

My name is Luisa Maria Flores. The reason why I'm
here in this woman's jail on Rikers Island today is that
I have been treated worse than a criminal by the Police
Department and the Bronx District Attorney's office.

I can no longer keep my mouth shut because this has
been such a bad thing. Not only am I fearful that my
life is in jeopardy, but also it has put me in a state of
grief. I am scared, hurt, but most of all angry to what
has happen to me.

If I am Jewish, Irish or Italian chances are this
wouldn't have happen to me, but because I was Spanish they thought I wouldn't complain.

This all started when I agreed to meet a detective by
the name of Crofton and that was last week. He started
to ask me questions like, did I know Teenager or
Benny or Albertito. I answered yes. He knew that anyway. But I answered yes. I knew them because I was
the barmaid at Ana's Bar at East 138th Street and that
they used to hang out in the bar. I never have anything
to do with them. But they used to confide in me about

the murders that Teenager, Benny, Albertito, Santos Rivera and others, that they committed. Teenager was going to let a girlfriend named Ramonita kill me and this got me so scared I went to tell the Detective Crofton about this.

Well, that was the beginning of my problems on March 14, 1977. I told them this day about all the murders made by Teenager. When I told them this, Crofton and the DA put his left hand on a Bible and raised his right hand and swore to me that as long as I cooperated that he would keep me out of trouble. That night I was at home and Detective Crofton and Hansen, a black color detective, came to my apartment. Crofton screamed and yelled at me that he was going to kick my ass, that they had just found out that I was the girl who was at the precinct the day when Octavio Turin and Boogaloo got killed in the Myruggia Bar. They say I was the girl who run away. I was scared and crying hysterically. Crofton says the deal is off because I am involved in a murder of my own. I told them I am not involved in the murder of Octavio Turin and Boogaloo. I never shoot a gun. I only point to them in the bar.

I was held prisoner in my own house. My girlfriend from across the hall, Rosie Woods, her telephone # is 933–3741, came to visit me at my apartment when Crofton and Hansen were there.

Then sometime the next day Crofton said to me that he wanted to put me before a grand jury. I told Crofton that he could go fuck himself and to tell Hansen that he could go fuck himself and to tell the grand jury to go fuck themselves also.

At no time was I advised I was under arrest or allowed to make phone calls to my lawyer. Instead they kept me in my apartment for seven days always in the company of two detectives.

Then one day about 3:00 P.M. they said to me that I had to go to Rikers Island to be a material witness and that they would put me in jail each night and that every day they would come and take me out and I would show them how Teenager, Benny, Albertito and the others, the murders they committed.

They said that if I did not do all this, then they would put me on trial for the murders of Octavio Turin and Boogaloo. I told them they cannot do that. I never shot Octavio Turin or Boogaloo. I just pointed to them in a bar. But these detectives say they can do this to me.

I want the government civil rights to come and help me because I am a Puerto Rican and not a Jew with people to help. I am here in Rikers Island all night with a lesbian girl. She tries to feel me up without permission.

Thank you,
Luisa Maria Flores.

Eddie Hernandez put the boxes down when Maximo walked in. "I got a problem," he said. "I didn't know who to call so I called you."

"Fine," Maximo said.

"The cops came in here before with the barmaid from up the block. They asked me about some clothes she bought for Teenager."

"What did you tell them?"

"I said I thought I remembered."

"And?"

"They want sales slips."

"What clothes are they talking about?" Maximo said.

"Two wedding suits. The barmaid told the cops she bought a formal suit from me for Teenager and some other guy."

"What did they want to know for?" Maximo said.

"They didn't tell me," Eddie said.

"I know why," Weinstein said. "I heard the detectives saying these bums wore the suits so they could cut up people in the cellar someplace."

"You're telling me detectives were in here?" Maximo said.

"Two of them. With the barmaid. I had to tell them I was pretty sure I remembered. What could I do?"

"And you have the sales slips?" Maximo said.

"Of course he has the sales slips," Weinstein said.

"Eddie keeps records. I taught him how to keep records."

"And what barmaid was it?" Maximo asked.

"The one with the long black hair. What's her name, Luisa or something. She bought the suits, all right."

"Let him keep it at that," Weinstein said. "I don't think Eddie ought to do anything past that."

"Get out the sales slips and call the police and give them to them," Maximo said.

"You think so?" Eddie said.

"You'll get in more trouble if you don't," Maximo said. He pointed at Eddie. "Do just what I say. Don't talk to anybody about what you're doing. Pick up the phone and call the detectives. I can tell you right now, without even knowing it, that you're in trouble if you don't. And then you can tell people around here that they grabbed your records. There was nothing you could do."

"You think so?" Weinstein said.

"Do what I tell you," Maximo said. "If you don't, do you know what they'll say?"

"What?" Eddie said.

"That you're in with Teenager."

Eddie Hernandez' eyes said that he knew everything that this meant.

Maximo, feeling as if he had just climbed a long flight of stairs, clapped his hands together and reached for the door.

"Thanks, Maximo," Eddie said.

"Say hello to Fela for me," Maximo said. It was the first time he had mentioned aloud the name that had bothered him for two years.

"I will. I'll say hello to her for you tonight," Eddie said. His voice was a chime in Maximo's ear.

Outside, a kid sat atop the mailbox in front of Cutti's Superette. The kid's legs drummed against the mailbox. Maximo was almost up to the steamed windows of the San Juan coffee shop when two detectives came out of the shop and walked to a Plymouth Fury at the curb. Maximo saw that there were two more detectives sitting in the car. One of the detectives looked across the street and waved a hand. A hand waved back from inside a

Plymouth that was double-parked. Maximo could see
that this car, too, had four people in it. They would strangle Eddie Hernandez if he tried to fool around with sales
slips or stories about the suits, Maximo thought. Eddie
owed him one. He headed home the long way, so he
wouldn't pass Ana's Bar.

The purpose of the operation was, first, getting even:
they believed Teenager had shot at Crofton and Hansen.
Then they wanted to catch Teenager and his immediate
gang, fourteen of them, for simple form. Martin intended
to catch Teenager when he was most vulnerable, probably during daylight hours, preferably either getting in or
out of a car. A Wackenhut detection device had been
fixed to the muffler of Teenager's car when he left it
unprotected earlier in the evening in the lightless parking
lot behind Julito's Latin Casino on Westchester Avenue.
    Throughout the next day, Martin told them, a police
helicopter would follow the beeps of the Wackenhut and
direct cars on the ground. In that way, Teenager of the
many left turns would have no idea he was being followed. As Myles was the one who had been shot at, he
was to get the honor of flying in the helicopter, Myles
tried to appear nonchalant about his assignment, but the
envy of others, and the thrill inside his own chest, caused
his face to flush visibly. The dozen detectives now milled
about the room, which had flak jackets and shotguns on
the desks.
    "I want to say something," Martin called out. In the
offices of the Twenty-ninth Homicide, the dozen men
became silent. "I don't know about you guys, but I love
this city. I'm here to defend it." Of the thirteen present,
including Martin, whose back twinged from further work
on his sundeck, only one, Hansen, black, did not live in
the suburbs. "More important," Martin called out,
"every man in this room is now on overtime until the
conclusion of this operation. I mean cash overtime. You
won't get compensated with time off. You'll get cash and
I got this cleared all the way through the Chief of Operations office. The money will be on your next check. You
won't have to wait three months for the bastards to add

it on.'' Whitecaps of excitement appeared in all eyes around him.

They were too filled with the thrill of the chase to go home. They stopped first at a bar, the Captain Bligh, where Martin delivered a lecture to the effect that it was truly man's finest work, chasing a gangster by helicopter. At the mention of the prized helicopter, Myles threw down several drinks. The group then went for Italian food, where Myles tried to chase the liquor with a half dozen cups of espresso, which he gulped as if they were lemonade.

Hansen drove Myles over to Baker Field in Manhattan, Myles left his shotgun in the car, but took the flak jacket for effect. Hansen left him on the football practice field and drove off. Myles stretched out with the flak jacket under his head and dozed for a few minutes. Soon a noise in the sky caused him to sit up. A Bell helicopter, a two-seater, beat its way through the sky and came down on the football practice field. Myles walked through the dust and got on.

''You all right?'' the pilot said.

''Just,'' Myles said.

''My kid got a flu home. I must've caught it from him. I feel terrible,'' the pilot said.

As the helicopter rose, Myles positioned his feet about an attaché case that carried the Wackenhut receiver. A steady beeping sound came from it. The helicopter turned over onto its side and headed for the Bronx. Myles' stomach also turned. There now was discomfort in Myles' chest, the heart seeming to beat too rapidly, and an aching growing in intensity beneath the left side of his rib cage. The closer the helicopter came to the South Bronx, where Teenager lived, the louder the beeping from the Wackenhut. High in the sky over the streets about Teenager's house, the helicopter was filled with the beeping sound, and the pilot turned the glass bulb on its side and swooped down at busy Gun Hill Road, then righted the copter, zoomed up out of the dive, and caused Myles to throw up on the attaché case. Myles picked up his head. He now threw up on the plexiglass.

''Fuck this!'' the pilot said.

The helicopter swooped into a sudden turn. Myles heaved again against the plexiglass. The helicopter rushed through the Bronx air, descending on a football field in Van Cortlandt Park.

Myles got out and stood on the grass, coughing, his eyes filled with water. He tried to throw up some more but could not.

"Over there," the pilot said. He pointed to Broadway, where a gray El train, its outsides covered with red and blue graffiti, every bone of its insides creaking painfully, ran slowly and noisily.

"Take the train?" Myles said.

"No. Go into one of the joints under the El there and get us some water to clean this thing off," the pilot said.

Myles walked over to a bar under the El, took a breath of fresh beer being poured from the tap and the night before's crushed cigarettes and cigars sitting in ashtrays, retched and went into the men's room. When he came out, he fished in his pocket for his badge, bringing it out on the long chain, and showed it to the bartender, who cheerfully gave him a couple of rags and a plastic bucket of water. Back at the helicopter, the one pail of water became hardly enough to wash away the mess. Working with wet rags, Myles cleaned away nearly all the traces, but could not cover the smell: the inside of the helicopter was somewhere between a nursery and a subway toilet. Taking off, the pilot flew the machine with his mouth open. The moment the helicopter attained any height, Myles' stomach again turned and he felt too weak to control it.

The beep on the Wackenhut insisted that they move away from the South Bronx.

The helicopter pilot said, "Subject on the move."

"We know that," Martin's voice came back. "Make sure you stay up there this time."

Following the beeps, the helicopter came over Fordham Road. Dropping low, the helicopter ran high over the car tops, but the Wackenhut noise was at such a pitch that Myles leaned forward and watched intently as the car roofs below raced past his eyes. To his own surprise, he saw the Mercedes.

"Subject is on Fordham Road," the pilot said.

"Which direction is he heading?" Martin said.

"Gee, I don't know the Bronx," the pilot said.

"Put Crofton on."

"Yes."

"Which direction is he going?"

"Well, I don't know. Like he's going south, but then the road goes up. I don't know, is it east, too?"

"Will you tell me in which direction he's going?"

"Do you know Belfast's Heaven?" Myles said.

"Yes," Martin's voice roared back.

"I can see that he's by Belfast's Heaven and he's heading toward, now let me see, where is he going?" Myles was so worried about his stomach that he could hardly concentrate.

"Crofton!"

"Yes?"

"Is he heading toward Billy Sheridan's?"

"No, he's going the other way."

"Toward McKittrick's or JP's Lounge?"

"JP's Lounge."

"At least now I know where the subject is," Martin said.

Myles' stomach rolled and he threw up again, this time over part of the attaché case, then his shoes and, head rising, the lower part of the plexiglass.

Alongside him, the pilot dropped his head and threw up on the floor.

"I told you I think my kid gave me the flu," the pilot said. "Look what you done to me."

The helicopter landed this time on a vacant space behind a shopping center that was a block away from the precinct.

"Do you think you could get a new pilot?" the pilot asked a furious Martin.

"You mean you're dogging it on us?" Martin said.

"I told them that my kid got a flu and gave it to me," the pilot said.

Myles was weak. "You could get another pilot, but I can't fly in this thing anymore."

"That means I can't track him by helicopter," Martin said.

"You can pick up the Wackenhut by car," the pilot said.

"What the hell, a car is ordinary. I wanted to do it special," Martin said, his lips compressed in great anger.

In disdain, Martin left the pilot standing guard over his helicopter. He and Myles got into the car and Martin immediately went over a list, tapped a finger on it and said to Myles, "You can cover a pusher's place over on St. Anselm's Avenue. I got McTaggart and Feeley there now. We already carried the dirty pusher out of there. You should've heard him. 'I only sell reefer.' I says to him, 'Well, I'm sorry. I only got homicide warrants. So I guess I got to arrest you for murder.'"

When the detectives on guard let Myles into the apartment, Indio's wife was sitting with her two children on the plastic-covered living room couch. She glanced out the window at the squad cars across the street where the forms of strangers, rat cops like the ones here in her house, could be seen. The whole day is wrong, she told herself. Right away, before anybody was out of bed, Teenager was banging on the door. "They are following me with a helicopter," he said. "Indio, give me your rifle. I am going up on a roof and I will shoot the motherfucking helicopter." Indio's wife noticed that Teenager had a glassy look and did not seem to listen when Indio said that he had no rifle. "Get me the rifle," Teenager said. "I'll come back for the rifle." Teenager went away. Her husband Indio sat on the edge of the bed and tried to think of where he could get a rifle. Ten minutes later, detectives crashed into the apartment, picked up her husband from the edge of the bed and showed him a murder warrant. "Was Teenager here?" a detective shouted. "He went away," Indio's wife said, hoping the information would cause them to forget about her husband. Instead, they carried him out of the place, cursing that they had missed Teenager. Indio's wife had only one satisfaction: the detectives were so mad about missing Teenager that they had not gone into Indio's shirt drawer and found the half los of heroin.

Now, the two detectives who had remained with Indio's wife picked up their shotguns and left. Martin, standing in the doorway, told Myles that he would send Hansen around in a few minutes.

"Shouldn't I have a shotgun?" Myles said.

"What for?" Martin said. "The guy's been here. You won't see him again around here. I'm not even sure there's a reason for having anybody here. Grab the phones maybe. We know where Teenager is. We're tracking him precisely."

"Where is he now?" Myles asked.

"How should I know? I'm standing here with you. When I go out and speak to the men tracking him precisely, then I'll know where he is."

Martin left, and Myles tried to lock the door after him, only to find that it had been loosened from all moorings by the police break-in. He shut the door, tipped a kitchen chair against it, which he knew was useless, and sank into an easy chair that allowed him to guard the door, see both Indio's wife and kids, and also the late morning cartoons on television.

In the middle of a Popeye cartoon the door swung open and the chair holding it fell. Myles' hand went for his gun and did not make it. A junkie as dirty as an oilrag walked in.

"S'up, man?" the junkie said.

"Get out of here," Myles said.

"Somebody just get me a little," the junkie said.

"Get out," Myles said.

The junkie wandered past him as Myles, growling, pulled himself out of the chair. First, he reached for the open door. Close this, he thought. Make sure nobody else walks in. He heard somebody else walking up to the door and Myles stepped through the door to stop whoever it was, another junkie surely, from walking in, and he came out into the hallway outside the door and was one long step away from Teenager.

Teenager's eyes went into a mean squint and his body rose into his chest and his heels came off the floor, ready to spring. Then he paused. The thought of garlic bullets froze Teenager's coiled body. He had just driven to see

Mama, and she listened to the shells and said that the spirits said it was all right to shoot a helicopter down with a rifle. But she said the spirits in the shells said again that he should be very afraid of the police shooting garlic bullets. "The spirits do not accept blood that is bad," Mama had said. "Your soul will fly through all the nights in pain and no one will take the soul in." Then she had told him, "Be distrustful. Carry water in a straw basket." Teenager had not understood this. He had stopped in his car and done cocaine in order to clear his mind so he could think about this proverb. No answer had come to him. And now he stood in the hallway and called on Changó for help. He waited for a sign, for a whisper from his god that it was all right to reach out and snap this person's neck.

Myles did not know what caused this hesitation, but he knew that if he reached for his gun he would precipitate an explosion that would end him. Carefully, he put his right hand into his pants pocket, making it obvious that he was not going for a gun. In the pocket, his fingers grasped the lengthy silver chain. At the most desperate moment of his life he was relying on his institutions, a prayer of his church, the badge of his civil service job. Slowly, so as not to alarm, he began pulling the chain out of his pocket. He wanted to produce the badge that would show Teenager that there was more than merely some gun to contend with, that he was facing the majesty and meaning of an entire city founded by Irish.

When the first section of chain spilled out of Myles' pocket, Teenager told himself to go, to jump Myles, to crack his windpipe. More of the chain began to emerge. More yet. Myles nervously had both hands at the pocket now, bringing out the chain hand over hand and he stood in the hallway like a plumber with an unruly snake. The chain now came down Myles' leg and began to coil on the floor. The growl at the bottom of Teenager's throat turned into a chuckle. Finally, Myles brought out the symbol of all his authority, his badge, and held it out for Teenager to inspect.

Teenager's eyes crinkled and his body shook with laughter. A fucking patrolman! He threw his head back and roared. I want my rifle inside Indio's apartment and they try to stop me with a fucking patrolman's badge! Teenager looked up at the ceiling and shouted a laugh and he was going to stop the laugh and kick Myles, kick him and then crack his windpipe, for he was certain that the badge was the sign from Changó that he was safe from garlic bullets. Then Teenager heard the noise behind him.

"How we doin'?" Hansen said.

"We have visitors," Myles said.

"Well, the visitor better get himself up against that wall," Hansen said.

Teenager turned his head and saw Hansen was well out of reach and held a shotgun. A shotgun that could put a thousand garlic pellets into his body.

"That's all right," Teenager said.

"I know it is," Hansen said. "Just put your hands against the wall."

"I don't do anything," Teenager said.

"Do what he says," Myles said. He now had his gun out.

Teenager waited for a sign from Changó but he felt none and he saw none.

"The wall," Hansen said.

Teenager turned and put his hands against the wall and felt Myles hand slap his thighs, spread the legs.

"Hands behind your back," Myles said.

"I'm a millionaire," Teenager said. "I go to court and the judge lets me walk out."

"I'm sure," Hansen said.

In the hallway there sounded the metallic zinnngggg! as Myles Crofton at last bound the steel cuffs around Teenager's huge wrists.

At central booking, there was a small bench for prisoners in the hallway outside the booking room and a uniformed patrolman was directing his prisoner, a black in ripped fatigues, to be seated.

Myles walked Teenager past the bench and to the booking room door.

"Hey, don't you see me here?" the patrolman on the bench said.

Myles paid no attention and started knocking on the booking room door. Hansen was standing to the side, humming.

A lieutenant looked through a small window in the booking room door. He waved his hands for Myles to go away. Myles gestured excitedly.

"Hey, you know?" the patrolman on the bench said.

Myles pretended not to hear him. He kept waving until, reluctantly, the lieutenant pressed a buzzer and opened the booking room door.

"What do you need?"

"We want to move this guy through right away," Myles said.

"I'm here first," the patrolman at the bench said.

"Neither of you goes anyplace until I let you," the lieutenant said.

"This is special," Myles said.

"What special?" the patrolman said.

"This guy is Teenager," Myles said, his hand on Teenager's arm. Teenager was cuffed with his hands behind his back, a fact of much comfort to Myles, whose fingers told him that Teenager's arm was maplewood.

The lieutenant looked at Teenager's face. "He's older than that," he said.

"He means that is my name," Teenager said.

"Oh, I see," the lieutenant said. "That's good that you got a name. Because that means you got a name."

"He also has a dozen homicides," Myles said.

"Good for him," the lieutenant said. "In the meantime, I got work to do here. I'll take you in a minute."

The patrolman standing at the bench ran a hand through his hair in agitation. "Hey. I got a prisoner, he got a prisoner. I was here first."

"I said this guy got a dozen homicides," Myles said. "We got things to do."

"So this guy committed a crime too," the patrolman said.

"Twelve homicides?" Myles said.

"We got him in a girls' room in a grammar school. Trying to fuck all the little girls. What do you call that, disorderly conduct?"

The lieutenant looking through the partially open door said, "If this is what you bothered me for." There was a loud snap as the door shut.

"How do you like this?" Myles said.

Hansen smiled. "Almost three o'clock now. We're lucky there's not a dozen ahead of us. The man's just waiting out the change of shifts. He'll leave us for the next group."

"He makes me wait like a beggar," Teenager said.

"Why don't you just sit down?" Hansen said.

"I don't sit with a piece of shit like that," Teenager said.

Hansen smiled. "I feel better if you're sitting."

"Not with him," Teenager said.

"Just keep things centralized."

Myles pushed Teenager's arm but Teenager held his position. "Come on," Myles said.

There was a loud clicking sound at the end of the hallway and there were voices and feet shuffling and four young blacks appeared, strung on a chain, with three transit policemen in leather jackets herding them along.

"Either you take a seat now or you'll have to stand waiting with them," Hansen said.

Teenager looked at the blacks on the chain and then stepped to the bench. He wiggled his body to make more room for himself.

"Stop pushing, man," the black next to him said.

"Shut up, you black nigger bastard," Teenager said.

The patrolman spun around. "You keep your mouth shut," he said to Teenager.

"This guy is a bum," Teenager said.

"Let me tell you something," the patrolman said. "He's shit and you're shit. There's no difference between yez."

Hansen took out his pipe and smiled as he filled it.

A half hour later, the shift in the central booking room changed and the door was opened and somebody said, "Next," and Teenager started to stand, but the patrolman resolutely led his girl-molester into the room first and the two kids on the end of the chain tried to slump onto the bench with Teenager. He stood up in disgust.

Then the booking room door buzzed open again and
Myles tapped Teenager's arm and led him inside.

A patrolman sat at an old typewriter at the first desk.

"All right," he said, typing, "you're arrest number
32,672."

"I'm Teenager."

"To me, you're arrest number 32,672," the patrolman
said.

Hansen took the pipe out of his mouth and held it out.
"It's just like the officer said outside. You're just shit to
us."

The sound of the old typewriter caused the last excitement in Myles to go away. He felt tired and sat down. In
the cells in the rear a voice was complaining that nobody
had brought the orange soda he had paid for.

.... Chapter 30

It was Friday night and Nicki was in the kitchen making bacon and eggs at eight o'clock when her husband came home.

"I figured I'd find you here," he said.

"Why?"

"Because you don't stay out shopping last three weeks."

"So that's why you decided to come home?"

"I don't know."

"Make you something to eat?"

"No. I got to meet some people later."

"Then why did you bother to come home?"

"I don't know. I figured you'd be here."

"Well, I am."

She took the bacon and eggs on a tray and went out and sat on the couch and watched television as she ate. She sat on the end of the couch nearest the window. Her husband sat on the opposite end. Both studied the television, a musical game show, as if it were important. Neither saw any of it.

"If it's that job that's bothering you, I told you to give it up," her husband said.

"It isn't the job."

"Something's bothering you, and I'm bettin' it's that freaking job. I told you to quit."

"It's not the job."

They sat in silence and pretended to watch television.

"Well, if it isn't the job, then it's something else," he said.

"It is."

"What?"

"Something died when you were in jail. I don't know how to explain it, but something died."

"Is there some other guy?" He asked it calmly, but she knew the simple thought of such a thing caused him to seethe. An affirmative answer would have produced immediate murder.

"No," she said.

"Do you love me?" he asked.

She wanted to tell him that she loved him for the past, for her family, for her way of life, but not as a husband she loved. Instead, staring straight ahead, she just said, "Yes."

"Then we need time," her husband said.

"I don't know," she said.

There was no more conversation. Nicki curled up on the sofa, keeping her face away from his, and cried without her body moving. Her husband sat and smoked cigarettes slowly, deliberately, and watched television. In posture and thought, he was prepared to pass the time as easily as a municipal building. He had done this before with her: let her flail until, tired of herself, she crept back to him.

At the other end of the couch, Nicki, her face turned from him, but constricted more by the feeling of his presence than she would be by his sight, continued crying. She wanted to ask out loud for a pill that would put her to sleep. Silently, she wept more. She would be asking her husband for drugs. After a while, she fell asleep. She woke up once halfway through the night and saw her husband was out of the house. She put her head back and remained on the couch. At 5:00 A.M., she awoke again and walked into the bedroom where he was asleep, or pretending to be asleep. She undressed and went to bed and lay awake until morning.

They exchanged few words in the morning, and he left while she was cleaning the house. At noon, she went out

to her new car, a red Buick with mag wheels, and drove
to Angela's house.

"I was just doing my map," Angela said at the door.
She walked happily down her hallway to the dinette
where she had a large street map of Manhattan spread on
the table.

"See?" Angela said proudly. Many of the streets had
been colored with orange crayon. "Every street I can
remember being on in Manhattan is going to get colored
in."

"So what does that mean?" Nicki said.

"Then I'm going to frame it and hang it up. It'll be like
a record of every place I've been in Manhattan. I think
it'll look very interesting."

"Or demented."

"Why do you say that?"

"Well, why would you want to know where you've had
to be in a crummy city?"

"I think it's nice," Angela said. "See, 52nd Street. I
was to the Alvin to see *Annie* and then we went to Gallagher's. That was with Joey."

"What would you want to remember a night with him
for?"

"Nicki, I've had three dates in two years. This was
one of them. He took me to see *Annie* and then we went
to Gallagher's. I can even remember what I had. I had
tomato and onion salad, thumb bits and that sauce they
have there, and three Scotches. I look at my map and I
remember the whole night."

Nicki pointed to West 44th Street, between Sixth and
Seventh avenues. Laughing, she said, "What were you
doing on a street like that?"

Angela said, "I don't know. I just remember walking
down it once. I never was in anyplace there, but I remember walking down it."

"Well, that's stupid to keep a record of West 44th
Street," Nicki said.

"What makes you say that?"

Nicki was laughing loudly now. "Because only some
moron would want to remember he walked down that
street."

"Why are you saying that?" Angela said.

Nicki was busy laughing and tracing other streets with her finger. "Oh, look at this," she said, her laugh louder. "Angela, how could you ever even want to admit you know this street?"

"Which one?" Angela said.

"Avenue C."

"I went walking there one Sunday."

"You had nothing better to do than go walking on Avenue C and instead of trying to keep it a secret, you're hanging up a map to tell it to the whole world. I think this is stupid."

"Nicki, please don't say that."

"Well, it is stupid."

Angela didn't answer.

"Avenue C," Nicki said. She laughed.

Angela picked up the map and took it into her bedroom and then walked past Nicki into the kitchen. "Have a cup of coffee?" she called out.

"Sure. As long as it's not on Avenue C."

She was laughing as she slumped into a kitchen chair. "Oh, Angela."

Angela, face straight, put out two cups of coffee, sat down and lit a cigarette.

"Avenue C," Nicki said. Her laughter reached a high pitch.

"Nicki, that's me you're laughing at," Angela said evenly. "Let's talk about something else. Tell me what's doing."

"I want to talk about stupid Avenue C," Nicki said. She stood up. "Let me go look and see all the other waste of times you colored in."

She started out of the kitchen. "Nicki, leave it alone," Angela said. When Nicki did not stop, Angela got up and walked briskly after her into the bedroom, then grabbed the map, which was atop the dresser.

"I want to see some more," Nicki said.

"Nicki."

"I want to see all the stupid places."

"Nicki, I happen to have something here I like. If you

think there's something the matter with it, that's your business. But please, don't make fun of a friend."

"What am I supposed to do when I see somebody color in Avenue C?"

"You're supposed to be a friend."

"But I am being a friend when I tell you you're doing something stupid."

"Nicki, if you feel that way, then why not just leave me alone?"

"No, I want to see some other streets."

"Let's forget about it," Angela said.

"I don't want to."

"I'm sorry, but I do."

"What's the matter with you, Angela?"

"I am sure I don't know," Angela said. "I'm also sure that if you don't mind, I'd like to be alone for a while today."

Nicki laughed. "Angela, come on."

"No, I won't come on. If it's all right with you, I'd like to be alone."

Nicki stopped laughing and walked through the strained silence to the door and left without saying anything.

That next week, at three o'clock on Friday afternoon, Nicki sat at her desk, with her face reflecting the hollowness inside her, and she abruptly compressed her lips, grabbed the phone as if it were a person to strangle, and dialed Maximo's office. He wasn't in. She asked if he could be reached. The woman on the phone said she knew he would be in much later, at four-thirty.

"You're sure?" Nicki said.

"Oh, yes. He has an appointment with the director."

Nicki hung up, lit a cigarette and stared through the smoke; it was the first day that she could remember having no interest in what was going on in front of her in the office. She was interested only in time dying as rapidly as possible, so she could be at this office where Maximo worked.

At this hour, twelve blocks away, Maximo Escobar

stepped off the elevator at the thirty-second floor, the executive office floor, of the Mobil Oil Company.

A security guard with his hands folded behind him stood in front of double glass doors leading to a reception area. When the guard saw Maximo coming off the elevator, the hands swung out from behind the back. Maximo smiled at this.

"Help you?" the guard said.

"Mr. Watson," Maximo said.

"And?"

"I've an appointment to see him."

"You say to see him?"

"That's right."

"What's your name?"

Maximo gave the name and watched as the guard called it over the radio in a skeptical voice that gave way to surprise when the voice in his ear told him, yes, this Puerto Rican certainly is expected. The guard went to the glass doors, waited until there was a buzzing sound and then pushed one in and nodded for Maximo to enter.

As Maximo's foot had the unfamiliar sensation of sinking into carpet, tight gray hair looked up from a reception desk and a small female mouth pursed and a detached voice said, "Yes?"

"Mr. Watson."

A hand started to come out to accept the package that the Puerto Rican carried, but then the tight gray hair realized that he would not have got this far if he did not have some mission more advanced than delivery.

She picked up the phone and dialed a number. She asked Maximo for his name and then announced it into the phone. Once again, Maximo watched the look of surprise cross a face as it learned the Puerto Rican was not there to kill.

Another gray-haired woman soundlessly appeared in a doorway. Her hands were clasped in front of her black skirt and her smile was too sweet for the eyes.

"Mr. Escobar, would you please come with me?"

She led Maximo down a hallway lined with hotel room paintings of mallards sitting among frozen reeds. At the end of the passageway, there was a heavy wooden office door that was open, and standing in light of such intensity that the windows it was coming through had to be high and wide was Bo Watson.

"Well, it's good to see *you*," he called out to Maximo. Watson smiled and the gray-haired woman in the black skirt smiled too. Both smiles were those of people on a charity committee whose role at this time called for them to actually mingle with the urchins they had been extolling at midtown luncheons.

"Nice to see you," Maximo said to Watson.

"I hope you're not just here paying a visit," Watson said. He laughed and the gray-haired woman laughed.

"I guess I'm not," Maximo said in a flat voice. Watson's arms extended in invitation and Maximo stepped into a small reception room and then into a large office with high, wide windows. He kept noticing how his toes dipped into the thick green office carpet. I guess this is what they mean by feet on the ground, Maximo told himself. He sat in a high-backed easy chair, which bothered him because it felt so comfortable.

At the end of the day, he was back in his office in the Bronx. At four-thirty he would go in and tell the director that he was leaving on vacation and would not be back. He was bent over, cleaning out the bottom drawer of the desk, pausing to read a note that said, "We have not recieved heat," and throwing it away, defeated by both spelling and the fact he could spend two days getting heat for them, while two hundred thousand others froze, and now he heard deliberate steps of high-heels entering his cubicle.

"I'm just here to see you for a minute," Nicki said. She stood in the doorway with a face that showed nothing. When she saw Maximo's surprise, her eyes smiled.

"How did you get up here?"

"I got here. Isn't that all that counts."

"I guess so," he said. He stood up.

"Sit down and do your work," she said. "I don't have any time. I want to ask you one thing in person. I want to know if I can see you again."

"Sit down for a minute," Maximo said. "I just have to go in and tell the boss what I'm doing. I'm leaving."

"Oh, I'm sure you can leave all your wonderful people. I don't have time for that. I just want to know if I can see you again."

Her old insulting style caused Maximo to smile. "It'll only take me a couple of minutes," he said.

Lefkind, the director, stuck his head in. "You had something on your mind?"

"Sure do," Maximo said.

"Can we do it now?" Lefkind said. "I've got to get out of here."

"Sure," Maximo said. Lefkind was gone.

"I've got to get out of here too," Nicki said. "So answer me. Am I going to see you?"

"Yes, but why don't you wait?"

"I said I can't."

"When am I going to see you?" Maximo said.

"When belongs to me," she said.

"So what does that mean?"

"Just don't try to call me and don't try to call Angela. You're still home?"

"Of course."

"Good. That's where you'll see me."

She walked out. Maximo, shaking the surprise out of his head, went inside to tell Lefkind that he was finished working.

Outside, as Nicki walked to her mother's car, a young guy sitting on an iron railing said, "Loose joints, lady?"

Nicki stopped. She hadn't done this in months. She started to go for her purse and then quickly backed away, frightened that the kid was looking to steal her purse rather than sell her anything.

"Relax, lady, loose joints only," the kid said.

"How much?" Nicki said.

"Dollar."

She bought the joint, put it in her purse and drove home. When she walked into the house, she was reaching for her cleaning clothes. Later, she was in bed unable to sleep, but immediately pretended to be when her husband came home at five o'clock. He got into bed wearing his underwear. Nicki waited until she was sure he was asleep, then she looked at him and started to go over their life together, and became confused at this. She put her head back and went to sleep.

In the morning, they both were in bed when Nicki said, "I can't make it."

"You told me that," her husband said.

"No, I really can't make it. I want to leave," she said. He did not answer.

"Not to have anything against you," she said.

"Well, what is it then?"

"I told you, I don't know. Something died when you were in jail."

"I know I'm not leaving here," he said. "I need the apartment for the fucking parole guy. Stable living environment. Some bullshit."

"And you just give me the car and let me use it to try and clear out my head. Who knows what could happen? Oh, I'm *so* confused."

He shrugged.

She got out of bed and started cleaning again. When he got up, she was scrubbing the bathroom. She put everything down and ran to the kitchen.

"What do you want to eat?"

"Nothing this morning."

"You've got to eat."

"I got no time. I've got to go meet somebody."

"At least have juice."

"I'm going. I'll see you." He started to walk into the kitchen to kiss her, but an ancient strategy, in his blood at birth, caused him to smile and walk out on her.

She cleaned the house until midafternoon. Then she went into the bedroom, reached into her closet and pulled the *Times* out from under the shoeboxes. She folded it and put it in her large shoulder bag. Her hand reached into the bag to feel the bankbook. Then methodically, she cleaned her clothes out of the closet and drawers, piled them on the bed and waited for darkness, so nobody would see her carrying the clothes out to the car. The last things she carried out were two clean orange towels.

It was eight-thirty when she was going along the road on the Palisades that led to the George Washington Bridge. Up ahead, high over the tops of the houses, the bridge towers were powder blue in the spotlights playing on them. She thought of Maximo, just on the other side of the bridge, and the excitement of going up the stairs to his door. She drove until there was a diner, and alongside it an access road to the bridge going to New York. She drove past the diner, past the entrance to the access road, onto an overpass and then onto another access road that took her onto Route 4 and the drive to her father and mother.

Her mother stood in the kitchen door and watched her carry clothes down the hall to her room.

"You'll end up alone," the mother said.

Nicki said nothing and went to her room, dropped the clothes on the bed, then turned around and went back out to the car.

When she came back in with the second armful of clothes, the mother said, "You'll have no babies. Do you realize that?"

Nicki carried her clothes to the bedroom, threw them on the bed, turned and went out for more. She was upset as she came into the house this time. She was carrying her beige silk dress, still in the plastic from the cleaners, and it had uneven creases across the front from being carelessly thrown in the car. The dress and the shirt beneath it would both have to be pressed again without being worn.

"Look at this," she said to her mother.

"You got a right to be more careful with your clothes," her mother said.

"I just got it out of the cleaners," Nicki said.

"You got a right to be more careful with your clothes."

Nicki walked to her room before the mother could right herself and return to talking about babies.

Maximo threw his clothes on the floor and, thinking of her, picked them up. He hung the pants on the hanger and put his shirt and underwear in the bathroom hamper. The shower was warm rain on the back of his neck and he leaned against the wall, closed his eyes and stood for many minutes, and then suddenly he turned the water off and got out. When he came out of the shower and reached for the towel, its bright orange caused him to feel that she was in the apartment with him, waiting right outside the bathroom door. He put on his denim court-room suit and a new yellow shirt he had bought at Eddie Hernandez' for twenty-five dollars. A courtroom suit for courting, he said to himself. Smiling at the pun, he fed the dog and went downstairs.

It was almost six o'clock now and he was going out, just going out to see what women looked like, and he had no idea of where he was going, but he was certainly going to be out and about, maybe even downtown, for that was where he would wind up living, he knew that, and as he passed the phone booth he stopped and for some reason, in his mind he did not want to do it, his hand went for the phone. Again, Angela's phone did not answer. After a while, each unanswered ring caused a small pain some-where inside Maximo. He decided to walk over to the subway and go down to the Corso Ballroom on 86th Street. He walked to the kiosk on 138th and picked his way through the rush hour crowds, ducking his head in case there was anybody left across in Ana's Bar who would recognize him. The phone booth was at the foot of the stairs and he ran up to it without thought and found he was nervous as he dialed Angela. When there was no answer again, he slammed the phone down, angry at her, at Nicki, at himself for being so vulnerable. He walked to within a couple of steps of the change booth, changed direction and pushed on a metal door in the wall. Music and laughter came through the open doorway and into the dungeon of a subway station. Maximo walked into a room of gold.

A woman as wide as a piano, a grand piano, not an upright, a woman so short that her head barely came over the top of the bar she was behind, poured rum in a room that was covered with colored lights that splashed on the rows of bottles behind the bar. Her black hair was twisted into a spike on the top of her head. She wore a sweater

buttoned to the neck and served rum to several people
who sat on stools.

"*Cierra la puerta,*" she said to Maximo.

A scarred train was roaring into the station. Maximo
closed the door and shut out most of the noise of the
subway train and allowed the music from the juke box to
be heard.

"You want to drink?" the woman behind the bar said.

"Rum," Maximo said.

The woman poured rum into a plastic glass and held
the bottle high and started to put it back on the shelf and
then stopped her arm in midair, shrugged, and brought
the bottle down to the bar and filled her own glass to the
brim. She took a great slug of the rum before putting the
bottle back. She reached under the bar and brought up a
small bottle of beer and placed it in front of Maximo as a
chaser.

Maximo swallowed half the rum, swigged from the
beer bottle and, carrying it in his hand, went to the juke
box. He played a song called "Elena," and drank the
bottle of beer and listened to the singer, Miguelito Anto-
netti. He was a very good singer, Maximo remembered
seeing him once at the Bronx Latin Casino, and Maximo
drank the beer and first hummed and then began to sing
along with the record.

He put in money to play the record three more times
and he went back to the bar and ordered another rum. As
the woman was pouring it, Maximo took a dime and
opened the door and went out on the subway platform
and called Angela. Women coming from work brushed
past him. Six rings this time. He went back into the bar.

"What time is it?" he asked the woman.

"Ten after six."

This made Maximo feel better. He thought it was half
past six already. "*Yo,* Maximo, you've got plenty of
time," he told himself.

"*¿Qué?*" the woman behind the bar said.

"Talking to myself," Maximo said.

"You must be crazy," she said.

"I am."

"That's good," she said. She laughed. "We like all crazy people."

Maximo looked at his rum and sang to the juke box. He started for the door with the beer in his hand.

"Put down the bottle," the woman said.

On the platform, as he dialed, he felt the warmth of the rum. Too quick, he told himself. When there was no answer he slammed the phone down.

"You want another drink?" the woman said to him back in the bar.

"No, I better take it easy," he said. "I'm starting too fast."

"Did you eat?" the woman said.

"No."

"That's good. You get drunk on an empty stomach." She poured Maximo more rum and the others at the bar laughed.

He drank the rum slowly this time. Alongside him at the bar, a lanky guy Maximo knew as Angel talked to a chubby guy who worked at Cutti's Superette.

"You are wrong," Angel said.

"No, I am right," the chubby guy said.

"Jose Torres never was knocked out before he became champion," Angel said.

"Florentino Fernandez knocks him out," the chubby guy said.

"Never."

"Don't say that to me. I was there. In San Pedro. He hit Jose Torres with a hook and then the referee stops the fight."

"After he was champion he was knocked out. Never before," Angel said.

"Hey, man, I was there, man," the chubby guy said. "He fight Fernandez in San Pedro. In 1961. The fight was at Sixto Escobar Stadium. Five rounds it went."

"You were there?" Angel said.

"I can prove I was right in that place," the chubby guy said. "I take you to that place right now and show you the whore that gave me the clap disease that night."

"I cannot say no to you now," Angel said.

"On the same night, Jose Torres got his chin broke and I got my prick broke," the chubby guy said.

The woman behind the bar shrieked. She bent over and when she straightened up, she took out a pack of cigarettes and offered them to everybody at the bar before she took one for herself. Maximo walked over to the wall, where there was a huge calendar from Cutti's Superette, East 138th Street. The calendar girl wore great breasts and no clothes.

"How would you like to have a drink right now in this bar with this girl?" Angel called to Maximo.

"Love to," Maximo said absently. He was staring at the girl on the calendar, but his eyes went beyond the white thighs and breasts and he saw Nicki. The vision produced an ache inside him that he did not know how to deal with. He had been lonely for a couple of years among the strangers at school, but it was a longing for his mother and the place where he lived, the street and the people he was used to seeing on it, the atmosphere that caused him to be whatever it was that he was. This thing that he had in him now was different: the center of his body had turned into a hot, lonely Sunday afternoon. There was no reason for it, he told himself. Nobody has to live like this. It was a situation that required defiance, not compliance. If he had trespassed on all the ancient customs to gather this woman into his arms in the first place, then why should he now force his heart to live unnaturally, to wander in search of pity because that is the way others say that it is supposed to be done?

"What's the matter, man?" one of them at the bar said.

"Woman," the barmaid said.

At the end of the bar, El Viejo read the Spanish paper aloud to himself. "This is a very sad thing," he said.

"What?" Maximo asked him.

"This man Ernesto in the projects on Alexander Avenue."

"What did he do?" Maximo asked.

"He had this woman who was married. He came over to her house when her husband went away. Now Ernesto is in the house and the husband comes back. The husband hits on the door. The wife says he can't come in. The husband says, 'What is this, I can't come in my own house?' Ernesto hides in the closet and the woman opens the door for her husband. The husband says, 'I can feel someone is here in my house.' The husband starts walking through the house and Ernesto gets so afraid that he opens the door of the closet where he is and he shoots the husband. Bang! Dead.''

"That's no good," Maximo said.

"It is wrong," El Viejo said. "The woman is supposed to be dead, not the husband. Ernesto should have come out of the closet and shot the woman and made her husband happy.''

Maximo looked at himself in the mirror behind the bar. No, he said to himself, that's exactly what I've lived my life to be against. It's thousands of years old and thousands of years crazy. Nobody hurts anybody, if you live properly, he said to himself. He saw Nicki with her head in the stars and he started climbing toward her. He loved her and he knew that she loved him. Why live in desolation, live in envy, when all you have to do is walk out of this place and call her on the phone, call her at her own house, forget this system of calling Angela. Let me call her at her own house and tell her that I am in love with her and that I am going to marry her and live with her and have children with her. Let me tell this to her and let her hear it and there is no way that she will say no to me. I am going to go out and call her and marry her, call all night and call all day. Get her on the phone and then into my arms for the rest of my life.

He pushed the rum away, picked up his bar-wet money and went out the heavy metal door and onto the subway platform, which now in the night was completely empty. He found he had only quarters. He walked the couple of steps to the change booth and put a wet dollar on the counter. When the clerk kept his head down counting change, Maximo became irritated. He could hear no train coming; the only sound in the station was someone coming off the staircase.

"Change, please," Maximo said.

"How many tokens?" the clerk said, without looking up.

· "Just change of a dollar, in dimes, please," Maximo said.

The clerk looked up, aggravated. He took the wet dollar bill and flicked the dimes back. Maximo took the dimes and, head down, started for the phone. He almost bumped into the man who had just come from the stairs, but he rolled his body away from the man and was walking up to the phone, a dime in his hand, Nicki's voice in his ear, when the man took a step after Maximo and the man's hand rose and put a black .22 Magnum Derringer behind Maximo's right ear and pulled the trigger twice. Maximo pitched onto his face.

The subway clerk looked up, but now Corky had wheeled, stuffed the gun into his pocket and had his head down and the brim of his hat well over the eyes and the clerk could see none of his face. Corky went up the stairs, stepped out into the car at the curb, which took off immediately, made a turn and headed for the traffic down on the Bruckner Expressway.

"You could say one thing about us," Corky said. "It took a long time maybe. The law gets Teenager, but that don't stop us. We still had a show them we bite too. Don't matter who as long as they know it's from us."

"He got no complaints about us today," the thug driving said.

"I'm on the subway steps almost three hours waiting for the guy to come out," Corky said.

As the car blended in with the expressway traffic, Corky sat back and slapped the Derringer. "This is a nice piece."

"When I got it off Jackie he told me, don't worry, it gives the best bang for a job like this."

"He's not kidding. You should've seen it. The back of the guy's head turned into tomato soup," Corky said.

Myles was home in his kitchen, throwing away the last can of beer of the night, when the phone rang. Martin, chuckling, said, "Do you know that Spic that give you all the abuse? The little guy with Teenager?"

"Yeah?"

"They just whacked his brains out on the subway station, 138th Street."

"Did they really," Myles said. "Oh, what a shame."

"Yeah, I just thought I'd let you know so you could cry," Martin said. "He was so innocent he got killed in a dope war."

"I'll bet he forgot to ask them if they had a warrant," Myles said.

They both laughed and Myles hung up and went into the refrigerator for another beer.

It was after midnight when Nicki finished straightening up the room. She had two things on the bed. The *Times* and two clean, fluffy folded orange towels. She took the *Times* and put it under the shoeboxes. Staring at the towels she imagined using one of them gently to rub the head of a baby she had just bathed. Sure she could. The towel was soft enough for any baby. Rub him dry, ruffle the hair with the towel. Make him laugh. Maximo's baby. Oh, you're crazy. No, I'm not. Maximo's baby. Suddenly, she was unashamed. Her body shivered at the idea. She looked around the lovely, neat room and could see only its vacantness, that she was standing here isolated and desolate, as she would be for all the days she remained in it.

"Are you all right?" Her father was not smoking a cigar so she had no warning of his arrival. He stood in the doorway with his hands in his pockets.

"I don't think so," Nicki said.

"Of course you're not," he said. "This is a terrible thing. My poor little girl has to leave a husband like this."

"It's no fun," she said.

"But at least you're home," he said. He began to reach into his shirt pocket for a cigar. The cellophane crackled as his hands fumbled to get it off. Nicki had never seen him this nervous before.

"I don't know if I'm going to stay here," she said.

"Where would you go?" he said. The fingers now were unable to deal with the cigar and he put it back in his shirt pocket.

"I have someone I love," she told him.

"You're not supposed to do that to a husband just home from jail," her father said.

Nicki looked steadily at him. His eyes looked down, then to the sides. The words came off troubled lips. The man supposed to spread fear stood in alarm in the room of his daughter and did not know how to protect himself.

"I've got a life," Nicki said.

"Sure you have. Nobody ever said my baby don't have a life."

"And I intend to live it."

"Well, you mean you're leaving here too?"

"I think so. I told you I love somebody. I want to go with him. I want to marry him."

"When?"

"I don't know."

"Right now?"

"I don't know."

"You're supposed to stay here," he said. She noticed his eyes glistening.

"I'm supposed to do what I want to do."

"That's right. That's my baby. You could do whatever you want."

"I'm sorry, Daddy, but that's what it's going to be."

"But you can't leave right now," he said.

"Maybe I will."

"No, you can't."

"Daddy. Let's not—"

"You got to have something to eat first. Lasagna. I got lasagna inside. I'll go heat it up. You got a bad thing happening to you. You got to eat something. Let me get my little girl something to eat."

"Thanks, Daddy."

"But you'll eat it?"

"I don't know. If I come out and eat it, I come out and eat it. I feel like being alone."

"I'll go get it ready," he said. "You'll come eat with your father."

As he went down the hallway, she picked up the orange towels and put them on her bureau. She would have these in her arms when she went back to Maximo. She felt in her bag for the bankbook. In doing so, her fingers came

upon a joint. She picked up the matches and went into
the bathroom. As she walked, she felt the corn leaves
brushing off her arms. She was walking with Maximo
through a cornfield. In the bathroom, she opened the window and lit the joint. She blew the smoke out the window
and looked out at the night. She wished there were somebody who could clean the house for her husband. The
poor guy was in jail for so long, he deserves a clean
house. As she smoked, the pot made her sleepy. She was
surprised that the pot was any good. She began to think
of the day she and her husband rode the speedboat in
Long Island Sound. The sun was bright and caused the
white spray to glisten like thousands of rich stones. She
thought that she was living in freedom that day, riding
through the water in the boat. Then right after it, he was
gone and here was Maximo. I love Maximo, she said to
herself. I am going to *marry* Maximo. She could not believe that she was saying this, and for a moment she
thought it was the pot, but then she reminded herself that,
no, this thought had been with her maybe from the day
she first saw him.

Say the truth: you always loved him, even if you didn't
admit it, even if you were *afraid* to. Afraid of what? I
spent my life worrying about my father and now he's
heating lasagna so I don't walk out tonight.

She thought of Maximo. She would call him tomorrow
morning. No, she would punish him and wait until the
next day before she spoke to him. Spoke to him and then
brought him his clean towels and herself. After all, first
she had to punish him because she had told him not to
see Teenager and he had broken his word to her. It didn't
matter why. He had told her he would do something and
he did not. In one more day after tomorrow I will live
with Maximo, she told herself. She blew more smoke into
the night air, took the last drag, flicked the joint out the
window and went to bed.

She fell asleep immediately. She never heard her father
calling to her to come and eat the food he had prepared.
She dreamed of Maximo and all the tomorrows.

About the Author

Jimmy Breslin was born and raised in the borough of Queens, New York, and was educated there and in the city rooms of New York newspapers. He has worked on some of the worst and best papers and has written three best sellers. In 1969, he ran for New York City council president in the Democratic primary. He lives in Queens and has six children. Mr. Breslin is best known for his bad habits.